THE SILENT DRUM

Hear the beat... feel the pain.

THE SILENT DRUM

Hear the beat... feel the pain

ISBN: 978-1-910181-09-6

First edition published in February 2015

Second edition published in November 2017

Published in Great Britain by the Anchor Print Group Ltd

Illustration and pictures by Raquel Precious Walker

Acknowledgements

I would like to give my most sincere thanks to many people with regards to their support and assistance with this novel.

Firstly I wish to give enormous thanks and praise to my Mother and Father who have always been there to encourage me and guide me, not only with this project but life in general.

I would also like to give a massive thank you to my daughter Raquel who has supported me from the start and designed the front cover of 'The Silent Drum'. I would like to thank Charlene Lewis who was kind enough to be the face of Esi on the front cover.

Two friends I wish to give special credit to are Les Kendrick, who would say he did not do a lot, and his partner Sue Bricknell who would say she did even less. To them both I give many thanks for their encouragement, suggestions and support.

Finally many thanks to you the reader for picking my novel to read. Hope that you enjoy it.

Andrew N Walker

CHAPTERS

1. Control 7
2. Tribe 17
3 Ohema (Queen) 29
4. ƆdƆ (Love) 51
5. Verdict 71
6. Stolen 87
7. Abjection 99
8. Captive 119
9 Maintained 133
10. Chosen 141
11. Journey 161
12. Arrival 183
13. Trinity 201
14. Punishment 213
15. Plantation 223
16. Workers 231
17. Market 245
18. Craft 259
19. Tranquillity 273
20. Collection 287
21. Hole 303
22. Pockets 321
23. Shock! 333
24. Scion 347
25. Expulsion 363
26. Malice 379
27. Guests 395
28. Wedding 413
29. Abolition 429

CHAPTER 1: Control

Silence.

Do you hear it?

Here I am in this still and quiet place with nothing but my ability to control. I don't exercise my listening sense to receive any noise, yet I feel the sound in my head and I sense the bam of a drumbeat. In my silence I feel the racing pace of a repeated strike from the players hand on animal skin stretched over its patterned, carved dark wooden frame, as it is thumped to a continuous rhythm.

This powerful and enchanted thrashing stroke reaches the highest and deepest part of my emotions. This bam bam bam sound and continued pace came to my thoughts early in my life, before I could speak my mother tongue or to even understand this type of rhythmic expression. I felt the beat as it spoke to me in my own language. It told me how to feel and how to control myself.

It took my thoughts and captured them holding them within. When the drum beat played I wished for all my dreams to come true. The question that I had to ask myself was this. Were the drum and the dreams of a good future inside my thoughts or were these thoughts and dreams inside the drum?

A drumbeat had a power more than anything I knew. So much it almost entwined itself around my inner body like the leaved tentacles of growing vines.

If you close your eyes and think about your favourite beat, and work beyond any light tapping of a drum skin you will soon train your thoughts to make this work very well. If you succeed then maybe your profound listening has time to occupy more.

With the strongest of your thought pounding ability you will find a most peaceful and tranquil sanctuary. If only you know where to look. It is there and you will find it deep inside you.

You need to train your concentration once you have captured it for it to become real and to discover it again when it is needed and at short notice you will find what you are wishing for, and at speed.

If you do not understand what is happening then you have not reached the end and cannot imagine my life without this drumbeat. You should try and reach to the depths within your head at every chance you get. Although for now it does not matter.

However, if you do understand then you will know all things needed to control any emotion. The drum beat will keep you focused on a journey of good times as this noise simply comes from a shallow surface. It can be as easy as scooping a shellfish from a small rock pool.

I am now ready to share with you more than my secret of control. I have to tell how I came to be where I am today.

Right now as I stand, beneath my feet the hard rocks are unmoved by the crashing of the sea dispersing into a light spray, sprinkling salt water showering to cool my hot skin.

I look out to this vast open water. Then I look at my animal skinned handmade drum held firmly underneath my arm, it is an odd shape for a drum but it is what makes it unique.

Looking back out to the sea I close my eyes slowly and find the beat in my head which has brought me this far in my life journey.

A journey which could never have been predicted when I was young. One I never thought was my destiny. I will be sharing with you an experience which should be forgotten but needs to be told for my sanity.

I am drawn away from my thoughts and I am left standing on these rocks wondering how I ever got here. I open my eyes to see reality again and look deep into the fierceness of the sea and I am reminded how it very nearly became my exit from this world I am alive in.

Closing my eyes once more I breathe in hard and take the salty air to my nose. A salubrious fresh breeze lifts the scent of the water to my nostrils and I make several jutted movements with my chin as I desire to capture more of this cleansing delight. I find it very interesting of the five senses we have, the sense of smell without the other four can explode thoughts to retrieve the strongest memories. It reaches a profound level as I imbibe deeper to feed my concentration.

At first my thoughts are focused, and then start running strong before they return vividly to my mind. I am searching for my drumbeat. My right hand reaches to feel for my drum under my left arm. I feel the stretch of skin tight across the top which signals me to begin tapping. Firstly with one finger then two, until I am in full rhythm. As I tap my drum and I remember the beat, which was the first thing to hold my attention in my world. This drum is real this time and it is truly delightful. I start to tap the skin.

"Bam ba ba, bam ba ba bam ba ba bam, ba ba bam ba ba bam, ba ba bam ba ba bam bam ba ba, bam ba ba bam."

"Du ga da, du ga da, du ga da" my voice sings, to the rhythm.

I ask the moment to "give me the spirit of this drum."

This beat makes me excited and warms my soul. My heart races and I breathe in again but this time with more control. I slowly feel the intakes of cool air blowing in from the sea in through my nose careful not to take too much in as I did before which nearly made me faint.

This drum beat given to the skin on the frame makes a pleasant rhythmic sound and I find my strength. It gives me hope. It gives me the sense of sight in a darkened room. A glow of warmness like the early morning sun as it starts the day. I tap louder and louder and remember what I experienced in my life. I think harder and deeper until I mentally capture the clear thoughts of my life experience.

I recall how this beat made my forefathers get excited and how they would laugh and tease each other and I remember my joy as I first learned to dance with my friends.

All the passion of being a part of our tribe made me strong, it made me fight. It made me whole. It kept my mind together. It kept my hopes and spirit high. It kept my sanity. It kept me alive. It made me the woman I am today. Who am I, Well, let me introduce myself.

I am Esi Takyiwaa Kwaku.

My name Esi means Sunday born and I am from the African people who are known as Fante and I was born in the year of 1779.

Our people were the Mfantsefo and my tribe were originally from an ancient place a long way north from where they are now. We are now the Fante and we are a proud people who keep our village in good order and secure.

My surname is quite strange as it is Kwaku which is a boy's first name and it means Wednesday born, yet now it is my family name. My middle name Takyiwaa was the name of my grandmother and I was named this by our tradition.

Many years ago we were given only one name until the arrival of the light skinned people who we called the "obroni" who came from a different land far away. We however are dark in our skin, our word is "tum tum", and we are "bibini" meaning African. These words were ours which we used between ourselves and kept them from the light skinned "obroni" ears.

The names and days of the week were brought to us by the obroni. They were from a faith told to our people of a Lord of the heaven above and this was the religion of Christian teachings. We use the word "Nyame" for the obroni word "Lord" and his name is Onyankopon. Onyankopon is God.

These obroni were friendly and they came to preach us their beliefs and ideas and they were gentle and peaceful whilst on their mission of their teachings.

Preachers encouraged some of our people to take names from the Christian faith and many of our tribe called their children Edward and Charles for boys and Mary and Catherine for girls. We were taught that these names were used by the leaders of the obroni we knew who they called "kings and queens." Our name for a king is "ohene" and for a queen it is "ohema."

We gained many things from the obroni. They taught us a lot of fine ways and we learned their traditions, yet not all were good and at an early age I had heard some stories which made me afraid of them. One of which scared me the most.

This memory was when I was very young and I was going to collect some water from close by. I strolled past some goats in their pen in our village then approached a hut when I heard a huge shout from inside which made me stop in my stride.

I walked over to this hut but before I got too close I slowed down and then I crept up to it. I looked through the gap to the side of the cloth hanging in front of the entrance and saw one of our tribe's men called Bobo and he was lying down on his sleeping mat on the ground.

Bobo was crying real tears and his wife was trying to serve him with hot leaf water and then she wiped his brow.

I then saw two of the elders of our tribe sitting on stools at the foot end of where Bobo was lying and I overheard them talking about what had happened.

They said that some obroni were cruel which I remember vividly. I wanted to hear more of what they were saying and so I kept myself very still as they talked. I was young and curious with a desire to learn everything I could and I wondered why these elders spoke like this.

They were talking loud enough for me to hear and said that Bobo was asked to escort some younger boys from our village to a river not too far away and show them some ways of catching fish there. Then as he got close to his destination he saw a group of obroni men who started to chase them.

At this point Bobo told the boys to run back to our village as he knew there was trouble coming.

Bobo made a distraction and these men chased after him whilst the boys were too fast and escaped in a different direction.

The elders continued to talk and they spoke about the group of obroni who finally caught up with Bobo and they started to attack him and they shouted at him in a language he did not understand. He was so frightened he started shaking and he was breathing hard.

These obroni trapped Bobo like a hunted animal between them and eventually snared their prey with what appeared to be a large fishing net. After a struggle Bobo became tired and his exhausted body slumped to defeat.

The obroni men took him to a tree where they bound his hands behind his back and then his feet with a thick twine and then they placed a cloth covering over his eyes.

I listened further as the elders spoke. As they did this Bobo screamed and tried to sit up and he nearly knocked the hot leaf water from his wife's hand. The tears ran down his cheeks just as water pours from the top of the hut during the rain and his throat choked. He then coughed and he appeared to gag. He complained his feet were giving him so much discomfort he wanted to take a cutlass and hack them off.

The elders continued with the story. They talked of how these obroni then threw the twine over a branch and hoisted Bobo feet first and hung him upside down in an inverted suspension.

This caused Bobo to become disorientated and frightened. He was already exhausted and had no strength to fight his ensnared tether. The obroni men laughed and pushed him making him swing which made him even dizzier. After what seemed to be a long time the obroni men all walked away and left Bobo dangling by himself.

Bobo had explained he tried to free himself but the more he struggled the tighter his feet were held. After a while his strength evaporated and he grew tired and then his feet went numb. Soon after this he must have passed out.

I thought at this point the elders were telling stories as this sounded so awful but then I looked over at Bobo and he was clearly in a distressed state. I also saw there was somebody attending to Bobo's feet but one of the elders was blocking my full view.

The elders then spoke again about the ordeal of Bobo regaining his consciousness and lying with his face down in the red African dusty soil.

As he opened his eyes he could not see they were so gritty it took him a while to find any vision.

In all of this confusion Bobo did not remember that he had been suspended from the tree, dangling like a bat and as blinded as one too. After what seemed to be quite some time trying to visualise what happened to him and shaking his head he finally started to get his sight back again.

He realised then that he was attacked and needed to start making his journey back to our village which he knew would take him longer than his way there.

What he did not realise was that whilst he was still unconscious and with numb feet one of the obroni had made deep cuts between each of his toes almost severing them and he also had lacerations on the soles of his feet. They were bleeding without any knowledge of pain. This same obroni had dropped sand into Bobo's eyes so he could not see clearly.

As this wasn't enough torture the obroni had collected some fallen and rotting fruits from close by which had biting and stinging insects and ants feeding on their soft sweet pulp.

When these men had gathered enough sticky rotten overripe fruit they rubbed and squeezed their sweet slushy pulp between his toes and on the soles of his feet.

These insects did what they know best and they enjoyed the sweetness of the flesh of Bobo's feet underneath the sticky lure of the fruit. Bobo's feet were so numb he was unaware of what was happening. He could feel only feel them tingling.

When Bobo could eventually see he looked at his feet that were completely covered in stinging ants and biting insects.

Bobo brushed the insects off and tried to stand but it took him several attempts to maintain his balance from his disorientation. The feeling was now slowly coming back to his feet and he soon realised then the pain was so intense he could not place them on the ground. As Bobo recalled what had happened he compared the pain to walking over the tops of spears.

He ended up crawling his way home to our village. His hands and knees were cut and lacerated from this epic endurance and journey home.

As I observed this horror being spoken outside the hut I remember making a noise of pain I was feeling for Bobo and I took an intake of my breath. This made the elders glance towards me so I had to retract my head from the entrance of the hut.

I then slowly moved forward and carefully took another peek back into the hut and I looked at Bobo's feet. The elder man who was sitting on front of Bobo had moved from where he was sitting.

It was then that I saw what Bobo had been describing to the elders and I could not believe what I saw. Bobo's feet were the size of cooking pots and they were shredded and there was what I thought was the white bone showing through congealed dark red blood of his open wounds. I opened my eyes wider to what I thought was ones of Bobo's toes hanging by its skin and I felt like being sick.

I quickly pulled my head away and ran to collect the water which I had set out to do and I tried to forget what I had seen. This was too difficult as it had already engrained its image into my head.

Whenever I went to collect water after this day I avoided going along the route which took me past Bobo's hut as I could still hear the screams of his pain trigger my vivid haunts of this horror scene.

I did see Bobo around our village many times after wards but he never walked for long and he mostly dragged himself around on his behind. He also never spoke to anyone of what had happened to him but I had heard it and I knew what had happened. I did not tell anyone and I let this horror find a convenient place in the depths of my memory.

I was given an insight into the obroni and when I think about it they were quite brave to enter our world with a skin which suffered from the glaze of the sun and made them glow as red as a hot burning wooden log in a fire. This meant on many occasions they would need to sooth their skin with the cold leaves and the sap of plants.

The obroni preachers who came to our village however were different to the ones who abused Bobo and it was these preachers who gave our people a new way of thinking and a new belief which helped our elders build a better spirit among our tribe.

What I want to tell you now is how my life experience challenged my spirit, my honour and my name.

My spirit, which kept my physical form alive, my honour, what made me refuse to let humiliation overpower my dignity and my name, which became distorted and buried yet never forgotten and to rise again to the surface to be spoken again.

I wish to share with you my journey of life. I will offer you what I remember and I will tell it how it was. This will be without any high fences of exclusion, without any cushions of comfort, and without any masks of blindness.

Without telling my story I cannot move on. Not allowing my memories to be heard I feel this cruel world will never realise the extent of my story, well are you ready? It was like this.

CHAPTER 2: Tribe

I lived in a village with my tribe and our people were many and there were vast amounts of families.

My home was a hut built using the red soil for its walls and the roof was made from the long grass grown nearby. It stood near to the inner part of the village and close to our Odikro who was our leader whose home was the biggest of them all. The word 'Odikro' is the name we call him but we address him as Nana.

Nana's home stood right in the middle of the village huts and in front of this was a large open area for gatherings, children to play and announcements to be spoken from Nana himself. Nana's home was huge and it was one of a few with several rooms joined onto the main doorway entrance.

Most tribes had an Odikro and we respected ours for he was the man who controlled and guided us with his sage words and decisions. Our Odikro had his advisors and key men who were each responsible for their role within the village.

Firstly there was the leader and mentor of the warriors. He was in charge of the men who would shield us from any attack by outsiders which would happen from time to time by neighbouring tribes. The men of ours were brave and we were well protected as our warriors were fearless. They would go to a secret area and practice their fight styles and ideas on beating an opponent.

Secondly there was the leader of the hunters who would teach the stealth and sage and the patience of trapping a beast for our food. They would throw their spears at targets whilst hey perfected their hunting skills which would also be shown to us as a spectacle during events of celebration as their skill amazed the others in the village. Their everyday practice ensured them to aim with such accuracy when hunting so we always had the meat of a beast for our food.

Lastly there were the leaders who maintained the village. These members of our tribe helped to build huts and repair and keep huts from any damage.

The drum maker was another important member of our village and there was the man who used the herbs and leaves to cure anyone who had pains from any sickness hidden inside their bodies.

For me Esi, I lived with my family which consisted of my father Adofo, my mother, and my sister. My mother's name Abena meant she was born on a Tuesday. She was a very good woman and she had a lot of respect in our village.

She was quite tiny and she was the last born of thirteen children and of these children ten were girls. There were actually five more but they died at the time they were born.

There were many people in our tribe who were related to me, but this was the same for most families. My mother (Maame) worked very hard and was very loyal to my father. She always made him his food and she kept him happy in their lives together.

She always plaited my short hair to keep me looking smart. It hurt when she did, but I got used to it after a while. I always had my silent drum to help me of course. I would sit down on the ground with my back to her as she sat on a stool. I sat between her knees and let her tug my hair as she made it neat. This took quite a while so we had time to converse.

When she groomed my hair we would talk about what we thought of the others in our village. Especially Nana's wives and the way they behaved so fancy and false when they spoke to others.

We also spoke about the different characters who we thought were the funniest.

We would sometimes play a game where my mother would say a word of an object and I would have to name something related to it. She would say the word "hut" and I would say the word "roof."

This game was lots of fun until one occasion my mother said the word "gold" and I did not know what it was.

She told me this gold was the name of something of great value and it was the colour, according to her, that was the prettiest of all, it was the colour of the sun on a clear and bright day.

I thought about this and wanted to respond my answer in the game but I could not think of anything related to gold apart from the sun so I asked my mother if she had any gold to show me. She informed me she did not have any because it was very precious, but she did tell me Nana had some.

She then told me only Nana could keep the gold as he needed it to give to the people with the light skin, the obroni.

These people would come to visit and give Nana things in trade for his gold. I did not really understand but this gold thing must have held some special qualities if people wanted it so much. What did it do I thought to myself?

I asked my mother if this gold was the most valuable thing she knew of. She told me there was one thing more valuable than gold. I remember at this time trying to think of the one thing more important than this gold and I thought it must be Nana as he owned the gold and so I told my mother this.

My mother finished plaiting my hair and then told me to stand and I turned and looked at her.

She looked deep into my eyes and then kissed my forehead and told me the one thing more valuable than all of the gold in our land was me. I smiled and then threw my arms around my mother and gave her a great big hug. This was the best thing I had ever heard and I felt a great flow of warmth from inside of me tingle my skin.

I asked if we could eat this gold and my mother laughed at me. I asked if we could use it to build our homes and again she laughed and told me it was not to eat or be used to build with.

This was quite apt really because every time we played this game we always ended up talking about food, which was my favourite subject.

As we played this game my mother told me when I was younger

I could always smell the meat of a beast roasting over a fire and it made me excited.

I always knew when the meat was almost ready by it's tempting and appetising aroma, which I think came from the blend of spices and seasoning of the herbs, and when it was ready to eat I enjoyed the burnt black outside and often asked for a strip to be picked off and cooled so I could suck on it as I held in it my hand.

I was so cheeky but when my nose took in the tempting flavours of roasting of the bush meat I got so excited I rose from where ever I was and my feet skipped a little dance.

I once even walked up to our former Odikro who was known as Nana Kuntu and I took his food from his bowl. This made Nana Kuntu laugh so hard he called me "The smart one." You see, to take the food of an Odikro was something you could never do, yet how could he refuse a child?

Nana Kuntu always asked me if I wanted some of his food when he was eating after this. For a while I did until I learned to say no, but it was the talk of our village at the time.

Unfortunately one morning Nana Kuntu was found lying motionless on his bed and his rule passed to his son whose name was Nana Apane.

My father was called Adofo Kwaku and his name Adofo meant "Brave warrior." However his last name of Kwaku was the name for a boy born on a Wednesday which confused me in early life. When I was young I thought that he was a brave warrior on a Wednesday only. Yet he was given this name and it was what I was also known as by tradition. Why did I have the last name of a boy's first name I thought to myself?

My father, in contrast to my mother was a very big man and would eat a lot of food when it was brought to him by my mother. My father had been a warrior in our tribe but now he was past his fighting days. He would help with many different teachings in our tribe. He would put his hand to anything from the building of new huts and fences to giving his knowledgeable advice to the hunters and warriors.

He was from a family of eight. Most of my father's family were male as he only had one sister. Three of his brothers had been killed when they were younger whilst hunting but my father never forgot them and spoke of them and when he did he looked to the ground as though he knew they were listening.

I heard my father say once when he was talking in his sleep he hoped his brothers were safe and well and I sensed they were not finished with this world at all but in some way they had just left the village. The strange thing was they were all lost from the same hunting trip. I think the truth was my father did not know what had happened to them and he chose to close his eyes from the pain and worry about them.

My father was tall and broad and I remember when I was very young I had to look up at him as he was like a giant. Now, however, his stomach was larger and his hair was turning grey and he was losing it at the top. His shoulders were still broad but they were now slightly rounded but he still had huge arms and he was very strong.

Finally there was my little sister, she was a little sweet smiling child who had started to lose her teeth and her smile had a gap at the front. Her name was given to one who was the youngest born. Her name was Kakraba. She was just like how I used to be and she looked just like me when I was her age, so they tell me.

Kakraba was also very smart and one day she was playing with some stones and a wooden cup in a bowl of muddy water and she had her hands in it for quite a long time. I was asked by my mother to get her to take her hands from the water as her food was about ready to be served.

I told Kakraba to stop and then went to get some clean bowls ready for the light soup my mother had prepared. I returned to see Kakraba was still playing in the muddy water. I asked her if she had taken her hands from the bowl and she turned around and put her hands behind her and out of my view as she stood up. She looked innocent of any wrong doing as she looked straight at me.

Kakraba was now standing with her back to a wall and there was a cloth behind her hanging on a hook.

I asked Kakraba if she was still playing in the water and she told me she was not. I then asked to see her hands and she looked at me with a frown. I sensed the thoughts running through her head were working quickly as she found a solution. The cloth behind her back then started to move and then shortly after her right hand appeared slowly and we both looked at it and it was dry.

Her face looked very pleased as she told me "You see", in an excited voice.

I asked to see the other hand and she returned the first hand and then the cloth behind her back moved again and then she brought out the left hand.

Again it came out carefully as we both looked and then, when she knew it was dry, she thrust it towards me. I laughed as I knew what she had done so I could not be upset with her.

This was so clever Kakraba my little sister, you saw the problem and you tricked your way out.

Kakraba was so cheeky and on some occasions she would chase the yard fowl around and they clucked and cried as she ran after them. The reality was when she got near to one she turned around and ran away screaming. She was also afraid of spiders and there was a time when she came screaming from our hut when she found one in her bed and wanted me to take it away. Seeing my little sister's scared face had an effect on me to face up to this eight legged menace. It was as though her fear for the spider became my strength and not to be alarmed. So whenever we found a spider after that it was left for me to rescue Kakraba from her dilemma.

My usual routine was that firstly I collected a wooden bowl. Then I would find the little pest and then slam the vessel over the top of the scurrying little pest and catch it.

Kakraba always checked her bed before she went to sleep after this and called me if I was needed which was not very often.

My mother had given birth to seven children in total from my father. Two of us had survived. Myself and Kakraba, I was the second born, behind a brother who died early of a sickness. Kakraba was the seventh and last born.

The brothers and sisters my mother gave birth to had died when they were born or early in their life without growing feet large enough to stand on our hot and dusty red soil.

This was sad but was accepted and these children were taken by our ancestors and were at rest in the earth.

We had a custom in our tribe where one day a year people made food for the dead to feast. This was done a week before a festival as we believed our ancestors watched over us and protected us.

My mother also took part in this and she made some peanut soup (agyina aduane) or ghost food which by tradition had salt but no onion or pepper. She also made pounded yam which was called fufu and there was cooked meat as well and she laid it out for them to eat during the night. This was placed in the centre of the village and covered. This food was very bland and had no taste. Some children who did not understand this would sneak to the food during the night and eat some. One year I did the same and the food did not have any flavour. My Father saw me just as I dipped my finger into a pot and his rage bellowed at me with a high volume of words which made him look like fire came from his mouth.

My father sat me down the next morning and he explained to me the importance of this tradition and I never did it again.

In the middle of our village in front of Nana Apane's hut was a large open area where we would come together and sometimes make a large fire. This was where the drummers would play their drums and their beats invited everyone to dance.

The people of my tribe used to come together for discussions concerning the village such as the outbreak of diseases, any announcements by the Odikro, or celebrating a birth and festivals that we were going to have.

This large fire was also for everyone in the village to keep warm, and to cook the meat caught by the hunters.

As my family home which was our hut was on the inner part of the village my family were well thought of. However all of the huts looked the same and were the same size and the same colour. I remember once wishing our hut could stand out bigger and taller than all of the other huts and not be of a dull colour like red clay from the soil with a brown thatch roof.

I hoped I could live in a house which was tall, big and white, just something to stand out and to make me feel different.

I tried as a young girl to understand everything that would happen among our people and most of the time I did, yet every now and again I saw some strange things which I was told to ignore.

One of the things which left a vivid memory in my head was one early morning I saw some of our current Odikro's main protectors leading away a woman from a hut nearby.

The yard fowl were gathered in a fenced pen and they clucked and squawked as the woman was led away from Nana Kuntu's hut and she was screaming. This noise woke me and my mother. My mother quickly put on a loose robe over her head and ran towards the group of men who surrounded this woman after she had broken free from their clutches.

As our hut was near to the centre of our village the noise was quite loud. I stood up and walked to our door entrance which was shielded with a cloth flap. I peeked through a gap and saw the group of men push my mother away as she was trying to pull this woman by the arm. One of the men finally pushed my mother heavily to the ground.

I did not really understand what was happening on this occasion but when my mother tried to stand she had blood coming from her head and she then fell back to the ground.

I ran over to where my father was still sleeping and I shook his shoulders until his eyes flickered open and his mouth opened with a large yawn.

My father soon rose from his bed and I pointed towards the spot where my mother was. She was still lying on the ground and he went to attend to her. My father ran to my mother and he carried her back to our home and laid her down.

I sat down and just looked as my father cradled my mother in his arms.

My mother did open her eyes and my father put her to rest on some soft straw and gave her some juice from a local berry mixed with water.

My mother lay down for many days and seemed to be getting better as she started to stand and go for short walks.

I remember holding my mother's hand on every occasion I could as I knew she was weak and my father took on her duties to carry water for us. My father tried to keep my mother with food which she took, but on some occasions she returned this nourishment to the red soil.

I remember my mother said to me these words and they were the last I heard, from her,

"Onyankopon aniwa hu asumasem biara,"

This spoken word gave the message,

"God's eye sees all things."

My mother passed away when Kakraba was still young and I was barely ten years old. She slowly drifted away after what happened to her left her weak and unable to keep food inside her. This took her from a well-rounded and solid shape to one which left with almost no shape to her body except for the frame of her bones. With her hair becoming suddenly grey like the clouds in the sky she joined the ancestors in the land of the dead somewhere underneath the earth. My mother was at asomdwoee (peace).

My father wept for my mother and it was sad watching him cry.

He was without his love ƆdƆ and he never hid it very well.

I did not feel the full effect of losing my mother at this time because I did not know how I was supposed to feel and to compound this empty feeling, I did not understand it.

Gradually this loss built up especially when I saw my father behave strangely and drink more palm wine than he had ever done. As time went on I began to understand I would never see my mother again and I remember there were nights I woke up and looked for her thinking it was all in my head as I slept, but it never was and so I grew more stronger as I did this so did my silent drum.

My father asked me to make the peanut soup and fufu the next time the food was to be made for our ancestors and this time I was more understanding. I did this with vivid memories of my mother's words to me previously and I understood more.

I had to support my father and I took on the role of looking after Kakraba as she did not really understand what had happened. I simply told my sister our mother had gone to another village and this was normal. Kakraba just played as before but in reality this crushed my family. We were all numb from our loss but somehow we formed an invisible binding and we bonded strongly.

I had no replacement for the pain of losing my mother. I just had the reminder of the drum beats which played the night after she left my life in this lonely world to go to the earth with my ancestors. My silent drum grew day by day to try to heal the scars of pain at my loss. The pain never went away. It was always there yet it was a way of making my body numb enough to tolerate the torture of pain, both physical and emotional.

"Bam ba ba, bam ba ba bam ba ba bam, ba ba bam ba ba bam, ba ba bam ba ba bam bam ba ba, bam ba ba bam."

My silent drum played a lot for a long time after this and it had become stronger and I played with energy and profound control.

Life and time moved on and I approached the age of sixteen and I had started to develop more of the body of a woman.

When I was a very young girl my father had been respected in our tribe by Nana Kuntu and he was also given a place by the centre fire by the elders who kept his name high in their thoughts. My father would sit by the side of Nana Kuntu whenever there was food at celebrations.

However my father was a warrior under the old Odikro. Now we were under the rule of Nana Apane.

Nana Apane never really acknowledged my father with the same honour. He was young when my father was in his prime warrior days.

This hurt my father, who kept his bitterness to himself, even so, I saw through his quiet shield of pride. I knew in my akuma (heart) my father was really a hero to our village. My father wanted so much to be in favour of the Nana Apane, but he was shunned from sitting next to him on all occasions. Nana Apane saw my father as a used tribe member and he would call him “Opanyin gyengyan”, a useless old person.

I guess my father was pushed aside because the new warriors who stole the glory were now Nana Apane’s finest and they got Nana's attention and sat where my father once sat when food was given. This however was the way of our tribe and the wishes of the Odikro were to be respected.

CHAPTER 3: Queen (Ohema)

Nana Apane had three wives; they were firstly Ansaba and then Agyeiba. Both were cruel and spoke down to the rest of the tribe and they were the ones who he had married first. Then there was the best one of them all who he had lastly taken as his wife. Her name was Kesiwaa and she was my favourite, she was my "Ohema," my queen and she was "Ewuraba" a lady.

The obroni had preached to our tribe about the Christian values and they had spoken to Nana Apane and advised him that he was only to take one wife. Any more than one wife was against the Christians belief. Nana Apane did not take this into his way of rule. He was arrogant and he was not going to let the obroni over rule over his tradition as an Odikro.

As I gathered the years after I lost my mother I saw Kesiwaa as my role model. Without my mother, my father had done his best and I was proud of him, however he could not give me the words and thoughts of advice a mother could give a daughter. He tried so hard but he knew all the words of a warrior and a great one too but as I was growing I needed the sage of a woman's words.

Kesiwaa had seen my father cope to his best but she also identified there were times he could not advise me. My father could teach me to throw a spear and chase a beast but he could not show me how to wash clothes and cook or anything a girl needed.

Kesiwaa was quite tall and slim. She was actually taller than Nana Apane. She had a face so radiant and nubile and when her teeth broke a smile it induced her natural beauty and she would tell me to walk tall and she would teach me some of the ways of an Ohema.

Not like the other two queens who were disfigured by the folds of skin sagging from their waist and stomach.

They also had bad skin which they would cover with a powder which they blended into each other's face and they made this from the red African soil.

I think Kesiwaa wanted to call me her daughter after I lost my mother but she never did. She would refer to me as her "Precious one." Although she favoured me she always reminded me our relationship was as friends as she said she would never replace my mother who was one of the finest in the tribe. Kesiwaa also looked out for Kakraba too, but only when I needed some support. My little sister was my responsibility and Kesiwaa knew I struggled with her.

As I learned from Kesiwaa I developed some of her ways and without realising it I would sometimes walk in her style, which was to walk chin up in the air and with my eyes looking straight ahead.

My father would laugh at me when I pretended to be Kesiwaa and this became a joke between some of those close to us.

As I grew closer to Kesiwaa I discovered more and more secrets that she disclosed to me, from her cooking and washing, to her beliefs and the many remedies for healing which were passed down to her. She taught me about the leaves and plants to use for head pain, bush rash, fever and all the other sicknesses which would sometimes find their way into our tribe. So I learned as I was taught, from the best, after my mother of course.

Kesiwaa also told me she knew her husband Nana Apane could be cruel. If he treated her badly, she would put a secret and extra special ingredient in his food which would make him have a stomach cramp which would also make his run to a bush to release his bowls. She also told me she sprinkled sand in his bed and she once placed a dead spider in there as well which she knew he was afraid of.

She even tore some of his robes and said they snagged and ripped when she was washing them. Some she let float away in the local river to feed her desire for revenge.

Nana Apane favoured his first two wives and it was as though Kesiwaa was the maid to these two other queens. Nana Apane made Kesiwaa cook the food for Ansaba and Agyeiba. This was just not right so she waited for her moment to even things up and get her revenge.

Kesiwaa took a nettle plant known to irritate the skin and she rubbed it into the clothes of Nana Apane and his other two wives.

The next day Nana Apane was sitting on his stool enjoying the sun and he was talking with his advisors.

Ansaba and Agyeiba came outside to greet him and they started to scratch their skin. Ansaba complained to Agyeiba's and Agyeiba complained to Ansaba's and they were rubbing and scratching like a pair of mad monkeys.

Nana Apane saw these two queens and asked them if they had ticks or bugs crawling over them. This then set off Nana Apane and he started to scratch himself with a passion. He started to shout at his two wives to get to the river to bathe themselves. It was funny as the two queens stripped off their clothes as they ran towards the river to wash.

On another occasion after Kesiwaa had waited for quite some time, the opportunity came for her to take her revenge.

Nana Apane had been given a pendant from the son of a newly trained hunter which had the tooth of wild beast difficult to catch. This was quite a gift and Nana Apane liked his new pendant. Kesiwaa thought this was a pleasant gift as well until Nana Apane upset her.

You see Nana Apane had taken one of Kesiwaa's necklaces which had fancy beads on it and he gave it to one of his advisors for his wife who had given the Odikra some wise words.

Kesiwaa saw how Nana Apane treasured his tooth pendant and so she decided to act and thought what to do about this gift. After a few days of showing it off to our tribe, Nana Apane went for a walk around the village.

Whilst he was away from his hut Kesiwaa prised out the tooth from its clasp and ground it down then seasoned it to the flesh of a hunter's catch meant for his meal before she made it in to smoke meat. She then added some of the dried droppings from this animal for extra flavour and insult. Finally she disposed of the strap and holder of the tooth and then poured Nana Apane some palm wine so he would forget all about it. Nana Apane never knew what Kesiwaa had done which I found to be amusing.

Kesiwaa also told me Nana Apane liked his Palm wine so much he sometimes drank too much and he became a different man. He would become demanding and could get aggressive. She knew when this happened in time he would fall asleep. If Nana Apane demanded more palm wine she knew what to do.

When Nana Apane wanted a new flask of palm wine which had turned him into a sot Kesiwaa would offer to fetch the drink and she advised Nana Apane she would spill the drink as was expected into the earth for the dead as a mark of respect. This she did but she threw more than just a quick splash and then topped the vessel up with water. She knew then how to control Nana Apane's drinking habit. Kesiwaa knew all the tricks and she told me as she was my mentor.

I asked Kesiwaa why the drink was poured into the earth and she told me it was the custom and belief whenever you open a new flask of Palm wine you were supposed to throw some on the earth for the dead before you drank any yourself. This was a mark of respect and acknowledgement and you would not spill any of the drink after this was done.

This was done on a special occasion and was more formal. This could be a funeral, when a child was born or named, or when two people were married. This was called "Libation" and just as people went to the earth when they passed on so the drink would be poured into the earth as well for them. Firstly an elder would call on three things. He would take the drink and hold it up to the sky and call the name of Onyankopon. The drink was then poured into the earth and the speaker called "asaase abenaa" for the earth. He then called for the ancestors. The speaker then invites them to watch over the person who is at the centre of the special occasion. If a child was being named the speaker would ask for this name to be accepted and anyone who does not wish this they will be cursed.

I was so excited when Kesiwaa taught me these things as I found them to be fascinating and I took this knowledge seriously. I also listened to the lighter side of Kesiwaa's teachings when she said if someone treats you badly there was always a way to get even. You just have to find their weakness then "play" them like a drum. This guidance was absorbed by me and she told me the most revengeful things imaginable. On one occasion she even dropped a dead rat into the water pot of Ansaba and Agyeiba and it made them vomit within minutes. She told me never to use that one as it was very dangerous and could spread a disease around the village and it was our secret only. I informed her of my secret which was my silent drum.

Kesiwaa advised me my silent drum was not just to stave off pain or ward away anything which made me uncomfortable or distressed but it would also be my sage, my judgement and my protector.

Kesiwaa was impressed and smiled when she spoke of my gift of the silent drum and told me it would be very useful one day, so much so, it could give me what I always wanted. She added just as my silent drum comforted me then I would also strengthen others in their time of need if I taught them.

Nana Apane had many children from his first two wives and he wanted more with Kesiwaa. The fact is Nana Apane had nine official children and dare I say he had more who were not recognised by his first two wives.

In recognition of these children Nana Apane made sure all drums made had nine beads of decoration around the side. Each bead represented a child and each one was a different design and colour.

However, I knew also he had one beaded drum with a hidden extra bead to mark his first secret child with another woman among our tribe who was not his wife, two extra hidden beads for another and so on until he had, for one nine beaded drum, five extra hidden beads. I knew this because the drum maker was a friend of my father and his name was Yafeu and the name meant "Bold."

One day he slipped out the information after drinking some palm wine with my father and it was not watered down.

Yafeu was a very private man and had been the master drum maker in our village for many years. He would make the finest drums for Nana Apane and each one had a different design. Each one had a different sound and each one had a name. Most, in fact nearly all of the drums made by Yafeu were played until they lost their sound which was when he would make a new one to replace it.

Yafeu also taught the younger boys how to play the drum and they all had respect for him.

I always wanted to learn to play the drum but Nana Apane decided he did not want any girls to learn to play it.

Yafeu kept one of his drums in his hut and he never played it or let it be played by any of the drummers saying it was made many years ago to give to his first born son.

However, Yafeu had five girls and when his wife produced a son, he died within a week of being born and Yafeu's wife had no more children. She then passed her time of being able to create a child and so the drum made for a son of Yafeu remained quiet and silent.

One afternoon I was with my father and we visited Yafeu who spoke of this drum with respect. He told my father the drum he made for his son was never played as it held a spirit within it, of mystic qualities. Yafeu then looked down at my face and he told me the drum was special and if anyone were to place both hands on the skin of the drum and closed their eyes then they could make a wish and it would come true. Later as my father and Yafeu went to talk outside the hut I remembered what Yafeu told me and so I placed my hands onto the skin of the drum and I closed my eyes and all around went quiet. I then made my wish. Well what did I want I asked myself? Did I want a big tasty meal, made from a juicy bush meat? No I thought to myself. Did I want to be the Ohema? No (daabi). I know what I wanted, and you know what it was? I wanted to be in a big white hut of course. I laughed to myself as I opened my eyes and took my hands away from the drum. My father and Yafeu were laughing at me and we all had a great afternoon.

Kesiwaa was not providing Nana Apane with any children and there was talk among the tribe she was barren. There was ill talk of her by Ansaba and Agyeiba, the two other wives and they started to poison the ears of other villagers.

I remained loyal to my favourite Ohema and I saw this talk to be a cruel act of jealousy.

Every time I heard talk of this I would inform Kesiwaa who just shrugged it off and continued to be proud and positive which I adapted into my own character which had started to teach me to try to also be strong.

I liked to visit Kesiwaa in her hut but I had to get permission from a guard who stood outside. He let me in to visit Kesiwaa as he knew I just wanted to see her and talk. However I was not always allowed into Nana Apane's hut if he was there and this was a strict rule, so I also found a way of sneaking in as the guard sometimes fell asleep. I made my feet tread very lightly on the red soil and I became very good at it. I found it funny and so did Kesiwaa but we also knew if Nana Apane found me he would be furious with her.

One morning I woke up early and I had given some food to Kakraba and I went outside to smell the clean air of the new day. I saw Ansaba and Agyeiba leave Nana Apane's hut and Ansaba was carrying a water carrier on her head and Agyeiba had a basket under her arm. They walked towards the river and so I guessed they were going to collect some water and some provisions.

Soon after Nana Apane left the hut and I heard him tell his guard he was going with the hunters to do some spear throwing with them. He asked the guard to fetch him his spear from the guards own hut and so the entrance to Nana Apane's hut was clear.

I seized my chance to visit my Ohema and quickly ran to the entrance of Nana Apane's hut and slipped in through the cloth hanging from the top of the door way. I knew where Kesiwaa must be as she had taken me there before. It was through the door cloth to a side area which was linked to Nana Apane's main hut. There were several of these side rooms leading from the main area of Nana Apane's hut but I only wanted the one where my Ohema was.

As I went through the door cloth I saw Kesiwaa and she was dressing in a beautiful cloth which was a bright yellow in colour. It was not too heavy though as the sun was hot and she needed to stay cool when she was outside. I surprised her with a big scream, "Ohema Kesiwaa!"

Kesiwaa turned around and saw me and she threw her hands in the air and her face was lit up like the bright golden sun outside, warmed with a big smile, beaming down at me.

"Esi" she replied and I ran up to her and fell into her out stretched arms. She grabbed my body as I threw my arms around her.

Kesiwaa looked very pretty on this day and I asked her why she was dressing in a fancy outfit and she told me it was Nana Apane's birthday and there was going to be plenty of dancing later around the fire.

For now she told me Nana Apane had gone to do some spear throwing so he could show his skills at the celebrations which were going to be held in the evening.

I was really excited and Kesiwaa told me she would find a pretty necklace from the many she had to wear this evening.

This was when Kesiwaa knelt down next to the wall with a window just above her head which gave the room some light. She opened up a wooden box and I saw bracelets made from shells and necklaces with square wooden patterned blocks. Kesiwaa picked one out and placed it around my neck and I felt like I was a really big girl. She told me some of these necklaces were not just for appearance but some of them helped to ward off bad luck and ill health. She then picked up a very thin fancy chain which was quite long. I was puzzled as to what it was for and she told me they were waist beads. Kesiwaa told me that they would only be seen by her and her husband as they were worn underneath her garments.

Kesiwaa then took the bracelets made from shells and put them around my wrist and I was so excited.

I also saw a pair of shoes I knew she had worn and I looked at them and smiled.

Kesiwaa saw me and giggled and she reached over to them,

picked them up, knelt down in front of me and slid them under my feet. I laughed loudly and Kesiwaa watched me as I walked along the side of her bed like I was all grown up. The shoes did not fit but it did not matter as I clomped forward with my feet.

As I walked along the bed I wanted to walk further and started following the wall where I saw Nana Apane's bow and arrows and then I saw knives and sharp blades.

Some were in sheaths and these were brightly coloured with red, green and black stripes and they had golden patterns on them. There was one big gold square near to the middle of the blade and it had markings which looked like they were legs.

I asked Kesiwaa why this marking was on the sheath and she told me it was the marking of our tribe. She also explained different tribes had their own symbols on their blades and other items like their spears and shields.

Some of the blades were curved and some had fancy handles. Kesiwaa spoke to me of these blades and told me some were ceremonial swords and carried by Nana Apane to deliver messages.

I walked a little bit further along the wall around this room and I saw woven bags hanging on pegs.

These were also colourful and pretty and I asked to take one.

Kesiwaa said I could and so I reached up to get it but it was too high.

I saw a wooden box underneath the bags which was standing on the floor and it had a cloth over the top and next to this was a set of scales and some metal figures. I asked what these were and Kesiwaa told me the metal figures were weights and the scales were to weigh things with.

As I tried to reach the high bag I put my right foot up to step on the wooden box and the shoe fell away from my heel. I tried to scoop it back with my toe but I completely missed my footing on the box and it flipped onto its side. This sent me tumbling onto the floor leaving me dazed.

Kesiwaa screamed and quickly jumped up from her knees and raced over to pick me up from the ground. She looked concerned for me but I reassured her I was fine, however the box had spilled some bright gold looking stones and Kesiwaa looked at me and told me to turn my eyes away.

Although I did as I was told I took a sneaky peep back and saw Kesiwaa was picking up the gold stones and was blowing away the dry red dust which had clung to them as she placed them back in the box then she placed it upright again. Kesiwaa was shaking which gave made me think she was scared at what I had done and so I asked Kesiwaa if I could help.

She told me to collect the metal figure statues which she called 'Mrammuo' which were next to the box and place them upright. She then to stood the scales back on their base and set the balance trays level again and placed them next to mrammuo and back where they were originally.

I picked up the first one which was two figures sitting on what appeared to be a log which was quite light in weight.

The next one was a figure which looked like an Odikro sitting on a stool and it had a curved seat edge which had a heavy base. This figure had a hat just like Nana Apane but it was not with a big belly like him. The stool was a symbol of status in the village and this stool looked broad for an Odikro's bottom.

The last one looked like the figure of a female, also sitting on a stool which was a weight between the two others.

I wanted to know more about these weights and I asked what they were to weigh as they were only small so they were no good for weighing any bush meat. Kesiwaa smiled at my curiosity and then she opened up to the purpose of the scales and their use.

She told me they were the bronze weights used to measure Nana Apane's gold. Kesiwaa then told me the box was Nana Apane's Kuduo vessel and I should promise her I never saw it. This I did and nodded my head to agree. She told me the scales were to measure the gold when Nana Apane was buying and trading.

This box had a lid with figures of two animals and a bird. Although not much gold stones had spilled out of the box, it was the first time I had seen this shiny yellow stone which glistened from a small candle flame which lit the room.

I had heard that Nana Apane had some things that were valuable because I knew he traded with the obroni men for things he needed. He sometimes traded with the obroni preachers who came to our village but I did not know where he kept it.

I asked Kesiwaa if she had a stool like the one in the statue and she told me she did, and she smiled again.

I saw this as an inviting expression on her face so I and asked her if I could see it. Kesiwaa said no at first but then she agreed to show me. She took me to a part of the room where she had the stool and pointed to it.

I asked if I could sit on it and Kesiwaa gestured for me to go ahead. I sat down and wriggled my bottom into place and it felt just right.

I was beaming a big smile now and so was Kesiwaa. I put my hands down by my side and placed them on the raised side on the stool and I shuffled my behind again and I sat up right.

Kesiwaa told me I looked very elegant and she curtsied before me.

I giggled, and then as I went to stand up my bracelet hooked around the raised side of the stool. I lifted my body and felt the bracelet tugging.

As I stood upright I looked behind me and I saw the seat had tilted to one side then I glanced back at Kesiwaa.

Kesiwaa looked at me and she gave me a sharp stern face. She then paused for a moment and walked over to the stool. Then in a soft voice she told me to take a look and she pointed to a hollow part of the stool leg.

Here I saw some gold stones and Kesiwaa told me these were

hers. She quietly spoke when she said nobody knew about them, not even Nana Apane. This was her secret and now it was mine as well. I saw some golden discs which had very pretty patterns on them and Kesiwaa explained these were the coins of the obroni and they were of a great value. I knew this was something that I had to remember. I wanted to have some for myself but I dare not ask Kesiwaa for her coins.

I never had a secret before and this was a big one. I knew by the look on Kesiwaa's face this was something I was not supposed to see but the secret was now out. I saw Kesiwaa had hidden something very important to her and she did it by hiding in something which would never be suspected. How clever of you Kesiwaa I thought.

Kesiwaa then replaced the tilted seat back to its correct position and clipped a thin metal spring into place which made it stay shut.

Once everything was returned back how it was Kesiwaa laughed and so did I She cradled me and I closed my eyes and absorbed her embrace.

Kesiwaa patted my back in a comforting gesture and told me to replace the shoes and trinkets as she did not want to be caught by Nana Apane.

As I took off the necklace, bracelet and shoes Kesiwaa told me she would ask the drummers to pound a new drum beat and she would give me the sign during the celebration when the new beat was to be played. Kesiwaa knew my love for the sound of the drum was what I looked forward to the most and I soon found myself looking at my Ohema as the most special person in my life other than my father and Kakraba.

Kesiwaa then told me the drums were all part of our tradition and they were played at events which included rituals of epic stories, the singing of praises, funeral ceremonies and my favourite, the masked dance performances.

Kesiwaa added that some drums were known as talking drums in some ceremonies and these were known as Kete drums. These were tall and they had a handle at the side. She told me her favourite drum was the Djembe drum as it had her favourite sound and she pointed one out to me was in the room.

She knelt down on the ground and wrote on the floor in the dust a set of markings. I was puzzled by these lines laid out in the ground. Kesiwaa then told me these markings were symbols which spelt the word for the drum.

"Djemba"

Kesiwaa showed me how to write this word and I was amazed at how this scribble in the ground was written to mean the name of a drum.

Then I laughed because it was so clever. Kesiwaa advised me she would slowly teach me the words of the obroni and also how to write some of the words down so someone could read what was written, but I was never to let this be known to anyone as only Nana Apane and some of his advisors knew these things.

Kesiwaa then wrote in the ground the word KWAKU.

"This is your name Esi; this is how it is written. Remember your name always Esi as it is your identity, you must never ever forget it.

This was a real fascinating thing for me to see as these lines in the ground made the words we speak.

Kesiwaa told me some of the words the obroni spoke were from the first people who came from a land known as "Portugal." This was many hundreds of years ago and since then there were people from another land who were known as the "Dutch" and more recently the English obroni were in our lands. Kesiwaa then told me it was the language of the English obroni she knows best and this is the one she would teach me which she did until I could write these words and understand them to read.

Kesiwaa explained the Portuguese obroni liked the gold which was embedded in our earth. She told me in order to get this gold a man would have to dig deep into the soil which she called "bilock." He would then take away this earth from around the stone which contained the gold and the valuable treasure would be his.

She explained to me gold was very precious and it was as valuable as a man's blood.

She informed me that when a man finds gold, he will spill his blood over it. This was an ancient belief, and by doing this it would ensure that the gold would remain as his.

If a man tries to take the gold without spilling his blood over it then the gold had a power that would make the bilock collapse all around him and the man who was trying to take it would be killed.

The message here was to spill your blood on any gold that you come by and it will be always in your possession.

Kesiwaa told me also that when a man is taking the gold away from the bilock or as it is known 'mining' it, there is a noise can be heard which sounds like someone is chewing food. This sound would become louder when the gold was being removed without a man's blood spilled over it.

I listened carefully as she told me they just took the gold and more recently traded it, with Nana Apane. This was why Nana Apane had his gold and also why she had her secret gold which was hidden. She added she had spilled her blood over her gold and so she knew it would never be taken away from her. When she told me this she smiled at me and I saw her eyes glisten with her pleasure of what she disclosed.

I learned from Kesiwaa that this was the reason for the name of the land I lived in. It was known as "The Gold coast."

She added that I was to be careful as there was a detestable desire for gold which would make a man's head go wild and his decisions were known to alter his loyalties for those around him. This did not sound too good but I understood everything had a cost in some way and I had to look out for this twist of character in a man's thoughts when he had this gold in his hands.

She explained to me another obroni came from a land called

France and they traded with the people far away down the coast to a place called "The Ivory Coast" and these people speak yet another language. I did not know why Kesiwaa told me all of this but it was interesting to me to learn.

Kesiwaa and I talked about the evening and we were both excited about it. I told her about a new beat I had heard and I liked it and she smiled and told me she had heard it from one on the drummers who was practising that afternoon and she like it too.

I asked Kesiwaa about our tribe singing and she told me there was always a lead singer who would sing the main words and everybody else would chant and sing it together. This was our tradition and this was what was thought to be the best way for our tribe.

It was then we both looked at some drums clustered together next to the side of the wall and next to Nana Apane's stool. I pointed at the middle one and I said i thought it made the best sound. Kesiwaa acknowledged my choice as I had chosen the little calabash drum but she said that although it was a pleasant sound, it made a quiet high pitched tone.

She then told me there was one drum that gave a very unusual sound and it was not played for a reason.

I tilted my head as I wanted to know more. Kesiwaa said it was a silent drum. So I thought it was like mine, but it wasn't at all.

She then told me that if she were to talk to it and asked it for something when it was being played and if it was truly believed in, the wish may just come true.

I was really excited about this and tried to think what I would wish for. I closed my eyes as I tried to think smartly what to wish for.

What we did not realise was how much time had gone as we just talked for ages.

As I was thinking about my wish my concentration was broken by shouting from a loud voice.

"Kesiwaa, are you here my ƆdƆ? (Love)" This was the heavy and deep voice of Nana Apane, he had returned to his hut.

"Oh no Esi, quick it is Nana Apane, get behind those drums before he sees you here." Spoke Kesiwaa in a sharp voice.

Nana's Apane's voice became louder as he neared the entrance to his hut. I scrambled behind the drums and just managed to pull my head down a make myself hidden.

"Kesiwaa my Ohema!

The shout grew louder from Nana Apane as he entered the room. Kesiwaa greeted him with an embrace and he spoke of his great aim at the spear throwing practice and he then sat down on his bed and started to remove his garments.

He asked Kesiwaa to help him and she walked over to him and took away his head band first and then his robe.

I was a little scared but I was also too excited as I was hidden away from sight and it was like playing a game, although I knew I really needed to get away.

As I crouched behind the drums I tried to think of how each drum would sound and it was then I thought of what the new beat would be for the celebration this evening.

My ears then heard Kesiwaa's voice as she seemed to be struggling with something.

"No my Odikra I am just about ready to go to the river and wash", spoke Kesiwaa in an uneasy tone.

"Remove these garments Kesiwaa at once", spoke Nana Apane.

These words were joined by the noise of movement and I heard Kesiwaa breathing and wining like she was struggling with something. I dare not look but I wanted to know what was happening.

"Remove this now Kesiwaa", spoke Nana Apane in a forceful voice and the sound of a cloth tearing came soon after.

"Nana no!" was the voice of Kesiwaa and this time it was not a plea but a mere desperate cry. I cowered even more behind the drums and tried to remain calm but I was starting to get scared. Kesiwaa's cries for whatever was happening to stop were just ignored and Nana Apane just spoke a few meaningless odd words.

"Stay still Kesiwaa" was his first request and then I just heard

"Yes my Ohema yes."

I dare not imaging what was taking place only a short distance from where I was. My short years of life did not give me any insight as to what was happening and when I heard Kesiwaa's voice turn from a moan to a sound she was crying, it was then I lifted my head to just above the top of the middle drum. Slowly, slowly I saw first the head of Nana Apane and then slightly higher and then I lifted up a little more.

It was then I saw what remained in my vivid thoughts like things were in slow motion. Kesiwaa was kneeling with her head crushed into the cloths in front of her and she was barely clothed. The beautiful cloth she had been wearing was strewn around her. Nana Apane was completely bare and he was pressing his mid-section as if he was rubbing himself onto Kesiwaa.

I wondered if Kesiwaa was alright and then she turned her face towards my direction and she saw me. Her eyes caught mine and I saw tears falling from her cheeks.

I did not know what to do but I just crouched and watched what I thought was Kesiwaa receiving some kind of massage to her back as Nana Apane stroked his hands from the back of her head to her bottom. This went on for some time and then without warning Nana Apane raised his voice as if he was possessed by demons and then he fell away from Ohema Kesiwaa.

"Kesiwaa, a seed of my loins may now grow and a child must come now!"

Spoke Nana Apane and then he just lay still. I thought this was a time for me to show myself but it did not seem right and so I thought long and hard and stayed hidden.

Nana Apane laid on his back and looked perfectly still. Moments later Kesiwaa gave me the signal to leave and I crept from behind the drums and slipped through the door curtain.

I went through the main door cloth and out into the sun and ran straight back to my hut. I grabbed a straw doll and went to the place where I sleep and covered my eyes. I tried not to think about what I had seen and tried to think about the sound of the drums but this did not work and the vision of my Ohema crying and seeing Nana Apane massaging her pain scratched a mark into my thoughts and they stayed there.

It was here I thought Nana Apane was a good man as he was healing my Ohema with his Odikro strength and power.

This day was to bring the night of celebration and the new beat was to be played and my Ohema Kesiwaa was to give me the signal. However she did not show for the evening celebration and so I imagined she was resting from her healing. Oh my Kesiwaa we had a great day today I thought to myself.

Ansaba and Agyeiba were always complaining to Nana Apane and they would not hold their tongue but would rather insult you than apologise. They complimented each other as they spoke as though they knew what each was going to say and they would never talk to us unless it was for us to fetch them something or they just felt lazy and made us work for them. This style of order and demand was passed on to their children.

They were also arrogant and they would walk around with their noses in the air, speak rudely even to the elders without any mark of respect.

Kesiwaa was the only one who would always speak against them and side with the tribe member if she heard anything. This would get her in trouble with Nana Apane and I sometimes wished she would keep away from these issues. You see, Nana Apane could one minute be your best friend but the next minute you were no use to him.

Kesiwaa had tempered Nana Apane on quite a few occasions because of his children.

On one occasion a son of Nana Apane who was named Osei (which meant "Nobel") was near to our hut talking to some of the boys who lived in huts nearby. The boys were saying my father was supposed to fix the roof of their hut but he did not show and because of this they had to ask someone else.

This was not true and I knew the reason my father did not show was because he had not been too well at the time, and he had told them he would do it when he felt a lot stronger.

Osei twisted these words and told his mother Ansaba that my father was not doing his work among the tribe as my father was lazy. He then shouted an insult and he called him "W'enim tantan kuraseni", an ugly faced villager.

When Osei returned to talk to the local boys, my father heard Osei say my father was no longer needed in the tribe and he was an old fool "Kwaseampani". This kind of talk would be the way a "Bush boy", an uncultured boy would behave.

This angered my father who told Osei his words were cruel, and he shouted "Wo nnim nynsa", which meant "You have no sense."

Osei went back to Nana Apane and informed him what my father had said. However, he did not tell Nana the whole of the exchange of words between him and my father.

He did not say what he had said to my father and about his cruel goading and he claimed my father spoke badly of him without Osei saying anything at all. He added my father had laughed at him about the repair of the hut and this got my father a warning from Nana Apane. Osei lied to Nana Apane and deliberately gave my father a bad name with him.

The layout of the village meant our homes were gathered about twenty huts deep and they were spaced out to the outer part of our village and some of the men were building new ones for the newly coupled young men and women.

From a young age I played with my friends and we made images of each other with straw from the grass near to an area close to the trees and clay from the red soil around us. One of my friends I knew from an early age was a girl called Efua. (She was born on a Friday).

We would make tiny mud huts to pretend our straw and clay dolls had somewhere to live. We would put them to sleep in these tiny play huts during the night and cover them with large leaves to keep them warm.

We would even use old cloth to wrap around our straw dolls and gave them names to get a feel of them being real.

As the time went by Kesiwaa continued, as she had promised to teach me the words of the obroni and she visited me every week when my father was away from our hut. She would sometimes write the words down for me to learn and it was a funny day when she wrote the word "obroni." This was because she told me the obroni did not even know how to spell this word.

Kesiwaa made me happy on this day. I listened very keenly to her until I was starting to hold conversations in the language of the obroni with Kesiwaa. She had to tell me to stop so others would not hear me and I was learning fast. Yet even better was I was able to spell his words as well and as Kesiwaa informed me, not all obroni could even spell his own words. The one word which was still a mystery was the word "ƆdƆ" for love. I did not really know how this word was supposed to be used but Kesiwaa tried to tell me it would be a word I would find one day in my akuma (heart).

As I was now older than some of the other girls, it was my job to go to the river and help wash our clothes which got stained readily from the red soil, and clean the cooking pots. It was also my duty to collect some water from a stream of running water for our village and find some kindling and some firewood.

I brought the water and poured it into a clay pot that was buried in the ground which, when covered kept the water cool for drinking. A bright cloth was placed over the top to stop anybody walking over it. I did this duty as it was my contribution to my tribe and I got into the routine with regularity.

Kesiwaa began to teach me how to sow the material and repair any rips that were in the clothes of Nana Apane. As I learned how to do this she helped me to make clothes for myself and I even made some for Kakraba. I became very good at sewing material together and I even started to add patterns to the clothes I made. I made beads and bracelets and as I learned these things I sat with Kakraba and I showed her also. I got to be very good at this and I helped Kesiwaa if she needed me and I was always given a hot plantain and ground nuts for my trouble, although I would have done this for her anyway.

I also worked with my friend Efua and if we were to leave our hut we let the family in the hut next to us and my father, watch over Kakraba.

Each day brought something new and I never knew what was to be my duty ahead of me.

Over the years my body grew in size and my limbs were fuller and bigger and my height brought me to stand to the shoulder of Kesiwaa when we stood together.

Not long after this time my body changed from one of a child to a woman. My chest grew bigger and I had pain in my stomach which was unbearable. I knew this was to come as Kesiwaa had told me, but I never expected it to be so bad.

When this happened Kesiwaa made me a drink of hot water which she poured over the leaves taken from a local tree, this eased my stomach, but I was still in discomfort. I found a position when lying down that eased the pain but it was not just in my tummy, the pain reached through to my back as well. She also boiled a cloth on some water and once it had cooled slightly I held it against my belly.

This was when I first discovered about my 'puberty rites' which was a tradition for the girls to undergo. I was only fourteen years old when Kesiwaa told me I had to participate in this teaching which took a young woman into Adulthood and where she became a Lady (Ewuraba). With our tribe it is the women who represent the purity and dignity where the mother would ensure the young lady would be taught good morals and mentor her to develop her beauty.

The queen's, along with some of the leading women would seclude young girls who saw their first time of becoming a Lady (Ewuraba).

They took the girls from the village for two to three weeks during which they are taught the correct ways of being a woman and they mentored the girls of the qualities required for a woman to be a good wife to her husband.

This is where I was taught by Kesiwaa about birth control and how to be disciplined. To remain untouched and pure and to ensure a good marriage by not having an unwanted baby which I quickly understood. I was told without going through this ritual I would not be able to get married. This was also the time to learn how to be respectful to your husband.

After this there was of course dancing and drumming under the eyes of Onyankopon which made sure this was blessed and complete.

Once this was done I was recognised as a woman and continued with my dignity and purity.

So I had become a woman and the things that go with this I had to adjust to and accept. Kesiwaa made me tea when I needed it. Sometimes this eased the ache but most of the time my belly was asleep for just a brief spell, however, I knew how to make the pain go away with my own potion because I had my gift inside my head. My silent drum always blocked any discomfort or pain.

I started to count down to the days to which this time would come. I had to however continue with my duties, which was often difficult when trying to carry a pot of water on my head.

On one occasion I remember I did not wish to walk for water and did not want to ask the mother of the family in the hut next to ours for help as she was getting older. She still had to do all of the duties by herself in her hut, so I went to ask for someone else to fetch some water for me and I had a wander around the village.

CHAPTER 4: ƆdƆ (Love)

I wandered around my village and saw the new huts being built for the couples who have declared their commitment to each other. These are young men and women in love. This word Kesiwaa had taught me is about something which should happen to me one day. I was still waiting many years after Kesiwaa first told me about it. I still did not know what it was.

I loved Onyankopon, our God, and I understood the love for my family and the love for my friends and of course I loved Kesiwaa but this was a different type and I was curious in how many types there were. Kesiwaa told me one day it will find me and I will not have to look for it. This was a strange thing to me but I believe Kesiwaa which is why this thing "ƆdƆ", love puzzled me, maybe one day I will know the answer but I knew for now my love was for my food.

Kesiwaa had once taught me how to make some abenkwan, which is palm nut soup. Kesiwaa told me how to clean the palm nut and boil them until they were soft. After this I had to pound them until they were made into a pulp and I was finding it great fun.

Kesiwaa asked me if I enjoyed pounding the palm nut and I told her that it was fun and that palm nut soup was my favourite meal. I just could not wait for it to be ready. As I was really excited about being able to make this soup and then ready and waiting to eat it, I asked if this was the love which I would find as I grew older. Kesiwaa reminded me the ƆdƆ I will find will be in my akuma (heart) and not my stomach.

I asked her if it was not the love for Onyankopon, or the love of my family or friends and now the enjoyment of pounding the palm nut and eating the soup then I did not know what it was. Kesiwaa laughed at me and continued to laugh as I pounded another palm nut until I asked her if the ƆdƆ she had was for Nana. Of course I was guessing but I said something wrong and Kesiwaa's face dropped like a falling fruit from a tree.

"Esi, daabi! Onyankopon aniwa hu asumasem biara!"(Esi, no! God's eyes see all secrets). I had stopped Kesiwaa's smile with my question and I felt terrible within myself.

I never asked her again and my search for this type of love remained a far distance away from my life.

I carried on walking around the village and was ready to give up looking and I had tried to get one of the boys who were just a little younger than me to help as all of the girls were doing their own duties. He just told me he was looking after his mother who was sick and his father had to help the other elder men with the new huts.

Most of the other boys were busy making and repairing their bows and sharpening their spears and so I assumed they would not help but I asked anyway.

As I looked around I came to an area favoured with the boys who liked to play their games. This was an open savannah and was away from any huts.

I passed by a group of five girls who were sitting on the ground. One of them was a girl called Kuukuwa (born on a Wednesday). She was one of Nana Apane's unrecognised children, yet everybody knew who she was. She was about fourteen years old and I guess she had just started to look at the boys as there were some of them throwing spears nearby. As I passed they just looked at me without anything other than a stare.

I saw the group of five boys who were practising with their spears by throwing them at targets made from large bundles of dry grass and I walked up to get a closer look.

They did look funny as one boy pulled the bundle by a length of plaited grass. It was wrapped around his wrist at one end and tied to the bale of straw at the other. He then ran across the hunter to make the target harder to hit. As he ran it was his part of the deal to make sure he ran quick enough to be like the escaping beast. He also pulled the bale with a sharp tug every so often to make the task more difficult.

To add to the escaping animal effect the pretend beast would make a noise. Not the noise of an animal though. No, these boys made this, just as boys do, into a game of "I am better than you" and so as the boy playing the beast ran across the boy hunter he sang words of tease to him saying he was the "worst of all hunters " and "You cannot catch me," in a taunting and goading voice.

"I am the beast,

You want to feast,

Well you will only match me,

If you can catch me"

These boys were funny, and although this was just their game, there was a sense of pride hidden which was not really part of the rules.

The boy who was trying to hit the target stood with his back to me but he was tall and had a broad back. I watched as he followed the target with a steady stance. The spear was held above his head with his strong right arm. I watched this hunting practice with some admiration and a tiny smile. The other three boys stood watching the practice and also goaded the "bale hunter."

These boys were going to be the hunters of the future and were on the first stage of their journey. I watched with interest at the show I was viewing. Then suddenly as the bale beast was targeted. The boy with the spear held it above his head and he leaned back and bent the leg behind him and then he remained perfectly still. All went quiet among the boys except for the "bale beast." Waiting for the right moment seemed to be a time not going to end and then it happened.

"Shhhhhhhhhhtuuum!"

The spear flew, cutting the air in an almost perfect straight line which I saw from directly behind the broad shoulders the thrower.

The long sharp spike was thrown with such accuracy and weight it flew with speed and sharpness piercing through the bale pinning it into the ground. This then stopped the target moving which made the boy pulling the bale perform his part of the act. You see, he did not see what had happened behind him, as he was too busy singing his tease to the spear thrower which ended with him being pulled back with a sudden jolt and his feet shooting forwards and up in the air. This made him slam down on the ground with a thump. The song ended and the boy and bale remained still. The "bale beast" was killed.

"Woah," I shouted, and then I laughed at the funny sight I had just watched as this skill and exhibition amused me. I did not think this was really supposed to happen but it was good to see the other boys run to the aid of their fallen friend.

The boy with the spear looked concerned as he helped his "catch" from the ground and as soon as he saw he was well, he started to reply with taunts of his own. He then sings to the others and as he does he runs around the fallen beast.

"The hunt which I trail,

Is slow like a snail,

This catch is not sweet,

This beast is old meat."

I laughed so loud it reminded me why I was watching in the first place as I felt a dull ache in my belly. I was there to find somebody to help me with carrying water but this was not in my thoughts any more.

It was then the spear thrower turned around and I first saw his face.

He had heard my laughing and I looked at this fine looking boy with an interest never before to greet my eyes. This boy had stolen my attention with a look of instant pleasure.

The gaze he gave me was direct to my eyes which made me tingle inside. My skin shivered nerves of shyness which was a feeling new to me and the start of new excitement.

This caused my confident stand tall style to lower and I felt stripped from my strength of style as this spear thrower curled the corners of his mouth upwards to reveal his bright teeth as he grinned at me.

I thought for a short time about this attraction to his smile and his muscular form but I pushed it away and out of my head.

After all, these boys were too busy with their game, and they were not going to give it up to help me. As I was about to turn and walk away the spear thrower called out at me. I felt a bit embarrassed now but he told me to wait and I did.

I do not know why but I froze just like a startled tiny animal and his shout took a hold of me.

This spear thrower walked up towards me and as he did I bowed my head to think quickly what I am supposed to say.

As he got nearer to me it was clear he was very tall. So much so his muscular body blocked the sun from my eyes as I stood in his shadow.

He then introduced himself to me. His told me his name was Fiifi Mensah. Fiifi's name meant he was Friday born.

In my attempt to be polite I asked if the boy who was pulled to the ground was all right and he just laughed and said his friend was called Ato (Saturday born) and he needed the lesson to learn for himself how to hunt and be hunted.

Fiifi was of course showing me his pride in his skill when he threw the spear, however, now he was showing me his friendliness and charm.

Along with his broad grin with teeth which had gaps Fiifi also had a wide nose.

The other boys chased each other as they ran up to join Fiifi and myself and their interest in me was one of excitement but Fiifi stood taller than them and their body frames were not as broad. Fiifi stood tall like an Odikro with his advisors by his side.

I asked Fiifi how he managed to be so accurate with his target so he could hit the bale beast. He appeared almost proud to tell me as his body straightened up and his chest lifted up.

He then continued to show me and he stood with his feet apart and legs slightly bent and he held his hand level with his shoulder and slightly behind him. He advised me he had to be very watchful and just wait until the target is still for a tiny bit too long. Then, he added, he threw his hand forward as if he were going to place his first finger onto the place he wanted to hit the object or beast. If he was quick and his hand moved in a straight direction he should not miss.

As Fiifi taught me how to spear a beast the boys looked at me and they laughed. They asked me to try but I was not feeling ready to join this game and I asked them that if I did would they come and help me bake some plantains later which dissolved their mocking of me immediately.

Fiifi continued to talk to me but I had drifted into a mild daydream as I lost the other boys in my focus and just saw the spear thrower.

By now I had tried to relax again, and I straightened up to stand tall. I did this to impress Fiifi as I did not want to appear to be slumped over at my shoulders. I then readjusted my vision to see all of the boys and I asked them if any of them could help me for the day.

Of course I was really only asking Fiifi and I did not expect any help from any of them but I was then surprised and pleased when he offered to help.

I had thought for a quick moment Fiifi was the kind of boy who thought he was better than the others but he proved my judgement of him wrong and he was ready as prepared to take my duties as part of his. Of course I had seen Fiifi before in the village but not with the same eyes I now looked at him with.

The day was strange to me as my focus could not keep away from his attraction which resulted with me finding myself asking questions to myself. Sometimes when I was with him I held my stare for longer as I monitored his muscular frame and handsome face. I even saw his left ear lobe was split slightly but I dare not ask him why it was like this. It would be too much to ask this boy as I did not really know him, but I wanted to.

I noticed he had a habit of pushing his arms up and down from his waist then towards the ground. I thought this was funny, but it turned out to be a sign Fiifi was nervous and he was becoming stressed. On one occasion he started to do his arms thing as I was with him and it was as if he were trying to get a dance rhythm going. I don't know why he was getting stressed as I was just as nervous about being around Fiifi, probably more so.

Fiifi and I met regularly and he helped me with my duties and we continued to be friends.

I found out more each day about Fiifi. He was the son of a hunter as I was after my father and so although they knew each other they did not really talk very much as my father was slightly older than his was.

Fiifi had four brothers and three sisters. He was the eldest and so he had his responsibility as I did. His mother was a very quiet lady who kept herself to their hut. I think she just preferred to remain like this as she did not enjoy the gossiping and talk among the other women, but she also had her sister to watch over as she had a problem with walking which meant everything had to be carried for her.

For this reason, Fiifi's father would always be away from their hut either, maintaining other people's roofs, fixing fences or collecting fruits and ground provisions.

This left Fiifi to do the main work around his home which he passed quickly on to his next youngest brother. He told me he had no time for tasks at his home as he wanted to learn quickly to be a warrior as building a fire and chopping wood for the fire were jobs for younger boys.

Fiifi asked more about me and my family and he made it clear from his questioning, although he never actually told me at this time, he was showing a closer interest in me. I found this attracted me even more so to him. It was like we were being drawn together like two pretty birds in the sky flying together.

I knew he liked me, however, I had in the back of my mind he also desired to be a warrior and his bow and arrows were his other loyalty.

As the weeks passed I now could not think of anything more but Fiifi. I went to sleep thinking of him and woke up the same. Thinking of him became my first and last thoughts of the day. I soon got to see his little movements and varied facial expressions which made Fiifi the boy I liked.

The day I met Fiifi changed my life and after he had fetched my water on the first day it was soon we were seeing quite a lot of each other. To the tribe we were friends because of his choice for the secrecy. Fiifi wanted this to be between just the two of us as he did not want to spoil his chance to join the teachings from the elders for his learning with the others who wanted to follow after their fathers. Fiifi wanted to one day become a mighty tribal warrior.

We had both shown obvious feelings towards each other until the day he walked me to the edge of the water of the river nearby and expressed his desire for me to be his future. I thought for merely seconds before I answered an acknowledgement of my desire to be with him as well. He took me into his arms and my feet went all weak and by belly fluttered ripples of excitement.

The day was special for me and I was so excited about our future. Fiifi then paddled into the water and held his spear high and then stood calm. He then snapped his arm forward and the spear shot quickly from his hand into the water. As soon as this was done he pulled out the spear and there was a tilapia flapping on the spiked end.

Fiifi stepped from the water and told me the fish was for me and I just giggled with excitement at his sharp eye and skill.

We talked about the time ahead of us and although he wanted to be a warrior, for now, his duties would be to help the hut builders and watch them and learn what they did. He knew he had to progress through the ranks of duty in the village.

Firstly there were the hut builders and the men who repaired any damaged huts. These were usually the older men or younger boys who were soon to become men. These could also be bush boys

They would gather the straw for the roofs and work as teams to build the walls and then the roof to a new hut. They stayed within the village and would also help the women with the carrying of water if they needed it. The boys would use their spare time to practice their hunting skills. Fiifi must do all of this.

Then there were the hunters. These were the men who used their stealth to catch the beasts for our meat. They had to be vigilant, quiet and precise with their spears.

They would practice throwing their spears at a target made with the softest of wood so their weapons would not be damaged.

The only time they would use the bale of grass was if they were pretending the beast or target was moving just like Fiifi had been doing when I first saw him practicing his throwing with his friends.

They also had their bows to fire their arrows and they would practice until they were very accurate and precise. To fire an arrow at a beast and not kill it would mean the arrow would be taken and lost and another one had to be made.

Finally there were the warriors and these men were taught to fight. They were usually former hunters who went away with their mentors and other boys and were guided by a group of head warriors to learn the skills of combat. These warriors went to a nearby area every day the practice fighting skills and learning the wise teachings from the most experienced of men.

Fiifi was very strong and so he hoped he would make a fine warrior. However he was a bit shy underneath his big frame. He would need to bring out some fire from his heart if he was to succeed. Fiifi was a very good role model for the younger boys and he was ready to choose his future. He knew of the stories about my father and to gain my heart he knew he had to produce a profile of ambition. I was after all the daughter of a very fine former warrior.

Fiifi started to fetch my water more often although he was needed to do other duties and he was warned once by one of the elders for neglecting these.

Soon after this a girl called Kuukuwa came by to see me. She was the girl who I had walked past as she sat with her friends and they all stared at me without a comment.

Kuukuwa told me she had heard information from her mother that the elders thought Fiifi was neglecting his duties by helping me and she advised us to be careful of what was being spoken amongst them. She added she was only passing on a message to brief me and offer her knowledge and guidance.

She informed me the elders were talking highly of Fiifi but they noticed he was being distracted by visiting me. Kuukuwa then said whilst this situation was like it was the best thing Fiifi and I could do would be to keep our interest in each other a secret for now as it could jeopardise his chance to one day be a warrior.

I was very grateful Kuukuwa had offered her advice as I was determined not to get in Fiifi's way of his dream to achieve his dream. After all, she did have direct information from Nana Apane and his advisors as she and her mother would often take food to them and talk would be open to many ears.

I had to tell Fiifi immediately that I had to start collecting water for myself and I suggested I would only ask him if it was really needed. This I did and we agreed to be more discreet with our visits and interest towards each other.

As time went by Fiifi and I kept our desire for each other between us although the village saw us together a lot they thought we were just friends as we held our feelings out of the reach of listen ears as Kuukuwa advised.

This did not stop us talking just as strongly and passionately when we could about our future together.

It was clear to us we had fallen in love and we hid it very well. Not even my father knew about my feelings for Fiifi. In fact my father asked me on a couple of occasions if I had found anyone to settle down with in case he should start building a hut for me and my future husband.

Fiifi and I continued with our secret commitment and when we could we met at the end of the village near to an open water area where we discussed our future and things we enjoyed about each other.

One subject I always brought up was that although he was strong and handsome he still did not have a steady pace in his feet to dance.

I tried to teach him but he did not know how to dance around the fire at our drum beats nights.

Every step I showed him did not go past his ears to his feet.

When he did try, his movement was one of a frightened rodent that just scurried its feet in a frenzied shuffle.

The thoughts of his attempts to dance still bring a smile to my face as I think about this rapid movement. When the beat was racing he was too slow and when it was steady then his feet moved too fast.

As time went on both Fiifi and I grew older and it was time for him to start with his hunting training and after he made a new spear and bow he was shooting his arrows at the targets all the time. He usually arose earlier than normal to go to the river to get my water if I needed it then he started his hunting training. His strength and energy was in need of nourishment so I made sure he had some fruit as a supplement to his daily food.

During our many conversations Fiifi told me about the different tribes and he drew me pictures in the sand of the symbols each one put on their spears and shield and hunting arm bands he had learned about. Everything Fiifi was taught he usually came back and told me. I remembered all of his teachings to me and I absorbed this knowledge with a keen interest.

I was so proud of him and I soon started making extra food for him and as I made him some of his favourite light soup and banku.

I encouraged him to always practice his hunting skills so he could keep his mind focused and his aim sharp.

One afternoon when the sun was behind a grey cloud Fiifi brought me a "Grasscutter" which was a little rodent and it was very tasty when smoked. We called it bush meat. He told me he tracked it and then his spear stopped it still with one swift and powerful throw.

It was supposed to be for me but I insisted we share it. This was our first meal like this and we giggled together like children when we finished eating it as we were both still hungry. It was a small meat but it was a sweet gesture from Fiifi.

This was also the first time I cooked Fiifi my very special palm nut soup and as I pounded the palm nuts I felt a great sense of pleasure doing this for him knowing he would really enjoy it. In fact I was so happy he may even love it. I was delighted when he responded to tell me it was just like how his mother made it and his broad grin made me feel contented with my provision. If I can make his stomach content his akuma will follow.

A while went by then Fiifi was asked to join a group of young men which included Ato to go to the hunting teachings and at this time I was so proud of him.

I remember this was the day we had spent the late night by the central fire talking about his achievement of his hunting skills and he held my hand with the comfort and commitment of a boy who was already sure of his choice for a life with me.

He would come to see me and sit with me after the first part of his training and I put the pot on the fire ready to warm him for the evening and maybe warm some soup.

After what seemed to be a long training time which took several changes of a new moon Fiifi told me the day had come for him and he was ready to go out with his group of friends and of course with Ato to his first hunt.

Fiifi told me he would be gone for several days and each night I had to look for the brightest star in the sky. He added he too would be looking at it and thinking of me. If we did this then our thoughts would fly to the star and then it would sparkle and would reflect them back down to each other and then we would dream about our love we both received. Fiifi you are such a sweet man and you make me feel full with my love for you.

The next day I was sitting by my hut pounding some yams when Fiifi approached with his big smile and his chest was standing high. He informed me that he was going on his first hunt and he had passed by to see me before he left the village.

I remember vividly this day and I jumped up and fell into his arms and my akuma (my heart) raced like the legs of a fast beast as it raced away from being caught.

I was so proud of my Fiifi and I would continue to support him and my akuma was jumping around inside my chest. I started to understand what Kesiwaa had taught me and what my akuma was feeling for my Fiifi, or should I now call him my ƆdƆ?

Fiifi then left for his hunting and I watched as he wandered towards the open savannah with the others.

One morning I was with some of the other girls and women of the village who were grinding some cassava to make food.

Among these girls was my friend Efua and she was sitting next to me roasting some plantain over a small fire.

Now that Fiifi and Ato had gone for their first hunt with the elder hunters, I stayed in the village with Efua. I was excited as you can imagine but she was too and she had something to tell me.

Her information came as a surprise as she informed me she was making an arrangement with Ato for a future together. I had noticed them sitting alone on many occasions but I did not see this at all. I listened with interest but I kept my commitment to my Fiifi close to my chest so she never knew my feelings for my ƆdƆ.

As I listened to Efua I wanted to talk to her about Fiifi as it was the day of his first hunt too and I wanted to say how proud I was. I decided to keep my secret to myself as I had agreed with Fiifi.

Efua however was telling me about her ƆdƆ who was her love so I was obliged to listen.

I did not realise that her love with Ato had gone so far, so much so that they were making the plans to be joined in a new hut together, and very soon. So they were arranging their marriage I thought.

It was then I felt stronger about telling her how I felt about Fiifi but when she started talking there was no stopping her.

As this talk continued it made me even more certain I would hold out for the right time to inform her of my love for Fiifi.

Each time I spoke to Efua after this I wanted to talk about my Fiifi but she did not cease her conversation about her ƆdƆ. I listened to her at first, but after a while my thoughts soon drifted onto Fiifi. Although I did not want to be rude, I wanted to think of Fiifi. This was the perfect time for my silent drum to find my head.

I closed my eyes and thought of my Prince, my ƆdƆ, my special heart (akuma). I saw him with my beats of my drum pounding in my head. I picture my beloved hunter chasing a wild beast with excitement under the sparse tall trees out in the savannah.

The drumbeat which joined the vision in my head was the strongest I had brought to my eager desire for my Fiifi. As soon as this beat was there, the tranquillity was in my mind and was complete. This beat had an almost hypnotic spell to me. It cushioned any thoughts, and made me numb to the world. I still heard the words of Efua rambling on about her and Ato but I did not absorb them.

"Bam ba ba, bam ba ba bam ba ba bam, ba ba bam ba ba bam, ba ba bam ba ba bam bam ba ba, bam ba ba bam."

In my head I saw Fiifi hunting and he would skip through the bushes with his hunting spear in his hand raised high and his newly learned hunting skills ready to capture our food.

These skills which kept him away from the village and away

from me for so many days, learning from our village master teachers. I saw his face, as he looked at me with his big excited eyes. It is as if I was with him. I heard Efua still talking about her Ato and I somehow knew what she was saying to me but I was totally focused on my thoughts of Fiifi.

I had a vision of Fiifi and Ato with a good days work done seeing their smiling faces and I was confident they would walk into the village with success in their arms in the form of a beast to roast and feast on after their first day of hunting.

After this I thought one day about what Fiifi had told me. He informed me about the skill needed to throw a spear at an animal that was running for its life. So I took my father's hunting spike and made a target and practised just as Fiifi had done.

I put my feet apart and legs slightly bent and then I held the spear level to my shoulder and slightly behind me I imagined my target was still for a little bit too long and then I threw my hand forward trying to place my first finger onto the point on my target. Well as you can imagine I missed every time until one day I actually hit a tiny grass shrub I aimed for and I felt so good. I laughed so much but nobody knew why I was smiling to myself when I went back to our hut. Well I could not really tell anyone as girls never practised throwing spears but more so, no-one was interested anyway.

Fiifi and Ato had been absent for many days and the village was preparing for a celebration on their return with the other new hunters. Efua told me on this occasion she was going to announce her union with Ato.

Fiifi and I did not want to overshadow their night. I agreed with Fiifi to remain quiet and keep secret of our union and feelings for a short time longer until the next evening of the Nana Apane's dancing and drums.

You see, Fiifi and I were blessed with each other's commitment and we were strong. Fiifi and I even managed to create our own code of communication so we could signal each other and nobody would know.

Well actually we did not create it really as it was introduced to me by my mentor Kesiwaa one morning when she taught me about stealth and secrecy.

Kesiwaa not only taught me how to speak in code but also the way to walk around without making a noise. She taught me to be light on my toes which I told Fiifi to use when he was hunting. This was fun when I was teaching him as he kept losing his balance and he would fall over. I showed him how to move without making any noise and included controlled breathing and balancing his body weight with every stride taken. Then slowly each step was softly trodden with precision so nobody could hear you. I made sure I practised this until I had it just perfect. Fiifi was thankful that I taught him.

The visual code she taught me varied but it was to give a signal when a decision was needed.

The one we used to communicate the most was if you scratched your nose it was a signal your coded answer was "yes" and a "no" if you rubbed your left ear.

These were the main codes among many others Fiifi and I used and we used them as often as we could to keep our communication secretive.

"Oh Kesiwaa you know all the tricks and codes", I thought to myself. I thought about Kesiwaa for a brief spell and what she had taught me and then quickly forgot her again. Anyway I had my Fiifi now and it had been a long time since I had seen her.

What Fiifi and I also did was use a cipher which made the words we spoke switch to mean something different.

Only we knew the code so when I told Fiifi "I am hungry for my favourite food", it meant my hunger was my desire and love for him and not for anything to eat.

If then I asked him if he was still hungry for his favourite food, it was a code of me asking him if he still loved me. He would also ask the same of me which I found to be sweet when he did pose the question.

If I had wanted to tell Fiifi I needed something then I told him I was tired. This code meant I was tired of waiting for something.

When I had a secret to tell him I informed him I wanted to hear the sound of the drums play.

Lastly, when we spoke of "a pot of boiling water" This became our code for there may be danger ahead. These codes were just a bit of fun really but they were useful when they were used.

Fiifi made some proposals to me that he knew he couldn't keep just to make me happy and he even promised to give me the first catch of his inaugural hunt, even though he knew he had to give it to our Odikro.

Nana Apane had the first choice in everything and this was our village way and it could never be challenged by anyone. If you did challenge the Odikro's decision for anything then you would be punished.

The offer by my Fiifi was a sweet offer which made me proud and full of love for him.

Our pact of silence about our love for each other was our secret. We knew when we were ready to announce it to the village it would surprise everyone and make them scream with excitement. Our secret love was ours and ours alone. This was the one thing Nana Apane couldn't take that away from us at least.

As I listened to Efua, the words she spoke made my mouth open but I could not speak. My silent drum held my words behind the barrier against my mouth.

Efua's lips kept disclosing everything towards my tired ears and she went on and on and on. I absorbed all she said but filtered the bits that were unnecessary. Every now and again I took a breath to say something but she got in first with more chatter. She did not hear or see my attempts to speak and she just continued talking each time we prepared the food for ourselves and others.

On one occasion I did manage to say something when my tongue let itself go, "Oh Fiifi me daase," thank you, I said "me daase", I repeated as I thought of my Fiifi.

Efua was too centred with her conversation and she carried on without pausing.

When I had fulfilled my thoughts my eyes opened and I was again listening to Efua and my dreams for Fiifi soon evaporated temporarily and Efua never even knew I had switched off. How would she?

The day went by and the sun began to slowly sink into to ground.

Then Efua and I heard and great noise from the other villagers which turned into a chanting of song.

The hunters had returned from the day of success and they walked proudly into the village with their catch. I did not see Fiifi or Ato so my thoughts were where were they? The first hunters to arrive placed their beasts on the ground in front of the Odikro's hut, whose hut was the only one to accept the meat before all others.

These hunters then stood back and the Odikro's advisers were called.

I kept looking back for Fiifi and Ato. Efua carried on again just as before about her Ato and this started to become tiring.

I was concerned about Fiifi and Ato and I was just starting to get worried when all of a sudden I saw two figures in the distance. There he was. I saw him walking in the distance with Ato, carrying the biggest beast of all between them on poles made from the local wood.

Their tiny frames were in the distance, they grew as they got nearer and it was then I realised why they were far behind everyone else. The beast they caught was huge. So big that Fiifi and Ato looked almost slumped and rounded in their shoulders as they struggled to carry it.

They arrived to the excitement of the villagers. The beast was big and therefore it was heavy and they had to carry it between the two of them slowing their pace more than the other hunters.

There were about ten beasts in total, some were grasscutter little beasts but Fiifi and Ato's wilder beast was the biggest of them all.

The excitement raced through my body. I was so proud of my Fiifi. I looked at Efua and her smile was as broad as it could be.

Our hero hunters had returned with their offering to our tribe's folk.

CHAPTER 5: Verdict

After the gathering of villagers cheered all of the hunters as they walked into the main area, the loudest and last shout was for Fiifi and Ato. This signalled the time for Nana Apane to come out from his hut and he saw the hunter's gifts to him.

His eyes met a huge selection of slain lifeless beasts ready to be cooked over a hot fire and Nana Apane looked happy. He turned to one of his advisors and he slapped him on his back.

Nana informed everyone he was hungry by these words and he then looked at his hunters.

As he spoke he stood tall and proud and his eyes saw a treasure of a feast to be had. He looked around at the villagers and told them to thank the hunters and we all shouted our blessings.

He then raised his head up to make another announcement to us. Nana Apane appeared as though he had drunk some palm wine. He was smiling all of the time then he spoke to us and said.

"Tonight is a special night and I am required to deliver a message to all." Then he paused.

"The women shall take the catch the hunters have brought for us and prepare them for a special evening," he added.

"The drummers will bring me a new beat for this evening of celebration, and the fire makers will build a bigger fire than normal for today is one to be remembered." So spoke Nana Apane.

Why was it to be remembered I thought? Then I realised it was Fiifi's first day hunting and he may be given a reward for his catch.

Hunters do not normally get a catch for the first couple of hunts. So this was a great day for both Fiifi and Ato as they had caught the master beast of the hunt.

Everyone was excited and we returned to our huts to prepare the food on the fire and for the evenings feasting and dancing. Fiifi came with me as we had spent so many days apart and I wanted to hear his voice of excitement on this special day.

We talked about the evening and how there would be lots of dancing. I chuckled when I told Fiifi that as he was now a known hunter he had better dance a little sharper as the villagers would be watching him.

I loved dancing to the beat of the drums and my feet moved by their self when I heard a pound of the skin. There were times when I found the beat so easy the drummers would end up following me and my feet instead of me following them. This was very funny to those playing their rhythms. Fiifi also picked up on this and sometimes I would dance and others stopped to watch me and when this happened my eyes half closed and I became lost in my own rhythm until I managed to bring myself out of this state and see my audience.

This then made me think, 'What new beats will the drummers bring?' I was excited about the coming night's entertainment and festivities and I knew Efua was going to tell the village about her and Ato. I wished to do the same with my Fiifi but this evening was not mine and Fiifi and I agreed for the next night of feasting to be ours, and when it comes it will be magical.

I was looking forward to this evening and spoke to Fiifi about my admiration for him and also my happiness for Efua and Ato.

I was hoping Fiifi might get a word of appreciation from Nana Apane for his catch and this added even more impatience from us for the evening to start and the dance to commence.

I asked Fiifi how he managed to get his catch and his answer was simple. Fiifi spoke to me,

"I simply never gave up Esi. Some of the others did give up but I stayed eager and vigilant to the end and it was to prove to be the right decision. You see, if you give up, then you have lost. Never ever give up Esi, on anything. You will be amazed at what you can achieve. You can make it if you do not give up. I did not give up because of you. I did it for my beautiful Esi."

Once this was said Fiifi took my hand which did not really express how he was feeling and so he then took me into his arms. I wilted from his embrace even though his body odour was sour and his skin was clammy and dusty.

"I am so proud of you my Fiifi." I said.

I sunk my face into his chest and I felt his big arms around me. I then pulled my head away and looked at his face and stroked his cheek. My hand moved to the cut in his earlobe and I then found the courage to ask him about this.

Fiifi took my hand away and I suddenly felt like I had asked the wrong thing.

Fiifi looked serious in his face but then he smiled and said his Mother cut a mark on it when he was a baby because a woman in a nearby hut had lost her baby a few days after it was born and she was concerned her son would be taken and swapped for the dead child. The reason for the cut earlobe was so Fiifi could be recognised without fail. The strange thing was this woman and her husband who lost their baby were short people and Fiifi was tall which would have been very odd. To think if he was to be raised by them as her other children were also short made Fiifi laugh and it made me join in giggling with his humorous tale.

Fiifi then looked at me with his big eyes in the way he did when I first met him and the day when he was first fetched the water for me.

We kissed and I felt his strength flow through his lips and into my body. His touch sent a power surge through me which made me tingle. When he stopped kissing me I was still absorbed into his enchantment and I must have looked all dreamy as I savoured my Fiifi, my hunter and my ƆdƆ.

I was so proud of Fiifi and my head could not imagine the thought of how well he was to be praised by Nana Apane and not just some grateful hungry villagers. I knew one thing was for sure the evening was going to be special.

A single drum started to play and more joined in then we

ventured towards the middle of the village. As we arrived we saw the food was prepared by the best cooks from our village. From the ground provision of the cassava and other roots to the plantain, wild boar and Fiifi's beast roasting over their fires. The men had decorated their faces with celebration paint, and the women wore pretty cloths and beads of many shades and the whole thing looked very colourful.

Everyone talked of the success of Fiifi and Ato and I sat very proud among the tribe and the hunters who sat near to Nana Apane.

When the food was ready I loaded my wooded bowl with some pounded yam first and I watched as some meat was put into my bowl over the top.

On this occasion there was so much to eat, I over ate and I felt a bit sick. My tummy was so full, but this was Fiifi's first catch and the meat was the sweetest taste of all.

The fire roared the warmth of the hottest sun in the sky and my brow soon had beads of sweat on it. I was happy as I had a full belly and the feast was being enjoyed by all. I felt special as all ears listened to the stories of Fiifi's and Ato's adventure.

I knew Ato had spoken with Efua's father about the two of them becoming united to make a family and he had approved. Efua made sure I knew. I also knew an announcement was going to be made to Nana Apane.

Nana Apane was also going to make another speech about something else but he had not told us.

It was then that I noticed at this time that Kesiwaa was not present. In fact I had not seen Kesiwaa for a while.

I knew she would spend time away from view on her time for flowing of her blood but this had been for a long, long time. I had shown so much of my interest and time in Fiifi I never noticed it before. Where was she I thought? I had been so absorbed with my eyes focusing on my love that I forgot about my queen and mentor.

I guessed this was one of her tricks and I waited for the

conclusion where she would tell me she was at last with child and this was the reason for her absence from the others.

Whilst sitting around the main fire the first beast meat had been eaten, but although there was still plenty of cooked meat left, most bellies were full. After a resting time for our food to settle and the talk among all of us it was then the drummers started tapping to a new beat.

Fiifi and Ato were encouraged to start the men dancing and so they jumped up and began moving their hips and kicking their legs until everyone hailed them with cheers and roars of delight. Fiifi and Ato then asked the other hunters to join them in their rhythm which now had a Djemba drum playing along as well. They all started to dance.

They danced with the crazy feet they knew and I was enjoying the evening as the two new hunters were suddenly the talk of the tribe.

I stood up at this stage and Fiifi looked at me. I then started to tap my foot on the red soil to the beat of the drum with my heel on the ground and Fiifi observed me and he soon got the rhythm right and found the beat.

It was after a session of hard dancing Nana Apane stood up and stopped the music. He asked for Ato and Efua to stand and asked for Ato to make their announcement.

Ato looked at Efua's father and called for all to hear.

His voice had nervousness in it but other than the occasional stutter it was strong and all could hear.

"I wish to announce on this night I am giving the village and my family the decision I, Ato would like to choose Efua, for a life together." He said.

"We will be setting up our hut at the back of Nana Apane to the outer edge." He added with a voice which started shaky but ended with a strong and heavy tone.

Ato had broadcast his pledge to Efua for all to hear and it was greeted with a huge roar of pleasure.

I must admit I was surprised at first with the overwhelming reception and I thought about Fiifi and myself. We would be doing the same thing soon.

I was pleased for their decision and this made the drummers start tapping the new beat again which sent the dancer's feet stamping and kicking wildly.

The celebrations went into a new level and the beat hastened to a quicker, more rapid excitement.

My announcement will be the next one to be made at another feast and celebration and I looked over to my Fiifi and he smiled his usual grin of loyalty to me. I pointed to him and rubbed my belly as if to ask if he was still hungry to which he just smiled and scratched his nose.

"Ha ha Fiifi me daase me ƆdƆ." I spoke to myself. Our code made me feel content with our secret communication.

So the speech for the evening had been made and I looked forward to the rest of the night.

The drummer's finger pounded against the drum skins.

"Bam ba ba, bam ba ba bam ba ba bam, ba ba bam ba ba bam, ba ba bam ba ba bam bam ba ba, bam ba ba bam."

I sang with my excited voice which became raised in pitch as the excitement of this beat lifted my attention.

Fiifi was encouraged to join in again and so he picked himself up from the ground and stepped up to the other dancers. I could not believe my eyes. Fiifi had got the rhythm and he was good this time. It was as if these words from Ato about his decision to make their announcement had punched some strength into his head which now matched his body mass. Fiifi caught a fine beast with his first hunt and he was now a man. He was now a man to be proud of. He was my future partner and I was in love. Yes Kesiwaa I now understand what love is and you are right with everything you taught me.

I gave a big smile which was broken by a burst of laughter and tears of happiness in my eyes welled for joy. I sang to the drum and etched this beat into my memory. This was a good occasion and I wanted to remember it for always.

"Du ga da, du ga da, du ga da," I sang with my excited voice.

I heard clearly the tune and voices of many around me. I was getting into the spirit of the beat as the evening progressed. After a short time it suddenly all went quiet.

The drum had stopped. The men who were dancing stopped moving their feet and looked at each other. Fiifi was looking confused, and he turned his face towards mine. He wanted to dance again but they stopped with no music to drive them.

It was then Nana Apane stood tall in front of us all with his arms folded over his chest. His feet were astride proud as he prepared to speak. He raised his right arm and gestured us to be seated.

Every one sat down on the dusty red soil and all eyes focused on our Odikro.

He raised his head high and stuck out his chest proud and broad as he prepared to talk to us. With a great deep voice he spoke.

"I welcome you all to my gathering and hope you enjoy the new sounds of our blessed music maker. I also take this chance to thank the new hunters Ato and Fiifi for what they have given us this great feast for the evening. I also say I wish for Ato and Efua to be blessed from all of us."

The villagers cheered in agreement to our Odikro's words.

"With this I wish to announce that this evening I will take on a new wife. As your Odikro I have fine and strong children.

However an Odikro needs many children, so one of our tribe's women will be honoured with this duty and she will take her role tonight. The new wife of your Odikro will be treated as my queen and she will be respected by you all I have made my decision and it will be a good one for the tribe."

It was then I noticed Nana Apane had his first two wives by his side but where was Kesiwaa?

As I noticed earlier she was still not anywhere to be seen and she was not at this evening of celebration.

I must admit my thoughts were more now of Fiifi so I had blocked nearly everyone else out anyway. I had also been more interested in Ato and Efua and so had failed to notice Nana's third wife was still not present.

Come to think of it I tried to remember the last time I saw her and I could not. I guessed again that she must be inside the hut carrying a child for Nana Apane which must be the answer to my curiosity. Yes that must be it I said to myself. She has got to be in the first stages of being a mother I thought and I reassured myself of my favourite of our Odikro's wives whereabouts.

With this announcement due to be given we all got excited as to who the new wife would be. I looked around and I spotted some of the girls I knew Nana Apane liked and favoured, and they looked at each other with almost a rivalled stare.

These favoured girls were Afi (Friday born), Akosua (Sunday born) and a girl with the same name as me, Esi.

All three of these girls had their own beauty and yet each had sourness to their character.

Afi was tall, dark and lean and she had spoken all her young life of marrying our Odikro. However, Afi was also known for being lazy and she would often fake illness to get out of doing her duties. In a funny way I thought she would fit right in a new wife for Nana Apane.

Akosua was lighter in her complexion, and she was not as tall as Afi, but she had a face of beauty and was always spoken about among our people, well mainly the girls. Her lips were full, her nose small and round and she glowed an air of authority. The problem with Akosua was she just ate too much. Her full figure was round and curved which was going to become bigger if she was to marry Nana Apane

The third possible choice for Nana Apane was a girl by the name of Esi. Now Esi was beautiful and the boys in the tribe all saw this. She was a good catch as she was the daughter of Nana Apane's favourite warrior and advisor. The other two were also the daughters of warriors.

The problem here was she was devious. Esi walked about our village with the arrogance which made her somewhat intimidating to the other girls. Esi always looked down on us and she gained no respect from the girls among our tribe apart from her friends around her.

The three moved from where they were and they sat together at the centre of our audience that was addressing Nana Apane.

Each girl pulled fake smiles to each other which was clear for the girls of our age to see but this bitter visage on each girl was unseen from the blind lustful eyes of the boys.

Nana Apane drank some palm juice and cleared his throat then he returned to his hut and left us to think about this for a while.

He kept us in suspense and whilst he was away we were encouraged to dance to another beat and later he would announce his choice for his new wife. The drums then started again and Fiifi jumped in the air with excitement. He knew this was a good evening for all.

So Nana Apane had found another wife for his loins to spread his seed.

After a short time of dancing and drumbeats and chanting of songs from the tribe Nana Apane came from his hut and took his place at the main seat in front of everyone.

This time Nana Apane wore his robes for his announcement of his union to his new wife. These robes were the finest red and gold in colour and they were ones I had not seen before and these colours were quite new and clean.

Nana Apane then rose from his seat and everybody sat down again and we all waited for the Odikro to speak of his choice of his new bride. The favoured girls bowed their heads as others whispered to each other.

These whispers were spoken from behind the backs of hands of women and sniggers were passed between some girls mixed with the men, who knew one woman is to now be honoured above them.

As we sat waiting for a name from Nana Apane, we knew the choice of his new wife would gain a status that made them above those villagers who were merely the hut builder's, women and the hunters. The new wife would be immediately promoted to one of the highest and respected ranks of our tribe.

It was the wives who bore the children of our leader and it was the warrior's daughter's, who were the pedigree for our Odikro.

The choice of wife was to give the girl a new life and it was every girls dream to marry an Odikro. I was really pleased as the girls all looked around at each other then they nudged each other as they focused on the three favourites and tried to guess which one Nana Apane was going to choose.

With a loud and strong voice Nana Apane spoke and all went quiet.

"My people I wish to announce the ewura I have chosen as my new wife. This woman has been seen by my own eyes around our village as the perfect candidate. She has shown hard work and commitment to all of us. My new wife has not yet chosen a partner for her future and so it has been observed from many my choice will be one of a good woman for the bearing of many children and for being nubile.

I have chosen very wisely my people, and I trust you will agree my decision is good. It is therefore the choice of your Odikro I will take the hand of my new wife who will receive full support from my two other wives."

Two other wives I thought. What about Kesiwaa? Nobody said anything but there was a look on some of the faces of Nana Apane's audience.

Agyeiba and Ansaba both stared out among us and then they looked at each other with a glare of secrecy held between them. They returned their gaze to look at Nana Apane who stood tall and glorious in his bright robes.

What about Kesiwaa I thought again? Where was Kesiwaa I said to myself? I was starting to worry about Kesiwaa. Had she died without any declaration? I thought I might have missed the announcement as I was so focused on my Fiifi and maybe something was said whilst we were on one of our many walks to look over the water nearby. I looked around to try to locate Kesiwaa and she was not to be seen.

The favoured girls shuffled on their little stools with excitement as they looked at each other with eyes of curiosity. They did not even think about what Nana Apane had just said. Who was it to be, was the only thought inside their eager hopeful minds.

Which woman caught the eye of Nana Apane? Who was his choice of a new wife? Nana Apane says this woman is nubile, she is one who is beautiful and confidant, yet can fit in with his other wives, and finally someone who he sees as good queen potential. All of the favourite three girls have these qualities.

Afi, Akousua or Esi who will it be? For a quick thought in my mind I was drawn to Afi and as I thought this she lifted her head and smiled as though she was ready to stand. This was noticed by the other two girls.

The words of Nana Apane's decision was about to be made and I sat nervous and looked at the favoured girls as they all now raised their heads in an almost uncomfortable posture.

Afi who was, now it seemed, the favourite girl sat confident. Many said when she was born she would one day be the wife of the Odikro and as she grew she developed into a very likely candidate. The whole village spoke often about the day she would be chosen to be a queen.

Akosua, however, sat with her head held high, and she was chewing on palm nuts. What a surprise she was eating at this time. She just couldn't stop could she? I shook my head at this and smiled to myself.

The girl called Esi appeared to think she had been chosen already and was looking at her friends and thanking them for their support.

Then Nana Apane who had kept the tribe waiting continued with his speech.

"The woman who will be my new wife has been chosen and her name is..."

The pause kept everyone muttering about the three favourite women as people got excited with the new announcement of Nana Apane's new wife.

"It is Afi," shouted one voice from the back which made Afi bow her head from view,

"No the Odikro will take Akosua for his wife it is obvious," came another voice. Those who thought Esi would be the choice voiced their prediction for all to hear and all three girls looked at each other in anticipation for the result.

"My tribe, I wish to name the woman who I will take as my new wife, it will be....."

A short pause of silence followed again which created a complete silence.

I sat as nervous as the three candidates and was excited for all of them. For me any of them were good choices and could provide children for the Odikro. Then Nana Apane raised his chin and spoke.

"Tribe of the Fante who live in this good village, I choose the woman who will suit very well for a new wife. I have spoken about this choice with the father this evening and my chosen wife has not yet made her decision for a future husband and so she is available for marriage. I will take her for myself and you as my tribe will also agree with me the choice I have made.

Another pause of silence as the three favourites now looked at each other with a touch of confidence between them.

Nana Apane spoke again.

"I have decided to take as my next wife...... Esi..."

The tribe roared with approval and I did too.

All voices screamed with excitement as Esi stood up to greet the people as the new chosen wife of the Odikro.

The noise was cut short Nana Apane was still shouting something over the screams for of new queen. Then it became clearer.

"Takyiwaa Kwaku!"

Groans of confusion came from the crowd as Nana Apane repeated.

"I have chosen Esi Takyiwaa Kwaku!" "Onyakopon Ka yen bom"

(God unite us), spoke Nana Apane.

"Yay Esi Takyiwaa." I shouted, I stopped, shocked, bewildered. I shouted half-heartedly a second time until I paused and recalled what I had heard in my ears.

"Wait, it's me? Esi Takyiwaa Kwaku is me?"

I spoke these thoughts to myself with a sudden realisation of what I had just heard. I looked all around me and those who knew the villagers were looking at me with smiles of excitement. I was confused right now and I had a mixed feeling of goodness which shrouded something with sourness to it.

Then before I could understand what had just happened, I had been lifted from my seated position and taken by some of the girls towards Nana Apane, who had a huge grin which showed his large gap in his front teeth.

My heart at first was raging with excitement like the beat of the drum and it started to race quickly but it soon slowed down to almost stopping as I realised I was going to be stolen from Fiifi.

I looked over the fire at Fiifi and saw him bow his head. As he did this I saw beyond him the face of Kuukuwa who was with her friends and she had the biggest smile of them all which made something collapse inside my stomach for a reason I did not know.

I wanted Fiifi to rise up and object to the announcement but he kept his head low. I stood for a brief moment to juggle my thoughts in my head into a sensible order. What to do? I then stood up tall onto my toes and shouted,

"Fiifi, Fiifi, what do you say to this?"

Fiifi rose from his seated position and all eyes were on him. The three favoured girls all sighed with disappointment at not being chosen but then looked excitingly at Fiifi as he stood tall and strong.

Fiifi looked around at them and with this he folded his big arms in a mark of defiance and I was certain of a positive response from him of objection.

There suddenly there was a big silence. I looked around to others and knew I had their union to my reaction as Fiifi unfolded his arms then he spoke.

"All give praise to the Nana Apane's new wife!"

As Fiifi spoke he gestured with his hands then he also joined in the approval of Nana Apane's choice.

Fiifi's voice had a tinge of edginess to it and I knew he was as surprised as me at what was happening.

"What Fiifi? I shouted to Fiifi. "You are going to accept this?" I screamed at him again.

I knew deep in my heart he would do this, but I was hoping for a different reaction. He really had no choice. To go against the Odikro was unthinkable, but I wanted a stance to be made. To speak out against our Odikro was a very dangerous thing to do.

I still wanted Fiifi to do something though, even if it was just to say we are in love, but the reality was Fiifi's noxious response was all I heard.

"Say something Fiifi," was pouring heavily in my head, anything,

"Fiifi say anything ƆdƆ me pa wo kyew" (please). I spoke with a pleading voice.

I looked at my ƆdƆ as I was being pulled towards Nana Apane's hut by Ansaba and Agyeiba. At this juncture, before I went through the entrance of Nana Apane's hut, I broke the wrist hold of the two women and I turned and walked back towards the tribe and towards the direction of Fiifi and shouted,

"Fiifi Mensah! Fiifi Mensah! Are you still hungry for your favourite food?"

I could not see my Fiifi and I sensed Agyeiba and Ansaba were coming near to me.

Just as I was about to turn away from the crowd the frame of my ƆdƆ stood tall. His raised his right hand towards his head and I waited to see his signal.

It was as if everything was in slow motion as he went to give me his coded response. His hand move gently towards his face and towards his nose then my view was blocked by one of Nana Apane's advisors and I missed the signal before I was encouraged to enter his hut.

My heart felt like it was crushed which drew me into state of shock. I tried to think about what I had just heard. I almost fainted with the decision as I stood broken from my future with my ƆdƆ.

I looked back through the entrance to the crowd of villagers and they all started to stand. One by one they cheered me saying they were proud of me and they will serve me as their queen as best they could.

My life had just dealt its most cruel blow to me and I sensed a shiver run through my already frightened and trembling body.

I felt a little neglected but I knew Fiifi could not do anything. He stood up to the moment but not to Nana Apane and I knew he could not do anything anyway.

He could only watch as I was taken for the Odikro, which under any other circumstances, would be the happiest day of any girl's life and a dream, however in this instance for me, it was the beginning of the end of my life and my future with my love.

Fiifi was going to give me a signal and I did not see it. I did not know what to do or what he was going to do. You see, to challenge the Odikro would mean disrespect and we both knew it.

Fiifi could take the easy path and not do anything and just look after himself and his family.

The other route, which was almost unheard of, was for Fiifi to challenge Nana Apane for me. I have never seen this before as this was an option not usually taken wisely. Yet something inside me felt this challenge would be made, or if not, I sensed Fiifi would find a way to prevent this. I am sure he will fight until he gets this resolved, and I remembered then, as he told me, he never gives up.

CHAPTER 6: Stolen

I stood at the entrance of Nana Apane's hut and two of his advisors were behind me. A girl came through a beaded arch to the side of the entrance as I arrived and she held some robes in her arms.

Nana Apane then came over to me and took my hand. At first I pulled away as I did not want to accept this agreement nor his control.

"Come with me now," spoke his heavy tone.

I did not understand what was to happen but I walked with him through the beaded entrance to the left of where the girl with the robes had appeared. This was also the room where I had seen my queen Kesiwaa before and I wished now to see her again.

I could hear the sound of the drums race their beat away with one of my favourite sounds playing outside.

"Bam ba ba, bam ba ba bam ba ba bam, ba ba bam ba ba bam, ba ba bam ba ba bam bam ba ba, bam ba ba bam,

Bam ba ba, bam ba ba bam ba ba bam, ba ba bam ba ba bam, ba ba bam ba ba bam bam ba ba, bam ba ba bam."

The drums played their beat and I imagined the dancers were working their excitement with their feet, into the red soil, and I wished I was among them, but I was not and here I stood, in Nana's Apane's hut and I was nervous.

Once through this door way I was welcomed by two girls. Nana Apane's wives Ansaba and Agyeiba stayed outside beside the fire and the music.

Nana Apane then left and the girls walked up to me and started to remove my waist garment. I felt really uncomfortable with this and I put my hand on the first girl to stop her. She replied with a look of shock and looked at the other girl who removed my hand.

Now I was scared, and felt my belly rumble even though full with food I felt the shaking inside me.

As my waist garment dropped to the floor I just looked ahead and tried to find something to help me hide away from this. I thought about my silent drum but I could not remove myself away from what was happening. The girls then removed my necklaces and wrist decorations. The only thing I had on my naked body was my waist beads.

Once my skin was bare the first girl took my hand and helped me step into a large wooded trough filled with water that had been warmed over the fire.

These girls then washed me with this freshly warmed water from the river.

As I stood naked in the water I looked straight ahead and I saw the three drums I had hidden behind on the day Kesiwaa had been healed by Nana Apane.

I felt embarrassed as one girl took a moist cloth and swiped between my legs as the other girl cleaned me from behind all over my back.

This was when I started to try to think about what was expected of me? Was I going to be dressed as a queen with fancy robes now? I thought to myself; was this all a dream and if so when do I wake up?

I was nervous but I stayed calm. I did not know what was expected of me you see I was untouched by any man, even my Fiifi, and I was not aware of anything I was supposed to do. The only thing I knew was what I was taught during my learning of my puberty rites.

The girls dried my moist skin and placed a loose light robe over my right shoulder. They worked together and placed a simple cloth over my head and tied a waist braid and attached a long cloth and this was left to fall from my waist to the ground.

The girls then stood in front of me and looked. The first girl walked around me. She pulled the cloth around my waist to adjust it and then she stood again alongside the second girl. After this was done they looked at each other and then left.

It was here I started to get worried and my "akuma", my heart started to speed up like the drum beat I knew.

I then heard the voice of Nana Apane and he came through the door curtain dividing the room.

"Well my Esi you are proof my choice was correct as I see before me a true queen ready to start her new and happy life with her Odikro." Spoke Nana Apane without any thought for how I was feeling. It was as though this was just normal to him yet I was almost unable to breathe with the amount of nerves racing around my body.

Nana Apane asked me to lay on his bed with him, which was huge and bigger than anybody else's resting place and it was lifted from the ground with soft straw and covered in animal skin for softness.

The bed looked very relaxing, unlike my own which was basic and on the hard ground.

I sat on Nana Apane's soft bed and saw his delight as he smiled at me and I saw the huge gap in his teeth which were also crooked and reminded me of twisted sticks lying on a fire. Nana then lowered my body to a laying position. The smell of his breath was overpowering as it invited itself into my nose. It was the sweet smell of palm wine he had been drinking and it made me feel sick.

My thoughts at this time were of my Fiifi and what he might be thinking. Fiifi is my only vision in my head and before I knew what was going on in this situation Nana Apane had invited his body to lay next to mine.

As he touched me on my arm and stroked it I trembled and I closed my eyes to try to lose the vision of Nana Apane but my eyes opened as soon as I felt his hands on my inner thigh. This alerted him and he asked me to remain calm.

I told Nana Apane I was untouched and he said he had me observed for a while and he knew which was why I was perfect for him. He loosened his robes which made me even more scared than I already was.

I started then to think about the person who had betrayed me. Who had watched me and had given the information to Nana Apane I was pure and unattached in love?

I asked Nana Apane who he had watching over me and he told me the name of the traitor without any hesitation.

"Well my Esi, it was Fiifi Mensah of course. He was making sure you remained pure for me and for this I paid him very well and his family are now being rewarded for his good work."

When I heard this I fell in to a state of sudden shock and I almost fainted as I gasped for air and my mouth went very dry. I found myself dazed by what Nana Apane had told me and after I let the words absorb into my thoughts I felt used and lied to by Fiifi. How could he set me up like this? Everything he told me was all lies.

All of his special words he spoke to me at the water's edge on those early evenings where he held me, and kissed for the first time. When he made my heart flutter like the wings of a bird as it takes to the air. This was just all an act for Nana Apane.

At this point I felt Fiifi had taken my akuma out of my chest and trodden it into the ground before taking his spear and spiking it with the joy of a hunter killing a defenceless beast.

Nana Apane told me to relax. I asked for more time to prepare myself for him and he just smiled and said I was welcome to use another room to prepare myself and he would be waiting for me.

Nana Apane told me he was going to get some palm wine and he was going out to the villagers and the celebrations which were now reaching their peak. The drumbeats played faster and with more excitement. He stood up and adjusted his robes he had loosened and then left through the beaded curtain doorway.

I sat up and climbed off the bed then I stood and took a good look all around me to see if there was a way of getting out of the sleeping area.

As I remained alone in this room I felt completely deflated, betrayed and broken.

Fiifi was still my deepest thought as I kept asking to myself, why did he do this to me? It made no sense at all. I did not see this coming and what more where was Kesiwaa? This was all wrong and to be in this position made me feel confused and uncomfortable.

The days sun was taken away by the darkness of the night quite soon after and Nana Apane was just enjoying the celebration and his palm wine. He seemed to have forgotten about me as I thought profoundly about what I should do. I tried to think about what Kesiwaa would have advised me and I remember that she once told me that I should use the things that she had taught me and I remembered the stealth and skill of walking unnoticed and treading quietly.

“That’s it” I said to myself as I looked around the room.

It was here I did what I thought was right at the time. I looked at my clothes and I knew being in this room was not my destiny. I did not want to be used as a child maker for my Odikro.

I wanted my love, my ƆdƆ, my Fiifi, but he betrayed me and I needed to get away. I did not feel safe around anyone at this time so I decided to take my chance.

I removed the robes given to me by Nana Apane’s dressers and

I grabbed my robe cloth and pulled it around my waist. I then took another cloth for my shoulders, to ensure I had covered all of my body. I then pulled this cloth over my head so I could just see out of a tiny part of it.

Shaking, I crept out of the entrance to Nana Apane’s dwelling easily as most of the tribe were celebrating. My every step was soft and delicate. I never created any attention and made myself as small as possible just as I was taught by Kesiwaa.

Once I was away I quickly scampered towards the back of the hut and out of sight of the rest of the village.

I went past the food store hut and then increased my pace until I was running. I soon came to a wooded area and I hid low to the ground shaking with worry at my actions.

I stood behind a tree and saw the dark of the night and this made my escape difficult through the thick flora. I had the moonlight as my only guide for direction as I walked away from the sound I could hear behind me. Rarely had I had gone beyond the village outer edge but I had to do this now and there was no reason or choice for me to return now.

I felt a desire to speak to Fiifi and ask him why he had lied to me. Why did he set me up like bait used for trapping an animal which was going to be used as food for another animal?

This thought crushed my akuma and I tried not to work out his reasons why, other than he was rewarded and now stands well in Nana Apane's favour.

He was my only thought at this time, however I knew I had to stay away and hope I was forgotten. In my panic I had all the desires of what to do but no real answers.

I just had to get away but I could not go too far though as a neighbouring tribe were our enemy and they were cruel to their own let alone other tribes.

I was also cold and afraid of the beasts and biting and stinging insect around at night and my body shook. There were also the snakes, oh my goodness I don't like snakes I thought.

I ran as fast as I could which was not quick as I wished. I knew Nana Apane would discover I was missing.

After a while I needed to rest and as I squatted behind a bush. I felt the cold of the night wrap its arm around my shivering body.

I was far from the fire warming the tribe and it was going to be a long and lonely night for me. I was definitely not going to lay down with Nana Apane and I had made my decision. So I stood up once more and moved further away from my village.

I found some soft grass in a remote area and I needed to rest again. My breathing was loud and I was gasping for air from running so long and hard and so I had to stop for a while.

I almost dropped with exhaustion but managed to place my body against the ground. I was now hot and the perspiration of my body dripped from my forehead. My head was scrambled and I felt dizzy. So much had happened and I felt confused which made me weary so I rested.

As I lay still I thought I could hear something like a rustling of bushes so I pulled myself underneath a big leafed plant that was next to a rock to hide.

Then shouting from some of the warriors made me wonder whether they were worried for my safety or chasing me with anger. One of the voices sounded like Fiifi. I wanted to yell for him to take care of me but as he gave me away to our Odikro I knew now he was not to be trusted.

However I still loved Fiifi and this was the most painful thing. He had no power over Nana Apane and he did this for an opportunity to secure his family with a better future within our tribe.

The warriors ran past me and I remained as quiet as I could.

I lay as still as I could but I could not stop shaking, not from being exhausted, but from being cold and frightened.

I thought of how I got to be in this position, from when I was having a good time watching the evening of dancing and new beats on the drums.

As I lay down I looked up at the moon through the trees and wrapped my clothes tight around my body. I closed my eyes and shivered and just thought about my drumbeats and Fiifi dancing to them. I thought of the new beat I heard earlier before I was the choice from Nana Apane and it played in my mind on my silent drum to calm me.

I slowed down my breathing with deep intakes drawn through my dry mouth. I relaxed as best I could and then I was at ease. I was so tired and drained that I was soon embraced by the arms of slumber.

I woke with a stem of coldness running through the core of my body. My first thoughts were "Where was I?" Then I remembered I had run like the beasts and the warriors chased me.

I looked through the trees to the sky. The sun was just coming up so it was the early part of a new day. The light shone shafts of golden beams through the trees, long spears spiking the ground all around me.

What was I to do now? I thought. My stomach felt the need for food but it was stored in the village. I slowly picked myself up and looked around for signs of anyone who was trying to find me. I wanted to give up and return to my villagers but was it a good idea? I did not know what to do as I could not hunt and the only water was in the river near our tribe where I would surely be seen.

My visions and thoughts were playing tricks with my head. I decided as Fiifi had told me, I should never give up. Yet I could not stay in this place, so after a lot of thinking, I decided to try to go back to the village and get some nourishment. After all, it was early and no one would be around after a special evening of dancing. The cooked meat would be still near the fire and the yams and plantain would be in the store hut.

I tried to remember the route I had taken in my panic and dragged my weary body through the trees and undergrowth.

The long walk had me drifting away from my path but I soon found the track I had used to escape the night before. I slowly made my way back to the edge of the tribe as the hot sun grabbed my body with its heat. If I was really careful I could take some yams and plantains from the store hut I though. As it was early in the morning there was no sign of anyone around. I made a long observation and everyone was sleeping from the late night of celebration having returned to their huts to rest.

I crept towards the store hut and pushed back the curtain covering the way in and slowly entered. I looked for the food and saw some in front of me. I reached to gather some yams with an eagerness matching my feet that rescued me from my original dilemma.

As I gathered some yams and plantains into my robes I felt a presence had joined me. The curtain over the door made a flicker of a tiny ray of sunlight and I felt someone was close by.

Before I could look around I was grabbed from behind. I struggled with all of my weak strength.

My feet left the ground and I was being crushed around my waist. I kicked, like I was dancing to a crazy beat of the drum in the air. My vision was then shrouded like a hood was placed over my head and I felt my body jostling around and my waist was so tight I could hardly breathe. I looked down and saw the feet of whoever was carrying me.

Before I could identify my captor my feet landed on the ground and the hood was removed from my face. It was then I saw where I was. I was standing in front of Nana Apane my Odikro and leader.

I knew they were waiting for me. They guessed I would return so they never pursued their hunt for me during the night.

He looked angry, as his jaw tightened which gave his face an ugly look and he clenched his hands to form fists.

"Why did you run away Esi?" Spoke the Odikro in a harsh tone.

My heart raced as I knew the answer but dared not speak. All I thought about was the feelings I had for Fiifi. These could not be abandoned or discarded, or transferred like the trading of goods.

My inexperience with lying down with anyone was a worry, because my body was untouched and this was something I knew would come one day. However I dreamt it would be Fiifi and the thoughts of us making children excited me. Now I stood in front of the Odikro and thinking of him lying next to me, smothering me, induced a feeling of sickness in my stomach. I needed to reply and I did.

I told my Odikro the truth, how could I not? I could not lie, and did not lie to him as I spoke.

"My Odikro, I dearly respect you and know you are the strongest man among the tribe, but my akuma is, er well it was with Fiifi Mensah.

The reason I ran away was because Fiifi and I were wishing to announce our commitment to each other but Ato and Efua took the occasion away from us. Now I know Fiifi betrayed me it made me feel even less attractive and bitter. I am confused and I am hurting at Fiifi's betrayal of me."

I felt pleased but nervous about my answer and felt I was saying the words I wanted my Odikro to be told but it was clear from the look on his face it was not what he wished to hear.

He replied with a cruel harsh voice and told me I was lying to him.

"Esi, I know your words are untrue because Fiifi is promised to the girl who is called Kuukuwa. She came to me and informed me of their intention yet she told me they wanted it to remain a secret."

My Odikro, Nana Apane continued to explain.

"This is why three moons ago I asked Fiifi if he had yet shown his interest in a woman and he said he had someone in his heart but he wanted to keep it away from the others in our village. I asked him what interest he had in you and he said he helped you to collect water and nothing more.

I asked him if he had seen you with anybody else and he told me he had not and he could confirm you were pure and untouched.

This made you the ideal woman Esi Kwaku to be my wife."

He went on.

"Fiifi confirmed everything for me and from his advice I chose you. You now tell me Fiifi promised himself to you and not Kuukuwa which makes Fiifi a liar as well. Well in this tribe we do not want liars and so you will be dealt with in the correct way."

As Nana Apane spoke these words I felt confused but it was clear the information was falsehood and the traitor was Kuukuwa.

Fiifi's secret was with me and not Kuukuwa. She had seen it from the first day I had taken the attention of Fiifi and she had deliberately set her plan to drive a wedge between us. Kuukuwa had worked out what Fiifi and I were doing and she used it against us. As she was the illegitimate daughter of Nana Apane he believed her over me. I was shocked but as my thoughts sewed up the loose ends of cloth torn apart in my head I calmed and was taken away to a hut at the edge of the village.

Here I remained in a dark guarded empty room and was unsure what would now happen to me. Will Nana Apane announce my union with Fiifi? I had no idea of what was going to happen to me, but whatever it was I felt my life was about to change again.

As I sat awaiting my fate my stomach rumbled with hunger but it did not matter because I had lost my will and desire for anything now anyway.

CHAPTER 7: Abjection

After a short while I heard voices approaching. Then into the hut walked the Nana Apane with two of his main guards and three other men who I had seen many times before. Of these three, two I noticed were warriors and one was a hunter. The warriors were wearing the same style of blades in the bright coloured sheaths at their waist side I had seen the day I was with Kesiwaa in her room.

Then there was Fiifi who stood between the guards. He was being held with a binding around his wrists and a length of rope hanging in front of him. The guards then pulled me from the ground and bound my wrists with the other end of Fiifi's tether and I stood in front of him.

I was even more puzzled at this and now started to worry. I thought of what I had done but nothing came to mind. I was chosen for the greatest honour against my wishes and then I told the truth of why I rejected my Odikro. I now knew Fiifi also answered truthfully to the questions put to him. Yet nobody would hear me and I was now feeling the effect of the poison which had found its way to me from Kuukuwa's mouth. She had deceived her own father to claim Fiifi for herself but it appears now it was like an arrow caught in the wind as it return back to her.

The hunter made a signal and led the first of the two warrior guards who in turn led me and Fiifi, followed behind by the second warrior and then behind all of us followed Nana Apane's two guards.

The hunter led us out from the hut and he took us to exit the village. I looked around the village to check if anyone could help us to alert someone but there was still no one to be seen. It was still early and everyone was asleep.

I looked for my father and could not remember seeing him from when I left our hut the night before.

As we reached the edge of our village Nana Apane's guards walked up to the leading hunter and spoke to him. They then walked passed us all and returned back towards our village.

The hunter then led the way and Fiifi and I followed and we were trailed by the warriors armed with their spears and shields.

We strode right past the same area I had hidden in for the night and then beyond and walked for most of the day.

I had rejected my Odikro, Nana Apane, but Fiifi, why was he being forced along with my cruel abjection? This never made any sense at all as he never broke any rules of the village and he had not betrayed our Odikro.

Kuukuwa was the one who lied to him and he believed her. He believed my Fiifi had promised himself to her and I knew this was not true. This ambiguity played on my thoughts as we walked further away from my village.

This journey was the start of a great trek as we walked for a long time to territory I was sure not even Fiifi had known. As he spoke to me with a shake in his head to confirm my thoughts he said,

"Esi, I have not been this far before."

Fiifi was told to be quiet by the warrior behind us who spoke with a sharp tone in his voice.

I did not know whether to speak to Fiifi or not for fear of maddening our escort but I thought about what to ask him. I could not see him as he was behind me.

We continued further and further and the hot sun in the sky moved across from casting a shadow on my left side to making one on my right telling me we were heading South wards.

Where were we going I kept asking myself? As a child I had heard stories of a place where people could go and are never seen again. Some said this was because they chose to leave. It was only children's talk though as young voices we would tease each other about it and try to scare one another.

As we walked my thoughts explored all avenues of mine and

Fiifi's destiny so much so I was almost plotting my future of doom with every step I made.

Fiifi tried to talk to me again but he was told to keep quiet by our escorts who had now shown a new side to their character as they started to become more concerned the further we progressed. The two warriors were particularly edgy at times and they became more vigilant of the area we were in and the surroundings in which they knew very little, but the hunter pressed onwards.

I thought about my destiny and the one place I knew I would not want to find myself which I had heard about, was a big white building near to the sea.

This situation I was placed in with my Fiifi made me scared. This new place for my destiny was constantly in my thoughts as I wondered what to expect. I also thought about my Fiifi as he would not be here if I had not informed Nana Apane of my ƆdƆ.

I questioned my loyalty to him and I started to blame myself for this situation.

I betrayed him as equally as I felt Kuukuwa had betrayed me. However mine was far more serious and if I had not spoken my honesty to my Odikro then we would not be in this situation. It was scaring me. If I had only just gone ahead with my Odikro then I would not be here. Thinking this on reflection made me angry with myself, yet I wanted my perfect life with my ƆdƆ and not someone who would just use me to plant his seed with.

'Forget it,' came to my head. 'Why am I blaming myself for something which happened so suddenly? After all, I did not even get to think what the best option would have been to avoid all this. I questioned it all and ran the past events through my head time and time again thinking what would have happened if I said yes to my Odikro and denied my love for Fiifi.

Which was right my head or my akuma?

We walked for a long time and the bindings around my wrists were rubbing harshly. Every time the warrior ahead of me pulled forwards I was given another pain on my wrists which had taken them to the point of swelling. As we walked my body was draining of energy and my stomach was soon feeling for food and water.

I asked Fiifi where we were going again although I knew it was a pointless question and with no surprise he gave me no answer. As I followed the warrior in front of me I watched him from behind and I noticed his shoulders started to round with his tiredness.

I spoke softly again to Fiifi so our escorts could not hear me. They seemed to know where they were going as if this was a trail taken before.

"Fiifi are you all right?" My question was not answered.

I assumed as Fiifi never replied to me it was because he had not heard me. I did not repeat my question, as there was not going to be an answer the second time either.

I did however, say to myself, Fiifi must know what is happening and will look after me. I had my trust and faith with him.

I then began to trick myself everything was going to be fine and wondered if we were going to be left among the thickest of the trees for us to start our family, which was another story we used to say as children. If this was going to happen then Fiifi and I were just left to our own defences. I knew, however I was only fooling myself to another conclusion to what was, in reality, the tiredness of the walking affecting my judgment.

We walked all day and as we did the trees got taller. It was quite cool though as they shaded our bodies from the sun. Our escorts walked us to a pool of water where we drank to quench our thirst and cool ourselves down. We sat down to rest.

My wrists were still sore and my eyes met my Fiifi. He looked as drained as I felt and he shook his head. His expression was one of a walk of doom. He knew something but he kept his thoughts behind his mouth and away from his tongue.

I managed to talk with Fiifi when one of our escorts went to find a bush to drain his water. The other two sat nearby.

I asked Fiifi if and why he had betrayed me. Why he did what he did. Fiifi looked at me with a face of disbelief.

“Esi I did nothing but love you, I do not know what you are saying. This was just as much of a surprise to me as it was to you.” He replied.

I opened my mouth at what Fiifi said. I don’t even know why I even asked him this as I knew he had not done or said anything wrong but right now I was not thinking straight and wanted to just lay down and fall asleep as my feet were sore and the binding around my wrists were biting them.

As the escort returned I asked Fiifi about the situation we were in and if we would be safe.

Fiifi looked into my eyes and told me there was boiling water ahead of us, which told me he sensed danger ahead. I then raised my hand and slowly scratched the tip of my nose which replied to him my answer was “yes”, as I agreed with his code.

I asked Fiifi if he was hungry for his favourite food. He raised his hand to his face and he scratched his nose. He did still love me.

Fiifi then told me the reason he was here now was because he did in fact challenge Nana Apane for me to be his wife and because of this Fiifi was taken to a hut and kept under guard until the morning and he knew then we were both to be removed from our village.

“Oh my ƆdƆ.” I said to Fiifi. I was about to throw my arms around my Fiifi but the escorts shouted for us to stand. We did as we were sternly ordered and then we continued to walk.

It all made sense now why Fiifi was with me. He had challenged Nana Apane for me. My Fiifi never betrayed me at all, it was quite the opposite. He actually fought for his right to be with me and our Odikro knew he was never going to win a fight with such a strong man as my Fiifi.

So my Fiifi did not betray me at all and Nana Apane believed his daughter above anything else.

If Fiifi had not challenged Nana Apane and had he accepted his bribe of gifts and rewards I would never have known the truth. This did not solve the situation we were in but it eased the pain and feeling of emptiness of Fiifi's loyalty to me.

I asked again about where we were going. Fiifi prepared his words carefully and told me he thought we were to be traded with another village. He had heard about this from when he was out with the other hunters. He said sometimes the hunters from another village met up with them, where they were friendly and wanted no trouble. They also told him they had heard of a place where the people were of a light skin and these people were dangerous. These were the obroni but not like the ones spreading the word of faith and religion.

He was told these people needed to be avoided and you would be better to be with your biggest enemy than these people.

Now this part I did not understand because the obroni brought peace and the word of the Lord to our people and showed us how gentle he can be. It is a far contrast to the obroni I was hearing about from Fiifi.

Our escorts stopped and stood a short distance in front of Fiifi and me then they gathered together in front of us to look at the path ahead. As our escorts were now not looking at us I took my chance to show my love how I was feeling for him.

Fiifi tried to make me learn of his sage words as quickly as he could and while he was speaking I brushed his face with my hand and we drew close and kissed. This was a kiss of the most powerful love and his mouth felt sweet against my lips.

This special moment was a stolen one. We kissed and I felt my body lift from the soil. I was totally and completely in love.

This moment of our embrace was curtailed as one of the escorts looked back and saw us. We then lost our physical contact as the escort pulled us apart.

I loved my Fiifi and I knew my judgement of him was right and my ƆdƆ was a good man. He was my shield from danger. The fact was, I was completely naive to what was going to happen to us.

Fiifi and I were told to start moving so we carried on walking. The night came and drew it's covering on us so our escorts decided it was time to rest.

We were given food for our nourishment which was baked plantain brought by our escorts in a cloth sack over their backs. This food was a little stale now but it was all we had and so we ate to restore the strength drained from our tired bodies and sore feet.

We settled under the night sky. I was restless but managed token sleep spells as I snatched every occasion to gather stock on my energy. It was on this night I also took every opportunity to look at the face of my ƆdƆ Fiifi. I thought to myself, you know what Esi, he really does love you.

I woke from my second night under the stars where I did not really sleep, I looked and I saw Fiifi was lying on his back facing towards the sky.

Fiifi and I were told to stand by our guides. We started to walk again and this time my feet were hurting from the first steps I took. As we progressed for what was most of the day I noticed the trees started to thin out. This journey seemed to be never ending and I watched again how the sun which before had cast a shadow towards my left side move to my right, telling me we were still walking South. The air smelt slightly cleaner and freshness greeted my nose.

Although my strength and energy kept me walking my wrists were now chaffing from the bindings quite badly now and they were very sore. My legs were aching and I felt as if I was walking on sharp splinters. In fact the bottom of my feet had shredded from the rough ground but I had walked to the point they were numb.

I also needed to wash as the sweat from walking for so far had drenched my body all over and I was sticky which made me feel quite dirty. I would normally bathe in the river local to our village early every morning and evening but so far I had not had the chance to do so since preparing for the night of Nana Apane's announcement.

I asked Fiifi to walk in front of me this time and told him not to pull on the rope as the binding was cutting my wrists. We walked further onward under the hot sun and the red soil started to become softer under my swollen feet and the flora looked different too. Eventually in the distance I could see over Fiifi's sullen shoulders, a rising of the smoke.

Further on I looked to the ground from where the smoulder of a fire was coming from and this is where I saw a huge gathering of people. There were patches of smog climbing to the sky from several areas now.

We were led towards this smoke and things started to become clearer as we approached. Firstly we attracted a group of obroni men who came to greet us and then they marched us towards the settlement.

We walked by many cages which held bibini men and women within them. They looked as weak and distressed as I felt.

They were being guarded by obroni men but these were not the same as the men who had visited my village and spoke of the teachings of Christianity.

These obroni were not friendly which I could sense in their aggressive voices. They held onto spears of a strange shape which were pointed at one end with a silver metal and wider at the other end which looked wooden. They carried these sticks over their shoulders with a strap.

They marched Fiifi and I towards a cage and the gate was opened. We were pushed in and as I felt a shove in my lower back I nearly fell to the ground. I couldn't fall though as we were roughly packed in among other people.

Our escorts were then taken aside and I saw an exchange of several heavy cloth bags given to them.

One of them opened up the bag and took out a red and gold

cloth. It looked very similar to the one Nana Apane was wearing on the day of the announcement of my choosing. This was all done in a few moments before the three escorts who led us here turned away and started to return from where we came.

Fiifi began to talk to me about his concerns and a voice recognised our language spoken to us.

This man introduced himself as Cudjoe and he said he was a member of a tribe close to ours. He told us he was caught many days previous whilst out hunting alone.

Cudjoe was tall and he had a big frame. He was so big he made Fiifi look like the young man he was.

He told us he had tried to escape his captors for many hours but there were too many of them and eventually he became tired and it was then they threw a net over him.

Cudjoe spoke about many things and he said what he found to be the most confusing thing of all was his obroni captors were being assisted by other bibini, and some spoke in our language as well. He also informed us these speakers tended to get their translations wrong so we were to watch out for them.

He told us we had arrived at a place called "Assin Manso" and we were at the Nnonkonsuo River or as it was otherwise known as "Donko Nsuo", the river of slaves. This water flowed from the river Ochi.

I thought of Bobo and I wondered if this was the place he had brought the young boys when I was a little girl. It must have scared him so much he ran away. I started to also feel very afraid I let some of my water release without any control.

Cudjoe informed us we were expected to bathe in this river and clean up for the long walk to another place of captivity within the walls of a castle.

I looked around and I noticed some people were carrying lifeless bodies to a place in the distance. Cudjoe told us they were brothers and sisters whose spirits had found themselves in the heaven of the Lord but whose captive bodies were to be taken to Nnonokosie (burial site) to be laid to rest in the earth.

I asked Fiifi what was the meaning of "Slave?" He gave me an intense stare and he was about to speak.

At this point a man sitting down in the corner of our cage looked up with a tired stare and spoke. He said "You will wear the epa (handcuffs) of the obroni. Onii a ne epa da wo nsa no, ne akowa ne wo." (You are the slave of him whose handcuffs you wear.)

I became more scared at these words and I moved to stand closer to Fiifi.

Fiifi asked if it was possible for a slave to escape from this place. Cudjoe replied with a harsh voice.

"Firstly we are not donko! (Slaves) We are captives and you had better not get the two confused. You are a free man taken against your will and your freedom will one day return to you. It will be a matter of time."

I took notice straight away of these words as he added.

"I will never be a slave. I will die before I am ever a slave."

Cudjoe also told us we would be joined by other bibini from the Salaga slave market where other captives were collected, bought and sold before joining us.

We would then, after another long walk, be taken to a castle at a place called "Elmina."

Cudjoe informed Fiifi and I this building was built by the people from a land known as "Portugal" and the word for its name meant "The Mine."

This was where, many years ago, they came to dig out the rocks on our land and turn it into a shiny golden material which had a value in their lands. This was the same gold Nana Apane had in his kuduo vessel, and that Kesiwaa had hidden. This was a valuable metal and the obroni like it very much.

He then added these people lost this fort to another land of obroni who were called "Dutch" and it was these people who were now in control of Elmina castle.

Cudjoe also informed us there was another possibility of where we could be going to. This was a large castle at a place called Cape Coast. This was owned by the British and this was the same as Elmina as it was a holding place for captives. Cudjoe said there was no difference between the two places. They just belonged to obroni speaking a different language. Cudjoe then spoke of being taken over the sea in a large vessel called a ship which would carry us to a new land where we were to be sold and made to work for the obroni. We would be lined up and sold in a market and this would be our destiny. I asked Cudjoe how he knew this and he told me he had learned the language of the obroni from the missionaries and they told him. He also advised me to listen to every word spoken by them and remember it. He was quite harsh with his words when he told me to learn to speak the language of the obroni in order to a better chance to survive the future. I kept this advice in my thoughts. Fiifi did hear this but he did not care for the advice. I think Fiifi saw Cudjoe as a storyteller and he turned his head away.

As I listened to the voice of Cudjoe who said he had been in the cage for many days, I looked out towards the river and I saw at the edges many naked men and women washing themselves whilst others were cleaning their clothes and drying them on the rocks on the sides of the bank. This was all done under the vigilance of the obroni with the silver metal sticks who had now taken them off their shoulders and they were holding them in both hands.

There were many different people here. There was a line of people who were being coupled into pairs, joined by a metal neck collar.

I could not believe what I saw as a similar linked line passed by our cage. This line had girls who looked younger than my sister Kakraba. They looked confused and innocent and I caught the stare of one little girl who looked at me with the eyes of fear. As she walked by I saw a trickle of blood run down the inside of her leg and she could do nothing about it as her hands were tied in front of her and the girl in front of her tugged her along by a neck collar. This young girl had not only earlier cleaned her skin and clothes in the Nnonkonsuo River but after this she had her dignity washed away from her by these unfeeling bastards, her captors.

My ears were attracted to the snarls and barking of hounds (Ɔkraman) but I could not locate where it was coming from. I looked in the direction of this noise and saw an obroni holding onto a captive by his shoulder and arm and they stood next to a small cage.

This captive man wore no collar around his neck and his hands were tied behind his back. He wore only a waist garment and arm and leg decorations. I tried to see if I could identify his tribe from these items from what Fiifi had taught me. All I could see was the colour red but I saw no tribe symbol. The snarls and growls continued from the same area and I still could not see where it came from.

It was then two other obroni men joined them and they walked next to the small cage. The obroni holding on to the captive cut the man's hands free from its binding and released him.

The obroni then assisted the captive to turn around and I saw the decorations were on his upper arms and against his shins. They were no decoration symbols from any tribe Fiifi had told me about. These decorations were bones! These bones looked fresh and there was still some flesh attached. The red colour I saw was the blood which was dripping and running down the bibini man's arms.

The obroni shouted at the captive and gave him a lash from a long black whip which cracked a "snap" on his back. The captive fell forwards and the obroni then pulled back the whip and again cracked it over the captive man's back and he shouted again at the man who looked like he was shaking.

This time the captive understood and he started to walk away. The obroni shouted again and the snarling and growling from the cage grew louder. I then saw the snouts of the hounds poking through the cage and they were aggressive and restless.

The bibini captive man started to trot and then run and quickly he was racing away on the hot red soil. It just did not make any sense to let him run anywhere as he would not get far.

Then the two obroni men took a bamboo bar away from the cage and four black hounds sprung out barking like mad beasts. They caught their prey in a matter of seconds and dragged him to the ground. The man's screams were a sharp and frightened shrill full of painful agony. One hound was ripping at the man's throat and the others had hold of his arms and a leg. These beasts growled and snagged at his skin as the captive screamed with the pain. I could not imagine the suffering of this wretch but my skin felt a tingle shiver over me.

Within a few seconds one hound had severed the man's hand and was tossing it in its strong jaws.

The man fought with the beasts but he soon lost his battle. This scene made me sick in my stomach, other captives just looked away. It was then I saw the hungry pack of hounds pulling at the man's lifeless body. His throat was missing to show an open wound to the length of his chest with a line of deep red blood against his dark skin.

Moments later these animals took their prize meat to their own area to nourish. What was left of the captive was nothing more than a ripped mass of bloody flesh and bone. This man never had a chance and he was trying to scream but he had no voice as he was slowly slaughtered in front of my watery eyes.

The obroni men who looked on just laughed at the man as his life was barbarically stolen then butchered in what appeared to be for nothing but food for their hounds.

This sight made me unsteady, my knees buckled and I went fuzzy in my head. My body felt a warm pulse race through it and I shuddered at what I had seen. The poor man was scared and confused and he was sent to a most gruesome end. This was when I had to wake up to the reality of my situation. I needed to calm my thoughts as I felt instantly like throwing up but I did not want to bring attention to myself. I slumped to the red soil and looked ahead of me. I felt the beat of my silent drumming calling me and for the first time let it beat hard and strong as it invaded my head with a beat as fast as my heart.

"Bam ba ba, bam ba ba bam ba ba bam, ba ba bam ba ba bam, ba ba bam ba ba bam bam ba ba, bam ba ba bam."

As I sat down I could not look at any more shackles, neck braces dead bodies and humiliation. I needed to control myself of this emotion. I looked at Fiifi and he also looked stressed. He stared at me with a strange look which I had to turn away from. I felt he was blaming me for our situation. I sensed his fear as he lowered his head.

I was trying to think of the right words to speak to Fiifi, but an obroni came to our cage and pulled us out. My body trembled as we walked past the ripped flesh of the man's carcass and towards the river. Here a man who spoke our language told us we were to bathe in the water.

Fiifi and I were untied and we made our way towards the river on the instructions given to us by a bibini collaborator of the obroni.

We were asked to go into the water and so I walked into the coldness and drifted into it up to my waist and then I dipped my whole body underneath and I bathed my body. This felt so refreshing. I cleaned between my legs and cleansed my sore feet. I let my wrists float in the water and soak up as much as I could and this eased the pain of where the bindings had been.

I also managed to taste the water and although it was very gritty from the mud having been disturbed from the many feet in it, this was my only chance to take a drink and so I took a bellyful until I could drink no more.

Fiifi was calm and quiet, although I had sensed his nervousness as he washed his skin, whilst keeping his watch over me. His eyes were fixed in a stare. He never blinked and he was observing my every move. I sensed he was planning to try and escape. I was right as he gestured for us to run as he pushed his arms up and down in his nervous twitch I knew.

At first I thought this was a good idea, however my feet were so sore so I would not get far. I shook my head at Fiifi who looked out to the river before holding his head in his hands. I could see a strange look on Fiifi's face at this moment and I did not like it. It was then he fell forwards into the water. I could only imagine Fiifi had seen enough and he was broken and he never resurfaced from the river.

This was noticed by the obroni guards who raced into the water and scooped Fiifi from his plea for a fatal freedom.

Fiifi was then hit around the head with the thick end of the obroni's pointed stick and it drew blood which ran down his cheek from a wound around his left eye. Fiifi dropped to the ground with a heavy thump and his head bashed against the hot dusty red soil.

I was so angry with Fiifi accepting this treatment from the obroni but I knew he was feeling weak. How much do we have to suffer? Were my thoughts as I saw my ƆdƆ lying like a slain lifeless animal?

It was then my ƆdƆ was taken to a small tree and tied to it. I watched him being lashed across his back with the tail of a severe whip. His blood dripped as readily as his cries of pain. His head hung down but I could see the wound from his eye continued to swell.

He screamed from the hurt as ten lashes tore into his dark skin. The strong man I had fallen in love with was becoming a tortured and withered man with sores on his body and a broken honour which was once strength and pride. I did wonder why the obroni stopped a man from taking his own life only to save him and then beat him to almost to the point of the same result.

I was taken from the river and Fiifi was chained by his neck to a line of men nearby to me where I became part of a line of women. My neck chain was tight and dug into my chin. The girl in front of me turned around and spoke something I did not understand. She looked like she was about ten years old. She looked frightened and I rested my hand on her shoulder before an obroni pushed it off and shouted at me.

I tried to tell the obroni the girl was with me. I wanted to protect her by my gesture.

It was then the obroni unchained this girl and removed her and took her away and joined her to another girl of the same size and what seemed to be the same age on another line. They had deliberately split us up.

Once she was chained to her new captive they set off and I never saw her again. Another taller girl replaced her in front of me.

There were many other bibini around and they sat with each other in lines linked together and chained by the necks.

It was here our bibini guards communicated with the obroni watching over us and they exchanged words and signals and this made me aware this was not a new practice. What I was seeing was just organised rape of freedom and humiliation.

How many of my people from our tribe knew of this? I think they have been sheltered from reality in our village as this would have been something we would have been taught to avoid. I was never made fully aware of this awful trade unfolding it's horror in front of my eyes.

Indeed, I was now part of it and Fiifi and I were joined to the other sad souls, our freedom taken away.

Our new guards joined the obroni who were in control of this torture and they told us to stand. I and my fellow captives were ordered to walk. I was drained under the hot sun but I had no choice but to do as I was ordered. I saw Fiifi was in a line a short distance in front of my line and so I kept my eyes on him. Just as we started to walk I heard two obroni say some words I did not understand. Then one word I had recently heard. This word was "Elmina." Another obroni repeated it back to him and they shouted it towards the captives walking in front of me.

We started our journey once more. I was fresh from the water which had caressed my skin with a new feeling of cleanliness, but I was still tired.

We walked on and on, and then further more until my feet were so numb they felt like they had shredded and it was only by lowering my weary eyes I saw my feet were still there but there were cuts all over them.

I did wonder how I was moving my languid body and I thought long and hard as to why I was even bothering to walk as I was quite clearly heading towards a most terrible fate.

I knew the answer was to keep walking as I have seen other bibini fall to the ground only to be put to sleep from the obroni's stick which they pointed at their target then a loud bang followed by a puff of smoke which instantly drew blood to explode from their heads and leave them lifeless.

My legs were sore and my lower back started to hurt. The brace around my neck was uncomfortable and heavy and it was rubbing against my chin and digging in which made my teeth remain clasped together.

This was another pain added to my breaking body as I became weaker with every step. However, I could not stop walking and kept the words of Fiifi in my head. Never give up.

We walked further on and I could see beyond Fiifi in the distance beyond the leading guards there was a vast area of water. We went beyond the last of the coconut trees and as I looked ahead I saw the biggest of buildings ever!

It was the big white building of the obroni. It was straight ahead and to the left sitting next to the sea high on some rocks. It stood right next to this vast stretch of water which disappeared on the horizon.

I got scared which made me jolt in my step and I pulled back on my neck chain. This made the girl in front nearly fall over. It also made the collar around my neck pinch the skin on my neck which was very sore. The metal sitting around my neck had become hot from the sun and it started to be more and more uncomfortable.

We approached this huge building and it was then I realised how big it was as it grew in size with every step nearer to it.

This was where the obroni came on to this land with his huge floating vessel and it was docked next to the big white building I knew now as Elmina castle and was now a short distance ahead. I knew now where I was going to be a captive.

Fiifi turned back and looked at me and his face was showing signs of panic as he also knew this was our fate.

It was enough to make my stomach collapse with worry as another wave of fear ran through my body too and my step slowed its pace.

A guard behind me shouted at me as he pushed into my back and forced me to move on quicker.

My heart again pounded rapidly in my chest and my stomach felt so empty, not only from food, but from the loss of hope of seeing a future of happiness.

We walked along the coastline and I looked out at this vast expanse of water.

I had heard of the sea but never seen it or heard the noise it made and I had heard it said the ground next to it was golden and it was soft under foot. As we approached it I never felt the warmth I had been told of or the prickles from the rough plants scratch my tired and sore toes as they pressed into the soft grainy ground, but just the heat travelling through my feet towards my shins.

We walked along this soft sand next to the sea and we were approached by another gathering of obroni men.

As we joined this group we stopped and I then felt the heat of the soft grain on the top of my feet and it hurt them with the sharp bite of the heat. This awoke them to a new pain which added to my hunger and my extreme dehydration and fatigue. I tried to shuffle around but was told to keep still. I was falling into spells of dizziness and at times I almost collapsed.

The pain was burning but my thoughts to block it out were the beat of the drum, which made things temporarily disappear.

My silent drum was my temporary cure as we walked on. I closed my eyes and thought of the beat to ease my pain

"Bam ba ba, bam ba ba bam ba ba bam, ba ba bam ba ba bam, ba ba bam ba ba bam bam ba ba, bam ba ba bam."

This was my painkiller, my trance, my way of blocking out anything I did not like. This was my silent drum and I needed to find it and play it.

I was pulled out of my temporary trance by the voices of the men.

The first of our captors walked up to the first of the three new obroni and they spoke in a strange language to our guard. I did not know what was being said, I could only see the gestures made by my captors. I noticed Fiifi was tired and the sores on his back were crusted with the covering of several lines which had dried under the sun. He was in pain and I knew he was suffering from his punishment. My body was sore and numb and I merely existed now to see the abuse of my fellow captives.

Our guard spoke back to the other obroni and he appeared to agree with the few words exchanged. The new obroni then turned towards the white building and we all walked behind them.

We followed the coastline around the front and then to the side of this huge white building rising high as it over looked the sea.

The sound of the water crashed around the rocks on which it was built. There were local huts nearby and these were similar to our tribe huts. I saw bibini men and women stand and watch as we were led up a steep slope towards this vast building.

I looked up lifting my head on my weakened neck and saw this huge white building and thought to myself. "Oh my Nyame." (Oh my Lord). This is my big white building, this is it. I wanted to live in a big white building and here it is stood right in front of me as if it were built from my wishes. I remember how I made the request when I was younger and the dream came true. I thought about this again and again as I approached it. Once I had a choice of a big meal, but I turned it down. I could have been a queen, but I said no. I wished for a big white building and I got what I asked for.

There were steps leading up to the entrance of this building and we were taken towards them. My pain increased with each step as now I was completely exhausted and needed to rest. There was no sound except for the water from the sea crashing against the rocks behind the castle. Fiifi was quiet and the obroni men just stared at us as we steadily walked in our pathetic stride towards our incarceration like animals. As I ascended the incline I saw something small move against the base of the large white wall and the ramp entering the castle. A little brown scurrying rat was making its way in before me. My escort to my hell was no more than a filthy flea ridden vermin probably waiting for me to rest before bringing its twitchy nose to my skin. Probably then transferring fleas and ticks to my body.

My line of captives who were weak from their chain and neck collars followed Fiifi's line of sluggish shapes up a slope and then some steps where we stopped as the gate was opened up. I was ordered forward by the obroni in to this huge white building and through a side arched doorway. The castle guards at the entrance then stood aside without any expression with their grey sullen and moist faces that were clearly struggling from the heat of the sun. Our guards also stepped inside the doorway.

I followed the line without any choice. The rat entered unnoticed and if fact it looked eager at watching us as if it was trailing our presence. I walked under an arch way and then through a side door that was behind slammed shut.

The rat was inside the walls too and sitting upright looking at me. It started to scratch itself and I imagined how many tick and fleas it brought in under its dirty fur. This was a vermin that roamed as free as a bird. I was a proud African woman enslaved and captive.

The rat however ventured into Elmina castle unharmed and free unlike me. I entered clean, but shackled with heavy chains and a metal collar.

CHAPTER 8: Captive

The castle guards then separated the men from the women and some were you girls. Fiifi stood against a wall on the right and I stood against a wall opposite with the other female captives. Two obroni with the wood and silver sticks pointing at us stood and watched us. One of the obroni who we had followed from outside went to a door way and came out with two bags of what appeared to me to be full of some kind of payment. This obroni put his hand in the bag and I saw him take out some glistening yellow gold coins.

The obroni who had walked Fiifi and me to this building had in his arms the finest of materials of several colours and they were all rolled neatly.

I looked at the obroni who had the bright yellow pieces in the bag and he smiled at me which showed most of his front teeth were missing.

I transferred my stare beyond the smile from him as I focused at the wall behind.

I saw what looked like to be some shackles that were fixed to the bricks. As the wall was covered with a white paint it showed clearly that there were deep red stains on the wall and the ground. It was fresh as if some barbaric event had taken place earlier. I looked at the floor to avoid trying to imagine what had happened here but I glared at something on the ground that was wrapped in a dusty fabric. It was the length of a body and there was blood seeping through the top end of the cloth which made a small deep red puddle in the dusty ground.

I just wanted to try and get beyond the unforeseen future now taking my life into a new unknown.

Another obroni with a funny hat came over to us and unchained my neck brace and the removal of the weight gave me strength to at last stand up straight. I was hunched over with exhaustion but I managed to straighten up my body and I took in a large breath of air and breathed in the salty smell of the sea.

This guard then grabbed my arm and led me away to the left of the courtyard. I looked at Fiifi who was having his neck brace removed and he winced with pain as he stood straight. The crusted scab formed over his back cracked open and a trickle of blood ran down his back.

As I walked away I heard a noise and looked back to see Fiifi had run out of the door in which we came, only to be stopped, and dragged back, kicking and fighting against two men twice his size. I watched as Fiifi was carried away to a far side of the large courtyard.

I was led through a doorway into a smaller courtyard. It was behind a gate and I was beckoned by the obroni guard to go through where there were many women all just walking around and some talking to each other. The other women with me entered into this area and we just looked at each other without knowing what to do.

One thing that invaded my senses was a strange stench. It was filtered by the sea air, which first got my senses alert. I did not recognise at first but soon realised it was a sour smell of stale air of human excrement.

A girl came over to me as she saw me and gave me a bowl with what seemed to be food for which I was grateful. I had forgotten about my hunger but the pain in my belly soon returned. My head was more interested in where I was and the purpose for all of this. I started to eat the food, which was quite tasteless but still it was something to nourish my emptiness. My feet were numb, I needed to rest them.

The girl who greeted me tried to talk to me but I did not understand what she was saying. I smiled in a way of saying thank you and then mingled among the others.

I spoke my language at random to the women to see if there were any of my tribe here and they just gave looks of emptiness as if they would not say if they were anyway. Every face I saw was the same. Every face had a blank expression of a person with no emotion.

I walked to the corner of the yard and saw some water in a

trough. I scooped some with my hands and felt the refreshment fall down my dry throat. As I turned around to again circle the women I looked ahead and I saw a face I recognised.

"Hey I know you," I said with a hope of a reply.

The face was not exactly as I remember. It was more drawn and gaunt. I walked towards this woman and noticed she was holding something. It looked heavy and she looked like she was about to fall so I ran to her and she slumped to the ground and dropped the large round stone in front of her. The other women never moved to her aid they never even looked like they were interested. I cradled this woman's head and I looked at her face with more detail. I saw a face of beauty yet one which wore a frightened and weary frown. Indeed it was the only face I could ever wish to see right now yet one I did not think I would look at again.

"Oh my Ohemaa, my Kesiwaa," I said with a dry croaky voice.

It was Nana Apane's third wife, the queen who I had not seen for a while. I thought about this and realised she had been taken from our village and I was supposed to replace her. I spoke out to her again.

"Kesiwaa, are you well? Please talk to me. Open your eyes."

I spoke in a panic to my queen. All of my energy was gone but for a short moment it came back to me as I needed to attend to my queen.

As I looked down at her I saw she had been holding a ball of rock attached to a chain and tethered to the ground. I saw her eyes glisten open as she widened them in an attempt to see me. She knew my voice and it was a last attempt from her to remind me of her good memories. She looked a bit confused and then she looked at me deeper and said in a soft voice,

"Esi, is it you? Esi Takyiwaa Kwaku?"

"Yes it is Kesiwaa, it is me Esi" I said with a comforting reply.

"Where are we Kesiwaa? Why are we here and why are you

holding a rock?"

Kesiwaa spoke with a soft husky and delicate voice.

"Esi, do not try to help me. I am to be left alone. Please leave me now. Go on get yourself away, the day is getting on and night will fall soon."

"No Kesiwaa, You are not well," I replied to her, with authority against my queen.

"I will get you some water." I added.

I went to the same place that I had found my refreshment and used a half broken and abandoned coconut shell to contain some of the discoloured liquid from the wooden feeder box.

I helped Kesiwaa to sit up and she insisted on standing. I tried to bring the water to her mouth but she resisted. It was getting dark and I noticed that the sun had started to lower in the sky as dusk drew in the night.

I tried again to spill some water into Kesiwaa's mouth but as I did this, a man shouted from a balcony in a language I did not recognise.

This man was dressed in a very bright coloured yellow waist jacket and his shirt was as white as a cloud when the sky is blue. His hair was dark and grey at the sides and he had a mixed grey and dark beard.

I was summoned to stand and join the other women so I rested Kesiwaa's head to the ground gently and made my way to join the gathering of the women.

All of the girls moved towards the centre of the courtyard and looked up at the obroni above. Some other obroni men came from a door way and stood in front of us with their silver and wooden deadly sticks. I saw they had holes at the front. I now knew these sticks were rifles.

The man on the balcony shouted something and above us there

were some windows with shutters. All of these shutters suddenly slammed and closed.

"Thud, thud, thud, thud, thud, thud," the sound of the window shutters made some girls bow their sorrowful faces as they looked to the floor. One of the obroni men walked around us and amongst us and he lifted some of the bowed girl's heads to look at the obroni on the balcony. I noticed on these shutters there was a sign of a cross. It was the same as the obroni Christian men carried to our village. This must be a place of worship I thought so these people were Christians.

This obroni on the balcony walked along from one end to the other and looked at us women.

He stroked his beard many times before pointing to one of the women near me. She took a sharp intake of breath and put her hand to her chest.

Two men with the wooden and silver sticks came among us and pulled the girl away and she never resisted. I did not know what was going on here but kept looking for Kesiwaa who was again lying on the hard stone floor. The obroni on the balcony then chose two more women and disappeared.

The girls were taken through a door to the side of us and the window shutter above us opened up and soon after voices could be heard singing songs of a similar style to the songs from the obroni preachers. The songs were hymns sung by women's voices.

Another two men with sticks of wood and silver ushered us out of the sun and into the building to the side where the obroni had been on the balcony.

As I neared this room the smell from my first sense here grew stronger and stronger and the room was dark. I looked back to Kesiwaa and saw an obroni man removing the rock attached to her by a chain to her ankle. The sun was starting to fall low in the sky now. Night was approaching and the guards started light flares on stick for a light in the courtyard.

I reached the entrance to the building but I held back for

Kesiwaa as I wanted to see her safe and well. She had looked drawn and was coughing and she was obviously weak.

I stayed by the door to this dark room to breathe as much fresh air as possible. The stench from inside was stomach churning and at first I gagged but I was not sick as there was little food in my stomach to bring up.

I waited for Kesiwaa as her feet shuffled towards me and slowly she made her way to join me and the other women.

Once all the women were inside they found their space and sat down. Some of the women were already in the building and had found a space and they were lying down on the hard floor. As Kesiwaa came through the door I put my arm around her waist and supported her.

I escorted her to a space which only really had room for one person. We were crammed together tightly and the stench of the room along with the smell of unwashed women was horrendous. Then the door to our prison shut and locked.

I helped Kesiwaa to the ground then comforted her best I could. The floor was cold. It was hard stone. It was also uneven and so it dug into my body. Some of the bumps made the floor uneven and had crumbled away and it gave of a sour smell and I soon identified it as human waste which had dried solid. There were also tiny pools of deep red liquid dotted around which were an attraction to flies and bugs.

"Kesiwaa, what is going on, why are we here?" I asked.

"Esi, you are held captive of the obroni, this is a terrible place. This is worse than being lost among the thickest of forest with all the creatures you fear.

Our Odikro had sent us to this place of misery. He sent me away because I bore him no children. I tried Esi, to be a mother but the child never came. Our Odikro rejected me and he had me taken from our village."

Kesiwaa was finding the talking difficult, so I asked her to not speak too much.

I was supposed to be the replacement to my favourite queen because I behaved just like her and Nana Apane saw me as his future potential queen.

I had created my own destiny without realising it. The days I spent playing the role of a queen and walking tall and delicate had been observed by Nana Apane and I had not realised it. However I also met the same fate and I too was rejected by the cruel and fickle bastard Nana Apane.

It was now obvious Nana Apane was not the man I had learned to respect and my father was right to be wary of him. I had not seen him for what he truly was. He had been in contact with these obroni before which I knew but not to this extent.

Kesiwaa spoke to me in a soft voice which had little strength. I did not want to ask too much but I needed to know some things.

"Why did he send us Kesiwaa? It has to be something really bad as nobody should be brought here."

I asked this with a delicate voice so as not to stress her.

"He sent me because I gave him no children, but I don't know about you, but you must have done something wrong to offend him." She spoke softly in response but she struggled with her breath.

I replied, "He wanted me as his new wife Kesiwaa. I realise now, after he sent you away from the village, he was looking for a replacement to give him more children. I was with my Fiifi and I thought the village had some idea about us. We had never spoken of our love to anyone and I guess we should have. We never announced our commitment and then it was too late for my ƆdƆ Fiifi and me."

Kesiwaa and I pieced together the recent events. This was when I spoke of Kuukuwa and Kesiwaa's face looked stressed.

"This little girl has caused trouble from the day she was born." Spoke Kesiwaa with some venom in her tone.

I continued, "Anyway Nana Apane ordered everyone from our tribe to an evening to announce his new wife. I sat down excited as did all the other women. The Odikrio then made his announcement and he chose me. I was shocked Kesiwaa.

Nana Apane chose me? He then took me to his sleeping place, had me undressed and washed and then told me to lie down", I informed Kesiwaa.

"All of this was fine but when he touched me I froze then panicked and ran away. I ran into the trees and slept next to a large rock under a bush. I was very scared but thought about my favourite drumbeats. They help me to relax and I soon slept.

When I woke up I was cold and hungry and so I tried to creep back to the village to the food store.

A warrior found me and took me to Nana Apane who asked me why I fled and I told him the truth. My love was for Fiifi. He then got two of his men to bring Fiifi and myself here."

Kesiwaa then said something making me feel even more emotional.

"Esi, I have managed to survive this place because I found something whilst I was here." She quietly spoke.

"What did you find my queen Kesiwaa? I asked curiously.

Kesiwaa spoke as the tears behind my eyes built up rapidly.

"I found my silent drum Esi; I remember when you told me about it many years ago I could not find it then. Well I have now and it kept me beyond the time I should have been with the pain and torture I have endured here. You were the daughter I never had Esi. I also say this to you Esi the obroni on the balcony is the devil himself."

I saw a look of desperation from Kesiwaa as she laid her head in my arms. She was a tired and weary woman.

I looked around and the recollection of what I had gone through over the last few days brought my eyes to swell and they were on the cusp for them to release my tears until one tear managed to escape and left my eye to trickle down my cheek and reach my mouth.

Kesiwaa's eyes opened and she wiped away this tear which had appeared on my cheek with her hand. I dripped many more tears straight afterwards as I thought of my love for Fiifi and our situation. Then the tears dam burst and I was crying hard.

If I had just gone along with the Nana Apane, and had his children, then I would not be here, and Fiifi would have been safe too. What have I done? Yet I had found Kesiwaa who was already ejected from our village without anyone even asking for her.

At that moment I thought about Fiifi. Where was he?

"Kesiwaa, where would Fiifi be?" I asked in a mumbled tone.

"Esi, he will now be a prisoner with the men. They are in the main square in the cells around the walls." She informed me.

After a pause for breath she added.

"He must not talk of trying to escape Esi, because the obroni have our vernacular speaking traitors hidden next to where the captives are held. If they hear words of trouble they will tell the obroni who will remove the captives responsible and take them to a cell where they just close the door and leave them and open it after many weeks to remove the bodies. No food, no water, complete darkness Esi. If you don't die of madness then you starve to your fate slowly and cruelly."

I cried with fuller tears then my nose started to run and when I blew it on my own cloth the stench of the air was twice as powerful as it was before.

Kesiwaa was right this is the worse situation I could have been in. This was indeed the place you would see as your worst nightmare, barbaric inhumane torture of human life.

Life wasted and destroyed by another person's total disrespect and heartless attitude which makes them feel it gives the right to abuse and degrade another.

My captors had me in a room with about one hundred women. Some were standing some lay still, while others sat talking in their native tongue.

I saw a women squat down and urinate and another defecated on the floor. The first woman let her water trickle along the floor and the other woman picked up her mess and smeared it on the wall to ensure it was not on the floor for others to step on or roll into as they slept. Others just left their deposit and moved to another part of our confinement. Nobody really said anything about this and I felt to speak out would not be wise. There were no rules anyway.

When we were all in our sleeping area big doors slammed over the gated grills and blocked out the dwindling daylight and this minimised any fresh air coming in. There were slight cracks in the sides of these doors which let a little light through but they were tiny. Mostly it was complete darkness and the only noises were groans and nervous cries.

I lay down and cradled Kesiwaa. Our bodies kept each other warm and I felt comforted with her by my side. My queen needed me more now than ever to watch over her.

So with the floor hard, noises of all descriptions, a stench so stomach churning that I could taste the sourness in the air and not being able to see, made sure my senses all fought each other's for my attention.

Then there was a loud scream from one woman and there was shouting between two or three more voices at the other end of the long cell but it soon died down.

On this night I thought of my drums again but this time it was difficult as the women coughed and others cried out as their nightmares teased their heads.

So I thought of a new beat and imagined me tapping this time. Instead of the music makers, in my thoughts I myself took over and created my own beat.

Bam, bam, bam, bam, bam, bam bam bam, bam bam bam, bam bam bam.

Eventually I got to sleep with the pains of hunger in my stomach.

When I awoke it was dark and I cradled and held on to Kesiwaa. She was not awake and so I let her sleep. Some of the women were talking quite loudly and there were many moans and groans of them waking up. Another voice shouted again and more voices joined in and there was an air of aggression in their tone.

I thought of Fiifi sitting in his dungeon and how he would cope. He was a strong man and I was sure he would be able to take care of himself. However I was concerned about his back and the ripped flesh caused by the obroni's whip.

I thought of my family and my little sister Kakraba who was a pretty girl but sometimes a naughty one. I thought of how she would run around like she was a wild animal with complete innocence. I thought of how she made tiny mud huts out of the red soil and put dried grass on the top for roof just like I used to do. Then she would use some sticks and bind them together to make them look like people from the tribe. How was she? How was my father, surely he would find me?

This was all a mistake and I should not be here. Saying that, nor should my queen Kesiwaa. I was now yearning to be with my family.

I have so much responsibility with them and I am not there.

As I thought of these things, the reality of not being around my people hit me but it was soon washed away and started to evaporate, as I feel entombed around so many women that all must think the same and feel as confused and as lonely as I do.

These women with so many different languages continue to raise their voices as they try to fumble their way in the dark to find their friends or women they comfort and share their pains with. They all have their own lives and tribes. They have their own stories of why they are here and all have mothers and fathers who must worry where their children and daughters are.

The time had drifted by and dragged with it the struggle felt by all. The night time went by as I snatched short naps of sleep for the night and during this time my stomach throbbed with the pain of emptiness which made me feel weak and faint.

When small lights splintered through the tiny cracks the door to our dungeon opened up and a beam of brightness flashed in with greatness, and showed the women who were like animals in a pen.

It was morning and it marked the time for us to leave the cell. I tapped Kesiwaa on the shoulder to waken her and she did not move. The women were almost walking over her as they rushed to exit the squalor we were in. I shielded them away to stop her from being trampled on. During this rush to escape to the freshness of the air outside I turned Kesiwaa over to face me.

The light from the open door showed on her face flickering as women cross the light beam which allowed me to see her. Her eyes were open, but she still slept. The warmth I gave her back as I cuddled her was missing from her face. Her hands were cold and she gazed at nothing.

My eyes felt the swell and a rush of emotion build pressure behind them and this feeling ran through my entire body. I realised Kesiwaa had removed herself from her physical form and joined our ancestors.

She was away from this horror and she will not suffer anymore within these walls that kept her freedom away. I kissed her face and left her lifeless body to remain on the stone floor which was as cold as she was.

I stood with eyes swollen and with a glaze of tears over the top over them. I slowly walked to the door and joined the others outside. As I was nearly the last one to leave I looked back at Kesiwaa and saw she was one of many women not coming out of this vile place. Their bodies spotted around pools of liquid and tiny mounds from women who had been busy with squatting.

They were all free, all at peace. They were the lucky ones who had escaped this torturous stinking nightmare.

As I stepped outside and smelt the freshness of the sea air it was then I realised the extent of the rancid miasma contained within the walls of the dungeon.

Some of the girls had blood around their ankles and they held their stomachs as they bent over in terrible pain.

The tears in my eyes flowed down my face for Kesiwaa and this time my eyes were sore.

A group of guards came to the dungeon with their mouths and noses covered with a cloth and dragged out the corpses and pulled them with their feet.

The women's heads dragged over the cold stone causing their sores to open and their flesh to tear. Seeing this made me think this was the ultimate humiliation. This was worse than seeing an animal killed by a hunter. The hunters were told to strike and kill the beast they hunted and not make it suffer. My queen Kesiwaa had suffered and this was the work of sick and disgusting people.

Kesiwaa was brought out and she still had her eyes gazing, open and unmoving.

One of the guards vomited before he reached the freshness of outside air. All of them started coughing then gagging as they were trying to catch their breath as they choked. One obroni guard did throw the inside of his stomach over the floor and the others laughed at him as he gasped for air.

The women who were now outside this dungeon stood silent and each one knew a women being dragged away from inside.

I counted four women with various tribal marks and indications of their identity. Kesiwaa had a mark on her cheek, but this was not tribal but a recent cut.

She soon had another flesh wound as her face was scraped along the hard stone floor which sliced her just below her right eye.

Her head banged heavenly again until the wound snagged against the stone ground and opened up more and then poured deep red to lay a trail of her blood behind.

The bodies of these lifeless women now free from torture were taken through the gate and into the same main yard I saw when I first arrived. I could just see the guards to the side of the edge of the wall in front of our metal bars throw Kesiwaa's lifeless form onto a wooden cart like the straw dolls we made in our village.

It was then I felt the coldness of death touch my shoulders. Then it wrapped around me and a spiking shiver ran through my body. I bowed my head and gave my thoughts to my queen who had the worst treatment imaginable as she saw her last days in this hell on earth humiliate and then mortify her.

'May peace, now be upon your soul,' I spoke to myself. Kesiwaa, you are now with Onyankopon.

CHAPTER 9: Maintained

The next morning took a while for the sun to escape the clouds and when it did I heard the women start to speak their languages. The feeling of loneliness among many was difficult to describe yet it happened to me and all the women I observed.

I could not release the thought of Kesiwaa passing this life in the way she did from my head and as I stood outside thinking of her a tear welled up to greet my eyes. It became too much as it ran into a slow trickle until it was soon accompanied by a stream of tears running down my cheeks. My nose released its own contribution of mucus too as I collapsed to my knees realising the true horror of my experience which drew strength from my already weakened body.

My tears became stronger and I wailed with my sobbing. I was unaware of my volume.

I had attracted attention to myself and I felt a cradle of an arm around my shoulder and I was helped to my feet. I did not care who was taking an interest in me or why. My eyes were blurred from my tears and I could not smell the stench from the dungeon because my nose was so full of my mucus which ran into my mouth. I was now crying so hard I found it hard to breath and I started to choke.

Two women had taken me to a corner of the small enclosure away from the main site of the guards and furthest away from being seen. I began to feel some comfort and more secure and let these strangers enter my profound thoughts.

Here they sat me next to a wall and they helped me to become calm. They spoke a language I had heard before from the others in my tribe who had learned the words and used them as they tried to speak them in jest to each other.

These women spoke to me and I replied as best as I could until we managed to understand each other with some common words. I actually found that I understood Anulika more than she understood me. They were from a place further along the coastline than my area. A place where there was more hostility between tribes and the women were more used to comforting each other after battles between tribes as so often warriors and loved ones never came back.

I managed to clear my eyes and before me I saw a woman and a young girl. The girl was about twelve years old. They silenced my cries to a whimper and eventually they stopped my tears completely.

The older women told me her name was Anulika and then she said the other girl was her sister called Ifunanya. I looked at Ifunanya and she had the body of a young woman full to the bosom but her face gave away her youth.

I noticed earlier some women had specks of dried redness around their ankles and legs. Ifunanya showed no signs womanhood had flowed between them.

All of the women in the courtyard talked in their many languages but this was suddenly brought to a halt when they heard a call from a guard on the high balcony above the dungeon. They started to move towards an area next to the barred gate where I first stepped into this prison.

I watched the women who were pushing to assemble in some form of line, which was helped by more guards with their prodding sticks and rifles.

Anulika and Ifunanya helped me to my feet and escorted me to the line. As we progressed my stomach knew it was time to be relieved from the emptiness which ate away my strength from within.

I reached the point of the area where I was given a dirty wooden bowl and then I was given a handful of something looking as if a monkey had chewed up some nuts and spat it out.

Anulika took the bowl from me and gave me hers which tasted much the same.

I did not know whether to take it or drop it. My low energy was giving my arms no strength and my hands shook as I held the bowl in front of myself. Immediately Ifunanya raced around my side and relieved the bowl from my weak fingers and took my hand to guide me to the area where we could sit.

I sat down with Anulika and Ifunanya and we ate the cud which was our nourishment. It was tasteless, like the food which last touched my desperate lips. I struggled to swallow this pulped gritty mulch as my throat had swollen and my first attempt to swallow regurgitated it back to my mouth. I swallowed again and this time it stayed down.

After a while I managed to eat all of it and it then gave me the feeling of being stronger. So I scraped the bowl and cleaned every part of it and licked the extra from my fingers too.

Anulika told me in her tradition it was bad luck to take something from someone's left hand and the bowl was given to me this way. This was why she took the bowl from me and gave hers with her right hand which was the way it should be accepted.

At this time I was too weary to think too much about this but I remembered it was quite important to Anulika.

I asked Anulika how long they had been in captivity and she told me so far they had counted twenty two days and nights. They had seen many women come in and everyone was sick within the first day. They explained to me with the words they could make me understand, that I would get used to the smell of the dungeon and advised me to try to smear my defecation on the wall as much as possible to keep it off the floor where we all try to find space to sleep. The dungeon was swept and water thrown in every day to wash it but it was basic and it made it smell even worse.

The number of women grew more and more with about five to ten captives being interned each day which swelled to fill the space. This created more mess and more smell. Each woman who arrived went through the same torture of feeling alone among other feelings of despair and confusion.

I also asked Anulika about the girls who were taken away after the obroni on the balcony pointed them out. Anulika put her head down and said nothing. This seemed to be something known to her but she kept quiet. She went cold and did not want to talk for a while. This had hit a nerve with her and so I did not pursue it again. I quickly talked about her reason for being in this place to remove the subject from the stale air between us.

Anulika explained to me they were from a people called the "Igbo" and she was one of two girls who dressed the queen in their village. The queen in their tribe had a husband who they called an "Igwe" which was the same as our Odikro. Everything was fine and she was happy and she was devoted to her royal lady and they became friends until the Igwe, suddenly became ill and he spent a while hidden from his people. The Igwe only had the one wife and so she was thought highly of and they had three sons.

Everybody was saying their leader was soon going to be with Amadioha, the God of thunder.

They said he would be in front of them to speak to them and guide them. He would stand with his flywhisk, which was a short wooden pole with a handle bound in animal skin and the other end looked like a horse tail. This was used to shake in the face or tap on the hands of others in a form of greeting as it was forbidden for anyone to touch the Igwe. He would also hold his 'Mma Igbu' (ceremonial sword), as he spoke to his tribe but his return never came and this went for a while. The village never saw their Igwe until one day it was declared he was dead.

With this the eldest son became the new Igwe and in this case he was a young boy of nine years old. The problem then was that by tradition when a new Igwe takes his reign he has to kill his mother to be able to start from a fresh and new beginning.

This was because it was believed the wife of the Igwe would interfere with the ruling of the village and so it was a tradition the queen must die to prevent this.

Anulika stopped for a second and paused as if she was struggling to speak but then she continued to tell me more.

Her queen was still young and she was scared of her fate as she expected to live a long and good life. Her husband's father was old when he died and his wife then took her own life soon after, but she was also elderly.

Anulika spoke of the preparation for the killing of the queen which she saw as an act of senseless murder with no meaning. She told me of another tradition which was if a naked woman sits on the Igwe's throne then he is dethroned and stays so until he dies.

Anulika was not allowed to dress the queen in preparation for her death and so the royal robes were laid around the shoulders of the condemned lady by two newly appointed dressers in preparation for her death. Anulika saw this as her only way to save the life of her queen and she removed her clothes and ran towards the Igwe's stool.

She told me the royal stool was bare and clear for her to take her rest and remove the Igwe and stop the killing but in her haste she tripped and fell short of her aim. She was then picked up by some of the Igwe's guards and taken away to a hut where she was detained.

Anulika told me how about how she watched through the door curtain of the hut and said the queen was dressed in bright robes and then made to stand between two wooden poles with her hands tied to them.

The new Igwe, her son, then took his flywhisk and shook it over his mother's face. This was because an Igwe was not allowed to touch anybody with his hands and it was his way of kissing her goodbye. He then took his 'Mma Igbu' (ceremonial sword) to his mother's chest and with a sudden thrust he pierced the heart of his mother who then dripped deep red blood from her mouth as she slumped between the posts with her robes stained with the redness from her wound seeping into the cloth.

This then was the problem for Anulika and she was then stripped of her duties. She was responsible for trying to dethrone the new Igwe so Anulika and her sister Ifunanya were both then sent away from the village. The sisters had no parents to defend them as they had also passed beyond this world.

I listened in disbelief of this disturbing and sad story which was similar in its tragedy to my own.

I looked at Anulika who looked back at me and I introduced my name "Esi. " I added I was so named because I was Sunday born.

Anulika told me that her name meant "Joy is greater" and Ifunanya's name was "Love", but when they were sent away from the village they were given a last name of Nwosu which meant they had become outcast.

So Anulika was sent away from the life she knew also, just as I was and so we knew we were to support each other and I felt the warmth of comfort being with her and Ifunanya.

She informed me there were only a handful of women when they arrived and now there were around one hundred and fifty sad souls who have all lost their freedom to the unknown. Anulika wanted to know why we were all here and asked me yet I could not answer.

The unknown was the frightening part, why were we here? There was a story I heard when I was younger though which I remembered. It was the "obroni" would take you to a land far away and very different from our own. However, this was a rumour to scare us as children to keep us close by our village. What scared me was it appears to be true. What happens in these far-away lands? Why are they taking us? Why are we treated in such away?

Some of the women and young girls are just accepting their fate.

They just sit there with a sorrowful face and look at the sky. They like to watch the birds fly above in almost a cry for help as though their spirit could be carried away by the freedom they have.

I also wanted to be away from this stepping stone on the edge of life and death and I want to be back with my family.

Yet although I wanted some answers I am too weak to try and find out.

I listened to the voices around me and I heard some of the women speaking in words similar to my vernacular and I just about understand their plans to try and escape to their freedom.

I looked also to see the girls in this yard and I could recognise those who had been here for a while as they sat almost motionless and their limbs are skinny and their faces are sullen.

I also saw Anulika and Ifunanya are both quite skinny and under nourished. Unlike me as I was still quite solid and my body shape was full, as I had only just arrived.

There were women with thin limbs and those who looked healthy and the women with confusion on their faces, and those who just sat in acceptance of their plight whose spirit of hope was broken. These were also the women with the dried blood around their ankles which told me they were here for a while.

I sat with Anulika and Ifunanya and listened to their words and this then became my daily life. Anulika and Ifunanya watched me and guided me to build my strength again and I thanked them for this.

Over the next few days my eyes identified the women around me and they were drawn to one woman in particular who was here before me but she is still well rounded in her shape. This did not go with the pattern and so my concentration stayed with her.

This woman made sure she circulated with most of the others and appeared to speak many different languages and understand different tribes. There was something about this woman which did not seem to be right. I decided to keep my eyes on her.

I watched her for many days until one day she did not appear among us.

I told Anulika about my observations and she told me this girl was in our confinement before her. So this was when I asked myself, how come her limbs were not frail and lean?

One day as we were made to stand in the middle of the yard for the calling from the obroni on the balcony this woman appeared and made her way to the back of the courtyard, this time not speaking to anyone.

All of a sudden some guards approached and sifted through the women and pushed me aside. I watched these guards pulling the women and turning their heads around by their hair and looking at them with aggression.

They eventually found who they were looking for and six obroni men took three women and escorted them out of the courtyard through the gate which I first came in. These women were not as new to this place as I was but they were quite recently brought here, I thought, just before me. I saw they were always together and at times they would argue with each other over something. I did not know what it was as I did not know the language they used, but something made them aggressive.

It was then I remembered these were the women who I guessed were plotting to escape and it was this which triggered my answer to the mysterious woman among us.

She was a spy for the troublemakers. I asked Anulika about this and she had not thought about it before.

However Anulika did confirm every time a new group arrived to this place there were some women who talked of escape and they usually got taken away and did not return. Where were they taken to?

I later overheard one girl say they take them to a cell and push them inside and then only open the door after three full moons had past.

CHAPTER 10: Chosen

Many days came and went and I got to know more of the women, and although communication was sometimes difficult, we generally traded our view with an interpreter. I did get to speak to a couple of girls who spoke my language but I still remained closest to Anulika and Ifunanya and I felt their loyalty was genuine as we got more familiar with each.

The days drifted along and it was the same routine that greeted me from the morning to the night.

We were allowed to walk and stretch our wasting and frail limbs during the day and then we were served the minimum of the stodgy food which tasted of nothing.

Each evening arrived and drew the night shade to cover the sky then we were returned to find a space on the hard floor to rest.

Every time I entered this filthy dungeon the stench made me gag and I felt a rush to my head. Each night more bodies, more mess and the stink hit my nose. This meant less room to find to sleep, and more lifeless souls removed in the morning as they lost their fight to exist in this squalor.

As the days and nights alternated and shared the time between them one day blended in with the next. Each new morning moved on and it felt as if one day was no different to the other.

One day the morning was greeted by the voices of ladies singing.

These voices could be heard coming from the open windows above the gate through which I first stepped into my captivity. I noticed the ladies voices always started the singing and it was later joined by the deeper voices of men.

I then realised it was Sunday but it had been lost in my suffering before now. The singing happened every week on the Sunday and they always sang the songs I heard from the obroni preachers who came to our village. This was the thing I did not understand. The obroni preachers always told us at my village about the way to be civilized and the singing of the songs had words of being kind to others, yet this building was surely built by the devil as the angel's backs were turned.

This room had windows and they had shutters to cover them. These windows were always left open to greet the sunshine and then were closed in the evening. The only other time they were shut was when a girl was chosen by the obroni on the balcony.

The songs sung were of a Christian theme and this made me think about the values introduced to our tribe by the obroni. Yet no songs were sung as a girl was picked by the obroni on the balcony. Why was this I asked myself? The windows were shut and closed to this ritual to hide it away from the eyes of the obroni preacher and the women.

More captive women arrived and the dungeon stank even more than ever. The mixture of vomit, defecation, blood, sweat, urine, and sometimes death wreaked a dense mixture of the worst of smells ever inhaled. We all breathed the sea air every day with gasps of relief as we moved into our small yard. The first breath of the morning usually brought about coughing and spluttering as the clear air ran into our clammy mouths. We all grew used to this and once our throats were clear it was easier to breath until it all started again.

I sat with Anulika and Ifunanya and we talked about our families. I also talked about my Fiifi and my dream of my future with him. Anulika had asked me how long we were betrothed and I told her we had come from the same village. I told her we knew each other for a long time, and we had given loyalty to each other as I saw him as my future. We were perfect together and we had done everything as normal couples do.

Anulika tried to ask me how close had we actually been and I had to laugh. I informed her although we were close we had not ventured into trying to produce any children and I was pure from any carnal knowledge. Anulika smiled and brushed my hair. Ifunanya was unsure as to what we were talking about but Anulika knew and it was between us.

The day went well into the afternoon and we continued to talk about lots of things. Anulika was interesting but sometimes I fell under the spell of my silent drum if she was not capturing my interest. Well she would never know anyway would she? Nobody ever did and I just thought of my drumbeat to numb my body of the reality of my situation.

One day whilst I was with Anulika and Ifunanya and they were talking too fast for me to be bothered to listen I was suddenly being shaken and Anulika was pulling me to my feet. I had realised the tone in her voice had changed.

We stood up and many obroni guards made us face the balcony. The obroni dressed in fancy clothes came out and walked along the top behind the wooden barrier where he placed his hands before stroking his beard. His eyes focused on every one of the women and he was particularly looking at the new faces among us. So far my face had not captured the eyes of the obroni and I feared my time was running out.

Above us we heard the shutters to the windows slam closed.

"Thud, thud, thud, thud, thud, thud, thud," was the noise of the wooden shutters as they thumped closed, followed by two more, but louder straight after.

"Thud thud."

It was then the obroni pointed to several girls and they were removed from the yard by the guards. I did not know what this was but I had an idea and so did not try to think about it too much.

The obroni then scanned the area of the women and as always I bent my knees slightly to hide behind the girl in front of me, until the day I stood behind the girl who was the traitor. I stood still and hidden until she moved away to the side like a mask being removed from a dancer at a celebration around a fire and I was exposed to the obroni. The obroni's eyes saw me and his stare fixed and never wandered away. He slowly lifted his arm and his finger pointed directly towards me. I was chosen.

A guard took me by the arm and led me to the side and through a doorway. Here I was ordered to stand against a wall and I joined three other women who were taken before me.

In this room there were several beds all lined along the opposite wall and a couple of men were sleeping on them. These men had removed their uniforms and they were lying down in just their dingy white trousers and they used their shirt to cover their heads.

I stood in the line and dared not move. An obroni man then came up to us and spoke after first spitting on the floor at our feet.

He told us to remove our ragged and torn clothes and place them on the ground.

I was so scared at undressing as the only person to see my bare skin was my mother when I was a baby and the two girls at Nana Apane's hut. Definitely no man had seen me naked and I was shaking with the nervousness it gave me.

A door from another room opened and two obroni men carried in a large wooden container of water and they placed it next to us.

I nervously removed the ragged cloth hanging from my weak limbs and sensed the other girls doing the same.

I tried to cover myself with my arms as did the other girls but I covered very little of my body and the obroni guard looked at all of us with the eyes of a fevered animal.

With all of the girls naked we were directed to wash our skin in this old wooden barrel cut in half. As the first woman stepped into the water we helped her and held her arms and she was trembling which I assumed was from the cold water, then the obroni told us to wash her.

We scooped the water with our hands. She gasped as the cold water splashed around her shoulders. We finished with washing the grime and dust from her face and she then smiled and showed her large white teeth.

This smile was nervous though and it lasted only until the obroni made a grunting noise as he spoke something I did not understand. After this he handed me a dirty rag cloth then he turned and he walked away.

The second girl was quite tiny and she had a small frame and no breasts like those of a fully grown woman. She kept her head down and we washed her in the same way as the first girl. I scooped some water with my hands to cleanse the dirt from her face and as I pulled her head up I saw she was very young and was crying. The little trickles of the tear trail were delicate but they were there. I looked into this girl's eyes and they were empty of any emotion. She did not blink or give any sign of distress but I knew she was afraid. I splashed the water onto her face and washed away the tears and then dried her face with a little rag of torn cloth handed to me by the guard earlier. Her expression never changed as she stepped out of the water with the minimum of movement.

The next girl to step in to the barrel stomped into the water and decided she would wash herself. She pushed mine and the other girl's hands away and she cleansed her own body. This girl had full limbs and her belly was solid which I identified as the signs she was quite new to this place. She also had good teeth and I noticed she stood tall and upright and she was standing like she had some defiance in her.

I tried again to splash water onto her skin and she grabbed my wrist tightly and she squeezed it until it hurt.

She spoke to me and she told me her name was Yenmah. I looked at her hand holding my wrist and I stared back at her face. She informed me she was the daughter of an Odikro from the upper East region. Her grip on my wrist started to feel painful but I remained unmoved by this until she let go. My eyes never left hers and after a short pause she apologised. I felt her sorrow as her upright body then stooped in despair and she placed her head in her hands and she started to sob. I stood looking at a woman of noble stock reduced to a broken one. Yenmah then held out her hand to mine and I reached up and I took it as she stepped out of the water.

She thanked me and asked me my name. I told her and she smiled. She was about the same age as me and as we stood and looked at each other and I saw behind her womanly face the worry of a young girl. I think she saw the same reflected by me as well.

I had not bathed as yet and I noticed the first girl in the barrel got the clean water and it was going to be the last girl who was to douche who got the stale water of the others, however it was still fresher than having a sour skin which had layers of dirt upon dirt.

I was the last to wash and I stepped into the water and its coldness gave a sharp sting to my skin and I shivered until the cold bumps rose on my skin.

The girls splashed water over my naked body and they washed me all over as I adjusted to the feel of the cold water. It soon felt so refreshing. I could not wait to get the water between my legs and when I did it stung me as I had developed some sores at the top of my legs from the sticky sweat that had not been washed properly away for weeks. As I washed I smelt the stink of my body release itself from my skin and how good it felt.

Once I had cleansed myself I climbed out of the cold water barrel and felt the air tingle me like the softest of cloth caressing me.

The obroni guard returned and he stood in front of us and he looked at us with lust in his eyes and then he placed his hand on his groin.

After we were all dry the guard asked us to stand against the wall opposite the guard's beds.

As I stood with the others against the wall I heard the door to this room open again and somebody entered. I wanted to see who it was but I dare not turn my head. As our obroni guard looked towards the door I stole a glimpse of who it was and I soon saw it was Ifunanya.

She was accompanied by a guard who brought her to join us and he was holding her arm so tightly her face was wincing. Our guard placed her next to the water, and the he gestured for her to wash.

Ifunanya looked over at me with a deep stare and I knew she was asking for a sign to acknowledge she should bathe. I dropped my chin down with a quick nod to agree to what the obroni was asking.

Ifunanya took her robe from her shoulders and it fell onto the floor and revealed a young woman's body perfectly formed. Her neckline was straight and sharp, her breasts were ripe and her slim waist showed the figure of a young girl who was on the cusp of being a very fine and beautiful young woman who had the face of what an Igwe would choose for his wife.

Ifunanya was left to wash herself as the others girls and I were made to remain against the wall. Ifunanya stepped into the barrel, as she did the 'splodge' noise of the water woke one of the guards from sleeping on his bed. He pulled his shirt from over his face and looked over to where the noise was and his eyes fixed on Ifunanya's glistening form. A ray of sun shine beaming through a gap in the door helped the water sparkle against her skin.

As Ifunanya bent down to collect more water from around her feet, the guard who had just woken up prodded the other guard who was on the bed next to him and woke him up.

They both stared at Ifunanya bathing with epicurean lust and they started to talk to each other as they watched her.

I wished Ifunanya to hurry up and finish and end this voyeuristic show and she looked nervous as she stepped out of the tub shaking.

After she had cleansed her skin in the water Ifunanya took the cloth to dry her skin and she was taken by the guard to join us.

We all stood silent as we were inspected by the guard who was watching over us. He walked down the line and then he told us to follow him through a door along to the end of the guards sleeping area.

This room was small and it had some stairs to the left side that rose to the ceiling and led to nowhere which made no sense. It seemed to have no purpose as if something was blocked. We all stood away from the stairs and again lined up against the wall opposite these stairs.

The guard then climbed the stairs and knocked three hard blows against the ceiling and shouted at it before he climbed down again.

There were heavy footsteps above our heads and these seemed to be heading towards us near to the top of these stairs.

Then the ceiling opened up and there were a pair of feet climbing through and down the stairs.

Through this trap door came the obroni in fancy clothes who was from the balcony and he spoke to the guard and then he came over to us.

This obroni in fancy clothes walked down the line of women inspecting us. I could not dare turn my head but I could just see from the side of my vision he was stopping at the first girl and then the next.

He approached me a paused and looked long and hard into my eyes. He opened my mouth and then did something I could not believe. He groped my breast with his large obroni hands. I tried to pull away but I was standing against a wall. So I could not recoil from this intrusion. I started shaking and my heart raced with a panic.

I wanted to scream at the top of my voice. The rage behind my voice was an explosion of anger and it was croaking my throat.

This action made my stomach curdle and I felt disgusted. I was untouched by anyone and this was a shock to me. He coldly ran his hands down my body. I dare not move and I froze. It must have been only seconds but it felt like longer. My breathing stopped suddenly with the shock and I found myself feeling faint.

After he had removed his hands from me I began again to breathe heavily then he moved to the girl next to me who was not even a woman as it was Ifunanya. As he touched her I felt her intrusion as if it were mine as she was only a child. My stomach gurgled and I started to tremble. The obroni then chose three of us. I was one along with Ifunanya and the small girl with the young vacant face and pretty features. Yenmah and the other women went back into the guards sleeping area and I heard a door slam. Ifunanya, this other girl and I were allowed to sit against a wall of this room with the stairway of the strange ceiling door. The obroni in the fancy clothes climbed back up the stairs and through to the place above us.

We were made to wait as we sat quiet on the hard stone floor not daring to move. Ifunanya moved up to me and I placed my arm around her to comfort her. The other girl saw this and she did the same and so I placed my arm around her as well.

Then I saw through a tiny window at a top corner of this room that darkness of night had started to fall. I just embraced Ifunanya and brushed her hair with my hand. I stroked the hair of the other girl but she remained empty and lifeless as I cradled her. I assured her we would be fine and she tried hard to smile. She was confused and I was beginning to realise our fate. We kept each other warm as we were still naked and my skin felt the shiver of both of the girls.

As I sat I was falling asleep with Ifunanya and the other girl in my arms. I was awoken suddenly and pulled to my feet.

The obroni guard pushed us towards the foot of the stairs that ascended up to the ceiling. I started to climb the staircase as the trapdoor opened up then I stepped through followed by Ifunanya and the other girl.

As I climbed through I noticed another open door in front right of me. We followed our guard through this door and I saw the big obroni of the fancy clothes now in a large baggy white gown.

He was drinking from a silver metal cup and he was big like Nana Apane in his stomach area.

We were pushed into a line facing a huge bed with thick poles on each corner reaching upwards and there were cloth drapes hanging from them.

The big obroni approached and stood before us. He then walked up to the first girl and stopped in front of her. This was the young girl whose name I did not know.

Here the big obroni towered above her so much he needed to bow down to look at her face as it was glaring at the floor. He pulled her head up from her chin and stared closely at her face.

The obroni spoke to the girl then he brushed her lips with his finger. He then reached down and kissed her before releasing his grip from her raised expressionless face.

He moved to me and said something to one of the guards who started laughing.

The obroni looked from my eyes down to the length of my body. He was biting his lip which looked like he was getting hungry and he then licked his lips with a slow movement that made me wonder what he was thinking. I knew the first girl did not have the curves of a woman like mine and he saw this for himself as my flesh was bare to his attention. His gaze then left me and he focused on Ifunanya and he held a long stare over her. I felt sick in my stomach at the thought of what could be done to her. He reached out to take her arm and I knew it was wrong.

I could not let anything happen to her and so I acted quickly and moved in front of her and blocked his hand, which caught my breast.

This distracted him and one of the guards shouted something. The obroni spoke to him and then he took my breast again.

As before when the obroni touched me he smiled and I froze, but while he gave me his attention he was distracted from Ifunanya. My palms were hot as I tighten my fists and my stomach felt like it was on fire. The air was silent and only the sound of the wind blowing through an open window could be heard.

I was so scared I wanted to lose water from between my legs and I was shaking.

It was then I became a little bit dizzy from the rush of fear that overcame me. I wanted to run but where would I go. Anyway I could not leave as my life was not my choice anymore. I was in the control of my captors and right now I could not leave Ifunanya.

The obroni smiled at me and it was then I fully realised I had been chosen by him.

He took hold of my arm and led me to his huge bed and he pulled together the drapes on each side. As I approached it I turned around and just saw Ifunanya disappearing down through the trapdoor, with the other girl and the guard.

The trapdoor slammed shut over their heads. I felt desolate and helpless.

I was now in a closed room with the big obroni. He came and stood in front of me.

The other girls were gone, I stood alone naked and I felt like I was a skinned animal ready to be seasoned for the cooking pot. He stood towering his form over my slight frame then spoke to me in a language I did not quite understand. I did hear the odd word which I guessed was being spoken to me. These few words were those spoken by some of the obroni preachers from when I was at home.

The obroni gestured to me if I wished to have a drink and I refused by shaking my head. In truth my mouth was so dry I could have drunk water from the bathing tub but I did not want to take anything from this obroni in case I was duped into being accused of stealing.

I felt so uncomfortable thinking this situation had visited my head before. I thought back to when I was on my own with Nana Apane in his hut. I stood still, and as I did not know what he wanted me to do, my body became numb. The obroni just stared at me, his eyes not leaving mine as though he was looking into my mind.

The only movement in the room was a lonely candle flame flickering from a small breeze coming through the open window. Joining the air was the salty smell of the sea and the noise of the waves crashing against the rocks.

The obroni walk over and drew the wooden shutter from its wide open position to half closed to prevent the breeze cooling the room from the wind. This also blocked some of the evening light which was disappearing quickly.

Which was the better of these two situations, the Odikro or the obroni? They were both against my wishes. They were both against my dreams. They were both against my understanding.

The obroni walked over to a large wooden desk and started to close some books and tidy the area. He then put a book neatly on a shelf and then came over to me and spoke something to me and smiled. I dare not make a retort as I did not know if this would offend him. I was scared.

This time I could not run away. This time I was more afraid than before, so much so I started to have the nerves rage in my stomach.

If I were with Nana Apane at least I would still know Fiifi was safe. However, people in the village did not know how I had loved Fiifi and to lay down with Nana Apane would be a duty only for my Odikro and not a choice through love of any kind. I could have hoped my tribe and villagers knew of my real feelings and I would at least still see Fiifi and my family.

Being with the obroni nobody could see the pain and humiliation of my plight. Nobody would ever know my suffering or know of my real love and dreams.

Nobody in my village would ever know the shame and dishonour of how I felt. I have gone from the potential wife of an Odikro, which should have been every girls pride and joy, to what I was about to face and about to have forced upon me.

The obroni climbed onto his bed and beckoned me to join him. This time I had nowhere to run and to hide. I shivered with fright but did not show it. I walked slowly forward and carefully climbed onto the soft mattress which had a deep red cloth draped over it.

Once I was on the bed the obroni moved over and pulled me nearer to him. He first looked at my eyes then at my breasts then my whole body. His jaw jutted in and out and his cheeks clenched as he looked at my mid-section. At this point I wanted to fight and use my arms and legs to lash out and punch, but I knew my strength would not be powerful enough to end my situation and I would most probably pass out. I had to remain with a strong head.

I immediately covered myself with my hands as the obroni took off his gown. The obroni had a large belly which hid his manhood which was a relief but his flesh was as bare as mine. His skin was so pale and it was a shock to see.

I was naked with shame and humility lying next to a man I did not know. I saw a stranger lusting over me so I closed my eyes almost shut to get his vision away from me. I felt his hand touch my shoulder and this made me tremble.

I tried to ignore tactile intrusion on my body but then I heard his groan. His was breathing heavily.

I kept my focus on not letting this disturb me and I just about managed to block my ears by calling for my silent drum but the stench and the sour sweet smell of his breath hit my nose like a breeze of rotting fruit which was unbearable. This smell broke me from all concentration and my eyes opened.

The obroni was so close to my face I could see the tiny black spots around his nose and the tiny hairs on the end of it.

What had meant to be a time when I was to give my body to Fiifi as the dream of my akuma for my ƆdƆ, has turned into one of complete horror.

I looked into the eyes of the obroni in a hope he would stop but I knew this was not going to be curtailed. The only thing I could do was to go along with the expectations of the obroni and be calm. I also needed Kesiwaa's strength and discipline if I was to do this.

I wanted my Fiifi to save me but he was not here and I knew it was not going to happen and so I prepared for this savage and humiliating indulgence from this obroni.

My eyes were swollen and behind them were the tears of everything I wished for being held back as my dreams are shattered. I felt this was my death sentence, as my life was about to end. My future was no longer a dream but a curse of a witch doctor disguised in the name of Nana Apane.

I took a deep breath as the obroni took my hands away from my shoulders I had crossed over my breasts. I felt his cold fingers against my bosom and I stared straight ahead. The obroni then pulled me down by my arms to lay on my back, so the he could look at me.

His eyes looked deep into mine and then he gazed down at my body. He then closed in on me and started to kiss my neck, as he did this I froze and then I looked at the ceiling.

Touching my body could only be compared to being eaten alive by a beast from the hunting grounds. The fear was intense as my legs almost shrivelled up as I wanted to protect myself. I wanted to cover my body and felt as exposed as a new born baby would be to a vicious beast.

The obroni pushed my legs apart and he started to breathe heavier and quicker.

I started to shake at this point and my mouth went dry. I tried to swallow and nervously failed as my throat tightened with a spasm.

A moistening of saliva to my mouth was welcome but it never came. My fingers clasped a fist as I prepared for my slaughter.

He placed his hand directly onto the part of my body which was the only place a man who I was married to was allowed to do when we decided to create a family. I instantly felt sick and my stomach tightened and I wanted to scream.

My teeth clenched tight and my body went ridged and my knees closed. The obroni just pulled them apart again without any thought for me as his breathing got heavier and the sour stink of his breath invaded my air space. I felt sick, but had to contain myself. The obroni man's breath smelled like a sour nut from the drink he had swallowed and his skin was clammy and sweaty.

He then invited his hips inside my thighs and fumbled around again with the inside at the top of my legs.

Then I felt something other than his hand. It hurt and I felt as if I had been stabbed with a knife below. This physical pain was equal to the emotional pain I felt. Both seemed to fuse together and fortified each other for the ultimate invasion of my life.

The obroni's body was crushing me and he had me pinned underneath his huge shape. The tears behind my eyes were there but they would not come out. My feet started tapping uncontrollably from trembling which was coming from my mid-section. This was a fight against the beast was one I would never win.

I was about to wish my life was over and I wanted to be with Kesiwaa. My head started to spin and the scream in my throat would have been heard by my ancestors. I remembered what Fiifi had told me about not giving up and so I tried to stay strong.

I called my silent drum remembering the beat that moved Fiifi's feet during his dance from the hunt. All I could do was let the beat control my mind and the obroni pressed his big stomach against mine then up and down to a rhythm.

"Bam ba ba, bam ba ba bam ba ba bam, ba ba bam ba ba bam, ba ba bam ba ba bam bam ba ba, bam ba ba bam."

My eyes were open and I felt the obroni as he lay over me and rocked himself to his own rhythm. I felt his body on mine but I was numb. I was in agony but without any pain as I fought for my silent drum to block it out.

"Bam ba ba, bam ba ba bam ba ba bam, ba ba bam ba ba bam, ba ba bam ba ba bam bam ba ba, bam ba ba bam."

The crying wall of the dam behind my eyes was becoming stronger yet still no tears fell from them.

The candle flame was dancing around and was causing images to flicker on the ceiling. In my head I saw a vision of Fiifi dancing to this beat.

However it was taken over by the thought that I wished I could grab this flame from the candle and set the flame onto cloths around the room and set it to roar a blazing fire. To burn down and remove everything including my tortured body from this world and the bastard obroni who was destroying my life with this unwanted invasion and assault.

The feeling between my legs was an intrusion to my inside, both my body and mind. At first it was a painful feeling which made me want to scream but I controlled it with my silent drum. This was a very different drum. This drum was louder in my head yet it was as silent as death.

I tried to keep positive thoughts in my head and wondered how Ifunanya was. At least this was not her, lying here. I could not have let Ifunanya go through this as she would have been broken.

As I was being savaged I thought she would not have coped with this mauling by the monster that lay over me.

My silent drum played its beat for quite a while before it was no longer needed. The obroni finished the slaughter of his prey then he removed himself from crushing me which made me draw a huge breath.

I had not realised my body had been under so much weight. It was as if I had been trapped and then released.

This had taken the pain between my legs and made it numb.

The obroni rolled and turned away from me as if I did not exist then he was quiet. He was still and he rested. I knew he was less of a danger this way. I heard men talking in the room below and there was laughing from deep voices.

I felt that between my legs was moist but I did not want to touch it. I tried to sleep myself, to remove myself from this evening's theft of my body, but the stench of the dungeon had no competition to the stench this obroni passed to me. This was by far the worst smell to abuse my nose. One that will forever make me feel and sick disgusted.

I lay on my back and looked at the ceiling for as long as I could remember. What had just happened to me was abuse of the worse kind. In my tribe the men did not behave in this way. Not that I knew as there was never any talk of it. Looking at the ceiling I gaze beyond the high ceiling and I was transfixed to one stop for so long I became still and unmoved.

Then as I was staring in a trance that took over my mind the obroni turned over and coughed into my ear.

It alarmed me as I wondered if he was going to wake up but then his snoring confirmed to me that he was asleep. I started to feel tired and the softness of the bed was kind to my aching body.

After staring around the room and slipping in and out of slumber from the exhaustion I had to endure I fell into the arms of my sleep.

The morning sun came to greet me through the crack in the shutter by the window and I dare not move. As I stared at the ceiling from a night of disgust and rape I looked over at the obroni. He slowly awoke from his nights rest.

The guards below had been making a noise for most of the night in their sleeping quarters below, and they were still groaning as I remained motionless flickering between light sleep and bouts of tiredness from my ordeal.

I closed my eyes to pretend to be asleep as the obroni turned over to face me. He then threw his big lazy arm over me and when he realised I was next to him he spoke to me in his strange language. He then coughed into my face and his breath released the vapours of a wild animal.

I knew to remain still would be my safest option so I kept my eyes closed and my body still. However I soon felt he was shuffling closer to me and my nose smelt his breath again, this time more sour than before.

I tried to turn away from him onto my side. This just made things worse and he pressed my shoulder down and moved close to me from behind. When this started I closed my eyes and called my silent drum as I knew again the filth of his loins was going to fill my stomach.

I managed to stay strong until I felt his body on mine and again I was numb. I was pushed on to my front as the obroni adjusted my hips and pulled my behind up from the bed.

This was to be another encounter of the worst kind as I felt his body thrust into me without any gentleness.

This time however the walls of the crying damn burst that was behind my eyes and the tears trickled from my eyes and then dripped onto the soft cushion cradling my painful face.

The obroni moved aggressively behind me as he reached his end. I let my stomach down onto the bed and as I did I felt him leaving me. He had gone to open his window and he shouted to his guard.

I wiped my tears against the soft pillow I rested my head on. I turned this soft wet cushion over to the other side without being noticed by the obroni. I felt dirty and disgusted and I sensed my body was not my own anymore. I wanted to sit in a river for as long as I could bear the cold. I wanted to scrub my skin so hard until the blood seeped through. I wanted to cover my body with tight robes and never take them off to expose my skin to anyone ever again.

The obroni picked up a cloth and dropped it over me telling me to cover myself and he also gave me a rope to use to tie the robe around my waist.

I dressed quickly and I felt the trickle of his mess running down the inside of my leg. I could smell this filth quite strongly. His stench was like a rotten dead animal and it covered my body.

Once I had wrapped the cloth around myself I felt more dignified but it somehow made me feel still exposed inside.

There was a knock on the door and the big obroni shouted his command and the guard came into the room. I was then ordered to leave by a half-hearted hand gesture by him as if he had just eaten some food and had no desire for any more. I followed the guard down through the trapdoor and then it hit me. I went dizzy, I was drained. I nearly fell down the steps. I heard my stomach rumble and

I needed to eat. It was painful and continued to make a noise.

I could not fall, were my thoughts as I needed my strength to carry me through the day ahead.

I was taken through to the guards sleeping area and I saw that every bed this time had a guard lying in it with some who were sleeping and others who were awake. Their eyes watched me walk past them and I felt this sick parade was a show of shame as I counted quickly twenty or so guards.

As I progressed towards the door I saw the skin of a dark coloured arm underneath poking out from underneath a bed sheet on the last bed.

This cover was then removed by one of the obroni guards as he woke to the noise made from the trapdoor slamming shut and what I saw made me have a rush of horror and disgust.

On this bed as the obroni climbed off of it, I saw the body was Ifunanya. She was lying on her back her arms crossed her just under her chin with blood all around her and between her legs. She lay motionless with her legs open and her mid-section was exposed. Her eyes showed a fixed stare at the ceiling and the white traces of where salty tear tracks having run dry down her cheeks were visible.

These guards had all taken her. As they woke all of them laughed at me when I saw this and I walked over to her and picked up the exhausted body of this child, she was limp, dazed and silent.

I lifted her head and looked at her face and her eyes were both open but shut. I could see behind her empty stare she was still alive but exhausted.

I wrapped her listless inert body in her clothes hurriedly and made my way to the door to exit this area of massacre until I was back into the main yard.

What had I done? I thought I had saved Ifunanya from the obroni, but instead I had sent her to an onslaught of savagery. I had sent her to a lair of obdurate ferity.

I carried Ifunanya to the middle of the yard where the women had been summoned.

I looked to find Anulika who saw me step through door from where she last saw us and then I was faint, weak and about to fall. With my last steps I fought to put one foot in front of the other. Anulika hurried towards me and grabbed Ifunanya and held her tight.

I looked for some support to keep myself standing and knew I needed somewhere to lie down and I looked for help from someone.

The women however were more interested in a bowl of food for their empty stomachs than to be bothered by my needs and I couldn't blame them.

Anulika looked at me and the tears flowed from her eyes as they did mine. Anulika took Ifunanya inside the rotten room where the women slept. The blood around her ankles dripped slowly from them which sourced from her mid-section.

My tears were now stronger than before. More intense as I saw the result of an act of continuous brutal and barbaric rape this poor girl had gone through. It was in my mind this should have happened to me.

I could not speak to Anulika so I remained silent.

I sat for the rest of the day in a state of shock just outside the room and looked on constantly and kept an eye on Ifunanya who was cradled by her sister as she cupped water to her dry mouth.

I felt faint and so I crawled in to the room and found a space that was not so damp. The darkness came as I passed out.

Chapter 11: Journey

I woke to the stench of the cell as I lay on the hard floor.

I turned my aching body over to my side and tried to pull myself up and stand but I was feeling dizzy.

I managed to find some strength until I stood but my legs did not carry me more than three strides before I fell down again. I was so weak I could have laid there on the cold stone forever I was so weak and dirty.

One of the women came over to me and helped me to sit. She spoke in her language but I did not understand her. She had brought me some food and helped to feed me like I was a child.

The food I was given was a light soup with little taste.

I struggled to let this tiny amount of nourishment pass my swollen throat.

As this woman was from another tribe she tried again to speak to me but again I never understood her words.

I thanked her with a forced smile and she wrapped the cloth around my shoulders that had fallen away. I could see outside the dungeon there were a new group of women who had arrived.

Against the wall near the back I just made out the figure of Anulika and Ifunanya. They were lying down together and Anulika had her arm as a cushion for her sister's head.

The woman who fed me helped me to my feet and took me out side into the courtyard for some air. The women, as usual, were talking in their native tongues the languages they knew. This new friend who fed me went to join in a conversation with other women who spoke her language.

I saw the woman who never loses weight walking between them.

This spy, this rotten collaborator who betrays the women with poisonous words to the guards if she hears talk of rebellion. She needed to be watched as she was the ears of the devil.

I had noticed her actions to the guards as she gave the ciphers and showed them signals. She gave codes to inform them of the captive women who speak against them. I believed she deliberately stood in front of me and then she moved when the bastard obroni was looking for his night time company.

She was very sly and I watched her with vigilance which is why I hid behind her. I guessed she knew what I was doing and I tried to remain secretive. Her codes were so simple queen Kesiwaa would mock her if she saw what she was doing.

I noticed she would scratch her left shoulder whilst she stood behind anyone talking of a rebellion. She would touch her right shoulder if there was a woman who was causing trouble.

I had seen many women get taken away after these signs and they never returned. Where they went I did not know. This became the fate of the girl I met called Yemnah. She was starting to talk about fighting against the guards and some of the women she spoke to were either weak or too young to take action with her.

Once the guards were notified of this they took her away and she was not seen again. As she was taken she was screaming about her father who was a very powerful Odikro but this meant nothing to the guards who did not listen. As she was escorted past me she looked over and her eyes caught mine then she spoke calmly to tell me.

"As my name means the mother of Onyankopon, then I will go and meet her and I embrace her calling me."

Yenmah was never going to be able to accept these conditions and so she chose to rebel. I think she knew what she was doing and she had decided to leave her living hell within the walls of the white building.

I spoke to Anulika later on this day and she told me Ifunanya's body was giving her pain from the waist down and I knew why.

Anulika spoke about her hurt inside at what had happened to her sister and she told me she was sorry she had neglected talking to me for the last couple of days but I reassured her I understood. I also told her there were a lot of devious things happening in this confinement which kept my eyes constantly looking for tricks.

Ifunanya needed her sister's full attention and I let her take it. I could care for myself now and I was available to talk to her if she needed me.

I was aching too and had bled from my skin being broken between my legs however Ifunanya was ripped apart and I saw her dazed face wince as she tried to move on the cold stone floor.

Over the next few days I managed to gain some strength and was able to walk around more. I was losing weight however and it was noticeable. My arms and legs grew thinner each day from lack of nourishment and movement which made me feel weak.

Anulika continued to nurse Ifunanya who just lay on the hard ground each day. She stayed in the same spot and only moved when she had to defecate, which Anulika gathered and pressed into the wall.

Over the next few weeks the women had grown to such a number, the gathering in the dungeon room we slept in was unbearable.

Anulika continued to watch over Ifunanya and I helped when I could. I also offered to help these women who had come from the room of the obroni. I offered this help even though they had not helped me but I chose to do this. I had no loyalty but I felt I should show my care for the women I shared my torment with.

On one morning when I woke I offered to get some water for

Anulika I suddenly became very faint and dizzy. I was throwing what little food I had onto the ground. This caused the other girls to groan at me in their languages.

This carried on for a while and I imagined I was starting to get the sickness which has made so many women just want to lie on the squalid stone ground and never wake up. I had to keep my chin up as Kesiwaa had taught me so even though some mornings I doubled over with vomit I cleared my mouth then I picked myself up from the hard ground and stood tall.

One morning soon after came and I went outside to the courtyard and through the bars to the main courtyard I noticed the guards were carrying fresh fruit and provisions. They carried barrels and various other materials.

Cloths of many colours and more rifles and smaller sticks with the hole in one end and the wooden and silver colour which I had been told were hand pistols.

These sticks or pistols as I have come to know them would kill you if they faced you and when the guards raised them you made sure you would stand still. This I learned from the other women.

I knew something important was happening as the guards were singing. They carried the provisions in for most of the day and the women approached the bars of our enclosure each wanting to see these items.

The women started talking about what they thought was going to happen and their minds were full of the ideas from the new captives. These new arrivals had their health and were still strong. How I kept my strength I will never know.

Those who had been in this filthy, dirty and disgusting place for some time, were tired women, some so weak they just lay on the floor among the sludge inside this stone dungeon.

Flies, and insects were rife, little bugs crawled over the floor, so many of them some of the women trapped them because of their hunger.

The obroni would throw in water every day to sluice the dungeon but the stench still remained. The filth darkened the white walls which shaded downwards to meet the stagnant puddles.

Open wounds on the flesh of others who needed treatment were ignored. Their moans were unheard as the fight for survival was now a personal battle for each woman.

They did not see this new stock being taken to the stores. They just slept and faded into a sleep of darkness, some not even knowing or seeing daylight. They lay down and started the first stages of their descent to join their ancestors in the earth.

This day ended with the night closing fast. Over the next few days the supplies kept coming in and the smell of fresh food and spices was blown our way and I breathed it in with my head pressed against the bars. The sea wind encouraged a sweet smell to kiss my nose and for a few choice moments I was back in my village.

My eyes closed and my vision saw a memory.

"Bam ba ba, bam ba ba bam ba ba bam, ba ba bam ba ba bam, ba ba bam ba ba bam bam ba ba, bam ba ba bam."

There was my Father sitting with Nana Kuntu. My Mother was cooking over a fire and my sister was playing with her straw dolls. I was singing and dancing by myself and my enjoyment was with those I loved and who loved me.

The next morning greeted me with groans from the many women who were pressed into this dungeon of squalor. I managed to stand and made my way towards the door of light that opened. In the court yard the guards had dressed smartly and things looked tidy.

I felt tired but strong enough to take on another day. This was short lived though as I threw what little food from my stomach and I was gagging and retching so hard I was choking and coughing. I had suffered a sickness for some days now.

The women slowly started to release themselves from inside the messy room and then the shouting from the guards began.

We were pushed and barged to line up as we were counted. The amount of women was so many I gave up after two hundred. I was weary but we had to stand and listen, my ears became deaf to the numbers being called.

I looked for Anulika and Ifunanya. I noticed Anulika was stood at the front to the left of me. My eyes were still tired and the bright sun made me squint to see her form. She was sullen and her body drooped. I saw bodies being dragged by the guards from inside the stench enclosure that had trapped us each and every night. I counted about five lifeless souls and then I recognised the one I did not wish to see.

It was Ifunanya being pulled by her bare legs and around her mid-section the only small cloth that kept here pride fell to the ground.

She looked like she was sleeping as her head banged against the hard stone ground but she was now on her way to join her ancestors in the earth. My Onyankopon lifted her away to be at peace and it was her only sanctuary from this misery.

My eyes glazed over with a layer of water and dripped a fall of emotion. I clench my fists in anger and I wanted to scream. What good would it do? This cruel world that let these beasts roam had allowed this brutality as these monsters took Ifunanya and killed her with their evil lust.

As I looked on I saw Anulika was swaying in the heat but I knew it was distress for her sister.

I wanted to run and capture her as I knew she was ready to fall but it was too late. She dropped heavily to the ground with a thud.

The guards were alert and quickly scooped her from the floor and took her away as they did the others. She had passed out from the constant caring of her sister. She had no energy and this prison had swallowed all the strength she had. I did not realise it then but it was the last time I would see Anulika. I did not know if she had managed to keep herself alive or if her akuma had broken and all her strength evaporated from her exhausted body. I felt her sorrow from losing Ifunanya and shared her pain from living in such an appalling place.

My heart sank in my chest as I remembered the words Fiifi had told me to keep going and fight for my life. For this reason I stood in the heat and kept my body straight and tall as Kesiwaa had taught me.

The women were all drained and their withered bodies had reduced to a size some would say was that of a child. I myself was without any build and my limbs were empty of strength and volume.

A guard made an announcement in a language I was just beginning to understand. The mumblings among the women's interpreta tion filtered then translated through to my ears. We were being moved to another place of imprisonment. Where we were going to I could not tell but I sensed something was happening.

We were pushed into a long room which had high walls and there were gaps at the top where the light shone through. A young girl grabbed my hand and I sensed she was scared. She gripped my hand tightly and I felt her concern about our fate. We were densely packed together and there was pushing from all sides. We stood for what seemed to be quite a while and the heat was becoming intense. The girl holding my hand looked up to me and she had a look of fright in her eyes. She was a girl I had seen before but she always stayed by herself and never spoke to anyone. I did not think she could talk so I made no attempt to try. I wanted to reassure her that all was going to be fine but I did not know myself what we were to expect. The tired smile that I gave was helped by a dry gulp in my throat. This was all I could offer her.

A guard spoke again and we were ordered to move forward to a point where we were made to form a single file. I nudged the mute girl holding my hand in front of me so I could keep her in my sight. As I neared the front of the line I saw the women were stopping for a few seconds as some guards placed something around their necks. I reached this point and I had a collar of strong metal clipped around mine. Then a trail of chains was snapped around my feet. This time we were not linked together with others.

This took a while for the guards to do but I soon found this heavy necklace weighted me down. As I walked forward between these stone walls I just followed the girl in front of me. I had not been in this part of my enclosure and as I moved on I saw other people ahead entering from a side entrance. They joined us and the amount of captives swelled.

"Is that Cudjoe?" I asked myself so I spoke his name for him to hear me. He reacted and turned around but was quickly prompted to face forward and he was encouraged to do so by the sting of a whip to his back. He had lost a lot of his size and he was gaunt and he looked unwell.

We made our way forward towards a darkened area which had a shaft of light shining through a hole in the wall to the right hand side.

We shuffled even further towards our destiny. Everyone who approached seemed to pause before they went towards the light. The young mute girl in front of me looked back and I nodded and gently pushed her forward. The girl then slipped into the beam of light shining through the hole in the wall. I clenched my fists and my akuma raced with panic as I was to be next.

The light was now really bright now. I was told to move to it and I smelled the salty air of the sea. I closed my eyes and I turned towards the direction of it. I could almost see the brightness from behind my eyelids. I opened them to view my destiny. I saw what looked like a wooden walkway that led the direction I was supposed to walk.

I was ushered through a very small gap, a tiny hole in a wall, I now know as the "Door of no return," to start the next journey of my stolen freedom. I stepped nervously forward and the route ahead led out of the walls of the stinking hell that had been my prison for two moons. I saw the outside world again. I looked at the sea next to the sand and then I saw a tall vessel sitting like a sea bird on the water. It was huge.

How I managed to fit through this tiny slot in the wall that held my captivity I will never know. I realised the time of being in this hell, my body had wasted away with malnutrition. I watched as each captive slipped easily through this dark slit towards the beacon of brightness, some even walking straight through as their bodies were slender, frail and weak.

It was when I was outside these terrible walls that had held me for many weeks I realised my next journey was to be in the huge craft sat on the vast water before me.

What I saw was a trail of confused, weary and thin people being led to a vessel sitting on the sea by a wooden ramp descending towards the ground then further along another ramp ascending towards it. My fellow captives were being directed onto this huge wooden husk with poles in the middle and large cloths wrapped around them pointing to the sky. They walked down the wooden slope and then up again onto this floating giant structure which was pointed on one end.

The back of the vessel was finely painted and there were flags along the ropes which held the poles in the air. Right at the top was a solitary flag with many colours. This was the ship of the obroni and it was going to carry me away.

I looked at the huge wooden shape awaiting us and suddenly felt afraid.

As I slowly progressed forward the ship became ever bigger. I tried to imagine my fate but I was too weary.

I walked carefully towards the steps of this giant monster of the sea. I heard the creaking from its caress with the seawater and I got the blow of the cool clean sea air and it made my skin shiver and tingle.

I grabbed hold of the mute girls hand in front of me and I squeezed hard to keep hold of my fellow captor. She replied the same gesture with more strength than my tired fingers could match. So much so it hurt.

This was when I saw my love Fiifi. He was standing in the line of others in front of me, and he was joined by his neck with a chain to another man who looked frail. I knew my chance to speak to him was the only one then. I shouted his name.

"Fiifi my ƆdƆ!"

I yelled with the energy which exhausted me and he turned his head which was restricted in movement and then he looked down at the ground. He was broken as it appeared he had given up his fight.

He had told me to never give up and I was being let down by my mentor. I also held my head down for a brief while before I shouted again.

"Fiifi, do not ever forget me!"

I said with my last energy then I drew my last breath before I had to let go. I breathed in the salty air and my nose cleared and it made me dizzy.

I climbed onto the obroni boat and I entered the vessel with the last strength I had. The mute girl was parted from me and we were shown into different directions. My line approached an opening in the floor and we went down some wooden steps into the belly of the vessel.

As I looked to where I was going to be placed I saw that there were already some captives on this ship. They looked weary and most of them looked as they had vomit around their feet. This ship must have travelled from another slave castle further along the shore. It appeared that this vessel was filling up with our human cargo.

We were made to sit on wooden benches and then as the last captives entered, the groans joined the clink of our chains and I finally lay down and rested. An obroni man then slipped another long chain through each of our collars from one side to the other. This made us become linked together in a row. The short walk was as tiring as it was dramatic and my strength had left me. I looked for the mute girl and she was just behind me. I placed both of my hands against my cheek and gestured to her it was time for her to rest as it was with me too.

I looked around hoping to find Anulika but I could not see her. I would try to find her later if she were alive. She must have been weak and I would need to watch over her the best I could.

Once everyone was inside the sun was blocked by a cover over the hole from where we descended.

I lay my head to rest on the splintering wood as best I could as we were all cramped close together. I felt the sway of the ship and amongst the confusion I managed to close my eyes.

At first I was too aware of the noise around me. I could not rest, however the tiredness grabbed my mind and I gave in to the pillow of sleep.

I was woken by the scream of a woman which left me scared at first. It was the obroni removing some bodies by sliding away the chains that were restricting our movement.

One of the bodies carried away also bore the same signs of the fate of Ifunanya and I knew this young woman was met during the night by the beasts of the dark as she was removed for the lust of the obroni loins. This woman had held her last breath for freedom and lost the fight when she realised her sanctuary would never be seen again.

As I lay and looked around I saw men and women who also appeared to be losing their fight for their future. Many were vomiting and they were clearly distressed.

I wanted to help them but I was too weak and chained anyway.

I wanted to talk to some of the others who were looking stronger but when I had tried on other occasions I was given no response.

I heard many voices talking in different languages and I wished we all had one united way to understand each other's words. With our different languages for communication we could not connect and with this we had no power. The women had learned basic dialects from each other but many remained silent.

The ship I was contained in was rocking from side to side as the choppy waves from the sea crashed against it. This constant swaying our new cell made me feel like I wanted to throw up the little food I had in my shrunken belly. I managed to keep it within me but it had begun to bear me cramps. Many captives were constantly regurgitating stomach bile which soured the musty air.

This smell, along with the stench of stale blood, defecation and vomit, fortified its vile aroma .The strong odour of sweat made the mixture of this rank pungency sit in my nose and it never left it.

Captives were groaning and there were some who just lay down and shook with a fever, others were coughing and spitting the bitter taste away from their mouths as they struggled to breathe with heavy gasps.

For many days we floated in this husk on the choppy sea. Each day and night merged together until a light sprayed a shaft of brightness into my eyes. As I was weak I could not respond. I then heard the voices of the obroni and I knew I had to be conscious so I opened my eyes.

I sat up on the wooden seat and looked around. Then water was thrown at us and it was responded by cries and screams as it was so cold. A next guard arrived and we were given a piece of fruit and water from a coconut shell. I was given only one chance to drink which I was barely able to consume.

A line of us were then unshackled from the long chain that joined us in our seated rows and told to stand.

As I stood I saw the face of the full bodied girl who betrayed us lying against the wood. She had taken her position just like the rest of us on the obroni vessel. She had been tricked into doing her role for the obroni. This girl's payment for her collaboration with our captors was as fickle as her heart. She was also enchained and was now part of the battle for survival.

As I dragged my feet forward labouring against heavy legs chains, I saw her shoulder and back and there were deep lacerations that leaked blood. She had been given a beating and by the look of it, a severe one. She then had water thrown at her but she did not respond.

We were then forced to climb the steps to the top of this floating torture.

I dragged my weary and slender form to join the group of

women also taken out of the hole below. I looked at the sun for the first time in many days and my eyes were closed by it without my instruction.

A sway of the ship made me start to splutter and without warning putrid bile dribbled from my mouth and slopped in front of me.

I saw the young mute girl at the side of me and grabbed her hand. She was so slim and under nourished and I was surprised she could stand.

I noticed some girls looking around but I looked straight ahead and all I saw was the sea.

As we stood together I watched a girl in front of me slump to the floor. The obroni guards raced to her and they tried to arouse her from her unconscious state. They slapped her face and rolled her from side to side. A call from a man standing on a high platform gave and order to the men standing over her.

Without any delay they quickly picked her naked body up, carried her to the side of the boat, lifted her to their chests and then she was gone over the side and into the sea.

I pulled my body as straight as I could and stiffened my legs. They buckled at first and I felt myself sway but I locked my knees again and I looked ahead again.

A call was made from an obroni who stood nearby and I sensed a rhythm through the boards of the floor around me. I tried to recognise the beat but I did not feel my feet move. This beat was being thumped out by another bibini but he was not anyone from my tribe. We were gestured to move our feet by a big obroni guard and so my knees unlocked and I tried to pick up my sore feet.

I had no energy but I had to do as ordered without question. I was in a situation I did not know and so I conformed without any refusal.

Once all the women started to tap their feet there was a feeling of unity and we looked around at each other as we knew the movement tied us together unlike the chains binding us against our will.

My frail body grasped the last of my energy and as I danced to the unfamiliar beat. I then took my own minds decision and tried to bring on my silent drum yet I could not meet these inner comforts as the obroni gathered water from the sea and commenced to throw it over us. Each time the water splashed against me I shivered and I was getting colder but I knew this was keeping me alive.

This was my only way to rinse my body of the smell and filth from the hole that contained me for most of the time. I soon got used to this so I could cleanse the sores developed around my elbows and I knew splinters had ripped into my skin from where I had been placed during this tortuous journey. My feet stung from broken blisters but although the sea water had its bite on them, I felt it also washed away any pain after a while. I took the full force of many buckets of sea water and it was refreshing.

I washed with the passion of a woman almost mad. I rubbed my skin with the swiftness of a desperate animal. I shook my body like the animals of the jungle as I became cold from the sea breeze.

Once we had bathed and moved our feet we were once again led to our chamber of filth and squalor which not only removed our dignity but also our right for movement. I even lost any wish to know our destiny.

This journey made me constantly feel sick and nauseas and I dry gagged quite regularly. I also threw the little food up that I was given only to feel some slip back down my throat as I lay on my back. I felt increasingly weak to the point my will to continue was breaking.

I knew this vessel took me further and further away from my home and I came to the point of wanting to let my stomach remain in one place.

When we danced and washed I saw no other land and was scared and tired of just water all around.

This carried on for what seemed to be never ending. I tried to reserve all of my energy and my silent drum carried me through. Each night I found it. It floated me away from the reality of my prison to a temporary place of safety.

As this journey removed me from my home the sickness took over. I was so weak to the point I was vomiting each day. The water carried our vessel up and down constantly. My vision became blurred after days of being without light and then suddenly taken into the brightness of the sun for the dancing to the obroni drum for our exercise.

I often thought about the girl who had slumped in front of me and was thrown into the sea. I thought about dropping on the floor and letting the obroni do the same to me and join her in a place of sanctuary but I was too determined to swap my captivity to freedom by giving in so easily.

Some girls swallowed the sea water and then threw it straight back onto the wooden floor. They were desperate for liquid. These girls claimed they saw images of the worst kind of spirit. They saw images and shouted in their language. The obroni mocked their madness with laughter and ridicule.

One girl was rolling around in our wooden confined area and she became restless to the point she claimed to see a 'grasscutter' bush meat rodent roasting on a spike over a fire. She reached down and grabbed a rat from the wooden floor and held it in the air before she screamed as it bit her finger.

This only angered the girl who bit into the vermin's face with her sharp and crooked teethed. This punctured the wretched rats face and spattered its blood over her and people nearby.

She then tore at its head like she was ripping cooked meat from its bone as it squeaked a dying cry of pain. Her teeth were still clenched, bleeding filthy blood down her throat when she opened her mouth and licked her lips for more nourishment of this raw and spontaneous feast. After this she lay still.

This girl kept this flesh and fur meal inside her stomach, but the bitten finger became infected. After a few days she was crying from a swelling in her stomach. The same as what started her appetite days before.

She was in so much agony she took the chain between her feet and smashed it over the swollen finger so many times it eventually fell off. I saw the girl raise her hand to look at it with her palm to her face and the damaged finger dangled by the girls flesh towards the floor. She shrieked before her body fell back wards and her head was heard to thump hard against the wood she was sitting on. Soon after with twitches of her limbs, she lay still. The obroni guards simply took away the chains, wrapped her in a cloth and carried her away.

This was sad to see and it now made me more determined to survive. I was however becoming more slender and my limbs withered, apart from my stomach, which was now bloated. I felt my head was pounding from inside, my hair was falling out and my eyes felt as though they were gritted. My mouth was dry.

I was in need of food; more than the piece of fruit we were given each day but I was not going to take the rats and mice scuttling around the floor. I did not even pick the bugs and insects around me to suppress my hunger as I did not want to feel any worse than I already did. My pain was my hunger. I did not want to be greedy and live on vermin and seawater that way I would surely lose my fight for thinking clearly.

I continued to absorb this disgusting nightmare. This was a sick and humiliating situation for me. I thought so hard and long at what I was observing. I took into my thoughts my mother and how she gave me my life. I thought about my father and how he was a great warrior. I thought of my sister Kakraba who was not only my best friend but the one who needed me more than most. I also thought about my queen Kesiwaa and I could not let her down. I needed to recharge myself with a belief this would soon come to an end and I called to myself to let my stomach fill with not just food but my belief in Onyankopon.

I called in my head and my mutterings for as long as I could manage, then slowly I felt my throat became moist. I opened my eyes and the grit had filtered away. My head was no longer being invaded with pain.

Out of nowhere I felt Onyankopon reach towards my akuma and tell me to be strong. This was my lift, my own message from my Nyame to be determined to fight for my mortality. I had to follow this to its end and I was more determined to keep alive and one day speak the reality of the foul and disturbing life I was living. I was not going to slump to the floor or let the obroni take my lifeless corpse away and even more so, eat vermin from madness invading my sanity. I needed to remain in the world and see the future. My name needed to live on as the name of Kwaku must be heard in future generations to show I existed. This was my destiny to speak my story to others.

For now I had to remain strong and whole. I had to keep the strength of a warrior, the sage of a hunter and the commitment of the tribe's workers in my mind.

I had to take the words of my love Fiifi and never give up. I also had to take the words of Onyankopon who had spoken to me with the words I needed to survive this journey.

"Onyankopon na ahy me den". God gave me strength.

I felt my body lift from the ground and my akuma filled with excitement. My vision became clear and my limbs felt as though they had blossomed. I was alive and I was not going not leave this world yet.

I continued to hold my new surge of spiritual energy within me. Each time we climbed onto the deck of the vessel I kept my hope of health.

I was as lucky as most of the remaining women around me as they held onto their own lives whilst others fell. It was also noticeable the more people who were not able to stay with us on this tortuous journey the more space was available for those still wearing the cloth of resistance around their shoulders. More space yes, but no more fruit.

If I were to achieve this survival I needed to remain away from any trouble from the obroni as I started to hear words of rebellion. The men were talking of fighting when they were in the open air at the top of the steps.

The men spoke with words and signals about overcoming the guards. I understood some of the men were great warriors and some were young men.

I watched and listened and there was one man who was creating unrest among many men. He was very aggressive in his tone of voice. I do not know what he was saying but as the languages filtered around he was talking about fighting the obroni guards and taking over the vessel. He stood up and spoke to all and said he would make a signal for his line to run at our captors and over power them. The men appeared to agree with him and others spoke up to announce that they also wanted to fight.

I laid back and closed my eyes to rest then I heard a voice speak in my language.

"They will not succeed with this foolish plan. This is doomed for failure. They will lose any attempt to overcome these men who hold us captive and as much as I am as angry and furious about what has happened to us it is better we stay alive than be thrown into the sea."

I sat up and looked at the speaker and I saw it was Cudjoe. He stood strong and tall and he spoke with the authority of an Odikro. He looked around then he made his final words known to all.

He spoke with passion and leadership.

"I say to you my fellow captives. The obroni has captured your body. Do not let him now steal your wisdom. The only way we can see our freedom from capture now is to stay alive and unite at the right time. That time may not be during your lives but it will be in your descendant's lives. Your future is not to be ended on this vessel, but your legacy will be from your offspring."

With his speech done Cudjoe sat down and there was quiet for a while. Then there was further talk of rebellion from the aggressive man and this seemed to be encouraged by many who appeared to agree with him.

I left them to make their fate and continued my own personal path to my future and remained focused on my new inner belief.

Soon after this day I was taken above the containment area for my water splash and feet moving.

I stood as usual with the other women waiting for the guards with the buckets to haul the water from the sea. There was a shout by one of the obroni to a man who was dressed in fancy clothes with a hat. He was standing in front of two other men similar to him.

I had not seen these men before and I noticed the cover to the steps leading to our confinement was still open and this was normally closed once we out in the open air.

Then a shout was made by a guard and out of the opening to our confinement stepped another guard and he had with him the aggressive man who was speaking of rebellion.

The aggressive man was taken to a place near to the edge of the vessel. His chain around his neck was removed and his feet were bound with a rope. His hands were bound separately. He was then lifted to stand onto the side of the vessel. I could not see where the rope he was attached to was tied. I was expecting him to be hauled into the air. Before he could even prepare for his doom he dropped like a stone over the edge and into the water.

Obroni men hauled on a rope from the sea on the opposite side of this floating hell. I saw the fallen man as he rose again on this side of the vessel being pulled feet first. His skin was sliced to shreds and his flesh was scraped away from the underneath sharpness of the ship. He was left still and bleeding on the floor. The aggressive man was then placed in front of us for all to see. The obroni with the hat then spoke to a bibini speaker who spoke many languages. His translation to mine was not very good and he appeared to speak with a bad understanding. When he spoke my language he got things wrong about certain words. This was something I expected.

I made myself ready to move my feet and I looked at the drummer. There was no beat being played. Instead there was another shout from the guard and out of the opening to our confinement stepped another guard and another captive.

They walked to the same place the aggressive man had been before his torture and bound his feet and hands as before. It was then I noticed the captive was Cudjoe. He followed the same steps as the first man and within no time he was over the side and into the sea.

He came back on the other side of the vessel being hauled by his feet. He was not moving and he was also laid down in front of us.

Cudjoe had water pouring from his mouth and he had cuts and wounds all over him. I thought back to what he done or said wrong by deserving this treatment and I looked at the bibini speaker. It was because he did not translate Cudjoe's words correctly and he thought he was also plotting to rebel.

Cudjoe and the other man were then picked up and thrown into the sea this time with no rope to bring them back.

The fish would surely sense the blood of these captives as it seeped into the sea. Their punishment was for talking of escaping their hell but Cudjoe only wanted to live and leave a legacy after his ordeal. Cudjoe was right. The translators were not to be trusted. He never was a slave. He was born free and he was 'captured' and that is how he died, as a captive. He was now at asomdwoee (peace).

I saw a strong man with a good akuma taken away and it was distressing to see but I would not let this beat me. I do not know how but I remained alive until we had eventually reached our destination.

After a few days we were ordered to climb the steps and back onto the open area and this is when I saw the land of my destiny. It was just like the land I had left, the sun was hot in the sky and the trees held their coconuts up under their leafy arms.

Our vessel stood still for the first time and the obroni men gathered in the large sails as I stood at the edge. The water looked clear and light blue and there were several other boats already resting near to the sand.

The vessel we had arrived on was next to a wooded landing structure that was assembled for us to exit the ship. We climbed the stairs through to the outside of the ship then we were ordered to walk down the ramp so I drew on my weariness to drag myself down the slope to a new land and then I felt the hot sand bite my delicate feet. My feet welcomed the earth like a bird which landed on a branch after it ran out of wind in the sky.

I thought then of what atrocities we had endured on this treacherous journey of death and torture.

CHAPTER 12: Arrival

As the rise and fall of the vessel had become bearable now without it also made me also feel dizzy. After barely being able to stand I found myself among the others chained and manacled again to another girl.

I was so drained my vision was blurred and my hearing was not responding too well to noises to make any sense of them. I was constantly feeling sick and I threw up many times during this horrendous journey. My stomach continued to hurt and my arms and legs felt the aches of trying to rest on damp wood fighting for space and being knocked around by people around me.

As I stood with my feet on this new soil I looked around and I noticed it was very similar to my land except the soil on the ground was not red.

The bushes and trees looked just as it did at home in my world and this first drew my attention. This reminded me of my village surroundings and I wanted to know how far away I was. I missed my family and inside I cried bitter tears of sorrow.

I also noticed there were other vessels next to the one I had arrived on and there were men carrying large sacks onto them.

I inhaled the clean air into my wide nostrils with several breaths. I was trying to exchange the stench and sickness which invaded my body with the cleansing nourishing freshness in the sea breeze. I was sweaty, the sun was hot and my body smelled of the sickness from my fellow captives.

We were told to sit down and I was welcome for this rest. During this time I looked at fellow captives who had made the journey.

I looked for my Fiifi, but I did not see him. As the last captive left the vessel I bowed my head and imagined of the worst horror that Fiifi had been thrown over the side and into the sea for plotting to escape. I was about to shed tears when suddenly another person was guided from the ship. It was my ƆdƆ.

My akuma lifted to a great height and I was ready to scream his name. However I understood there would be no point.

I knew to be careful as the obroni split up captives who were known to be family or friends in order to keep them separate. This was to break down the bond of strength in numbers. The obroni thought they were smart but I knew about this. I therefore remained quiet and kept my head down.

I looked up momentarily to see Fiifi's feet touch the ground of the new land and then again I buried my enchained head out of sight. My eyes were strained from the sun and I was struggling to see him so I chose to shut them.

I heard the chains of the captives as they chinked and opened my eyes. I saw Fiifi was sitting quite close to me and he looked drained. His large frame had withered away to a slender one. His shoulders were hunched over and his head was down. He looked up and I saw his cheeks drew in to show a skinny face.

I looked away from him to try to remember how he looked before and I closed my eyes again to reminisce. I then looked at him again and I saw his eyes meet mine. His face was sad and his eyes tired. He looked drawn and emaciated, but I guessed I looked the same. I felt exhausted and yet pleased to be away from the vessel. Not only to be away from the stench of filth but also the abundance of death.

I was taken away from my position and chained to another line mixed with men and women. This time I was linked to a girl I did not know. I think she was already in the ship when I arrived on it and she looked weak. I looked at her and she stared at me with a frown of tiredness and sickness. Her eyes looked only half open and her cheeks were sunken. She looked weary from the journey and she struggled to stand. I smiled at her to offer some kind of support in my gesture. She barely managed to give a smile in reply however this tiny curve of her mouth gave me some kind of hope she would be fine.

We were told to start walking. I looked over at Fiifi and he was about to start walking as well.

I felt a little bit better as I started to move but I felt my stomach had swelled during the journey on the obroni vessel. I had not seen any blood flow from my body in a long time and for a moment I suspected I was carrying a child. Then again I had not eaten and nourished myself and my energy was at its lowest. I knew my stomach was swollen but with emptiness. The ache that came with it confirmed this.

I looked to my side and saw the next line which included Fiifi so near to me I wanted to touch him. We were so close but so far apart. As we walked my only thought was wishing my ƆdƆ could join in the same line I was. Was it too much to desire? What a small and weak dream yet at this stage it was all I wanted. This was something so simple and yet it was impossible for me to think it would happen.

In my thoughts I took the last of my energy and fortified it with my Fiifi's words to never give up. "Never give up Esi Kwaku," I spoke inside my head.

We walked along the track parallel to the shoreline and I looked back at the vessel which became smaller.

As we made our way to our destiny I looked again at my Fiifi whose heavy collar weighed his frame down as his shoulder sagged.

The soil was as hot as was our own at home and I felt the sores sting my feet. The combination of the hot ground and walking after a journey on the sea took its toll. It was not a long walk but my body was drained and finding the ability to move difficult.

I found my silent drum during this short trek and kept up my strength with constant reminders of never giving up again and again.

We arrived to a gathering of obroni where several bibini people were dressed in clothes just like them. Some sat on carts and some stood with the obroni also.

We were taken past a platform where there was a bibini man

standing for all to see. He was dressed in the clothes of the obroni. Next to him was an obroni and he talked to the gathering in a language that I recognised from the preacher obroni at my home. The obroni was speaking about the bibini by informing them he was a good field worker, he was loyal and he gave no trouble. There was shouting and several obroni waved their arms. Then there was an almighty shout of "Sold".

It was here I was to find my destiny, just as I had heard when I was younger. I was at the slave market.

I was guided to a large wooden building and this is where we were told to remain. Fiifi and his line followed us and two obroni men and two bibini women joined us. The bibini women wore the same clothes as the obroni as well and they talked the same language.

After a short while I was unchained and pushed into a line against a wall. I knew what was happening and it was as though I had seen it before. I thought back to when I was with the girls in the white building called Elmina castle where I stood lined up ready to be chosen by the obroni who stole my innocence.

At this point I felt the strain of the journey and the walking and sleeping on a hard wooden vessel took me too my health limit.

I also continued to have this new worry as I knew the symptoms of a woman who was to grow a child inside. I was too weak, it couldn't be.

What if the obroni devil had planted his seed inside me? I was starting to think of my tortured future with his baby. This was his child, not mine. I never asked for it, it was forced upon me and one day I would look at the face of this thing and see the reminder of the monster who took my pride and my virginity.

I was told whilst captive in the castle in my land any woman who was carrying a child was prevented from leaving our soil but it wasn't explained to me as to why.

Children crossed with the seed of the obroni man and the bibini woman gave birth to mulatto children or as we would say "broni ba" (white man's child). These were taken with their mother to a place nearby to Elmina castle and raised there. They were not allowed to travel on the ship as it was seen as a bad thing to take a woman with child over the water. I just had to release my thoughts as I was about to have my future decided and I had not time to think of this problem.

However if I was carrying a child it was also my flesh and my blood. I was feeding it and making it grow, and I may face a life time of seeing my repulsive endurance. Carrying this child would send me a lifetime of smugness and ridicule to my eyes from the devil obroni.

My thoughts drifted back to the present and I was offered some water from an obroni who was watching over us. I took the water as the heat was exhausting me. I gagged and this vile fluid came straight back into my throat and onto the dusty soil. I saw Fiifi who was observing me and he winced at my action but my body had its own decisions.

I was taken by a bibini woman to a lit area who rubbed oils over my body which made my skin shine. I watched the sheen glow against my dark skin and I noticed it removed the dryness. She then took my feet and washed the dirt from them and around my legs before she made them glisten with the same oil. She took away the ragged cloth I had draped over my shoulders and placed a clean simple but rough garment over my head and she pulled my arms through the side.

I saw my limbs now were thin as she helped me into this garment. My arms hurt as she tugged them and I winched from her tight grasp around my wrist.

An obroni man then checked my teeth and the bibini woman groomed my short hair with a wooden claw. She forced me to stand up straight and gestured me to pull in my stomach and checked my body over. She then looked again into my mouth and poked her finger in. It tasted smoky and there was a tingling against the inside of my mouth as my sore gums felt this like a sharp scratch.

I wanted to bite these smoky fingers off and would have done it if my jaw had had the strength. When this was done she moved down the line and did the same to the girl next to me.

There were also some bibini men and women among us who wore similar clothes as the obroni and some of these were older than us captives. There was one man whose hair was grey at the sides. The obroni took some black greasy substance from a metal can and rubbed it to colour his hair black and then they groomed his face with the oil to also make it shine. This man looked tired and unhappy. He should not be in this place and he showed this with the frown on his face. I looked down the line of bibini and each one now stood straight and tidy.

I saw Fiifi get treated with the oils and the black powder. It was smeared around his neck and shoulders and down his back. I saw as he turned around he had been showered with a powder that covered his wounds. Fiifi was taken near to the door from where we came and he looked like he was going to be ahead of me.

I was taken outside and I was pushed near to the middle of this market with many people looking to see what was going to be the next sale on show. I saw on the platform again that some bibini were made to stand as the obroni shouted for their plea to claim them. I thought back to what Cudjoe had told me and he was right. I was going to be sold at a market and my destiny lay ahead of me.

Since the advice from Cudjoe invaded my ears I absorbed all words spoken by the obroni. I listened carefully to everything I heard and repeated it over and over in my head to try and remember it. Some words I knew from home and the obroni preaching man, but there were also new words I had to learn.

I stood waiting my turn to go onto a raised platform before the crowd and noticed Fiifi had now moved on and he had joined a line outside.

My attention on Fiifi was taken by a shout from the crowd.

The obroni who was on the platform shouted out to an obroni who he called Master Adams. This obroni called Adams had a stout frame and a keen eye. There was another shout this time for a Master Grant who was appearing to compete against Master Adams. There were several others involved but my tiredness prevented me from keeping much attention. After all I had no influence on what was to happen to me anyway.

I was weary and needed to eat. My throat was dry and the taste of what I had thrown up earlier still lingered in my mouth.

My belly was empty yet full being bloated and it gurgled to prove its point and I focused the best I could. My silent drum was available but I could not try to play it with all around making me unable to be focused.

I stood in my line with the others waiting for my turn. Each captive was made to stand on the platform and the obroni decided who they were to be with.

At this time I was certain my Fiifi and I were to finally part.

I looked at him through my tired eyes and saw his sullen frame.

As each sale was completed the sold bibini was led down the steps to the other side and taken to a cart.

Fiifi was next and he was taken to the platform. He looked weary. I observed him and saw a good warrior reduced to a thin and broken man, destroyed and stolen from his potential and successful future. He was once a great hunter and potentially a fine warrior, yet he was now nothing more than a slave with no honour and equally no ownership of his own life.

As the seller shouted the cries of the sale to the obroni I thought that Fiifi would have a rush to his thought and run, but he stayed still and lowered his head. It was as if he had become the captured beast who had given up. He looked like he was shaking and he had beads of sweat on his brow. He was nervous and scared and I knew it.

I saw the marks the obroni tried had to cover up with the oil and powder quite clearly on his back. The marks where his chained collar had ripped his skin from around his neck also bore the scars from where is cut his skin and his back bore marks from the whipping at Assin Manso.

I know the water from the sea thrown over his back on board the ship had soothed his wounds but he was now looking like his time to meet our ancestors was close. He looked ready to collapse and I saw his frame sway more than once. The obroni made Fiifi stand straight and he lifted Fiifi's chin and showed everyone in the crowd his teeth. There seemed to be an interest for him and it must have been because he was still a young man and he was tall.

The cry went out as the seller called his audience's attention.

"Right here we have the next sale, fresh from Africa a neat and tidy strong young man. This young man can do good field work and help with all the lifting needed. Take a look at his height he can even pick all the ripe fruit from your trees gentlemen."

Looking at an obroni in front of him he said.

"He is so strong he could carry all your sacks of stock at once Master Samuels."

Then to a man to his left he said

"Look Master Thomas this is the sale for you.

Then to another man he spoke

"Now this young man is a good choice for breeding Master Green."

Finally he asked

"Who will take this sale?"

The seller was talking to people who he knew took Africans and was encouraging them to buy Fiifi. There was a lot of inward chatter but nobody spoke up.

The man I saw being sold was not strong and tall but frail and his body was buckled but he got the attraction of Master Adams who gave a determined plea for him. Master Adams shouted out his claim for my ƆdƆ with a passion of his determined desire to take him for himself.

If this is where Fiifi was to go then he would be taken to be prepared for his new home. This was then competed with another voice in the crowd and then another until the shouting was constant and I could not understand what was happening, until it slowly died down and the last cry went out.

"Sold," was the shout from the obroni seller towards the man called Master Adams.

So there it was, Fiifi had his destiny decided for him and he was to start his new life. I was in a way happy for him as this way of living for the past few months was slowly killing him.

After the sale of Fiifi there were some bibini who were already dressed in the clothes as the obroni were. These bibini were being sold as there owner had died and they were no longer needed.

There was not much interest in them as they were older and they were sold in twos. There was an old man with a frown who looked like he just went along with his sale but I knew he was sad. He had probably done this many times before and he looked like he just kept quiet and accepted his destiny, which was just what I did not understand. He had grey hair which was not smartened and dyed with the black grease and he looked like an elder from my village. He was probably a wise man but what use was it to the men buying and selling him?

He was first to be sold and he was described as useful for feeding the chickens. The others had their own descriptions informing the buyers of their skills.

They were described as Florence, housework and nurse maid. Abel, field hand, eyesight poor, Sally, handy in the kitchen, Bessie, infirm, but sews, Flementina, good cook, stiff knee. These were the first I heard and after this I past caring for them. The list carried on of these sorry people and they were sold as they needed to be owned by somebody. If one slave was not sold they would be added for free with the next person. My thoughts were that some slaves were not even worthy to be exchanged for money.

Here was I and as before was Fiifi, so weary and languished yet these bibini looked like they had lived like this for many years. Why did they not fight or run away when they were younger? This was the next question to enter my thoughts. This was also my answer, as there was nowhere to run to.

My turn had come and I climbed the platform and I was pulled by my neck chain to climb the stage of my future.

I dragged my sorrowful body onto the wooden structure and pulled my head up to greet my audience who had moved around. I was given some attention from some of the buyers who saw me as a good purchase which made me embarrassed and made me drop my head.

When I was on the platform, I looked at Master Adams and lifted my head again and looked straight at him. He appeared a little unsure as I focused on to his face but I needed to get his attention even though I just wanted to collapse from the heat, but I remained strong.

My silent drum played with my thoughts but again there was no chance to concentrate as I needed to try to be with my Fiifi.

I searched deep inside my mind to give Master Adams my thoughts and kept my eyes focus on him in a constant stare. I was now making my eye contact obvious and he finally called to the man selling me who stood by my side. Master Adams had taken my Fiifi and I needed him to take me as well.

Master Adams came over to the platform I stood on and he stepped up to see me. He walked up to me and his eyes stared deep into my own. Master Adams had dark hair, but going grey which was circled around the side of his head and he was bald on the top. His eyes were dark brown and they were focused deep into mine.

He was very similar to the devil obroni who had taken my dignity away from me and stolen my chance of the choice I had made of a future with my Fiifi. His eyes were the colour of the dark wood and the sun had reduced his pupils just like the eyes of the devil obroni when he first looked upon me.

As I stood on the platform in front of all onlookers, Master Adams put his hand against my stomach. I pulled away as the reaction made me defend myself which he saw straight away.

Master Adams sensed I was withdrawing my body and this caught his attention and I guessed he knew why. He must then know also if he got me then he would probably get two of us. He knew a bump had developed in my mid-section, this was his investment. That is if I had a child inside me and this uncertainty constantly played with my head.

Maybe it could be a good thing for me but I also thought of the problems that could lie ahead. I thought hard and deep and then after a quick decision I conclude that I felt safe with this obroni.

He appeared to be gentle and he had a soft face. His approach to me seemed to be because he cared about me. Was this just his deception or was he genuine? I had to gamble and I chose to believe the latter and I looked again at Master Adams and felt this was my best option. I tried to gain his attention but his eyes diverted from me. Master Adams looked unsure and he turned to leave the platform. He descended the steps and shook his head and put his hand on his chin as if he was thinking deeply. I was then showed for sale to the gathering of the other obroni eyes.

I heard the sale carry on and my akuma sunk deep as I saw this was my only way of staying with my ƆdƆ and it was slipping away.

A shout came from a tall man with yellow hair from near the back of the crowd.

"I'll buy the African girl" came the cry.

Master Adams heard this and made his bid against this yellow haired man then he stood observing the sale again and the yellow haired man cried for another bid for me.

Suddenly again there was a shout from deep among the obroni men as they made their choice for their claim to my sorry soul then there was again a shout from the seller man who was in control of their decisions. A shout came from a big man with a grey beard, who had a woman standing by his side along with people of my colour who had just arrived.

I looked over at Master Adams who had Fiifi sitting on a cart with wheels and a horse at the front.

The man with the yellow hair called again and in my head I thought "Daabi, no!"

Then Master Adams yelled for his bid again. I could not shout and the drama rushed through my chest like a gust of wind and I was having thoughts of being with my Fiifi.

This was when something strange happened. There was a trouble growing between Master Adams and the man with the yellow hair.

They spoke something to each other which was not in the range of my hearing.

Master Adams then made a claim I was to be with him and I was so excited.

After a few shouts between the two men and the seller finally I was sold to Master Adams and the man with the yellow hair gave up.

I was going to be with my Fiifi. I wanted to laugh so much my face must have given away some kind of secret and all my fears were gone. My Fiifi and I had beaten our chances and we were going to see our destiny. My destiny with my ƆdƆ, it was always going to be. No matter what we could not be separated, not by Kuukuwa, not by Nana Apane, and not by the obroni. We had beaten them all, I was so happy I just wanted to laugh and cry at the same time and if it were possible I was doing it inside my head. Fiifi looked at me and nodded and I scratched my nose. Ha ha ha I thought we were never to be broken.

Then just as my excitement settled down I saw Fiifi being unchained and he was taken to sit on another cart with two horses at the front. He was carried to another part of the market. I watched him until I was taken down the steps by the seller and I was greeted by a bibini man who was wearing smart clothes.

He led away me away from the platform and I was taken to the cart Fiifi was on before. Master Adams then joined the yellow haired man and they shook hands. What has happened? I remembered the obroni clasp their hands this way for greeting but this made no sense. I then reminded myself the obroni do this to seal a deal. This was something I had seen Nana Apane do before with some obroni traders when they came to our village.

It then hit me. This could not be true I thought to myself, did the two men just trade Fiifi and me? This could not be happening. Panic rushed through me.

I saw what was happening but I just wished to not believe it. Fiifi was traded for me and we were going to be split up after all. My akuma sunk in my chest and I felt myself spinning and almost collapsed. My final ounce of strength helped me to climb aboard the obroni Adam's cart and I sat where Fiifi had been minutes before.

I looked over to see where he was and he was moving towards me in a cart with some of the older bibini who were sold in twos. The old man with the weary face sat next to him.

My eyes found Fiifi's and as their wagon approached ours to cross paths we did not look at anything else than each other. It seemed forever until the cart stopped and the yellow haired man climbed aboard with some other bibini's by his side. They rode away slowly. I looked at Fiifi until he went into the distance. He just simply disappeared into the horizon. Tears tricked from my eyes and so I bowed my head. I was well and truly on my own.

"Fiifi, me dowo. Fiifi, I love you. Asem a onyankopon adi asie no onipa ntumi nnane no. What God has fore-ordained, no human being can change. Nya akokooduro, have courage, kae me, remember me."

I spoke silently against my chest holding back any more crying so I did not draw any attention.

My silent drum was brought to play as I found my sanctuary in this painful parting. I was, within minutes, deep in my own world and do not know how long I was transfixed by my escape from reality, but, I had to try to swallow the thought of my Fiifi being gone.

"Bam ba ba, bam ba ba bam ba ba bam, ba ba bam ba ba bam, ba ba bam ba ba bam bam ba ba, bam ba ba bam. Du ga da, du ga da, du ga da"

My concentration was broken as the cart pulled away and I looked at Master Adams who was guiding the horses away from the market. Sitting next to him was a bibini who led me from the platform and he was talking to Master Adams and they were laughing about something. Master Adams spoke to this bibini and called him William Beckles. His reply was that he turned to say hello to me and he greeted me with a smile. This was the first pleasant face I had seen in many months and it felt genuine and for once I felt some comfort. William's smile looked friendly and it made me feel a little more relaxed which came as a relief. My strength was just about finished as I held on to my reserve breaths.

So Master Adams had bought me and as we travelled along the dirt track he gave the guiding ropes for the horse to William and then he took out some papers and I watched as he studied them. Master Adams then spoke to me to confirm who I was. He read a paper with my name on it.

"Esi Kwaku, hmmm, I just bought you Esi Kwaku. Now this name Kwaku does not seem correct."

Master Adams spoke to me but he did not require an answer as he had the answer himself anyway.

"Well I think those traders have spelt this name all wrong Esi Kwaku, Kwaku does not start with a K.W it is spelt with a "Q" surely?"

Master Adams spoke so I heard him but what he did not know was my name was spelt correctly and I should know as my queen Kesiwaa had taught me and I was quite aware of how it was written and it does not start with a Q.

"Now this is how the name is spelt, Q.U.A. then er Q, U and

then an A and yes it reads better." Spoke Master Adams with a delight in his voice as though he had achieved something.

Master Adams looked pleased with himself for being able to write my name, yet he had spelt it wrong. I knew my name and I was Esi Takyiwaa Kwaku. This name is my identity and I will never forget it.

"Well that's the first thing done William. We got the name corrected so at least we got the records correct. Those traders don't realise a name is important and we should get it correct. When we get back to the plantation I will transfer the records to my books. Take me there William. I am tired and the sun is heavy on my face drive on whilst I rest."

Spoke Master Adams as we rode along the track leading away from the market.

"Oh and just one thing young lady, this name Esi, you will need a different one. Mrs Adams won't remember it so she will give you a new one. I think Mrs Adams has a more suitable name for you young lady."

Here it seems not only had I lost my freedom and my dignity, but I was even going to lose my name. This was the most degrading insult I could ever imagine. My life was about to start again and what I was going to see could not be any worse than what I already been through.

Master Adams and William then spoke and they laughed again. I did not want to listen to them as they were probably mocking me. I was too tired to care. I wanted to go to sleep and the breaths of sleep were invading my mouth and I started yawning. I felt the heat rage down on me and then I drifted away and closed my eyes from the bright glare of the sun.

My slumber was broken by a sudden jolt as the cart stopped. I was jostled forward. The horse spluttered as we came to a halt. I woke up to see I had arrived at the house of Master Adams and what a building it was.

"My Nyame, (my Lord) this house is huge!"

The building stood so high it reached right up to the sky. I had never seen a structure so tall. It was so high the sun was blocked and there was a glow all around like an aura. The main thing was the colour of the building.

"And it is white." I spoke to myself. Is this my big white house I thought?

A shudder went through my body as I saw vivid sights in my head of the place where I was in my land. There were even steps leading to the front door way. I almost lost my will to carry on. My focus then became blurred as my strength had evaporated in the strong heat that had beaten down on me as I travelled in the cart. I began to imagine I had returned to the terrible building as before. I was confused now as to where I was and my vision started to play tricks on me.

I looked away and when I looked back again I saw two trees which reached high on either side of the steps at the front. There were two more at the end of the steps. These trees were the type we had in my country which grew the coconuts, and there were many clustered at the top and they made them look like a pretty necklaces around the long elegant neck. I saw beyond these trees and looked at the house again. It appeared to be standing on stilts. There was a large stair case reaching up to a balcony. I saw a vivid flash image of the bastard governor strolling along here on the platform stroking his beard in my head but it soon went away.

The bibini called William leapt from the cart and Master Adams climbed out more gracefully. William came around to the back of the cart and helped me climb down to the dusty ground.

A hound barked and ran towards us and Master Adams went over and tapped its head and he called its name "Blackie," and he added "That's my boy." The hound saw me step from the cart and it showed me its teeth as it snarled at me. The hound was all black. (Ɔkraman tum tum, Black hound)

Master Adams shouted for William to take me to my new home

then walked up the stairs first and then to the side of the house and headed towards the balcony that I had spotted minutes before.

William led me up the stairs and past the tall palm trees towards the back of the house and then he gestured me to follow him up a slope to the side of the house. This was where the house altered as it was built on a slope. There was a ground level and an upper level.

I looked at it again, the front of the house was at the lower end of a slight slope and the main part of the house at the back was at the top and this side had a ground floor and then another floor on the top.

"That is why the house looked so tall from the front." I spoke to myself as the illusion that had deceived me was revealed.

As I walked around there were fancy colours from flowers at each window.

At the back of the house where there was a large open area and a cluster of trees to one side. Along the middle were a row of palm trees leading towards another area and past a high fence that surrounded this big white building.

To the other side was what looked like a place for growing ground provision and there were rows of plants parted neatly to form lines. There was a Tamarind tree, then a mango, a citrus fruit with bright orange rounded fruit. There was a fowl pen and a fenced area where there were some goats. I was still weak and my head started to spin and I was struggling to breathe. I tried to hide it and struggle on.

I followed William between these variety of trees and we walked straight down the middle of this yard to the new area and to the left were two buildings and on the right was one more building.

I was exhausted but something kept my feet moving. I stepped my pace with the last of my energy.

To the side of the second building on the left was a fenced area. As we walked on, the fence stopped and I saw a bibini man sitting on a bench. The sun was hot and I thought at this time why was this man was sitting in the sun without a hat? The heat must surely be too much for him but there he was sitting down on his own. It was then I realised I was exhausted from the heat. My legs felt soft under my body like overripe plantains and could snap easily. I looked down at my feet and they were hard and dry and dirty from the soil.

I hoped there was not far to walk now and I pulled my sagging head back upright and I looked ahead again. Further on the right was a funny coned shaped structure on which four sails spun slowly around in a circle on arms blown by the wind. This looked like the sails on the big boat which brought me to this new land but there was no water and the building did not move.

We walked further until we came to a group of buildings lined up facing each other.

William guided me to the first building which was on the left side of two rows of buildings in a neat line, unlike the huts of my village which were scattered at random. When we reached the door he tapped it. This was answered by someone who I did not see and we walked inside.

The first thing to greet my nose was the strong smell of food and my throat gagged. I was so hungry my body could not absorb even a smell of what was cooking. I was invited to sit at a table towards one side. My tired legs stepped slowly towards a chair next to it and then, my vision became blurred started to sway again and then all went hazy around me. Then it went dark.

CHAPTER 13: Trinity

I saw many beautiful things and my vision was fine my pain had gone and from my toes to the hunger in my stomach I was now feeling comfortable. I saw my mother kiss my father before he left the hut and I heard the sound of the hunters get ready to go to the savannah. I played with my straw dolls and my sister was sleeping? Then Kesiwaa called me to give her a hug then she changed into Fiifi who in turn changed into Nana Apane. I started to walk very far and then the obroni, then Ifunanya, then my thoughts brought me to a feeling of something gentle.

My eyes broke their closure and through the slits of my eyelids I saw a sparkle of light. I quickly closed my vision to the intense flash that hit my sight but then the bright glistening went away. I waited for a short pause and then slowly opened them again.

I tried to feel my body but I could not move so I tried to lift my head but this also did not want to rise up. As my sight slowly became clearer I focused at a cloth against a wall.

This cloth moved slightly and I felt a cool breeze filter through, which let a sliver of light through and dazzle me again. A sharp and piercing beam blinded me before it disappeared again behind the fabric as it settled back to its start position.

The thought of my silent drum came to my mind and I tried to remember my favourite sound but the bam bam bam I heard was a faint one. It was distant like a drum being played far away. It was not the strong powerful energetic beat I had developed over the years of playing it.

I closed my eyes again started to think to myself of what was happening. Firstly I thought how I could not move my body and my arms and legs were leaden. This was a very unusual feeling as I felt nothing more than pain from as long as I could remember.

Pain in my feet from the hard dusty ground which had constantly shredded them causing endless wounds to develop and then try to mend before the healing wounds broke open again. Then there was the pain from my legs from carrying my body over many miles of land.

Then I thought of the ache in my stomach from the suffering of being a woman, which had not visited me for a while.

Then was the weakness in my arms from trying to cradle then comforting my fellow captives. The pain in my neck and my shoulder muscles, they were so tired from the heavy chain collar which they supported and hunched my shoulders over and not let me stand tall and straight as Kesiwaa had taught me.

Then I thought of the most painful of them all which was the one I had in my akuma from losing my Fiifi as I saw his beaten and worn body taken away. There was Kesiwaa from being invited to be with to my Onyankopon and then there was Ifunanya and Anulika whose fate was not their deserved destiny. I so cruelly saw their suffering.

I thought of all of these things yet this was different. I listened with my ears for any sound to greet them and there was nothing and I thought to myself.

Silence.

Do I hear it?

Here I am in this still and quiet place without my ability to control. I exercise my listening sense to receive any noise, yet I do not feel the sound in my head and I do not sense the bam of a drumbeat. In my silence I do not feel the racing pace of a repeated strike from the players hand on an animal skin stretched over its patterned, carved dark wooden frame, as it is thumped to a continuous rhythm.

It was not there anymore and I came to a question what was offered me. The only conclusion I came to was,

"Am I with my Onyankopon? Am I with God?"

This was my destiny and I was at last at asomdwoee (peace).

"Me Esi Takyiwaa Kwaku akwaaba Onyankopon. I Esi Takyiwaa Kwaku welcome my God. Onyankopon ka yen bom. God unite us."

My thoughts were profound as I accepted my place among my ancestors and my body could now rest from the tired and brutal world it once belonged to and was abused by so many. Now Esi Takyiwaa Kwaku can be left alone and the silent drum is no more.

As I slipped into my decadent comfort I sensed something was taking me back to my early years. I absorbed into my mind a thought which made me remember my life as a little girl. This was a kind of nourishment as it scented my nose and captured my drifting attention whilst it pulled me towards its delight. My thoughts were confused at this strange sense and my mind juggled constantly with this pleasure.

The more I breathed the more this comfort fed me until my mind suddenly retrieved the answer to the messages I was now receiving.

It was a smell to my nose which lifted my chin as it searched to feed a craving. It was a joy and it invaded my nostrils with more profound breaths which became stronger and stronger.

I opened my eyes and this time I never saw the light as I had before that had flashed over my eyes and this time the cloth was steady on the wall. I clawed my fingers to clench my hands and then released them again. I wiggled my toes and my legs felt the time to move. My shoulders relaxed and my arms wanted to open up and rise in the air. I tried to lift my torso and slowly I managed to take my head from its rest.

I realised the smell that greeted my nose was something I had not sensed in a long, long time. It was the smell of meat cooking over a fire and it made me realise I was not with my Onyankopon but I was alive. I was alive? My Nyame does not want me yet?

I felt a tiny pressure on my head and I reached up and removed a damp cloth that had been until then, unknown to me, sitting on my brow.

I raised my body gently and sat up and saw I was on a soft bed and a light cloth was draped over me. I was in a small room with a table at the side and there was basin, a jug and a glass. At the end of the bed there was a door and I saw it was slightly open.

I breathed in again and smelt the overpowering delight of the meat cooking and my throat moistened. I sensed the spices and herbs of seasoned meat from home and this made me feel lifted.

This helped me to rise from the bed and when I placed my feet to the floor I saw they had been cleaned around my ankles and my feet were bound in cloth. I was wearing clean robes and I felt my skin had also been cleansed. I sensed a slight stinging on my upper arm where I had a cloth wrapped around it. When I went to remove it I felt a sharp pain against my skin. I decided I would leave it and look at a later time.

I made my way to the door and pushed it slowly open and it creaked slightly, then I walked into the large area. This room had several beds around the side of the walls. At the far end was a table and chairs and there were bottles and jars and pots and utensils hanging from a rack. There was a jug on the table and there was a cup next to it. Beside this was a bowl of green and red oval fruit, and alongside were some similar but these were turning yellow. These of course were mangoes.

On the wall there were African symbols and face masks and there were some necklaces and beads.

There was a fire place in the one stone wall and I walked forward further into this room but I could not walk very fast as my feet felt I was walking on sharp bush needles.

"Ahah, welcome Missy, now come on over and sit yourself down." This voice was the softness of a woman's but it contained some of the gravel of a tired one.

This woman made herself visible from near to a bed as she stood up.

She spoke and I saw she was a bibini and she had an inviting smile. This eased my mind as she walked towards me.

The woman was quite large and quite light skinned. She took my arm and led me to the table and sat me down next to it.

She introduced herself as Martha Callendar and she told me my tiredness had made me sleep and she had washed my feet as I slept and she also cleansed my body with oils and plant extracts.

I listened to her voice and only just understood what she was saying as her accent was different than anything I had heard before. What she meant was I had collapsed with exhaustion. She also told me she had treated my wounds with some old remedies passed down to her.

Martha asked me my name and I told her it was Esi. She mumbled something about my African name to herself as though she did not expect me to speak back to her.

"My name means I am Sunday born," I told Martha and she grinned but then she quickly lost her smile and looked at me with a more serious face.

I felt nervous as at this moment. I did not know what to say and how to react as my life of recent has been one treated like an animal and a worthless one as well. I have been ignored before and this was potentially no different.

Martha poured me some water from a jug on the table into a cup and encouraged me to drink which I did. She gave me the jug as well and I poured some more as my throat was dry. She laughed at me then went to the fire and came back with a wooden bowl and you know what was in it? It was burnt meat, how did she know? Martha had laid some strips of the food in a bowl and this looked like my favourite treat from when I was a little girl. I almost expected Nana Kuntu to walk in through the door and steal some from me.

I took a hot strip of the cooked delight in my fingers and slowly fed my hungry mouth. It was the tastiest meat I had ever eaten. I ate with the hunger of a mad person and I tried to contain myself, but my cheeks swelled with the nourishment it gave me. The best thing about it was it really did taste like a meat from home called 'grasscutter', which was a type of rodent or as we called it bush meat.

Martha just laughed and told me I should take my time and I should take this moment to rest.

As I ate the meat I started to feel at ease and I decided to try and talk to Martha and so I asked her.

"What meat is this Martha, is it grasscutter?" I asked after swallowing a really dry piece forcing me to take more water.

Martha smiled and told me she had heard about the grasscutter and this meat was a similar thing called an agouti which was found on this land where we were.

She then told me to take a mango from the bowl in the middle of the table and said the yellow ones were ripe and really sweet. So after I ate the meat I took the mango and once I removed some of the skin I bit into it and the juice ran down my throat, inside and outside of my mouth, and Martha laughed at me again. I ate the succulent fruit and sucked the seed until it was almost dry and it was surely the taste of nectar. I grabbed another one to take with me but Martha told me they will still be there for later and I smiled and returned it to the wooden bowl.

Martha spoke about the stories she heard from her mother that were passed down from her ancestors about the foods of Africa.

She had cooked the agouti just for me as she knew my taste would find the meat succulent and she had guessed I would enjoy the burnt piece.

Martha then sat down with me and she took my hand and wiped it with a wet cloth, then she informed me I could continue to eat my food with my hands however the master would eat his food with a knife and a fork. I would learn to place them on the table for him and as she told me this she smiled at me. She then told me I would be taught what to do and everything would be fine now. I felt she was telling me the truth. I sensed a trust in a complete stranger for the first time since I left my home.

I felt her squeeze my hand before she started to talk to me about her grandmother who was part of a tribe called Igbo.

Martha told me I was on a plantation where they grew sugar and the owner was Master Adams. She then took a jar from a shelf and removed the cover. She picked up a small wooden paddle and dipped it into the jar.

She handed me the paddle and told me to taste it. I was a little bit nervous but I then thought how she had cared for me so my trust for her was not questioned. I took the wooden paddle to my tongue and I tasted it. I was the sweetest and sticky flavour and I had to smack my lips a few times as Martha informed me this was molasses. She added this was what the plantation produced.

She explained the workers were slaves from the same place as I was but they were third and fourth generation, and they went every day to work the fields. She told me she was the plantation workers root doctor and midwife for the slaves as she called them. She also told me some of the older workers spoke a different language which she called "Spanish" as the place where we were was taken over by the British only a few years previously. It was previously ruled by a country called Spain.

Martha informed me that if workers became ill she would care for them and try to get them back into the field as quickly as she could. She used traditional remedies and potions which were passed down to her by her mother, who had them passed to her by her mother. She added that these remedies were given by word of mouth and this was the only way they knew as she could not read or write. This was unlike the white healers who always wrote them down for reference. Martha said that the black folk always passed down their knowledge and she added that she knew how to read some words but only a few. I thought to myself about what Martha told me and wanted to say to her I could understand the words written but I thought better of it and I kept this to myself.

Martha said she took her orders and responsibility from the plantation mistress to determine if a slave's illness was genuine or not. This woman was the wife of Master Adams.

Martha then pointed at the bottles and pots and told me she made several remedies in preparation for some sicknesses but mostly she made them as and when they were needed for the slave workers. I then thought in my head at what Cudjoe had told me about people not being slaves but captives but I did not have the strength to make the point to Martha.

Martha continued to explain I was sent to her was so she could heal me.

I thanked Martha and I started to ease my worry. She continued to talk to me about her life on the plantation. I finished my food and then she made me a hot tea made from the leaves of the lime tree. As I drank I heard a call from a yard fowl and it reminded me of home.

After this Martha spoke to me about Master Adams and she told me he was a good and fair man but if I was to ever cross him I would pay a heavy price.

I took these words into my head but for now I was just relaxing and listening to Martha.

It was a long time since anybody had sat and talked to me in this way and I enjoyed listening to her speak and the twang of her accent.

I asked Martha where I was and she told me I was an Island named by the Arawak people and in their language it was called “Lere”, which meant the land of the humming bird.

She then told me a man called Columbus renamed it to the land it was known now and this was "La Ysla de la Trinidad" and this in the language of the Spanish meant The Island of the Trinity.

So I was in this land of Trinity which I remember Kesiwaa telling me according to the obroni preachers was the unity of the Father, the Son, and the Holy Spirit. I thought to myself and realised this was my destiny to be in this place and my worries started to be less concerning. Martha added that the land I was in was a part of a group of island known as the Caribbean. All of my stress was behind me now and my time now was to rest.

I asked Martha about the work in the field and she told me I did not have to worry about it as I was going to work as a house girl in Master Adams home.

I enquired if this was easy work and she advised me it would be as easy as I made it. Martha told me the master's house was big with lots of rooms and I was only to go into the ones where I was allowed and no other. She added if I went into a wrong room then he would

"Cut yo raas wid 'im caryne."

I did not really understand what this was but it sounded bad. I asked if the man called William worked in the field and Martha informed me he was a blacksmith which meant he would shoe the horses and keep the plantation maintained. He had skills worthy and valuable and this made him important to Master Adams.

My arm then became uncomfortable and I tried again to remove the cloth around it. Martha told me I had to leave it and she would take a look later and treat it. Treat what, I thought, I could not remember hurting my arm, but I guess I must have.

After my long talk with Martha I asked to get some air and she told me we could go and sit outside but to stay in shade. We stepped out in the yard area and I tried to locate where I was from my memory of when I came onto this plantation. I looked ahead and I saw a yard in front of me and there was a wooden bench with a wooden structure in front of it with holes in it.

Next to this were a couple of tree logs laid on the ground with a hole made in the soil between them. There was a water trough near to a building and there were various items hanging on the wall from pegs. There was one metal stick and it appeared to have some letters on the end which looked like an "A" and an "H" which was very strange I thought.

Next to this there looked like there had been a fire and the area had some burnt wood and ashes which was next to a metal box.

I looked to my right and I saw the fence I remembered walking before yet this time I was on the other side. I looked back at the bench and I remembered a bibini man was sitting on the seat earlier.

I asked Martha about this man and she dropped her head and then went back inside. I did not want to press her again and so I sat on the door step and breathed the fresh air into my nose and closed my eyes.

I felt safe and right now I thought if luck had touched my life then it had just kissed my heart. After all I was not hungry anymore and my body felt cleansed. I just enjoyed the lifting of the worry from my shoulders and I just watched the day go by.

During this day I tried to notice many things of my new world but my concentration took away a lot of my ability to remember.

As the day just slipped away the sun started to lower in the sky I returned to Martha's home when a voice shouted from outside. The voice called for her.

"Good night Miss Marta",

The voice I heard delivering the greeting was a man's deep tone and had the same accent as Martha.

I looked behind me and saw Martha open the door. She invited a bibini man who had crossed the yard in and he spoke something to her.

Martha walked over to where the jars were on the side of the room and she took out some leaves and gave them to the man.

"Put this in hot water Abel and tell your wife to drink it when it has cooled down."

Martha instructed the man with some authority in her tone.

"Yes Miss Martha Iza does dat."

The man replied then turned and left.

I asked Martha who the man was and she told me he was a field worker called Abel Bowleg and he needed some herbs for a tea as his wife had a fever. She added he was born with a deformed right leg which left him walking with a broad gait like he was riding a horse and this made him ridiculed by the others. Martha tried to teach him to close his legs when he walked but Abel always just passed it off with a sigh of and a look of anger.

It became apparent that Martha really did look after these workers so I was surely in good hands now. Although I did nothing, I enjoyed my day which was spent just looking at the yard and thinking about my nightmare I had endured and it was now over. I thought about my new future and what to expect. Whatever it was I had to start my life all over again. This time I had skills nobody knew about taught to me by Kesiwaa.

After a long and informative but uneventful and relaxing day I saw the moon appear in the sky. I tried to remember the last time I had seen it and I thought of the night where my life changed after I ran away from Nana Apane.

Martha wished me a good night and then she told me I would be woken in the morning by the noise of a conch shell. She told me when this is blown I would need to be ready and standing for the morning inspection. This is where everybody needs to be before they are ready to start work for the day. She added although I was not going to be ready to work yet, it would still be expected of me to get used to this morning call and what to do.

Martha added when the horn is blown for the second time I had to be stood in the line and if I was not there then Master Adams would,

"Bust down de door and drag you out."

This again was not yet for my concern, whilst I was with Martha, she would make sure I was there in the line anyway.

So there it was my first day without any pain or hunger and this was a day without seeing people crying, dying and suffering around me.

Well I was in Trinity after all and so I guessed I was safe from any harm.

I took one last look at the stars in the sky and I looked for the brightest one. I gave my eyes the time needed to see the one that glistened with a magical sparkle then I sent my love and thoughts to Fiifi. I then closed my eyes as I caught the ones he must have sent to me.

The day had gone and I made my way to the room where I saw the first morning in this land of Trinity. I could not believe how quiet it was. This was peace, and there was silence. I thought about my silent drum and it was stored inside of my head and it was not needed. Tonight I was going to enjoy my rest and I lay down my head with no concerns. I started to drift away I thought of my Fiifi and where he was. Is he sleeping in the same way as me, I said to myself? I let my body drift away and I had my first undisturbed rest since I could remember.

CHAPTER 14: Punishment

I was woken by a loud noise which stole me away from a comfortable night's sleep that had caressed my thoughts and kept me dormant without interruption. It was a horn blowing which encouraged a yard fowl to join with its own cry.

This noise was annoying and after a big yawn I heard Martha shouting at me.

"Esi, Esi, get yourself from your rest!"

Martha knocked my door and I called her in. She told me to put on the dress she had left for me quickly and go out to the yard with her. As I pulled a garment over my head I then slipped my arms into the sleeves and the cloth around my upper left arm fell off and I saw a crusted wound was hidden underneath on my skin. I touched it with my other hand and it hurt so I left it alone. Martha shouted at me to hurry so I quickly continued with pulling down the lower part of my dress to cover my legs. After I did this I followed Martha through the front door and out into the open area where I had walked the previous day.

I saw a number of bibini gathering in an area in the middle of the surrounding buildings. Most of them came from the two rows of buildings lined up facing each other.

Martha told me to stand next to her and I saw many people all lined up. I saw maybe eighty to ninety men and some women workers.

We all stood under the hot early sun and I kept my back straight and upright. After a short while I saw Master Adams as he approached us and he walked up the slight hill and when he arrived he was accompanied by William and the master's hound which immediately fouled on the ground in front of us. At this time I thought to myself, what a pleasant morning greeting to you too.

The horn blower was standing in the front of the line and Master

Adams gave him a nod with a touch of his hat. The horn blower sounded the conch shell a second time which was to announce everybody was standing correct and in line. Master Adams then spoke.

He announced to the workers his morning pleasantry first then he continued by telling them he was pleased with the recent sugar canes harvest and he was happy to know nobody was claiming to be sick.

Master Adams voice had quite a jolly tone and I was warming to his voice and then suddenly there was a disturbance behind me.

I could not turn my head to see and I looked straight ahead as ordered but it was Abel who was late. Master Adams shouted his name and shook his head as Abel ran to join the line whilst still putting on his boots.

I saw a fury in Master Adams face and he asked Abel why he was arriving at his own leisure. Abel replied by saying his wife was sick and so he had to feed his young child. I knew this to be true as I had seen Abel collect the leaves for the medication the night before and so I thought this was all correct, how wrong I was.

Master Adams had venom on his tongue and he ordered Abel to call his wife Violet from the house which he did and when she arrived she looked terrible, she was with a fever and she was shivering. Master Adams voice had a temper of fury as he shouted his order to William. This caused Master Adams to disturb his hound "Blackie" who had been lying on the dusty ground who howled and got excited. Blackie jumped in the air and wagged his tail. He snapped his jaw then walked away with his tongue hanging from his mouth and panting heavily.

We watched as the master ordered William to escort Abel to the side of the building where I had slept and he took him to the bench the man was sitting on the day before. He told Violet to join them.

William turned the bench around so when Abel sat down his back would face the sun as it was rising in the sky. William then took Abel's feet and laid them over the wooden foot rest in front and then he snapped another wooded piece over the top which trapped Abel's feet. A voice murmured from further down the line "Abel's been put in the foot stocks, Lord have mercy."

Master Adams then spoke quite loudly so that everyone could hear what he was saying and he ordered William to fetch a jar of molasses and a face mask. As William went to collect the items, the master turned to Violet and spoke to her. He told Violet she should not forget how to do a simple task as feeding another person especially her child.

He then told Violet her husband was late getting out of his bed because he was lazy and he was lying on his back when he should be up, which he added was not acceptable.

The master then said not even his hound was so lazy to lay on his back for too long because if he did it would eventually be lying in its own mess.

I was beginning by now to think something was not good which was compounded as Master Adams voice changed its tone.

It was now no more a shout of anger but one quiet and thoughtful as he delivered his malice.

William returned with the things he was ordered to bring held the molasses and face mask in front of him.

Master Adams then told Violet if she had forgotten how to feed her child then he would teach her how to remember what to do.

The master then took the jar of molasses from William and he gave it to Violet. This looked like a kind gesture as Master Adams would allow Violet to do the punishment which surely could not be right.

Master Adams then ordered Violet to pick up the fresh piece of foul sitting on the ground nearby which was left by the masters hound Blackie just in front of us.

Now it was here I thought the sweetness of the molasses was too strong for anybody's mouth to endure. Violet then picked up

Blackie's foul and the smell sent a rancid sour drift to our noses which made me gag.

When she disturbed it from the ground it was fresh from Blackie's body and it still steamed from the heat of the ground. You can imagine what we thought as we stood under the hot sun waiting to start our work for the day as this was taking too long.

We just wanted to get the day started and ended so we could be home to our relaxation.

Violet stood with one hand holding the hounds foul and the other hand was holding a jar of molasses and she swayed under the heat. What happened then made my throat swell and my stomach twist in knots. The master ordered Violet to walk with him to where Abel was sitting and as she did this William accompanied them.

We could all see Abel sitting in the heat and he was already restless and he was shuffling his bottom on the seat now heated from the hot sun.

It was here that I saw the most disgusting thing I could imagine as Master Adams ordered Violet to feed the hounds foul into Abel's mouth which would help her remember how to feed someone. As I heard this I closed my eyes and I shook my head in dismay.

Violets face winced first and then she trembled as she opened Abel's jaw and placed the hounds foul into his mouth. The master then told Violet to take the face mask from William and to place it over Abel's head which she did until it covered his mouth, but let his nose still breathe. Violet was then asked to tighten the face mask under his chin.

Master Adams told William to take off Abel's shirt which he ripped from his body to expose his bare dark skin.

Violet was then ordered to smear the molasses over Abel's back and he told her to spread it evenly. Master Adams then told Abel he was lazy and the molasses would ensure he would not lie down for too long on his back again.

I heard Abel gagging and I saw he was vomiting. His mouth dripped rapidly and it ran from under the mask down his neck and onto his bare chest. With the sun getting hotter giving a sweltering heat to the ground the molasses not only attracted the flies and other biting insects.

I thought then of what my mother had told me when she said,

"Onyankopon aniwa hu asumasem biara,"

"God's eyes see all things."

I remember these past words and advice I was taught and these made me think more profoundly as though they were words to help me during this new life.

Master Adams returned to the workers who were lined up and told them laziness would not be tolerated. He then told them to get to the field and work hard as any man caught being lazy would join Abel in this chair of discomfort.

The workers left for the field and Martha and I went back to our building. My eyes looked at Abel as he chocked, coughed and cried with the sick torture he had been given.

I looked at Martha with a stare of concern and I wanted to ask her to help but before any words came from my mouth she just shook her head and as we entered the building she went straight for her jars of leaves and roots.

I was so disturbed by what I observed I had to say something and I asked Martha if there was anything she could do for Abel. She told me she would prepare something for him after his trauma. Martha put some ingredients into a stone bowl and pounded and crushed the contents. Once she had done this Martha covered the paste and set it to one side.

I was quite interested in what Martha was making because it was obvious she had done it before and she knew exactly what she was doing.

Martha took some water from a jug and put it in a pot, placed it over the fire and she started to heat it up. She then stopped to come over to me she took my arm and looked at the crust that had layered on it. She just mumbled to herself and walked off again.

I wanted to go and sit on the step of the door at the side of the building as I had done the day before but Martha advised me if I did I would see Abel suffering and it would be harder for him.

He would not want to be seen like he was so I stayed away and the door stayed shut. Instead I sat on the chair next to the table and talked with Martha.

I thought hard about where I was and I guessed this was not the place I expected it was and so again I had to be vigilant of my actions as Martha had warned me. I thought about Abel who was born into this culture and he knew no different way of life. He was never free like me before this time of being a captive. I knew what it was like to be my own person, and not owned like a slave.

If I were to be punished like this I do not think I could be so strong.

Time went by slowly that morning and all I heard were the moans from Abel's tortured body in the yard which sounded like the moans of the women from the big white castle where I was once held, as they slept in their squalor.

During this morning Martha picked up a wooden bucket and she walked outside the front door. I stood up and followed her as she walked towards the yard. I had to see Abel who was still on the bench and he was rocking backwards and forward. I watched as I saw Martha carrying the bucket, then she set it down next to him. I saw she had filled it with water. I looked back at Abel but he did not know I saw him. I just closed the door and asked my Onyankopon in my thoughts to aid Abel during this time.

Martha came back in, a short while later, through the front door and she was carrying a strange block in her hand. She placed this lump into another wooden bucket and when the water was boiled she poured it into this bucket as well. Martha then added more ingredients, leaves and a root and stirred it gently, then let it settle.

Abel was left to sit in his punishment for five hours until William arrived.

As the sun hit the highest part of the day I walked over to a window and I pulled back the cloth that was covering it. I saw William remove the mask from Abel's face and then he unlocked the part of the bench that trapped his feet. I then watched as the wooden foot trap was being opened and William was helping Abel to stand. He led him towards the side of the door where Martha had placed the bucket of cold water previously. I stepped out to see if I could help but William told me to stay inside.

William put Abel's head into the cool bucket of water and Abel vomited violently. Abel spat constantly so hard that each time he did he gagged and strained with his retching. Abel coughed violently and he kept gagging and coughing for so long he struggled to breathe and he was gasping for air. He was spitting and clearing his throat so hard that after a while the muck seemed to have cleared but then I saw he was dripping blood from his mouth. He told William that he had bitten into his tongue so many times to try to squeeze out the filth in his mouth and it was now numb.

William then assisted Abel inside and sat him on one of the beds next to the wall. Martha brought over the mixture she had made earlier and folded it into a mint leaf parcel and then she placed it onto Abel's tongue.

Martha told Abel not to swallow the leaf as it would release a flavour which would overpower any other taste he had and it would also release the herbs into his mouth to give him some goodness into his body. She also tied a cloth soaked in vinegar around his forehead which she said would ease the pain.

As he sat in a daze Martha quietly spoke and asked Abel to lie down on his front on the bed, he did so with the help of William. Abel's body was now trembling and he looked weak and he had beads of sweat all over him. His body shook uncontrolled and he was in a state of despair.

Martha brought the bucket with the ingredients to the bed and she dropped in it a large cloth which she soaked.

Following this she took it out and placed it over Abel's back to cover the crust of dried molasses which had set hard onto his skin and told Abel to just rest and she will watch over him for the rest of the day.

This she did and as Abel rested Martha slowly took away the molasses layer by layer and piece by piece using the cloths she kept soaking in the water she kept boiling and let cool. Slowly the black crust dissolved during the treatment which took for the rest of the day and when it was done Abel's back was blistered and bleeding. The only thing left was a clear frame of raw and bloodied sore skin. Martha kept this bathed with the dampened cloths. She then used the juice of a plant she called an "Aloe" that she mashed into a paste to cool and soothe his skin.

Abel spent a few days recovering from his ordeal and during this time I tried to talk to him but he offered very little conversation in return except to say if this was to ever happen to him again he would take his revenge. It did not surprise me after this treatment from Master Adams.

I thought about the obroni guards from the first place I was held and I now saw another horror with this one. I told myself Master Adams would not touch me and scar me as the last obroni did. He will not mark me by Onyankopon's name I told myself he will not touch my skin.

I understood Abel holding back any conversation and as I really did not know what to say to him anyway it was of no matter. What could I say to a man who had just a horrendous punishment given to him?

I did however think hard about what he had endured and the thing which puzzled me was Abel was given this sickening torture in the same yard as the building he was then treated to help him recover. After that day Abel Bowleg was always the first person to stand in line and some even called him Abel BLOWLEG as his legs ran so fast he would move like the blow of a strong wind.

I spent the next few days with Martha until I was told it was time for me to go to my new home and get ready to start my duties. I asked Martha about the mark on my arm and she told me I had been branded with the initials of Henry Adams and I looked at this and saw the letters "HA" had become visible after the crust had flaked away. Martha told me this needed to be done because I belonged to this plantation and it would tell anyone who owned me should I decide to wander away. I was now branded with the mark of as a slave. I was owned and my life did not belong to me anymore.

Only days after my vow to myself that Master Adams would not touch me it became clear he already had, he had scarred my skin.

My destiny was not Trinity but 'HA' and I now have the mark to show where I belong. I thought about this and knew it was probably something Nana Apane would probably have done if he thought about it.

I was here to do a job and so I decided I may as well get on with it. In an odd way I was now looking forward to what I was bought at the market to do and I was ready to begin with my contribution. I was now part of the HA plantation and my new tribal marks were there to make sure I stayed.

CHAPTER 15: Plantation

Martha woke me up and I dressed then I followed her outside. We hurried as the conch sounded to join the line for inspection. I stood tall and straight. I remember thinking I had to keep my chin up and my tummy in just as Kesiwaa had taught me. The conch shell had blown its sound and all were there, still and quiet and I thought how, in my home we did not make plans at the same part of the day, but here it was each day the same thing with the same start. The day always began with the sound of the conch and after that everything went by the same process during the same time of the day until the sun went down.

Master Adams arrived to the morning line up with William and Blackie to deliver his message to the workers and once they had been spoken to they went to the field. I looked at Blackie who was always yapping at Master Adams feet and my eyes followed him where ever he went. I was still afraid of these hounds and I started to shake as I vividly remembered the bibini man who was savaged by the eager jaws of a similar kind of beast.

I was left standing with Martha who kept me calm but who then told me to keep myself well and she hoped she would not see too much more of me. This was a kind way of saying she did not want to see me get punished or treated for any sickness. I was only with Martha for seven days but I got to understand her.

I figured she was only there to treat people and not make friends. Saying that I knew she really cared for the workers and me. I saw that on my first day but she kept this stern image to everyone on the outside. She did not like any talk of emotion and she seemed very cold hearted but I knew she cared for her people. She had a big akuma (heart) but she had a job to do and she needed to stay unconnected which made her the way she was. When she treated Abel she made him very welcome and comfortable but it was just her position as root doctor on the plantation, to get the workers back in the field.

Martha was asked by Master Adams to return to her home and I saw her walk back to the building I had stayed in. Master Adams spoke then to William who told me to follow him. Master Adams returned to his big white house and I joined William.

We walked to the wooden building I first went to when I arrived where I had passed out.

I followed William through the front door into this building and there was the main room and a corridor in the centre leading further along the home. This building was larger than the huts the workers lived in.

This was where I was greeted by a bibini lady and William introduced me. Her name was Hannah De Leon and she gave me a warm smile and invited me to the house. Hannah seemed to be delighted to see me and I felt welcome. William then told me this was my new home and I was to go and settle in my room and that he would come to collect me later, then he left.

Hannah took me along the corridor and we went to the far end and to a door on the right. I opened to enter and I saw just a bed and a table then she showed me this was where I would be living and I felt I had come to settle in one place at last. Hannah added she needed to bring something for me and I was to wait for her.

She took only a short while before returning with some clothes for me. These were clean and I thought they were quite fancy. There was a light blue skirt and a thing Hannah called an apron and a white blouse.

Hannah told me to wear these clothes as I was going to Master Adams house later in the day and she told me I would be there to help look after his home and keep it clean and tidy. There were many new things I had to remember. Hannah told me I would need to tie a cloth around my head and she showed me how it was done. She told me that Mrs Adams did not like to see the short hair that us Negros had so it had to be covered.

She also told me a little bit about herself. She was once married to a man called Fernando De Leon and he was a worker in the field but he had passed on recently and this was the reason I was chosen to live with her. She added there would be a hot meal waiting for me when I returned later in the evening.

I followed Hannah back into the main area where I had arrived and she sat me down in front of her on the floor and she sat behind me. She told me that she was going to braid my hair.

I looked around to observe the style of African things I recognised. There were some wooden bowls on a table that had a marking around the side I had not seen before and they were disguised as patterns but I knew they had an African carving style.

There were some children's grass straw dolls against a wall and they were laid in their little made beds. I asked Hannah about these items and she told me they belonged to her children. Two girls she named as Abigail and Beatrice. She added that the girls had been sent to another home in a building further along the line of houses and the reason they were not with her was because Hannah had to dress me correctly and make me presentable for Master Adams.

It was then I thought of my sister Kakraba from seeing the straw dolls and I remember thinking of being children and I had the well of tears appear in my eyes. This reminded me I had not seen any children for a very long time and I then reminded myself about my own age. I was not too old either. I thought about my birthday which I did not even know myself.

These children of Hannah and Fernando were also born as captives or as I now realised were not quite as Cudjoe had told me, they were born as slaves and this was different.

I asked how old these children were and Hannah told me they were six and four years old.

Hannah continued to talk about the children and the more she did this the more I thought about my sister and I listened until I started to hear my drum. My eyelids lowered and then the thumping sound entered my head.

As she talked to me she braided my short hair and she pulled it really tight so much it made my eyes draw water. She used a hot comb she heated on the fire which added to the sting as she groomed me. I sat in my peaceful state until her words slowly faded behind my silent drum.

Bam bam bam bam, bam bam bam bam, du du du du bambam bam bam bam, du du du.

I was in my sanctuary until one sharp sting of the hot comb scorched my scalp like a hot coal had jumped from a fire and my eyes opened quickly.

Hannah was still talking to me and she had changed her subject as now as she told me about the rules of the plantation. Her words informed me about the strict behaviour expected of me. My ears heard her advice when she informed me that if anyone stepped out of line then they would be punished as I saw with Abel Bowleg.

She told me nobody was exempt from punishment and even women carrying a child which I found hard to imagine. This made me immediately place my hand over my belly and I felt how swollen it was.

Hannah informed me that if Master Adams wanted to give your skin to his cat claws he would. If this happened you were whipped over your back with a flail which had a tail of small shells at the end. I wondered how those who were due to be mothers could be not exempt from such barbaric behaviour. Hannah continued with braiding my hair and she made several tugs in all sorts of direction before she wrapped the cloth around my head and tied it over my forehead so it covered my ears.

Hannah told me she was caught rain water at the side of their home in a large barrel. This was the only water they had to use. She told me whenever it rained I must catch as much water in as many pots as possible and that the pots were kept in a corner of the main room.

She told me I needed to wash myself every morning and every night because if my skin became sour then the master would beat me, however I had to be careful how much water I used as it was needed for cooking as well. She added that at the rear of our home was a partitioned area behind a screen which was for our bathing.

I stood up and I was now ready for my first day of work for Master Adams my new obroni Nana.

Hannah spoke with direct instruction as she explained my day ahead.

I was advised not to not ask too many questions as people did not like anyone who likes to do too much "Maco'ing." She explained this was when somebody is too nosey and goes around getting into other people's business which makes them very angry. She added I should also not do too much "Eyeballing" which was somebody who watches someone all of the time as this makes them feel uneasy. I acknowledged what she told me and so I knew I had to be careful and obey these unwritten rules. She concluded that of all people I should not maco or eyeball Martha as she becomes very uneasy. This did not surprise me as Martha had a secretive side about her which added to her mystery.

Hannah told me many other things relating to the plantation. She inforemed me that they harvested sugar which was taken by the workers from the field. It was then crushed by the large windmill where I saw the conical shaped building with the rotating sails when I first arrived.

Hannah than admitted to me that she thought at first I was to be a part of the collection of field workers until she heard I was going to work in the home of Master Adams which she found to be strange. As a new arrival this was odd. Hannah looked at me and she told me my face was pretty and this was probably the reason I was chosen.

I questioned why this was so and Hannah responded that Master Adams liked a dark face and if he saw one so beautiful he would make sure it greeted him in the morning. Master Adams liked the African influence in his plantation and he wanted to visit our soil one day and so he tried to learn about our culture.

She then told me about Miss Sylvester who was Master Adams main house maid and she lived at the tiny wooden house at the far side of the yard.

This made me ask further questions of my duties on this trinity land that was now my home. I asked Hannah if Master Adams had any concern with her family having these African carvings. She told me they were made by some of the workers in their spare time as they tried to hold on to their crafts of tradition.

I tried to learn more from Hannah as I prepared for my first day. One thing that puzzled me was why those bibini who were dark in skin were treated with less respect than those of lighter colour. I did not understand this at first but it made sense as these were people who had been born with a mixed heritage had obroni blood.

I remember I was once told anyone from my home who was mixed in skin colour and was taken into this captivity in the white castle was taken back to our home land to serve the obroni in a place that would accommodate mulattos. There was a building not far from the white castle in my home land for these people. I tried to ask Hannah more about this but she did not really answer me. She was light in colour so maybe she chose to remain quiet. She looked like she was a mixture of black and white as well, like a mulatto.

Hannah appeared to be uncomfortable with this and she changed the subject and spoke about her husband Fernando and she told me he was darker than me and to her he was more important than anyone with light skin, which just contradicted what she had told me as it went against what was generally thought. I took this information into my head and wondered if I would need to know what this meant and why she told me.

She spoke about something quite interesting when she told me to never take anything not belonging to me. I knew this was a common rule but she fortified this by advising me firstly Master Adams does not tolerate it and then some of the workers have their own way of dealing with people who steal things.

I remained silent as lastly Hannah advised me about a thing called "Obeah" which was a form of magic. She warned me about a "Jumbie" which was an evil or lost spirit. I took note in my head and kept my mouth shut as I had heard of this from my own people.

Hannah told me to stand up as my hair was done and I heard the voice of William calling from outside in the yard. I was now ready for my first day and I walked towards the door and I took a deep breath and closed my eyes. I was very scared now and I tried to imagine what was to be my future ahead.

There was a knock at the door and as it was opened by Hannah I saw William standing outside and he was asking for me.

William spoke to Hannah and he told her Mr Adams requested for me to meet with him in front of his house. I left with William and I took my pride with me. I walked tall with every step just as Kesiwaa had taught me.

As we followed William to the house of Master Adams he did not speak to me which made me more nervous. I walked through the section of trees and then I saw the house of the master and my fingers tightened and closed to a fist as I was feeling nervous at this reception. William walked in front of me purposely and we arrived at the home of Master Adams in a time which escaped me as I was thinking about what Hannah had told me.

We arrived at the huge white house and my thoughts again returned of my prison at Elmina.

I stood outside in the yard waiting until Master Adams appeared in front of me with an obroni lady and his hound Blackie was snapping and barking at his feet. I started to get nervous again about the hound and started to think about the punishment of Abel. I watched again and Blackie decided to yap wildly as I looked at him in his face, then he stopped and lay down with his tongue out. Another friendly gesture from this hound I thought.

Master Adams approached me and greeted me with a smile and he introduced me to his wife Margaret.

She was a pretty lady and she wore a dress of a light sandy colour and lace. She wore her dark but greying hair pulled away from her face and her eyes were dark to match.

It was here Mr Adams told me my African name would no longer be used as he would now call me Elizabeth and I would take the last name of Adams.

So this was the day I became Elizabeth Adams. I had a new name but did this mean I was reborn? I remembered what Kesiwaa had told me about my name and how important it was to me and so I kept this in my heart. I would never forget my real name as I am Esi Takyiwaa Kwaku.

CHAPTER 16: Workers

I started my first day and I was introduced to Miss Sylvester. She was a stout light skinned woman. She only spoke the obroni language, and had the same accent as Master Adams, William and everyone else on this land, which I now knew to be in the Caribbean.

When she first saw me she looked at me with eyes of temper and this stare showed them open and big then she squinted to almost close them. She had a face peppered with dark marks but I later knew these to be 'freckles.' In fact I was a little bit envious as I at first wished I had them over my face as well.

Miss Sylvester stood in the doorway of the house with her legs astride and her hands on her waist. She looked like she wanted to start trouble with me before I even started my first day and I began to shake with nerves. I clenched my fists to a ball. She was neatly dressed with a white apron and her head was covered in a matching cloth. She had on a light blue dress which had a broad skirt. She was almost looking like a queen because she looked quite fancy and stood tall with her head high.

Miss Sylvester then invited me into the house with a hand gesture and I followed without hesitation. I noticed the master's hound Blackie watched me as it lay down in a low wooden box to the side of the door and as I stepped through it, he snarled and gave a growl at me.

I was given my instructions of my first job which was to tidy the house with her. She invited me to follow her to Master Adams bedroom to straighten the bed sheets and prepare the clothes for washing. We needed to go to the upper part of the house which meant climbing the stairs and as Miss Sylvester stepped on the first stair it creaked and I looked at her big fat bottom wiggle and wobble in front of me. She blew a few gasps of breath as we ascended to a floor above.

When we reached near to the top Miss Sylvester suddenly stopped and I walked right into her. She turned to face me and she looked at me with those dark eyes and told me to slow down. I was trembling now but I stood tall and looked right back at her. She was breathing quite heavily as the climbing of the stairs had taken her strength away.

I thought I was in big trouble as she took a pause before she spoke to me and she took her sleeves and rolled them up to her elbows.

Miss Sylvester informed me about some of the rules in the house. She warned me about whenever I go to a door I must always knock upon it even if I knew Master Adams and his wife were not in the house. She added if I ever walked into a room without tapping I would be treading a dangerous path. She then told me if anything is stolen from Master Adams, then, unless the item was recovered everyone on the plantation will be held responsible. This could be anything from longer days in the fields for the workers, to folk taken to sit down on the wooden structure just as Abel did until the item was found.

She added that if I ever raise my voice or answer back to Master Adams and his family then a whipping was the usual action taken. She told me it did not matter to Master Adams who it was and who's back felt the lash, just as long as it ripped the skin and embedded the message of discipline.

With this Miss Sylvester said we should start with a room she pointed to which was the first one along the upstairs hallway.

Miss Sylvester pointed to a table outside a door and she told me every morning Master Adams required his tea to be placed on it. She then told me the used teacups will be left on a table just inside the bedroom door ready for collection.

She added that this would be my duty to attend to and I would also be responsible for the bedrooms of Master Adams and any guests, as climbing the stairs was becoming difficult for her and the rooms needed a younger pair of hands to attend them. She would then take care of the rooms at the lower section of the house, the preparation of the meals and the garden outside, where the vegetables grew.

Miss Sylvester remembered she had forgotten to bring a brush to sweep the floor. She told me to get started with collecting the bed sheets and she would only be a few minutes before she returned. She did not explain where to find these bed sheets so I thought I had to find them for myself. Miss Sylvester turned and descended the stairs.

I was nervous as I thought Miss Sylvester had deliberately left me alone to observe me and I did not know where to look for the clean laundry. I knew then that I would have to make my search look like I was trying my best.

I walked up to the door she had pointed out to me and knocked on it, as I was told to. I then opened it and put my head around the door and inside I saw how beautiful it looked. There was a big bed in the middle and it had drapes just like the devil obroni had at the white castle at Elmina. I decided to go into this room and I looked around at the pretty cloths draped over the windows. Next to the bed were a table with some clear drinking vessels on it and a clear glass jug with a handle, which contained some water.

Beside this was a fancy vase with some colourful yellow flowers standing in it. I walked over to smell them and I felt someone was following me. I turned to see no one yet I thought somebody was watching me.

I looked to see a lovely table and I saw things I did not recognise. I picked up a handle and felt the bristles stuck to it. I pulled out the stool from under the table and sat down and saw my reflection in the glass in front of me. I saw myself looking right back and although I had seen my face in the water of a river I saw myself now clearer than I ever did before. I stared deep into my own eyes and spoke to myself about being me.

I asked myself who I was and where I was and why I was here.

Esi Takyiwaa Kwaku was the girl who left my land and now she had gone and I was starting a new life and with it was a new goal. Sadly my Fiifi was gone too and I had to let him go. I knew I would always love my ƆdƆ but I had to accept my situation to survive. Fiifi would want me to keep going and never give up and so I had to accept my new home and new people around me. This was not easy to do but I had to at least try.

My reflection gave me a new start as Elizabeth Adams. I looked again and saw the pretty dress I was wearing and I smiled to see my teeth. I wanted to sit there all day but I had now seen myself and I had to accept this and learn the rules and obey them so I put down the bristly thing and stood up and pushed the stool back under the table. As I was going to turn around I saw the reflection of my belly in the glass and it was starting to show a definite bulge. I rubbed my hand over the top of it and I tried to pull it in but when I relaxed it showed a round shape swelling out.

I looked away from the glass to take my thoughts from what I had seen and saw the room had another door, maybe to another room. I walked over and knocked on it then I opened it and I saw loads of pretty dresses. This was where Mrs Adams hung her clothes.

Here I saw the finest of fabrics and I thought how pretty Mrs Adams' dresses were. They were different to anything I had seen before and they got me excited. I wanted to wear them. I just wanted to try them on right there but I knew this would not be a good idea and knew this was silly but I remember giggling to myself. I looked again at these dresses and I tried to imagine being dressed up like a fine and dandy obroni. Well what girl would not feel the same when put in this position? I thought about what Hannah told me about 'maco'ing' but I did not think this would be the same so I dismissed it and I carried on.

I wanted to look at them closer but I needed to make sure that Miss Sylvester was not around so I went back and I listened at the door to hear if she was outside. I heard her singing and she sounded like she was down the stairs and so I went back to the wardrobe and separated the dresses on their rail. I decided to take a closer look. I pulled out each one and I felt the delicate cloth and fine lace around the collar.

After filtering through a few garments I saw one I liked which had a pretty colour of yellow just like the flowers in the vase and I wanted to see it closer. I tried to pull it out to look at it. It would not come. I tugged again. It was stuck and it was not moving like the other dresses. I gave it one harder pull and it released but it was caught on the back wooden panel and I heard the noise of something falling from behind the dress.

I saw a piece of wood had fallen down and I quickly tried to put it back. As I did this a noticed there was a shelf behind where the wooden panel was and I took a closer look. When I saw what was there I could not believe it. I pushed the dresses further apart and the light from the window shone onto a glass jar. I could see something inside and so I took a closer look and saw that it held coins of different sizes and colours. I thought this was strange place to keep the jar but then I remembered how Kesiwaa had hidden her valuable gold.

I felt my akuma start to speed up beating in my chest. I picked up the wooden panel and wedged it back into place and then I pulled the dresses back to a neat row together. I closed the door to the wardrobe then ran to the door and left the room.

My brow was beaded with sweat as I felt that I had discovered a secret that I shouldn't have. I thought at the time that I had seen something I should not and I thought if anybody saw me then I would be in trouble of the highest as these coins were stored clandestinely so they must be valuable.

I stood with my back against the door and took a deep breath. As I did this I closed my eyes to take in what I had just seen. I heard footsteps walking in the corridor towards the bedroom and so I busied myself around the bed. Miss Sylvester entered the room and her face was frosty. Her eyes squinted again as she looked at me intensely. I held my stare with an innocent face then Miss Sylvester just looked away.

She was carrying the brush she had been to collect and she also had bed sheets and together we made up the bed. My thoughts were of the coins in the jar and this interfered with my concentration. Miss Sylvester asked me to fold some corners of the bedding and I did as I was asked although my mind was elsewhere.

After we did this we picked out the obroni clothes we were to wash and made our way down to the kitchen. Soon it was time to prepare the lunch for Master and Mrs Adams.

When I followed Miss Sylvester around the house I could not stop thinking about the coins I had seen and I had to focus and take them away from my thoughts. I eventually calmed down and was able to give her my full attention with my duties.

I stood next to a water pipe in the kitchen and I cut the ground provisions which I now know were called carrots. I peeled potatoes and then I collected the water required to cook the food.

This day was not so difficult and I think I was worried for no reason. Miss Sylvester actually laughed with me when I spoke so guessed she was warming to me. I had a day where for once I felt I was coping with this routine. I was aware of the brutality but I knew this life could be made easier by simply following Miss Sylvester's lead.

After this day I returned to my new wooden home and ate a hot meal Hannah had made and it gave me the energy to enjoy the conversation with my new family. I had to think about my own situation now. I was brought back to thinking of Fiifi and I hoped he was also getting on with never giving up. Yes I loved him dearly and I always would but I had to keep his love in my akuma and never let it go. I had to survive without him but I would never forget my Fiifi Mensah.

This evening I walked out side of my home to see the day come to a close as the sun was just setting. There was a group gathered together sitting down and they were talking. I stood still and I felt tense as I did not know anyone and I felt nervous.

Just as I was about to turn and go back into my new home a voice shouted and a man jumped up from the group and he walked over to me. He smiled and introduced himself as Augustus George He was a little bit younger than me. He invited me to join him and the others and his greeting made me feel at ease and so I walked with him and I sat down on a stool. I asked him if they had gathered together for a discussion and he told me they were 'Limin.' I asked him what 'Limin' was and he informed me it was to sit together and chat or just be around friends.

The group were mostly men with a couple of young girls and they were talking and laughing.

These people were some of the workers from the field who harvested the sugar on this plantation and they were telling some of their stories.

I heard them talking but I did not have any idea what they were saying as they were speaking with a twang and they spoke too fast. These people all seemed to be very happy as they made their jokes and I tried to understand what they found funny. One boy came and sat next to me and he told me his name was Edward Garcia.

He seemed to be friendly and when he spoke he told me the workers were laughing about a field hand called Jack. He added that Jack was in the field in the afternoon and he was being attacked by a flying insect and it would not leave him alone. As the flying insect settled on the back of his neck it stung him and it made Jack fly into raging temper.

He told me that Jack then shouted "This is the work of obeah from Martha."

Edward then told me that Martha once caught him taking some water from her container one evening and the very next day his throat remained dry the whole time he was in the field. He kept drinking but he was parched in minutes. Edward claimed he knew Martha had a dark side but she never admitted it to anyone. I did not know what to think as I thought Martha was on the plantation to heal and cure people.

I looked over at Martha's home and in the dusky evening light I saw her placing some laundry onto a drying rope. She had been busy washing a lot of cloths and sheets and her basket was laden.

I told Edward to not speak of Martha that way as she became uneasy if people talked about her. I spoke of the 'maco'ing' and 'eyeballing' that I had heard about and I told him she would probably know he was talking about her. Edward told me did not really care what she thought. I looked back at Martha and she was not there, and neither was the laundry! I looked back at Edward and again at Martha and she was clearly not there. I was puzzled but I did not think too much about it.

Edward continued his story and spoke about what had happened. He told me the other workers told Jack to calm down but he went crazy and ran around like a chicken with its head cut off. He was flapping his arms and screaming. Edward started to laugh at his own words and I found myself laughing along as well. This encouraged the others to increase their roar of Jacks terrible moment.

Edward then added to this by saying this was just the start of the fun as Jack brushed off one insect then another one attacked him until it took it's sharp barbed tale and stung him on his hand.

He told me Jack waved his fist around as if he was fighting somebody with a sword. He was lashing his hand around and he was bobbing his head around just like a man who was fighting with his sharp weapon of pointed metal.

Edward informed me about the obroni who used to govern this land were from a place called Spain and they used these swords to fight with their enemies and they fought against the new governors of this land the English. The place where I arrived was in fact called "Port of Spain" and this was the main landing area for the ships bringing the captives like me.

One voice was from a man who was called Leopold Gonzales who shouted at this moment to say Jack was a Spaniard.

"Jack Spaniard "he hollered.

Just as the mocking of their friend reached it heights a door opened on the opposite side of the yard. A man came out and he stood at this front door. He did not look too pleased as he looked over to the group and shook his fist. Edward looked at me and informed me this was Jack.

"Jack Spaniard!" they all shouted and they laughed at the victim and sang abusive chants as they goaded each other to yell louder.

They laughed and pointed at Jack who shook his fist again before returning inside to his home.

This drew the loudest of laughs among the group. This flying insect which tormented the poor man with its sting was then known as the "Jack Spaniard!"

I actually laughed for the first time in a while and it made me feel good. I sat and tried to remember the last time I actually did laugh and I couldn't bring any thoughts of being able to even smile. Yet this came to me without even thinking about it although I knew it was down to this Jack Spaniard stinging flying pest. I felt a sense of security with these people and yet they were not ever going replace my home where I wished to return.

The workers continued to talk to each other and I tried to listen but their accent was too strong and I lost every other word so I continued to talk to Edward who spoke slower and he was a little clearer with his accent.

He spoke of their work and their lives and he advised me if I were to get on with my duties without any questions and if I gave no trouble then I would be fine.

Edward caught my attention as he spoke some of my language which he told me had been passed down by his mother and this immediately made me want to listen to him more.

He told me his mother came from my land on a huge ship but she had since passed on to be with Onyankopon which made me feel like we shared something as my mother was also passed.

I told Edward I had been taken from my village by the light skin men who brought me against my will and he told me this was the way it was and if I questioned it I would bring trouble to myself.

I felt at ease talking to Edward and so I told him about Fiifi and I, and how we had planned our future together. Edward listened with interest and his face reflected his knowledge of things he had heard before as he nodded to my words.

I asked Edward what he had learned from his mother and he told me she was similar to Martha and she had wisdom of herbal remedies and traditions that were passed down to her from her mother and her mother before her.

Edward's familiarity to my background made be bring a suspicion to my thoughts he could be just teasing me and so I asked further about these traditions.

I was very aware by now of everyone I had met and I felt the need to question the truth of a man's tongue before I fully accepted it. I had been betrayed by so many people recently. After all, I had just sat down with a group who were teasing a man for getting stung and so I chose my words carefully.

I asked Edward to tell me more about his mother and he spoke of the traditional ways to treat sickness his mother taught to Martha which as a child he claimed he also saw being made and he remembered them. This is why he knew Martha would not do any harm to him and why he had his views of her.

He told me the root doctor of the plantation was now Martha and she had learned all of her knowledge from his mother. He added this knowledge is by tradition always passed down by word of mouth, unlike the white folk who write down their remedies and cures.

The root doctor is usually a black woman and she is in charge of the black workers. Yet she would also be called if a herbal tea or remedy for a cure could be given to the plantation owner and his family.

He added the root doctor's interest would be to make sure the plantation workers were as healthy as they could be because they were of no use lying in a bed. This made me think back to poor Abel Bowleg. He was given his punishment right next to the place where he was treated to help him to recover, which to me was something I did not understand. Master Adams made him sick and then he wanted him treated quickly to raise him from his bed and back on his feet and working in the field.

Edward told me about some things believed by our ancestors which included when a woman was giving birth then the root doctor usually placed an axe underneath the bed as this would help take away the pain from the mother.

When the child was delivered into the world the placenta was buried in the ground and this was done to remind the child of where he or she was born. Now this I liked but it made me start to think about my own situation as I had not seen any release of blood from my body for a long time and my stomach was swelling and I felt bloated all of the time.

Edward told me he had learned from his mother that after the placenta was buried then a fruit tree would be planted over the top of it to grow. This was supposed to ensure the child would never go hungry. It was a good sign if the tree would also bear the finest fruit then the child would be healthy and strong. However, if the tree failed to grow and looked weak then the child would need a lot of support as it may suffer health problems.

I asked further about this as I wanted to know the type of fruit usually grown. Edward told me the tree was probably one bearing a fruit he called a "Portugal". This was an orange sweet fruit with a bitter peel.

I froze when he told me this word as I thought of the people who had started the trade that stole my life away. How ironic it was these Portugal obroni who removed people from their happiness and in a way take their life of freedom yet the fruit of the same name was there to show a sign it was a supporter of a new life.

Edward saw my discomfort with the answer to the question so he changed his conversation to talk about African carvings and crafts.

I asked Edward if he liked the sound of drums playing and he said he did and he had heard about the fine drums of my land from his mother and of the many carvings and masks that were traditionally made in African villages.

He told me he had learned to create useful items and decorations taught to him by his mother from our African home which reflected his mother's heritage.

Edward explained as a boy he started to twist the grass of some long leaf plants. He then made rolls from the plaits for which these were materials were used in various ways. These consisted of baskets, hats and various other useful things.

He said he had also made carvings of wood and he had even learned to make small African drums he had heard his mother speak about. These were made by using the skin of the animals available and he had sewn them together. What really surprised me was when he told me he had carved a mark on each one which made them each individual, just like my village's very own drum maker Yafeu.

This was too close to my own knowledge and so from this point I knew Edward was telling me the truth. How would he ever know about the secret mark on each drum if he had not been taught this and so he was to be believed?

I asked Edward if he knew how to play a drum and he laughed at me and queried as to why I offered him such a silly question.

He asked me if I knew how to dance to the beat of a drum and I responded with the same answer he gave me and he stared at me with a look of shock from my answer. I added my feet would just stay with the drummers beat and even the drummers would sometimes have to keep up with me.

I told Edward that sometimes the player just needed to watch my feet and they would find the rhythm I was looking for. I laughed at Edward and we saw each other's comfort was united in this subject.

Edward told me that when he was younger there was a girl whom he thought he would get married to. She was the same age as him but she was taken by Master Adams and sold at the market and they never saw each other again.

Edward added he remembered she came to this plantation also from the ship on the water when she was about fourteen years old. He smiled when he spoke of her and they liked each other as friends and they liked to make crafts together. He said she was good at plaiting the grass and also she liked to make objects with the bindings of materials using the plant twine. He then told me the stool I was sitting on was made by her. He said he was good at carving wood and they complemented each other with these skills.

As they got older they found their feelings had turned into more than carving and plaits and they had started to find the binding of their arms around each other was a more enjoyable craft.

He laughed at what he had just told me and my eyes withdrew from his stare and I looked beyond him and over his shoulder. I did this because I knew what he meant and I felt this was too similar to my feelings for Fiifi. Edward then told me this girls name was Catherine and she was named by Master Adams after a queen from England many years ago. This was the country which now ruled the land we were in.

He continued to tell me about Catherine and with this his smile slowly dropped and his face became more serious.

Edward said that one day his love was asked to work in the house of Master Adams and she was asked to go there with William after the morning line up.

He told me William made sure Hannah had dressed Catherine ready for the house and he took her about mid-day. It was the same morning Mrs Adams had left early in the day to visit another plantation. She would do every month and sometimes twice and was away for a couple of days.

Edward spoke with a frown on his face now and his voice became more aggressive as he told me William had just saddled a horse to go and ride around the plantation to check on the workers in the field when Catherine came dashing through the rear door with her dress ripped from her top half of her body and she was exposing her bare chest whilst sobbing uncontrollably.

Edward stopped talking and looked beyond my shoulder and then he looked down at the ground. He remained silent and in thought and then he fidgeted on his stool and he started bouncing his knees.

After this pause Edward lifted his head and looked into my eyes and told me on that very same day, Master Adams arranged for William to take him and Catherine to the market and he never saw his love again.

He never even had the chance to say goodbye to her. He just saw his love being carried away on a cart and his heart sank deep into his chest. I knew how Edward felt as again the same happened to me. I did not speak and I left the air in silence. Edward placed his head in his hands and his head shook from side to side.

I realised from this I also would not probably see my Fiifi again. I declared my goodnight to Edward and the others and walked back to home and made my way to my room and thought strong and profoundly about my ƆdƆ and what I had learned.

I heard a voice shouting for me and I did not realise it but it was Hannah. She came and found me sitting on my bed and I do not even know what she said. The only thing in my thoughts was my Fiifi, and as I thought about him my memory entwined with the blended comparison with the way Edward showed his pain for the loss of his love Catherine. Hannah seeing my mood left me alone.

I tried to sleep but my head was seeing images which fought like demons in my thoughts. I sensed Fiifi reacting just like Edward.

I saw him talking to someone and then his head sunk to his chest, after this his knees started to shake which ended with his head in his hands. I tried to think about my day ahead and the cleaning of Master Adams house, and the preparing of the meals with Miss Sylvester, which led to the bright yellow flowers, then the fancy dresses, which was the disguise to the clandestine coins sitting in the jar.

I thought about the plantation, the workers, Jack Spaniard and Edward, and finally Fiifi. I called my silent drum to take me to my rest.

CHAPTER 17: Market

The next day I woke very tired and I felt like I had worked through the night. My body ached. It was then I struggled to sit up and I realised this was because of my little roundness in my belly. This was also the first time I noticed I was not being sick in the mornings like I had done when I arose from my slumber in recent weeks.

I dressed myself in my new clothes and left for the house of Master Adams and this time I went alone as William did not collect me. Master Adams wanted to go to the market and so I would have to make my own way to the house. William had already been to the house and told Hannah he had to put the shoes on the two horses needed to pull the wagon in the morning before they left the plantation.

I saw Miss Sylvester waiting for me outside the front door on the steps in front of the house. I approached with my aching body and I just thought of the work load she had prepared for me. I saw her standing strong with her hands on her hips and as I walked to tread the first step Miss Sylvester told me I was going with Master Adams to the market to collect some provisions.

I heard this and my heart raced as I knew what was happening from what Edward had told me the night before. I looked at Miss Sylvester with a worry in my heart. Miss Sylvester sensed this and she just told me to go ahead and she will see me shortly and with this reassurance I felt more comfortable to continue. She held her stare at me but then a happy face appeared and this slowly lifted my concern from sinking into a pool of worry. I was about to smile as I thought she was just teasing me but of a sudden she hollered at me to hurry up and join Master Adams.

This blew away my ears and I stepped backwards as I heard the horses behind me. I turned to see William holding onto them with the cart and they were down the hill to the front of the house where I first came onto this plantation.

I made my way towards them. I walked slowly and felt my

stomach pull as I descended the sharp angle of the grassy slope.

William called me to sit on the waiting wagon and I quickly did as I was asked to do. I was nervous but also a little curious about this and so I just decided to keep my eyes facing forward. One of the horses was uneasy and it pulled sharply which tugged the straps William was holding onto and this caused him to holler at it.

I saw William had something in his hand and this dropped to the ground. It was a cloth. William picked it up and I observed it was stained with a red colour and I soon realised this was his blood leaking from a wound on his hand. He wrapped the cloth around his hand and took control of the horses again.

Master Adams arrived and he climbed onto the seat next to me and we were soon on our way. We went along the track and out towards the field where the workers had already started to cut the cane. We then went beyond this and away from the plantation.

The sun was raging with heat and my brow soon started to feel the intensity of it. I tried to fan my face with my hand until Master Adams gave me a straw hat that was next to him to wear. I used it first to waft some cool air over my face before I placed it on my head.

We travelled along the road and Master Adams started to talk to me about the Plantation. I listened as it was my place to and I heard what Master Adams said to me but I was more focused on my surroundings. I was keen to see our route as I had taken this journey on my way to the house. I did not see it then as I was too weary and I was asleep for most of the way.

I firstly noticed how the dirt track was being churned away as the horses clopped along in front of us. The horses spluttered away, their big tails trailing behind. Their hooves coiled back and flicked the earth behind and I saw underneath their light yellow, brown soles. As I saw them walking ahead their big bottoms gave me a reminder of Miss Sylvester's huge behind as I climbed the stairs of Master Adams house. I had a little smile to myself as it also wobbled just the same as the horses.

On the side of the track was dotted some small bush grasses very similar to what I knew from my home. These were just like the ones whose leaves we plaited and made mats and decorations with.

We travelled further under the hot sun and Master Adams just carried on talking to me. Everything he said was just ramblings about his friends on the several plantations local to him and the work they do. He started to talk about a forbidden practice involving a dark side to various beliefs, healing potions and remedies. I really could not keep up with his words and I was just happy to breathe the clean air and look at the bright flora all around me.

As we rolled on I looked from the ground to the sky and it was a beautiful colour of blue and beneath I saw a lot of trees very similar to those of my home.

I looked at these different leafy structures and I saw firstly the tall and elegant palm which held up its green and ripe coconuts clustered like a necklace around its top. I lifted my head and held onto my hat and saw the sun glisten through the gaps of the big overhanging leaves high in the air. The sun sparkled into my eyes so I had to pull my hat down.

Master Adams was still talking then he started to inform me about what he called 'The works of the devil.' I found this to be distracting me from the beauty that I saw all around which I was trying to enjoy.

Next there was a tree which displayed an abundance of green oval shaped fruit. These were the mangoes I enjoyed eating so much and I smacked my lips when I saw then. My mouth started to moisten with the thought of tasting the juice of the flesh. They were only sitting a short distance away and they were calling to be picked and eaten.

Next to these was a jagged leafed tree and hanging from its branches was a brown stick which curled up at the end. Martha had these back at her home and she told me this was tamarind. This was used in cooking and was very useful in many recipes.

Again Master Adams spoke about evil rituals and his voice

become louder. He was telling me something about trickery and a thing he described as a people being under the enchantment of witchcraft. Master Adams was disturbing my enjoyment of such a pleasant and bright day. The air was clean and the flora was bulging with many attractive colourful shades of greens, browns, yellows and this had a beautiful clear blue background of the sky above.

I saw lower to the ground, another bush tree from home which I knew as the calabash. This inedible nut was dangling on its cord as was the next one to it.

I remembered this was the nut that, in my home, we scooped out the middle pulp and made drinking vessels and storage pots with the shell. This was the type of gourd which stored Nana Apane's palm wine.

This made me think of home again and I felt the taste of the bitterness, from missing my family and my village, touch my lips. I tried to swallow these thoughts but they had already dulled the sweetness that the sight of the mangoes gave me.

I thought about how my family were and if I would ever see them again. I thought about my Fiifi and if he was coping with his new life. I wondered if he had been looking at the brightest star in the sky at night and thinking about me. I had to put these thoughts behind me but they were things held in my akuma and I was finding it difficult to release them.

I thought about freedom at this moment. There were no guards of Nana Apane, no cages as in Assin Manso at the Slave River.

I was not enchained by my neck, bound by my hands or had metal shackles around my ankles. There were no walls of a big white building with the stench of decay which choked me. No defecation of women in desperation smeared on walls to keep their sanitation from their pride. There were no manacles to hold me down to the splintered rough wood in the ship entombing me within its bowels.

I could smell the wild freshness which was carried by the slight wind as it lifted and greeted my nose.

It felt at this moment that this was my freedom now.

I thought to myself, “Would I one day be able to be as free as I was before?”

I was born free and I enjoyed it and now it was gone from me I had to learn a new way to live and it was to keep my mouth quiet and my body as best as I could.

I thought at this time if I could run away into those trees just as I ran away from Nana Apane, I only needed one chance and I could be gone.

How wonderful the feeling was. I could go onto a ship and sail back to my home. My dreams ran away inside my head and then my stomach gurgled and my hazy vision became clear again. I could not run away as I was carrying a child. Yes, I had to be honest with myself. I am not free, not yet, but one day I will be.

I saw the pretty pink flowers strung along in a thread of beautiful flora. This laced its way to where I saw another tall tree and as I looked up I saw a pretty bird flying. It came to rest on a branch and it puffed out its bright orange breast from its green feathered wings and blue tail. It had a sharp pointed black beak and the eyes looked like he was wearing a mask.

I gazed as it sat and I watched it wag its tail as we moved closer then Master Adams caught me smiling as it sat looking at us approaching.

He had a laugh to himself then he told me the bird was called a ‘mot mot’ bird. He stopped talking and the natural noises of its song became clearer. I thought to myself how sweet the pretty feathered bird was as it sang a happy melody in a couple of repeated tweets.

I saw this mot mot wag its tail again and again and then heard as it started croaking its tiny nasal and far crying tune. I closed my eyes and breathed in the clean air through my nose and out again through my mouth to flush this freshness through my lungs. I had only smelled the sour and bitter stench of human fluids while I was in the big white building and on the ship which carried me to this land so this was a pleasure to enjoy.

I let the mot mot delight my ears with its chirpy shrill as it repeated its delightful tune.

I was feeling the joys of the start of happiness again and it felt good and cleansing. I started to try to put a drum beat to the mot mot's peeps yet after trying I thought no drum could spoil this natural whistle. I held my head up facing the sky then I opened my eyes and the bright sun blinded my sight as I looked again for the little bird which sang for me.

I saw a feathered lump sitting on a branch and Master Adams told me this was called the 'jumbie bird.' He laughed again at this bird because he told me it causes trouble with other birds as it was known as a nest robber. I had heard this word 'jumbie' from Hannah and after Master Adams was talking of a dark side I knew I had to be careful of hearing it too often.

He continued with his talk of this bird and he told me if I were to hear the scream of the jumbie bird during the night, then according to local folklore, someone was about to die on the plantation. I did not know if he said this to scare me or if it was true. Master Adams then had a little giggle to himself.

I forced my strained, blurred eyes to open and I just looked under the brim of my hat until I saw the outline of a large tree against the sky. My vision slowly brought to view the fruit on the end of the thread, dangling, from the branch, into focus. This fruit was unusually big as my sight adjusted and corrected itself.

The breath I had just released was immediately stolen back as the fruit dissolved its form and remoulded into the shape of a lifeless human body hanging from the tree branch by a rope.

My eyes could not remove themselves from a still and harrowing image. As we rolled closer I felt as if my body was floating like the mot mot, hovering in the air, as I was moving but yet I was still sitting on the wagon. The body was a man who was naked and all of his dignity was exposed.

We drew almost level to this shocking man's suspension and my thoughts were reminded of how my village hung some of our beasts to drain its blood. This man had the features of a bibini but his skin was fair and his short hair was curly and tight yet he had a grey sheen over his face. This made him look older than he was. The shock of seeing this did not immediately absorb into my head. It was like I saw it but it was not real. Yet it was real alright, I just saw a man hanging by a rope by his neck in a tree at the side of the road and he was now right next to me.

My hands were drawn towards my mouth and I gasped out. I suddenly felt a wave of a tingling sensation run over my body and wrap around my shoulders which made me jiggle uncontrolled in my seat. I turned my eyes away then I closed them and listened as Master Adams made the horses speed up. In my head the man's face would not go away and his image engrained itself to stay inside there.

Master Adams realised I was disturbed by this and he spoke of this man.

"There is the husk of Cleophus Hornigold, hung for performing

Witch craft."

Master Adam's voice softened to the tone of the same one he spoke when we had set off on our journey before we had reached the lifeless body. I kept my eyes away and did not wish to see any more of this visual horror.

My curiosity made me look back at this hanging man until we had travelled far past and I turned my head back to look straight ahead. I did not want to see anymore.

Master Adams talked more of Cleophus and he told me he was from a nearby plantation and he was a hard worker. Unfortunately he had fallen into the trap of trying to perform Witchcraft on his master who he said had prevented him from his freedom. He then told me it was rumoured Cleophus was secretly in love and he wanted to tell everyone but the woman would not be able to see him as the master of the plantation she lived on was a ruthless man.

I listened carefully to this as I wanted to know why a man could get himself removed of his life for wanting sanctuary for himself.

Master Adams then told me Cleophus Hornigold's mother was supposed to be the granddaughter of an unlawful man of the seas of the islands close by. He added this was never proven, yet his mother swore it was true. His mother had the honest words of her mother which from an early age was passed on.

She claimed Cleophus's great grandfather was a pirate who turned pirate catcher after he was given a Kings pardon from England.

His ears had also been fed this knowledge from an early age and he felt as the only boy born since his great grandfather, he needed to stake his claim as a man of freedom and he spoke about it passionately.

He had run away many times before and tried to escape his destiny and search for his true heritage. This led him to be tracked down, caught and beaten several times until he finally decided to learn the ways of a trade passed down by a selected few people. Cleophus Hornigold chose to indulge in the art of witchcraft.

Cleophus set about his plan to blight his master and his family and it was seen as nothing more than the tedious and idle words of a fool.

This was a strange one for me to understand because Cleophus was born as a slave with the mind of a free man. I thought then how he must have been tortured in his desire to be without his chains of captivity. I knew this feeling and now it was gone but it was purely the greatest thing I had when it was mine. This belief of Cleophus must have had a vein of truth which fortified his intentions. He must have known he had evidence of how he could prove his claim, were he to be given the chance.

Master Adams continued to tell me the master of the plantation on which Cleophus worked, became violently ill very suddenly one day.

This was when Cleophus went missing again and when his room was searched there were various items such as bones, tribal carvings, bottles and jars of liquids and powders even the root doctor of the plantation had not seen.

There was a huge hunt for Cleophus who was not caught for many weeks. He was eventually located and hauled before his master and he admitted his crime. The master of the plantation had sent many of his trusted workers and friends out looking for Cleophus on several different occasions and they all wanted to be paid each time and finally the master ran out of patience.

After his mind was struck down by the witchcraft of Cleophus the master took his own course of punishment and he took his trouble maker to the tree at the side of the road and left him to look at the freedom he so much desired. The tree overlooked his escape route which was his final downfall.

So freedom came at a heavy price and this was one I dare not now consider and one I hoped Fiifi would not either. This shock gave me the warning against trying to ever dream of being free from my invisible chains.

After a good while under the sun where I sat and thought about poor Cleophus we arrived at the market where I had been bought by Master Adams.

Master Adams pulled in the wagon and took me to the area in the middle of an open square behind the same stage I walked when I was taken and paraded before being sold. This filthy wooden platform I saw as a vile and humiliating structure vividly brought back thoughts of my last site of my Fiifi and I felt the water build behind my eyes.

Master Adams removed his hat and met some other men who were standing chatting. He called me to stand at his side and so I did. I remained quiet and dropped my head. Master Adams quickly picked my face up and the men all looked at me and they never removed their stare. This seemed to be a time which never seemed to end until Master Adams finished his talk and he ushered me to a building near to where we arrived.

We went into a tall wooden building and there was a huge amount of items all around on the shelfs in front of me and on the floor.

I was introduced to a man inside and this time I kept my chin up and level to the floor and with this I remember what Kesiwaa had told me.

Master Adams walked around this place and picked up several items on the dividing racks in the store.

The man behind the counter then spoke to Master Adams and they seemed to agree on things to be taken.

Some of these were also from behind the counter and they are in bottles which were labelled. I could read the labels but I did not know what they said as these were not words I had seen or heard before. However I did notice some of these bottles had a picture of a skull and bones crossed over the middle to make an X and it said "Poison."

Once these were placed on the counter Master Adams took out a cloth bag and exchanged the goods for coins which were similar to the ones in the jar I had seen. These coins were traded for the items and were clearly of value.

After getting the provision supplies needed and fruits from another part of the market Master Adams had them loaded onto the back of the cart.

Once we had finished getting these goods I boarded the wagon with Master Adams and we were on our way back to the plantation.

We rumbled onto the dirt track and the wobbly horse bottoms jiggled and wagged their long tails and their feet churned up the dirt below flicking bits up behind from under their grey hooves underneath.

We approached the place of Cleophus Hornigold and I averted my eyes. I thought to myself this was the reason I was taken to the market. I was made to travel to see for myself, trying to escape to freedom was never going to be an option.

I heard the mot mot with its sweet tune and my eyes saw the colourful flowers below. Then as we progressed there he was and this time a light breeze swayed his body very slightly and the branch which held him in suspension creaked.

I decided to remember this moment and I took my sight from his face where I engrained this vision into my eyes and held my stare to capture it. I saw firstly his face was not even and I soon realised his left ear was missing. I looked right down his body trying to remember all I saw and I noticed he had brown marks around his wrists which were old wounds which had healed in a way his light skin could not repair without leaving scars. I then noticed his back was the same with former lines from lashes given from a whipping.

Further down there was a puncture wound from the back of his leg and through to the front which had ripped his skin open.

I kept my stare and then I felt my eyes were drained and so I turned away feeling that I had seen enough. Master Adams was quiet during this journey and I think he was feeling the tiring heat during this day.

We travelled on past the calabash, the tamarind and then the golden mangoes and soon after this the coconuts were still up high in the air.

Further along the journey back from the market I saw the top of the master's big white house through some trees in the distance ahead. We approached the plantation as I remembered from the last time and this time I felt comfort at being home.

William was there to greet us when we arrived back at the house and I stepped off the cart with Master Adams.

Master Adams went into his home and I followed behind and as soon as I stood at the steps to the front door I was greeted by Miss Sylvester who told me to follow her to the kitchen. Although I wanted to see the hanged man on the return journey I felt sick in my stomach from this and I needed to speak about it.

Miss Sylvester took a broom from a cupboard and gave it to me. She told me to firstly sweep the front of the house as it had gathered some dust and I acknowledged her.

I was about to go and start my duties but before I did I managed to ask Miss Sylvester why I had to go to the market that morning and she told me I was there because there was nobody else to go and Master Adams liked to have some company on his journey.

Miss Sylvester told me when I had finished with the brush I was to start with Master Adams room and she would be collecting the provisions from the cart to take them to the store.

I asked if she would be seeing me later and she added she needed to get the provisions from the cart quickly because William needed to shoe the two horses now they had returned.

I remembered then William had already changed the shoes on the horses before we left for the market so I was curious as to why it was needed to be done again. I needed to think about this as it did not seem to be right.

I wanted to know more about Cleophus and I tried to think of who I would approach about him. I wanted to know about the woman who he loved so much and why he kept running away. Should I ask Edward, as he was aware of the things happening here? Then I thought about Martha perhaps as she was a trusted person.

I kept thinking about it and as I already had started the enquiry with Miss Sylvester I decided she would be my choice.

I wanted to ask her more than Master Adams had informed me but I had to wait for another time as the day was coming to a close. I had in the back of my mind thoughts about the coins and I wanted to ask about these and so I decided to give this trust to Edward.

For the items bought in the shop marked with the picture of the skull and the bones which looked like a picture of something bad I decided I would speak to Martha to see if she knew anything, however for now this was not important.

I was still not sure about the horses and the need to shoe them again in the same day but this was not really a question which concerned me so I decided to just remember this and observe them another time to see if this is was correct.

Master Adams left and became busy with the workers in the field after the market and Mrs Adams had gone to visit Martha to check on those who were sick. I just got on with what I had to do and my duties took my thoughts away from my earlier part of the day.

I went to my duties in Master Adams Bedroom and I wanted to see the coins in the jar and so I took my chance quickly and this time the glass was full of coins. More had been added since I last looked which got me thinking.

Once my duties were done I returned to my home and ate for the evening. I then went to find Edward who was sitting after his day just as before with the other workers from the field.

I sat down with him and he was carving a piece of wood and I asked him for his full attention. He looked at me puzzled so I gestured for him to take a walk with me.

I had to talk of the coins and so after a deep breath I spoke to Edward about the large glass jar behind a hidden wooden panel where Mrs Adams kept here dresses. I told him I had seen this jar contained coins of different shades of metal. I added that I had looked a couple of times now and so far when I first saw through the clear glass it was half full yet the next time I looked it was full.

At first Edward remained silent and he let me finish with my information. Pausing for a moment he then stroked his chin before telling me this was something I should not know. He told me not to tell anyone else about what I had seen. I informed him as a young girl I was taught always to keep what I had seen to myself. I remembered as Kesiwaa had taught me. Yet this time had I broken the rule by speaking about it?

I sensed I had made a mistake at first but he then smiled and told me this was something I should not mention again. I felt as though talking about the coins was wrong but I had to tell someone but did I make a blunder by telling Edward? I went to my bed with some concern and I did not find my sleep for my worry. I also spent the night stroking my belly and thinking about my unborn child.

CHAPTER 18: Craft

I arrived for my duties the next morning at the house of Master Adams and I started with his bedroom, as ordered by Miss Sylvester. I carried the clean bed linen up the stairs and lay them on the chair at the side of the dresser that held the looking glass. I noticed that just inside the bedroom door was a table which had two teacups on it. They had been used and were placed there by Master and Mrs Adams to be taken away as Miss Sylvester had informed me.

I saw some fresh flowers were in the pretty vase and a pleasant fragrant smell lifted around the room being carried from the light breeze flowing through the open window.

I began my duties and started to tidy the bed and unfolded some clean sheets. I heard Miss Sylvester coming along the corridor towards the bedroom then the door opened.

I was about to greet her but then my thoughts changed and I wanted to ask her my question about Cleophus. My mouth opened then closed as Master Adams came through the door close behind her.

He greeted me with a smile and then he walked over to near the window and stuck a strip of dangling paper on a hook near to the underside of a high shelf containing some ornaments.

"There, that should do it Elizabeth", he said and I had to remember my new name for a moment. I did not know what was placed on the hook so as Master Adams walked away I briefly looked at the strip of unrolled paper hanging down with a cylinder weighting it down at the base. It reminded me of the same display of Cleophus as it was unsightly and lifeless in its held position.

I carried on changing the bed linen and then the hanging paper was disturbed by the wind from the open window and it blew off its fixture and fell to the ground. I saw this and I walked over to it and picked it up from the floor and hung it back to the hook where

Master Adams had first placed it.

I looked at my hand and I had some of the substance from this paper on my thumb and finger and so I smelled them and then started to lick it off. It tasted sweet.

Master Adams had seen what I had done and shouted at me to stop.

"Elizabeth that is poisonous. It is dangerous so you are not to touch it or it will kill you. I have had to put this poison up as there are too many flies and bugs at the moment, I cannot sleep in the heat without the window open at night. Now go and wash your hands Elizabeth, and wash them thoroughly." ordered Master Adams.

Master Adams voice was quite harsh and it frightened me to the point where I was almost shaking.

I obeyed my order and went straight to the sink to wash my hands and scrubbed them vigorously until they were almost sore.

After this I returned and carried on with my duties and I made sure I was careful not to touch anything similar to the dangling paper.

Later that morning Master Adams was sitting at a table and he was writing on some paper. I heard him mumbling things and it was as if he were counting to himself. I made sure I did not disturb him with any noise and left as soon as I had finished my duties.

I joined Miss Sylvester who was in the kitchen, she was chopping some meat. She told me to go and collect some ground provisions from the vegetable garden which was located at the side of the house. I was told to pull some carrots from the ground and collect some potatoes that William had dug up that morning. I saw the fur skin of an animal laid over a wooden partition near to the house and I guessed it was from the slaughtered goat Miss Sylvester was preparing.

I took the ground provision into the kitchen for Miss Sylvester and placed them on the table. I then chopped them and helped Miss Sylvester season the meat for the evening meal and salt the rest for preserving in storage.

I realised my time was ready to ask her about Cleophus and so I started with my question about going to the market with Master Adams.

Miss Sylvester looked at me in a strange way as if she wanted to question my enquiry. She thought about her reply and then she advised me Master Adams wanted someone to accompany him on the journey and he felt the day was right for me. She added then that she had advised me of this the day before.

She looked at me and almost admitted to me with her expression she had more to say and it was then she added Master Adams had taken me so his friends and others at the market could see my face. This was in case I was to think of trying to run away then they would know who to look for.

She told me all the new arrivals have it in their heads to run, so for his friends to see me would help them to identify me. I thought back to when I did think of jumping from the cart and running away when going to the market.

I enquired if this was done with everyone and she told me it was not usually, however Master Adams had paid a lot of money for me. I thought again about Fiifi and the trader at the market where I was bought and this made sense. Master Adams sold him to pay more for me.

She informed me if anyone runs away then they normally pay to find you and this can be sometimes also expensive.

If you constantly do this then they will just take their rifles and hunt you down and if you are killed then so be it.

I understood now what the reason was for me to go to the market and so I did not need to ask about Cleophus as I knew the conclusion to his life. I decided to let this man's interest leave my thoughts. I was of course thinking about Fiifi running away but he probably had a similar experience to me that would prevent any thoughts of it. I acknowledged what I had been told and so I continued with my duties and I salted the goat for its preservation.

The day went quickly after this and it ended with me still checking for the sticky substance on my fingers but it was completely gone. I was curious about this fixture which took away the bugs and was also curious of Master Adams concern of its poison.

After washing myself in the evening I took my meal made for me by Hannah and went to the yard and met with Edward. He was anxious to talk to me and he grabbed my arm and pulled me to walk with him.

I followed him and we strolled away from any listening ears. Edward advised me he had missed making African crafts he had talked about at our evening conversations. He told me he wanted to see the form of a drum again and he had a desire to make one to keep his skill alive.

Edward was going to make his craft and he added that he already asked William if he could use the tools he had in his barn.

He then told me he had also asked William to request from Master Adams his permission to make the drum. Later that day he responded to Edward and informed him permission was granted and it could be made. William added this had to be done without any effect on his work in the field and if there was then he would have to make him stop.

I smiled as Edward told me and he gave me a smile back which made me feel like I was being involved in this craft but I knew it was Edward's desire, and for him to be excited made me feel his joy.

Edward told me he would start making the drum the next evening after he had returned from the field. I asked Edward if he wanted some tea which he accepted. Once we had our beverages in our hands we sat together and spoke of the types of drums we knew.

Edward took a stick from the ground and drew a shape of a Djemba drum which he was thinking about making. This was a top heavy shape which had a half cone shape for a base.

He was quite accurate in the way he scratched the shape on the ground into the dirt. He then told me the skin of the drum would be from a goat and he already had this drying in Master Adam's yard.

I took the stick and drew a shape of a Gangon drum which was traditionally hung over the shoulder and played with a curved stick and I suggested this was a good one to craft. I laughed as I was excited when I drew it because it was quite a good style and I knew it made a good sound. I told Edward the Djemba drum made a louder sound and to play it late in the evening would probably disturb Master Adams. I added that he kept his window open already because he was not sleeping very well due to the heat.

Edward took the stick from my hand and scratched the soil to remove my drawing and I felt a little hurt by this. I lost my smile and then Edward lost his as well.

He pointed to his drawing and told me that it was the style of drum he would make. It was the Djemba drum and he stood over his marking scratched into the dry soil.

He looked long at it and then he lifted his chin and a slow smile arrived and this time I knew he was already decided in his design and he did not want a style from me he just wanted the approval of his own.

I struggled to join him in his pleasure at first but then I managed to smile as well and I was pleased for him.

We spent the evening talking about the sound the drum would make and the various tribal markings he knew. I shared the ones that I knew, the ones most popular and the ones most fitting for the pattern.

After this I felt tired and my stomach felt heavy so I took an early sleep and went to rest. After all the talk of the drum I had the sound of beats in my head as I relaxed and finally slept.

The next evening, soon after he ate his meal, Edward set about the making of his drum. He had collected the goat skin of a recently slaughtered animal from Master Adams herd; he then collected the wood from a tree nearby and the twine from the twisted sinews of the same goat to bind it all together. He took these items to William's barn and got to work.

From then Edward's day started in the field early and although he finished late, he first ate a meal, then, instead of joining the others and me for the evening chat after, he went to make the drum. He was always away in William's barn and over the next few weeks I never saw him, except when I took him a tea made from the leaves of the lime tree to drink.

He always came back to his home at the time we had to be inside of our wooden chambers as ordered by Master Adams as we had to turn out our lights and sleep.

I only saw Edward briefly during this time and I missed his evening talks which had comforted me before. I always made time for Edward if I saw him and he advised me he was making the drum to a traditional design and he needed it to be made with the correct measurements.

As the time went on I realised I missed Edward so much I had to make him some food for his evening meal as I wanted to bring his attention back to me. I soon started looking at the brightest star in the night sky and sending him a message of how I missed his company.

I also started to feel my body change as my baby grew inside my belly. Nobody as yet knew about my condition, I had hidden it well, but I did remember when Master Adams took a deep interest in me as I stood on the platform of shame when I was traded and then taken by him to work in his home. I still had my daily jobs to do in the house and I could not take my focus away from it.

I continued each day and I noticed the paper with the sticky touch had many flies and bugs attached to it. This was very clever, I thought, and wondered if I would be allowed to have one of my own in my room as the insects and flies were sometimes too much. When they sat on my skin they left a mark and it did not go away and they also made me scratch my skin. This irritated me especially with my stomach swelling.

One morning I finished my duties in Master Adams bedroom where I had been asked to change the flowers among many other things. Miss Sylvester told me that when I had swept the upstairs landing I was to accompany Mrs Adams to the market. Well, I did not really want to go but I had no choice. This time I was going to keep my eyes away from the sight along the journey where my stomach turned over for now was not the time.

It was late in the morning and I got myself ready and went to the yard. William had prepared the cart and I climbed on.

As I sat on board Mrs Adams came from the house with a basket and she climbed on next to me. This time William was going to take us and Master Adams would stay behind and he watched as the horses pulled us away on the cart.

As we moved away to leave something caught my eye and I looked at the house. I saw Miss Sylvester behind the curtain in Master Adams bedroom. I watched her pull away from the window as she saw me looking.

This got me thinking "Why was she in the bedroom when I had already tidied it and done all the duties needed already on that morning?" I had even been told to change the flowers in the vase which was not normally a job for me. Miss Sylvester was normally in the kitchen and the duties in Master Adams bedroom were mine. I left the thought to drift from my head and went to the market with Mrs Adams and William. I let my thoughts fall back onto Edward during this journey and I did not even notice when we passed Cleophus or even if he was still there. We were gone for some time and it was late when we returned. I was excited to get back and make some food for Edward. I took him some tea made from the lime leaves I knew he liked.

Edward continued with his craft and during this time several of the workers asked what he was doing in William's barn and they started to talk about him with jest in their voices.

I decided to inform them one evening he was making an African drum which was my mistake and I should have known this was wrong to announce.

I was probed for more about this by one of the workers called Leopold who was keen to tease me at what Edward was doing this for?

I responded in Edward's defence and told him he had a great skill and he wanted to exercise this to good use. I said he was "crafty."

I meant this to mean he was very good at making African things. Well this choice of a word evoked the biggest cry from Leopold.

"Of course he is, he is "Crafty Eddie!" He shouted and then he fell about laughing with the others at this title.

I felt so silly at this and believed it was my foolish tongue that resulted in Edward now being given this name.

During the next few weeks Edward continued to be vacant from our place of rest and talking after eating his meal until finally one evening he called me to William's barn.

I walked with him slowly and we approached the large wooden door. Edward told me to wait for a minute and he went inside the barn. When he came out and invited me to go closer I made some steps nearer to the door.

Edward asked me if I could close my eyes and I did. I heard the creak of the barn door and Edward prompted me to open them.

I let my eyelids open slowly and I saw Edwards craft in front of me. It was a fine Djemba drum with a style not only traditional, with tribal markings but one which had a few marks and features of its own.

I was so please at what I saw I raced up to Edward and threw my arms around him, he hugged me in return and his embrace felt so warm and comforting. I felt my bump in between us but the feeling of Edward's arms around me was to inviting to let it be released straight away and we both held on to each other until I let go. I looked at Edward and he stared at me as we both realised our actions.

I looked at the shape of the Djemba drum and it looked like it was made of two halves. The top appeared to resemble a large deep wooden water container. This sat on a conical shaped base which had the point cut off about half way down. Where they joined it made a ledge and they complimented each other to give this fine shape.

Looking at the detail I noticed it was made with precise bindings and the skin was stretched tightly at the top and it was tucked in neatly around the side. The twine binding was then pulled underneath the part where the top sat on the bottom half.

Edward had carved figures of people dancing around the top section and they were holding African masks, spears, shields, and lanterns. He had made the carved figures in his own style and it was a very beautiful pattern.

He had even added some decoration beads at the base of the top section which gave it his own mark and this also gave it some colour. I asked Edward what it sounded like and he pointed his finger for me to pat the skin. I walked up to the drum and stood beside it and it reached right up to my waist.

I don't know why but I was a bit nervous. I took my hand and with a sharp rap of my fingers I drew it down onto the skin at the side and I heard a low thud. I repeated this towards the middle and the sound became higher in its pitch and it had more of a sharp sound to it. I then told Edward I had never played a drum as my leader Nana Apane did not encourage girls to learn.

It was the first time I heard this sound in a long time and it was pleasant. I told Edward how well he had done and he gave the biggest smile I had seen from him.

Edward clasped his arms under the rim of the Djemba drum and with a quick side tilt of his head he beckoned me to follow him. He carried it to his home.

Edward placed the drum at the door of his home and a few of the children raced up to come and see it and they were led by Augustus. They were all keen to see what Edward had brought to them and he told them to sit down so he could tell them all about it.

He started to talk with the keen ears of the children giving him their full attention. Leopold was sitting with some of the workers relaxing and he noticed the sudden interest of the children and so he raised his voice and shouted out his ridicule of Edwards Drum.

"Hey Edward, what ya garna do wid dat ting, make the rain come?"

This made the workers laugh and some even rolled onto their sides.

I felt this was unfair and Leopold was just showing his ignorance and senseless humour.

"Hey Rain maker, give me some rain," shouted Jack Spaniard. Then another voice joined in with the mockery. "Help to keep those stinging flies away!" He shouted.

Edward replied back by telling them they should not mock him as he had made it for Master Adams.

This was the wrong response and it drew more shouting and ridicule.

"Hey Crafty Eddie a gift for Master Adams is it? You tink you are, de white man trading tings now boy Eddie?

He then kissed his teeth and added "Just make de rain come before Master Adams laugh's at you as well!" Leopold yelled and chuckled at the same time.

"I can do de rain dance for ya" shouted Jack Spaniard. They used to call me 'jiggle knees' for my style Eddie!"

That was it, as soon as I heard this comment I replied to Jack Spaniard to come and show us what he could do.

This just made Jack and Leopold start laughing harder and louder.

I looked at Edward and I gave him a sweet eye and told him to bring the Djemba drum to where Jack and Leopold were sitting.

Edward clutched his drum with his arms and lifted it up and we walked towards the workers. As we approached them I spoke quietly to Edward and I told him to play a beat and then watch my feet and follow me once he had it in his head. From then, I added, that he should switch the rhythm of the beat when I gave him the signal.

"When I take the cloth from my head it will be the signal to change the beat." I said.

Leopold was the first to comment with his bitter tongue as he spoke to Edward.

"Hey Edward your funny canoe will never float on the water!" He said with jest in his voice.

"Yeah, Edward, where are you going to then, the African jungle?" Jack Spaniard added his words teasing.

Edward placed the drum on the ground and I looked across at him. I pulled up my dress slightly to reveal my feet and then I signalled with my eyes for him to look at them. I started my foot tapping and Edward soon picked up and started to play the drum with a steady beat. The pounding of the animal skin rolled out at a steady pace and it slowly built to a louder and faster rhythm.

I turned my back to the workers and then back again and a clap soon came from one of them.

I quickened my feet and shook my body and for this moment I felt fine with my stomach. There was another hand clapping and then another, until I could see several workers had joined in and then some were stamping their feet on the ground.

I continued with this beat until it had reached its closure and so when the hands of Edward slapped and thumped the drum to a finale I took my hand to my head and with one swipe tore away my head scarf and waved it in the air and from side to side.

Edward quickly picked up on this and I drew him into my beat as my silent drum came flooding into my head.

"Bam ba ba, bam ba ba bam ba ba bam, ba ba bam ba ba bam,

ba ba bam ba ba bam bam ba ba, bam ba ba bam."

I let my voice open up and "Du ga da, du ga da, du ga da" I started to sing to the rhythm.

I was really feeling this drum beat and I closed my eyes. My feet worked by themselves. I was now out of control of movement as the drum took me with its pace. I cannot remember how long this went on for but suddenly there became a swirling in my head and I opened my eyes and I saw everyone was standing and clapping. I even saw William had joined the group and he was smiling and shaking hands with the others.

I looked over at Edward and he knew I wanted to stop and with another build up he slapped his hand down onto the goat skin and I stamped my foot to end the dance. I was breathing hard and my brow suddenly flowed with my sweat and ran down my cheeks.

I looked at Edward who was smiling and also wiping his brow. I looked at Leopold who stood clapping with an open mouth. Next to him Jack Spaniard was like Leopold's twin brother making the same face and clapping gesture. Some of the other workers were smiling and laughing at Leopold and Jack.

Finally I looked at my side and the children were all around me and they were holding onto my dress and pressing themselves against me. They were tugging at my hands and arms and they wanted me to show them again and I just laughed and told them I would do it another time.

The dancing had caused quite a show to all and I was the main attraction. What a strange feeling I had at this time and my akuma raced at a fast pace until it slowed down and the talking and clapping quietened down.

After all the noise was gone and the workers retired to their homes I went over to Edward who took me in his arms and held me close. He told me I did very well and I replied the same to him. I added that the drum made a good sound but it was too loud which was why I had drawn the picture of the other drum as a suggestion.

Edward reminded me the drum was for Master Adams and he would present it to him as he has to show what he had made. I told Edward I thought the drum was made so the workers and all could listen to the sounds for some dancing and enjoyment.

Edward responded and told me he could always make another one for the workers to listen to and dance and with this comment he stroked my cheek.

I spent a short time after the dancing being comforted by Edward until I realised I felt weak and needed to rest.

Edward kissed me above my eyes and then he walked me to my home.

That night I lay in my bed and my dreams were overwhelmed with Edward and his smile was engrained in my thoughts. I closed my eyes and said to myself "Good night Edward."

CHAPTER 19: Tranquillity

The next day saw the sun rise and I recalled the evening from the day before and thought about the fun we had. This was a Sunday and Master Adams was going to attend a church for his worship to his Onyankopon.

I went to step from my bed and my legs felt a pain from the dancing I had done the evening before. I then felt my belly and it was bigger now than I realised. I also saw how my breasts had swollen and they were fuller than I realised. My baby was developing now and I was aware it would soon be noticed and so when I dressed I pulled my top clothes loose to hide my secret.

I went for the morning line up and I stood next to Edward. Everyone was there on time. Leopold commented on Edward's drum playing and Jack Spaniard talked about my dancing. Edward took my hand and squeezed it gently which made my heart warm from his touch.

Master Adams arrived with his hound Blackie and he looked like he was in a happy mood. He was singing a song about the Lord. He walked down his line of workers and stopped to talk to some of them.

He then walked up to Edward and spoke to him asking about his craft. Master Adams wanted to see the drum Edward had made as he had been informed it was now complete. He asked for Edward to bring it for him to see and so as requested Edward went to his home to collect it.

He returned quickly with the Djemba drum for Master Adams and placed it on the ground.

Edward presented the African drum for Master Adams and it stood as it did the night before with all the workers looking on at it. At first Master Adams looked like he was not really interested as he stroked the head of his hound Blackie who sat next to him.

He then asked Edward about its sound and he asked him to play it.

Edward looked at me and I gave a simple nod of my head and he placed his hands on the skin of the drum. He then looked at my feet and I gave a single shake with my head to say no, this time, Edward had to play without me.

Edward looked back at me and then he played with a rhythm I had not heard before. The beat was slightly quicker than what was traditional but it was a good one.

Bam, Bam Bam, Bam, Bam Bam, Bam, Bam Bam, the drum sounded.

This beat got my feet tapping with a delight which made me feel my real home. All eyes looked at Edward and when he stopped they looked at Master Adams. His frown of being uninterested turned to a smile of delight.

Master Adams saw this beautifully made drum with its fancy patterns and carvings and by a surprise he actually liked it.

Master Adams then spoke,

"That was delightful Edward it sounds so good and you played it very well. When William told me you were making this drum I thought it was going to be one you could hold in your hand and not one this size. So tell me why did you make it?"

Edwards reply was long as he said,

"Thank you Masser Adams. Well, I made it as a gift for you. It is a drum in an African style which I have known about as a small boy and was taught to me many years ago. The drum has been played for you to let you hear its beautiful sound, but it has not been made for this purpose. You see this drum is by tradition a drum of tranquillity. This drum is designed to give off an outward appearance and feeling of relaxation and it will help you to sleep if it is placed in the room that has your bed. These tribal markings will channel your restless energy into it and it will absorb your worries and concerns. Here is a drum not to be played but kept for its peaceful emanation."

Edward looked at his wooden creation with a profound stare and he spoke again,

"This is a silent drum." He concluded.

Master Adams looked totally puzzled as did I and he walked up to the drum and looked at it a bit more closely.

I looked at Edward and raised my eyebrow in question at the total and utter nonsense he had just told Master Adams. Edward looked away from me and I briefly shook my head to myself.

Blackie then walked up to the drum and sniffed it then cocked his leg at the side of it. Master Adams shouted at Blackie and he scampered away and whimpered then he lay down with his tongue out, panting in a shade next to one of the workers homes.

Master Adams looked at Edward and he smiled at him and told him he was a very creative and skilful man and he was also amused by his funny story about the drum. He advised Edward he was not sleeping too well and he will try Edward's tranquil remedy.

Edward spoke to Master Adams and he asked him for one more thing. He told him for the silent drum to keep its air of tranquillity he would need to take it, and wash the wooden body of it, and to tighten the skin at every full moon as this was the African tradition passed down to him. As it was just past the last lunar circle then about a month would need to pass until this was to happen.

Master Adams seemed amused by this little story and so he told Edward he could take the silent drum every full moon and do whatever he needed to as long as he slept more peacefully.

After the presentation was over Master Adams told me to go and start my duties. He then ordered Edward to take the drum to his home.

I followed Master Adams to his home and Edward carried the drum behind us. When we got inside Master Adams home Mrs Adams greeted us and made a fuss over Edward. She asked him to take the drum to the sitting room at the rear of the house and she asked me to take him there.

I walked Edward down the centre hallway and opened the door leading to the sitting room. Edward set the drum down and then he made his way back out of the house.

Edward left and I carried on with my duties and Master and Mrs Adams went to their place of worship. Master Adams looked very fine and dandy with a gold and white coloured waist jacket and Mrs Adams wore a matching shawl.

Master Adams was in a jolly mood and left the house singing as if he were listening to the beat of the drum Edward had played earlier.

I continued with my day and then in the evening I left and met up with Edward. I was keen to listen to what he had to say.

I questioned him on what he had told Master Adams and he looked at me and smiled. I told him I knew the story about the tranquillity was nonsense and he replied he was merely showing Master Adams his African skills; in case he wanted him to one day learn from William about his trade and one day take over from him.

I informed Edward that I did not believe this and he laughed at me. I knew there was something more to this but, as yet, I did not know what to make of it and I did not care to pursue my questioning of him.

I realised Edward was a very skilful man and a lot more profound than I thought. I then compared him to Fiifi and it was then I started to realise my ƆdƆ had slowly slipped away from the front of my thoughts to be replaced with Edward. It was when I asked myself how I felt about Edward and I knew I was having the same rush of warmth in my akuma I had with Fiifi. Of course I always would love Fiifi but we were never going to be together in this world again and I accepted it.

This was a sad thought but I wanted to be loved and wanted to give my love also. I felt I was falling for Edward. I did not know how to talk to him about it though and, as for my baby, what would he say anyway? He would not want me with a baby of another man and a mulatto child as well. I was caught in between my akuma and my head. Another problem I had was time had brought the progression of a larger lump in my belly and I had got to the point where I was struggling to hide it.

I went for my duties to Master Adams house the next morning and when I walked into his bedroom I saw Edwards drum. It stood next to the table where the used crockery was placed for collection.

I smiled to myself and thought Edward really made Master Adams believe his story about tranquillity. I had a laugh to myself and continued my duties.

One day rolled into the next until the day came when I was cleaning Master Adams bedroom and I saw the tea cups and their saucers had been placed onto the Djemba drum skin and not on the table next to it. On the table Mrs Adams had placed a hat box and there was no room for the cups to stand there as well.

I tidied the room and then as I was finished I went to remove these tea cups to take them to be cleaned.

I picked up one cup and saucer but the other was stuck so I pulled at it. The saucer had stuck to the drum skin from some of the sugary sweet tea that had spilt onto it. Master Adams made plenty of use of the sugar he harvested and had a lot of it in his own beverages.

I had one cup and saucer in one hand and I tried to pull the other cup away with my other hand. It would not come so I gave it another tug.

This was my mistake as I watched the drum lean towards me as the saucer became free. The drum fell back and then it wobbled and spiralled around before it rocked forwards and fell to the floor with an almighty thump. The cup on the stuck saucer then fell and hit the wooden bedroom floor and smashed.

"Oh no" I cried as this happened. I knew it would bring the attention of Miss Sylvester.

I placed the cup and saucer I was holding onto the table next to the door and I quickly bent down to stand the drum back up. As I did this I positioned my hand on each side of the round top but I could not get a hold to lift it up. I reached around to get a better grip and more contact to lift it with my grasp and my hand felt a handle at the side just below the top section of the drum. I lifted it back upright, which was difficult to do, and I felt my stomach pulling me down.

I knew the crash was loud and I heard the bottom stair creak which told me Miss Sylvester was coming to see what had happened.

I pushed the drum back into its position and I saw the handle I had used to stand it up and I thought to myself I had not seen it before. I pressed it and it slotted back into the lower section of the drum and it was as if it was never there. I thought I had broken the drum but I had also just mended it as well so I was pleased with myself.

I started to pick up the pieces of crockery which had fallen and smashed when I heard a landing floor board make a noise of footsteps approaching the room. The door was knocked and the handle turned and in walked Miss Sylvester.

“What on earth is going on here?” She shouted whilst gasping for her breath from climbing the stairs in a hurry.

I explained the drum had fallen over and it was not suitable for holding cups of tea. I added that Master Adams had spilled the tea and it had stuck to the skin of the drum.

Miss Sylvester accepted my story and she started to help me pick some of the smashed tea cups from the floor. She was collecting a piece from just under the bed and suddenly she gave out a huge scream and ran out of the room. I wondered what was happening so I rushed after her and saw her big chest panting heavily, hand on her chest and the other fanning her face.

“Huh huh spider!” She said in a gasp of breath.

Oh a spider, I thought. Miss Sylvester’s brow started to bead with sweat and so I knew she was very scared. I asked her where it was and she told me it ran under the bed and it was huge.

I went back into the room and took a glass which was on a tray next to a jug of water and went to look for it. I saw it near to the leg of the bed against the wall. As this little creature did not worry me I took the glass and carefully placed it over the little beast's body and legs. I took a sheet of paper which was on a desk Master Adams had for his writing and slid it underneath the glass and caught the spider.

Miss Sylvester told me to kill it and I replied we did not need to and I would take it back outside which is what I did. I took the leggy invader out to the back yard and let it go under a coconut palm.

Miss Sylvester thanked me for what I had done and we soon got back to our duties. We started preparing the food for Master Adams lunch. I had a laugh to myself later about how scared Miss Sylvester had been of the spider.

I continued with the day and was pleased when my house work was done so I could go for my rest. I ate, then bathed and sat outside with Edward.

The sun had gone down, the night had arrived, there was a full moon and the crickets played their tiny shrill in the grass.

We talked about our day and I told him about Miss Sylvester and the spider. He smiled straight away because he knew a story was coming. He liked Miss Sylvester but he knew she was Master Adams favourite worker and he liked it when she had these moments.

I told him when she saw the spider she ran out of the door faster than Abel Bowleg running for morning line up after he was punished.

Well this released an almighty roar of laughter from him and he stood up, fell forward and bent over holding onto to his belly.

I told him she was so scared that she was fanning her face like Jack Spaniard was swatting the stinging fly.

Edward bellowed again, his eyes were crying and he told me his stomach hurt from laughing so hard.

When I informed him Miss Sylvester was panting like Blackie does when he sat in the sun, he roared like a wild beast and fell to the ground and was rolling on the floor.

Edward told me to stop as he could not take anymore and I started to giggle at him laughing at me. Whilst wiggling around on the dusty earth a small wooden half-finished carving fell from the pocket of his pants.

This made me laugh even more and I then told him he had fallen just like the drum did when it toppled over in Master Adams bedroom. Edward's laugh suddenly changed to a splutter and then he coughed.

Whilst my laughter grew I added that a carved wooden object had just dropped out of his pocket was just like the handle popping out of the drum when it hit the bedroom floor. I thought this was the funniest thing I had said to Edward but this stopped his laughter to an abrupt halt.

Edward questioned me about the drum and he asked me where it was. I informed him it was in Master Adams bedroom and it had fallen over. I added that it made such a noise that along with the breaking pots; it caused Miss Sylvester to put in an appearance and gather the broken pots which is where she saw the spider.

Edward looked at me and paused and then asked me about the handle that had popped out. I told him I had pushed it back into the drum and I added that, at the time, I thought I had broken it.

Edward asked me if Miss Sylvester saw this handle and I told him she did not. This seemed to bring a slight smile back to his face and then he asked me if Miss Sylvester still goes up the stairs and I answered the same.

I stood from my seat and walked over to Edward to help pick him from the ground and as I took his hand he pulled me towards him and I felt myself falling. I pushed against his hand and this pulled my stomach and I placed my hand over it. Edward noticed me do this and he stopped pulling me.

He let go of my hand and stood up and looked at me. He placed his hands together in a prayer position and then put them against his mouth and blew out his cheeks and told me with his eyes he knew about my baby. This could not be. How could he know I thought to myself? He stroked my cheek and then he took my hand and told me to join him for a walk. He added that we would not be long as he had to get back home for some cleaning duties of his own in his room.

We strolled away from the two rows of homes and then we turned towards the field where Edward worked. When we were just about at the edge of the sugar cane and away from the view of everyone Edward stopped and he looked at me. He took hold of both of my hands and stared into my eyes. The full moon shone the only light down on us both as we stood facing each other.

He spoke softly and he told me he knew I had a secret. My akuma immediately sped up and I felt myself trembling inside. I looked back at him right into his eyes and I was trying to read his thoughts. I felt his eyes reached deep inside of mine and they were going beyond and it was a though he was filtering what I was thinking. Edward told me that as he knew a secret of mine then I could share one of his.

This made a rush run over me and my hands started to feel moist. What did Edward know about me? What was the secret he was talking to me about, I asked myself? I told him about the coins and I told him about Fiifi so there was nothing I was hiding, except the baby inside me.

After a short pause and with my curiosity penetrating my guilt Edward spoke softly and he told me he knew I was carrying a child. I took a sudden breath and he squeezed my hands and I felt this was a worry that I knew I would one day have to face. I tried to swallow but my throat was dry. I wanted to speak and I opened my mouth and my voice could not speak and then Edward put his index finger against his lips.

Edward told me this was not really a secret as he knew for a long time but he chose not to tell me.

He said the signs were easy to recognise from the way I was holding my back when I walked and the way I always put my hand over my stomach when I was sitting down.

He told me because he knew this he would tell me a secret of his and I listened closely. He spoke softly then said the handle on the drum was not for lifting it when it fell to the ground. I was confused at this statement but he added that it was actually a clandestine opening to a concealed compartment.

I did not really understand this but it sounded very much like Leopold and Jack Spaniard were right and their epithet of him as he really was crafty Eddie.

I squeezed Edward's hands and it was like a trade of each other's thoughts as we now knew something about each other that nobody else did. Edward leaned down to kiss me on my left cheek and I closed my eyes and I let his sweet lips caress my skin.

I felt quite excited really and my inner shaking had evaporated.

Edward then spoke again and he informed me that telling me he knew of my baby and the hidden opening to the drum was not the only reason for our talk and so he continued.

He said he knew I could keep things to myself and I could be trusted because he was the only person I told about the coins. He asked me not to tell of what I saw and I kept my word and this was good.

He informed me the nonsense about the tranquilly of the silent drum was not true and he knew I did too, yet I did not tell anyone and a month had past. It was a big test as he should have had Master Adams questioning him the next day but he had not heard anything.

I did not really know what to say in reply but it was true. I just acted as Kesiwaa had told me to do. I would not reveal things I knew to anyone and I nodded my response to Edward. I spoke and told him this was the way I was taught. I felt very pleased with myself about Edward recognising this and I knew Kesiwaa had taught me well.

Edward informed me because of this he could trade another secret with me. He wanted to tell me something else and I was eager to listen.

He spoke softly again and said the silent drum had been placed in the bedroom of Master Adams to collect the coins being stored in the large glass. Once there were enough coins every full moon which came he would collect the drum. He would wash the wooden frame, tighten the skin and also empty the coins from the clandestine compartment concealed within it.

I could not believe what I was hearing as this brought back the memory of Kesiwaa and how she had hidden her treasure away from Nana Apane. I felt a bit excited but also a little scared. What I was hearing sounded like a really dangerous thing to do and, of course, it was, but the way Edward was telling me his plans made me feel safe with him.

Edward squeezed my hands and leaned forward and kissed me on my right cheek and I felt a softness touch my skin which made my chest rise and my eyes close, I felt a tingle of warmth run down my neck.

I really did start to feel quite a glow had entered my body now.

Edward spoke again and told me he had a third secret to trade and I could not think there were anymore. I looked at him as he gazed into my eyes again and he asked me to tell my secret of how I felt towards him. Edward asked me if I was in love with him as he had similar feelings for me as he did with Catherine. I closed my eyes and placed my head on his chest.

This was the most difficult question to answer because I did and did not know the answer. So I asked myself.

Did I feel Edward was just my friend or did I love him? Well I knew I loved him as my friend but any more than that was what I needed to know. I had to dig deep into my akuma and ask myself without making an immediate answer. To be in this position was something I had never expected.

To catch a spider for Miss Sylvester was easy as I had done it for Kakraba in my home. To hide knowledge of what I had seen was nothing but what I was taught. To respond to a question of love well that was difficult.

My real and first love was my Fiifi and I would always be in love with him and his love was never going to be matched or even compared to. I had to think that Fiifi was gone and I had to accept it.

I was now with a child and it was my first and until this happened I was untouched and pure. I had to face the reality that my unborn child's father was the devil obroni from the white castle. This was the man who stole my innocence and changed my whole world and left his legacy inside me. I had to face this and when my child was born I would see his face every day which would haunt me. I now had a man standing in front of me who had shown me interest and friendship, laughter and confidence. He shared my love of my country and he had just told me secrets. He knew about my child and he had not said anything to offend me with this. I shared with him my love for Fiifi as he offered his knowledge for his previous love for Catherine and I had his respect.

I therefore knew my answer and I opened my eyes to see him looking at me with the same silly smile I had grown to visualise. I thought about him as I slept and when I did my duties during the day. He even seemed to be able to read the messages I sent to him at night from the brightest star in the sky.

I took a deep breath before I spoke and then I took my courage from my akuma and I told Edward I loved him.

His smile widened and his eyes sparkled then he told me the last trade was his pleasure to announce he had fallen in love with me too.

I felt a rush of warmth run through my body and I closed my eyes again almost embarrassed to see him tell me. As I did this I felt Edward kiss my lips and my head went back which made me feel like my shoulders were taken by the hands of angels which lifted my feet from the ground. I was lost in a daze and a swirl of dizziness and then my eyes opened and he was looking at me with a sweet smile.

I fell into his arms and he told me to look into the night sky. He pointed to the brightest star and spoke to me that it was shining down on us both and it gave us a blessing from all the messages we sent between us.

I was in love and it felt good and as I stood under the moon with Edward I felt I had also found my tranquillity.

CHAPTER 20: Collection

The morning sun arose from the sky like a lighted torch which indicated another warm day.

I arrived at the house and I carried my smile with me from the night before. I was so happy and I felt secure for the first time since my abjection from my home by Nana Apane.

I was greeted at the rear door by Miss Sylvester who told me Mrs Adams was going away for a few days to a neighbouring island to take some documents and to trade with another plantation. She had already got herself ready by the time I arrived and William had made the horses fitted with their harnesses and he was going to travel with her as her chaperone.

Miss Sylvester looked tired and I asked if she was well. She said she was just feeling the aches of age before she ordered me to start my duties with her sharp Caribbean tongue. She seemed to be angry with me for something but I did not know why and she told me to change the flowers in Master Adams room.

I went to the garden and I collected some big orange petal colours and mixed them with some small white ones and took them to Master Adams bedroom.

I entered the room and a soft breeze greeted me as the wind blew cool air through the open window. I changed the flowers and then I started to tidy the linen on the bed.

I was so happy I felt like I wanted to sing and I was just thinking of a beat in my head when I looked around for the drum to inspire me and it was nowhere to be seen, where was the silent drum?

I was immediately concerned and I wondered if Edwards plan had been discovered and I felt a rush of worry fill my stomach. It would mean punishment like Abel Bowleg or Cleophus Hornigold? I was really worried and I then started to think back and Miss Sylvester who was quite sharp with me. Did she know something she did not tell me about? Did she see the concealed compartment of the drum and tell Master Adams? I was starting to think all of the worst things possible.

I thought about the morning line up and Master Adams never said anything so the missing drum was a mystery to me. I carried on with my duties and I knew Master Adams was in the field, Mrs Adams was away and Miss Sylvester was in the kitchen and so I took my chance to take a look at the coins. My worry made my stomach feel uneasy and my breathing become heavy.

I parted the dresses and pulled back the wooden panel behind and I saw the large glass jar. This time there were no coins contained within it. I looked away and then I looked again. It was clearly empty of coins and there was nothing at all to be seen other than an empty glass.

This was strange as well and so I put back the wooden panel and returned the dresses back to how they were hanging and continued with my duties. I controlled my breathing by thinking about my baby and my health which I needed to concentrate on. I managed to calm my worry down and my stomach released its fluttering from inside but I could not stop thinking about my concerns for the drum and Edward.

I finished with the Bedroom and took the tea cups from the table and joined Miss Sylvester in the kitchen. She ordered me to take the brush and sweep the decking at the rear of the house free of the heavy layer of dust that had settled and then I had to collect some fruits from the bushes and trees in the yard.

As I swept the wooden flooring I saw Blackie was resting and he looked up and snarled. As I swept next to him he snapped at me and he caught my apron and he was tugging at it.

I screamed and Miss Sylvester came out and shouted at Blackie and he let go of my cloth and ran into the yard.

Miss Sylvester reminded me she wanted some mangoes, some portugal and some limes. She also wanted me to collect some coconuts cut down by Augustus the day before that was adjacent to

Martha's home.

I spoke to Miss Sylvester and said I thought Augustus worked in the field and she told me he did but sometimes he worked around the residence as he was good for digging the garden and collecting the fruits from the trees. She told me the fruits were already picked and they were in the baskets next to the coconuts. She then rested my nerves when she told me Augustus also took Edwards silent drum back to his home, so he could wash the frame and tighten the skin a he had requested.

When I heard this I wanted to scream with laughter. Of course I thought to myself, it was a full moon the night before. I remembered also that Edward did tell me he had some cleaning duties to do in his room which I thought meant he was tidying his things or washing his clothes.

Miss Sylvester informed me Augustus would be back later to return the drum and she also spoke of her praise for Edward for his gift for Master Adams.

I felt my smile return to my face which drew a question from Miss Sylvester as to why was I looking so amused. I just said "I like to smile."

I collected the fruits and the coconuts and I helped Miss Sylvester during the day and then I returned to my home.

Later in the evening I was washing myself when there was a knock at the door. It was Hannah; she said Edward was asking for me. I gave instruction I would see him after my evening meal but Hannah told me I must go to his home straight away.

I quickly dried myself and put on some clothes and went to the home of Edward. I knocked on his door and he invited me in.

I wondered what the emergency was and I was a little bit annoyed with him for disturbing me during my bathing.

Edward apologised and he took my hand and led me to his room where I saw the silent drum standing in the corner. He asked me to enter and sit down on his bed which I did.

Edward looked at me with excitement in his stare and that is when he spoke to me about his plan.

He explained to me that ever since I told him about the coins he had not stopped thinking about them. He had to trust me and he knew now he could. He then spoke to me about the silly story he had told to Master Adams about the silent drum helping him to sleep better which I knew was a lie. That was when Edward stopped talking and paused. He looked at the ground and he was bracing himself as he was ready to speak to me. Then he lifted his head and looked at me directly in to my eyes and said,

"You are going to collect the coins." He said in a soft and whispering voice. He then told me the drum was the way to collect them but he needed to be quick.

I asked Edward what the rush was and he told me he had little time to show me the silent drum's clandestine secret as Augustus had been ordered to come and collect it to take it back to Master Adams house. He then pulled the drum close to me as I sat on the bed and he turned it on its base to show me all around the frame. He asked me if I could see anything that looked like a switch to open a hidden drawer. I answered by saying I could not see anything other than the fancy carvings and patterns around the top section and the African tribal markings around the base of the bottom section.

He told me to watch carefully and I saw his hand move to just under the top section of the drum to a carved picture of a figure who was throwing a spear. He moved this weapon in the man's hand from facing down to facing up and this released the compartment I mistook for a handle. I saw the spear thrower and it reminded me of Fiifi and so it was going to be easy for me to remember.

I thought then how cunning Edward was, he really was crafty Eddie. The proof was right in front of my eyes and I looked at him and I saw the shade of Kesiwaa watching him from behind and she was smiling at his trickery and stealth.

Edward then asked me to look closer and he pointed to a slot where coins were to be placed. He told me that when a coin was put into the gap and it was I released it would fall into the hidden section of the drum. He added that inside was a sack which would catch the coins. I asked him how does he get the coins out and he laughed and told me I did not need to know.

Edward closed the open section and he asked me to try it for myself. He turned the drum around and then I sat forward and turned it until I found the spear thrower. I took my thumb and index finger and with a simple twist and a click the embedded hidden drawer popped open.

I felt quite excited and pleased with myself and Edward did too and he asked if I was alright with opening it. I responded with a smile and nod and he told me he was so happy. I stood up and Edward then took me into his arms and kissed me.

He told me the drum was to go back that evening and I should start the collection the next day.

I was a bit worried about what I was being asked to do at first but with Edward looking excited with himself I felt it would be fine to join with the plan. I agreed but then I remembered the glass jar was empty and I told this to Edward.

He responded by telling me I should not worry as it will have coins in again soon.

Edward and I kissed again and it was getting to the point where my lips touching his made a glow run from my mouth, through my body, to my toes and I felt a release of dizziness in my head.

As this was happening Edward quickly stopped and I heard a voice shouting from outside

“Good night Edward” it said. It was Augustus greeting Edward from outside his window. He had come to take the drum back to the house, so Edward pushed back in the secret compartment. He then picked up the drum and took it outside where Augustus stood with a little cart on wheels and a handle for him to pull it.

Edward placed the drum onto it and sent Augustus to the house. Augustus told me Miss Sylvester had promised to give him some coconuts and mangoes for his trouble and he looked quite happy with his payment for returning the drum.

Edward took me to sit outside his home and I spent the evening talking to him. I wanted to talk more about his plans but he told me we had to be careful.

I remembered the codes I had used with Fiifi and so I thought it was a good time to teach them to Edward.

I tried to think what they were and then it came to me. If I scratched my nose it was a signal the answer was "yes" and if I rubbed my left ear the answer was "no." I told Edward about these and he liked them and he wanted more, so, I told him about the others I could remember.

I told Edward that when I had a secret to tell him then I would tell him I wanted to hear the sound of a drum played. This was just as the silent drum contained its own secret. I added if I said I was tired then it meant I wanted something and this was because I was tired of waiting for it. A pot of boiling water in the conversation meant danger and when I told him I was hungry then the cipher meant I was hungry for my love.

Edward liked these codes and we sat talking about how hungry we were for the rest of the evening and scratching our noses. This day ended and I was feeling so happy. This was something I had not felt in a long time.

The new day came and I walked the stairs to go to Master Adams room. On the table next to the door were one teacup and a headscarf and it looked like the one that was usually worn by Miss Sylvester and I wondered why it was there. I picked it up and put it into my apron pocket to give to her when I saw her.

The one teacup was because Mrs Adams had gone to visit another plantation and she had still not returned. I am sure Miss Sylvester said she had gone on a vessel onto the sea to another island but I was not sure where this was.

I continued tidying and I knew what I had to do. I just hoped there were some coins in the jar. I was ready to try so I parted the dresses and pulled back the wooden panel and the glass was still empty. This was nothing to concern me and so I finished my duties in the room and then I went to the lower part of the house to continue to assist Miss Sylvester.

I saw her in the kitchen and she was making bread on the table and she was folding over the dough. I walked into the kitchen and I greeted her with a smile. I told her I had found her headscarf on the table in Master Adams room. As I spoke of this I took her head scarf from my apron pocket and held it in front of me for her to take from me.

Miss Sylvester's face looked like a cloud of thunder ready to burst with rain. She slammed down the bread dough onto the table and walked over to me a snatched her headscarf from my hand. It caught my little finger and jarred it making it numb for a while.

I wanted to squeal from the sharp pain I felt but I kept myself quiet. I did not know what I had done wrong and so I asked Miss Sylvester what I was to do and she sent me to the garden to tend it. She told me to clear to the weeds and then to collect some eggs from the fowl pen. She wanted me out of her way with the duties she gave me. I did not know why but I did as I was ordered.

I ended my day as the sun was closing and I felt that Miss Sylvester wanted me to be away from the house as soon as possible. As I left and made my way back to my home I met Master Adams coming the other way.

As I walked by he asked me to pass on to Edward the message that he was sleeping a lot better recently. I turned to walk away and was excited to be on my way as I was hungry to eat. I turned back to say thank you to Master Adams and I saw Miss Sylvester in an upstairs window. She was pulling a curtain together to cover it. I remember thinking, why is Miss Sylvester upstairs? It made no sense as she had no reason to be there. When she saw me looking she pulled away from the window which seemed to show a sign of guilt, but of what I thought.

I returned back to my home and I spent my evening with Edward until my tiredness encouraged me to sleep and I retired to my bed. I was finding my days were becoming a lot harder with my stomach getting bigger.

I went for my duties each day and eventually Mrs Adams returned home. I continued to look often at the glass jar until a day arrived and I pulled the panel away and there they were; the jar had coins in it. I reached up and took the glass and then removed the top, and I dipped my hand into it and took out a fist full of these round flat metal discs. I then put the top back on and returned the jar to the shelf where it sat and then I replaced the wooden panel.

I walked over to the silent drum and looked for the spear throwing man, or as I called him, Fiifi. He was near to the back so I had to shuffle it around to the front. I found this to be difficult with the coins in one hand so I thought to myself to remember next time to arrange the drum before I had the coins in my grasp.

I was listening all the time for the bottom stair to creak in case Miss Sylvester was coming but it never sounded.

I continued with my secret task and lifted the spear and out popped the hidden compartment. I took the coins and I counted five. I slotted the first one into the thin gap and let it go and it disappeared. I did not hear anything and so I put the second one in and as I let go and this time I heard it chink. It hit the first one as it landed in the sack Edward had built inside. I placed the rest of the coins into the slot and then pressed back in the hidden compartment to conceal it again.

When I was done I felt I had just achieved something although I did not know what it was but it made me feel pleased with myself.

I continued with my day and I could not wait to get back to Edward and inform him of my success. Later that day I returned to our row of houses and I went straight to Edwards home and called for him through his window as Augustus had done.

He came out of his door and he was eating his meal from a wooden bowl. I raced towards him and I threw my arms up to collect a greeting from him and he laughed at me. Placing his bowl down he met my greeting with a sweet embrace and asked me why I was so happy. I told him I took five coins leaving at least twice that many. He was so pleased with me but also asked me to lower my voice. He then invited me inside his home and we went to his room.

I told him how easy it was and he just laughed and we spent the evening talking about how my day went. I told him I had also found Miss Sylvester's headscarf in Master Adams room on the table but he did not really seem bothered about it so neither was I.

What he was interested in however was my unborn child and he asked to feel my stomach which I let him do.

This was quite a strange feeling for me as nobody had taken any concern over my pregnancy until now and it made me feel cared for and wanted. This fortified my feelings towards Edward which made me feel the worry was not only my own but also shared with him.

I continued to take the coins from the glass jar when I saw them and, as advised by Edward, I did not take too many and I was always careful to take them when I was completely sure nobody would see me.

My collection went on continuously but not always every day. I soon became quick in my gathering of the coins. I was getting good at it and my timing was always crucial. I made sure Mrs Adams was away from the house, Master Adams was in the field with the workers and lastly, Miss Sylvester was down the stairs in the kitchen.

One day I had taken out the glass jar and I had five coins in my hand. This was the critical time for me as this was where I felt the most vulnerable and scared. I still had to put the glass jar back onto the shelf, replace the wooden panel then arranged the dresses into their original place.

However, on this occasion I heard a tread on the bottom stair as it creaked and I knew Miss Sylvester was coming up them.

I did not know why as it was not usual because she found them hard to climb which is why I was given the upstairs duties.

I panicked and I was clumsy in trying to get the glass jar back onto the shelf. I only just managed it. I straightened the dresses but I felt the coins slipping from my hand as I was in too much of a rush and I dropped them. I closed the door quickly to the wardrobe and then went to pick up the coins that were scattered around the floor.

I heard Miss Sylvester coming closer and I found one coin and picked it up directly below me. I saw another had rolled to just under the bed and another went across to near the table where Master Adams had placed his tea cup which he had not drunk, and it was just left and had gone cold. He had added the milk so it was like he was going to drink it but he must have changed his mind. Another coin rolled towards the window and one stopped in front of me.

I collected four of the dropped coins except the one under the bed. The door was knocked and Miss Sylvester opened it and walked in.

I stood with my back to the table with the teacup with the cold tea and I put my hands behind me and I held on to the four coins. Miss Sylvester told me that she needed to collect the paper with the poison that was hanging down as it had attracted so many flies and bugs and it needed to be changed.

She walked over to it. I did not know what to do so I just stood where I was. Miss Sylvester spoke to me as she unhooked the length of paper. She asked me why I was just standing still like I had grown some roots in my feet.

I just told her I was deciding what to do next as I had to sweep the floor and make the bed. Miss Sylvester acknowledged this and she went to leave but stopped at the door and turned around and came up to me. She asked me why I was standing with my hands behind my back like I was guarding something and she asked me to show her what I was holding. I said that I had nothing.

She asked me to show my hands and for a moment I froze and I felt I was caught.

She stood there right in front of me with her hands on her waist. She had me trapped like a frightened animal. I saw her eyes close slightly and her brow wrinkled and she spoke again and this time there was aggression in her voice.

I started to shake and my akuma raced and I thought of the situation I was in and what I should do. I thought about what Kesiwaa would tell me to do but the answer never came to my head. I was about to take my hand with the coins and place it in front of me when I remembered my sister Kakraba when she was playing in the water as a child when she deceived me.

I placed the coins in my left hand then I put my right hand in front of me and I opened it up to show my palm to Miss Sylvester. She looked at me in a hard stern way and the she laughed.

She told me she was not a simple minded woman and she asked me to show her my left hand.

I asked Miss Sylvester why I needed to show both of my hands as I was trying to gain some time. She told me I was going to be in serious trouble if I did not show her my left palm. I looked down at my right palm and then I looked at Miss Sylvester who also looked at my bare hand. She then took a deep breath and hollered at me

"Show me the other hand!"

Her voice was so loud it was almost like a storm had blown its wind through my hair.

I had to think quickly and I remembered the cold cup of tea that was behind me on the table and I pushed my hand backwards until I felt it.

I found the rim of the cup and then I pretended to cough and as I did this I carefully dropped the coins into the tea. My cough drowned out the sound of the tiny noise the coins made as I released them into the cup.

I traded eye contact with Miss Sylvester and then I moved my arm forward very slowly. My eyes never left hers and neither did hers leave the interest in my left hand that was appearing from behind me. I was trying hard to keep my nerves and the back of my hand came into view and her eyes looked straight at it. I kept my look direct on her eyes and then I thrust my empty palm towards her and lined it up next to my right hand.

Miss Sylvester's face was like a snarling beast and I could just about see the horns rising from her forehead as she snarled at me.

"Move out of the way!" She growled.

I stepped aside then she stomped up to the table and picked up the teacup with the cold beverage still in it and asked me why Master Adams did not drink it.

I did not answer which made Miss Sylvester want to rant at me more. She suggested that he must think I had poisoned the tea which was why he did not drink it. I found the comment to be unfair but Miss Sylvester then put the teacup down and walked to the door, gave me a frosty look then left.

I took a deep breath and dropped my hands and I then took my apron and wiped the sweat away which had appeared on my brow. Miss Sylvester's words were awful and her shouting at me made me feel like crying.

I was upset at what had happened as I nearly got caught but I had to keep working and put it away from my head for now and so I carried on with my duties. I had to collect some of Master Adams shirts and so I took the ones I needed to wash and placed them in the basket I had brought with me.

When I was done I remembered the coin that had rolled under the bed and I needed to look for it. I got onto my knees and saw it right in the middle and there was no way I could reach it easily.

I lay on my side and reached out to grab it but it was too far under the bed.

I looked for something I could use to pull it to me. Master Adams had a white shirt in the basket and so I took it out and placed it under the bed and then I cast one end of the shirt towards the coin whilst I held on to the other end.

I missed the first couple of times and then I covered the coin with the shirt sleeve. I pulled the shirt back towards me and the coin was being dragged underneath. I pulled slowly and then the shirt sleeve lost its grip on the coin and I had to cast the shirt back to cover it again. I did this and it landed on top of it first time. As the last attempt of dragging the shirt back slowly did not work I decided to give it a hard sharp tug instead.

I did this and I heard a ripping of cloth as the sleeve got caught on a snag on a floorboard. I closed my eyes and thought about what I had done and I could not believe it. I had torn Master Adam's shirt and it was one of his finest ones he wore to the church on a Sunday as well.

I moved the shirt around until the barb released the shirt and then I pulled it towards me and it brought with it the coin.

I placed the shirt back into the wash basket as I needed now to get moving. I took the coin and walked up to the silent drum, turned it around until I saw the spear thrower I named as 'Fiifi and I then bent down and moved the spear. The compartment opened so I slotted the coin into the gap.

I then went to the table and I put two fingers into the cold tea and took out the other four coins I had dropped into the beverage when my hands were behind me.

I dried them off and slotted them also into the gap and then pushed the drawer back into place.

I stood and rested against the door and I wiped my brow again as I was feeling hot from the extra worry caused by my recent encounter.

I now had to think of a solution try and fix the shirt problem so I took the basket down the stairs with me and into the kitchen and I placed it onto the table in the middle. I needed to think of something and fast.

I saw Miss Sylvester outside in the garden looking at her crop of ground provision. I went outside to ask her if I needed to wash the clothes and she told me I did.

I collected some hot water boiling over the fire in the kitchen and began washing Master Adams shirts. I came to the ripped shirt and it was worse than I first thought with the sleeve torn at the shoulder. I tried to think what to do and I remembered Kesiwaa lost some of Nana Apane's clothes in the local river or she blamed them on the rocks she washed them on. Well I could try that but I do not know where the local river is and there are no rocks to tear the material. I had to think quickly and so I took the sleeve and I ripped a small part off of the shirt and placed it in my apron pocket. I then took the washed shirts and I placed them out to dry over a hanging rope in the garden.

Miss Sylvester went into the house as I finished hanging the shirts. I returned also but before I stepped into the door I took the piece of cloth out of my apron pocket and dropped it into the flat wooden box where Blackie slept. I thought to myself that I will now watch to see the little monster get the blame for the shirt and I had a smile behind my cheeky smirk.

I continued my duties for the day and then I went to my home to rest. Later I went to visit Edward. He was worried when I told him about the coins rolling around the floor and when Miss Sylvester had me trapped but he smiled when I informed him of what I did. This smile developed into full laughter when I told him about the shirt and the piece I dropped in Blackie's box. We laughed until tears ran from our eyes.

This evening we spoke until it got quite late. I was lying down on Edward's bed and he joined me. We had talked for most of the evening and Edward placed his arm around me and I snuggled up to him. Edward spoke of a future as a free man one day and he told me he hoped this day would come, and soon. He added this was his dream and he would be able to leave this land and maybe see the big world he had heard of.

I knew why he felt like this and I informed him about my home village. As we spoke it allowed the night air to slowly infiltrate into my eyes. I yawned from its sleepy effect and I felt like I was in my sanctum. Edward then told me it felt good to have me with him and I thought the same about him. I felt a little cold this evening and I encouraged Edward to put his arm over me to warm me. Edward yawned and then he spoke. He said he wished every night I was with him so I could fall asleep in his arms. I knew exactly what he meant as I was so relaxed with his arm around me and my head on his chest.

It was so good and Edward advised me he would soon walk me across the yard in between our homes and take me back to my own place of dwelling. He blew out the candle and I slipped into the sleepy cushion of his comfortable embrace.

CHAPTER 21: Hole

I felt Edwards arm resting over my shoulder and I needed to move it as it was stifling me. Yet I was so settled in the slumber I was having so I just pushed his hand from resting over my chest and shuffled myself around and then I nestled against the comfort snuggling me.

This had a relaxing calm on my back which had started to ache from the weight of my unborn child which was reshaping my body. At this time I was aware I had to wake but I was so comfortable that the sleep kept my eyes closed and peaceful. I then shivered as I felt a chill run down my arm and I knew my body was slightly cold.

Edward must have relit the candle he put out because in my drowsiness I saw a light irritating my eyes.

I lifted my head and then I looked at the side of my bed to see where my clothes were and I saw Edward's shirt and pants. It was then I realised I was not in my room. I had slept with Edward on his bed. The candle was not lit as the light in the room was the sunlight shining a shaft of a golden beam through a slight gap in the window shutter of the room.

At first I placed my head back onto the cushion but then I realised the situation was not right and I raised myself from Edwards embrace and stood up from the bed.

Edward was disturbed from his sleep by me and he opened his eyes. He gave a big yawn which brought on one from me and I raised my arms to stretch. Edward told me I had to get back to my own home which was across the dividing yard on the other side of the row of homes.

I felt that I had stood up too quickly, as my head started to turn and spin around and I felt like I was going to fall.

I felt my legs buckling underneath me and I put my hand out and called Edward's name.

I felt his hands steady me and I sat back down on the bed. I touched my stomach. I was feeling weak in my body. I just wanted to lie down and sleep again but Edward kept talking to me and advising me to stand and go to my home. He saw I was weary so he relented and let me lay down again. He took a cloth and reached to a jug of water nearby, dampened it, it and placed it on my brow.

This refreshed me and was I able to open my eyes more clearly and I saw Edward stare back at me. His face caught the beam of light leaking through the window. It was like a beacon that lit his eyes and they sparkled like the glistening of water.

This image of Edward in my vision was long as I captured an expression of a person who really showed he cared about me.

He bit his lower lip and then he turned over the cloth on my brow before he kissed my mouth and he held this sweet touch until my eyes closed. I did not need the use of them as the touch from his lips increased the sense I experienced. I felt as though his kiss was taking away all of my feelings and sending them to my mouth.

It was as though the sun beam created a flash, then a spark, then a fire which raced down my spine.

He pulled his face back and my eyes released themselves from his lips they were drawn to. I looked at Edward's face and the beam was not shining into his eyes this time.

I looked at the window and so did Edward and there was something that had dimmed the sun's ray.

As we both noticed this Edward put his finger to his lips as a signal for me to not speak. Edward sensed there was somebody outside his home.

I was nervous as Edward crept towards the window and he slowly leaned towards it to see what or who was outside. Just as he got close the light appeared again from the sun and Edward pulled away. He then leaned again towards it and this time he managed to spy through the small gap and then after a brief moment of vigilance he turned away and gestured that he saw nothing.

Edward spoke softly and told me I should go back to my home. He helped me stand from his bed and then he took me into his arms, held me and kissed me, which calmed my worry for the moment and eased my head from spinning again.

We walked towards the door and Edward unlatched it. We stepped outside. I looked at the ground and noticed it had rained in the night. My eyes saw the low morning sun and Edward then looked to the sky and he told me the dark clouds above were the reason for the sun being blocked from the window as another heavy shower was coming. We were both worried over a rain cloud and I had a little smile to myself at our worry over nothing. As we stepped on to earth it felt soft and the soil was sodden and in the air there was a slight chill.

I then heard something which made the fright of worry strike me like I had felt before and I started to shake. This noise took me back to Assin Manso. I had a flashback of the sound of the hounds that tore the flesh whilst shredding the bibini as he tried to run from them fearing for his life. The spark of the fire ember that had just lit a torch to my mouth from Edward's lips now stung its fierce heat into my chest.

It was the yapping sound of Blackie and I looked towards the house.

"Howl!" He barked, with a full voice. There he was standing looking at us along the muddy path that led to Master Adams house. He started walking and he snarled as he looked in our direction. He ended his growl and came towards us and I felt my nerves deliver a shudder through my body.

I put my hands to my mouth and watched as Blackie picked up his pace. He started to run until he was racing at us faster and faster. He was at a speed quicker than any spears Fiifi could fly in the air.

Edward grabbed my waist and then stood in front of me with his arms behind him protecting me as Blackie charged right at us.

As I looked over the shoulder of Edward I saw Blackie take a stride just a short distance in front of us and then leap directly at us and his jaw took Edwards arm.

Edward was knocked back and he fell onto me. I lost my balance which caused me to drop to the ground.

Edward had Blackie's mouth over his forearm as he was protecting me from him and he told me to get inside his home. I managed to push my heavy body to stand and I staggered towards Edward's door and went in. I heard more barking from Blackie until Edward joined me inside. His forearm was bleeding and he slammed the door hard behind him.

Blackie was scratching the door and the yapping continuously. It felt like he was going crazy as his howling grew louder.

I covered my ears and squatted in a corner of the room while Edward stood with his back to the door.

Edwards bleeding arm dripped onto the floor and I started to panic. I knew he needed help but he looked like he could not move and his face gave a look of pain. I went to his room and found the cloth he had held to my head and took it to him and I tried to clear the blood. I saw there was a deep puncture wound in his forearm from Blackie's bite.

Edward was looking like he was in a state of shock and so I asked him to go to his bed to lie down. I did not know what to do. I could not leave his home and go to get help from Martha as the snarling and scratching at the door from Blackie prevented me. Edward lay down on his bed and I took his head and cradled him.

All I could do was to wait and keep his arm clear of the flow of his blood until it stopped. I wrapped the damp cloth around Edwards arm and made sure it was just short of tight.

I cannot remember how long we were sitting on his bed but the growls of Blackie eventually stopped. I heard the voice of Master Adams telling him to be quiet which was why the growling ended.

At last the vicious hound was silenced. It also reminded me of when the fallen bibini at Donkor Nsuo was stopped from making any noise but this time the savage attack had a different result and

Edward was still alive.

I heard Master Adam's voice as the door to Edwards home opened, he immediately spoke of the blood on the floor. His voice was quite tame and he was questioning what had happened and I prompted Edward to stand and go and see our master.

Edward was still shaking and he was looking quite disturbed by this mauling from Blackie. He looked afraid at being confronted by Master Adams and he tried to hide his arm.

I felt a relief from the initial worry as Master Adams walked towards Edward and William was with him.

The room went quiet for a brief time and then Master Adams made the enquiry to what disturbance had woken him at such an early hour.

I dare not speak and I left the talking to Edward who it seemed left the talking to me. The silence in the room made me feel uncomfortable and so I decided to speak. I needed to tell Master Adams of the behaviour of Blackie. I informed him that Blackie had been snarling and yapping then charged at us both as Edward walked me home. I looked at Edward for support.

Edward was not responding and he was still looking nervous. His eyes told the story of his horror.

Master Adams asked why I was being escorted back to my home at the early hour when I should be sleeping.

I looked at Edward and I saw his eyes were about to spark a fire and his body trembled. I sensed something was wrong and so I asked him if the pot of water he was supposed to boil for me was ready. This was our code for trouble was coming.

Edward waited before he answered me and he took his untouched arm and scratched his nose showing he understood me.

Master Adam's asked us both what the pot of water was that I was asking about and I responded by telling Master Adams that Edward had caught his arm on a sharp pointed cane shoot, whilst he was working in the field on the previous day, and he had asked me to take a look as it was still giving him some pain.

Master Adams then wanted to look at Edwards arm and I removed the cloth showing a blooded puncture to Edward's skin.

Master Adam's told me to see to Edward and to bind his wound and then he reminded us the line-up for the day was only a short time away and I should be quick.

He then spoke to William and they left. I looked again at Edwards arm and the wound made by Blackie and I started to my clean it with some water.

I was concerned as to why Edward was looking nervous and when I asked him he confirmed my suspicions.

Edward told me it was not acceptable for me to stay at his home after a certain time which was normally when everyone went back to their own retreat.

Edward explained that I could have been in trouble if I had not spoken about helping him with his arm. I smiled as Edward told me it was a smart reply and Master Adams had believed it. I felt quite pleased with my answer although it was really a mistake as the pot of boiling water was my code and it was taken by Master Adams as a real pot of boiling water for Edwards wound which I thought was quite funny. I spoke to Edward about this and he told me my words must have been coming through my voice from the grace of God, (Nyame Adom).

After a short while the light increased through the shuttered window and the day looked like it was to be another warm and wonderful one.

I never knew how wrong I was. A few moments past and then there was an almighty roar and it was the voice of Master Adams. I looked at Edward and he looked at me and we were both wondering what the problem was this time as he returned forcing the main door to slam against the wall.

Master Adams heavy steps brought him closer to Edward who was sitting on his bed and he was immediately followed by William.

Master Adams looked at me and his eyes focused directly into mine. He asked me when I had actually come to see Edward at his home.

I felt this question was meant to trick me and I also sensed Master Adams could not know the truth so I called his bluff. I answered that I had walked over early in the morning to make sure my care for Edward's injury did not affect my duties.

Master Adams took a long pause and then he informed me that however my journey was made, it was taken without my foot imprints in the wet soil. The only marks beyond the door in the sodden earth were the ones made by himself and William and among them were the paw prints of Blackie.

He told me how he knew I was light on my feet as he did not always hear my steps in his house. He added that only if I had the wings of an angel could I cross the yard and not leave my foot impression in the muddy earth.

Master Adams looked hard at me and I saw his eyes squint as he reached to the depth of my thoughts.

I looked right back at him and then I noticed William behind him shake his head sideways in warning.

Master Adams spoke to me in a different tone. This time his voice was soft. He asked me again when I had come to visit Edward and this time I was backed into a corner. I had no answer but the truth.

I saw Master Adams eyes and they appeared to have a fire behind them. His mouth was turned down and he stood rigid so I took a breath and I told him I had been in the home of Edward from the night before and was now ready to go back to my own home.

Master Adams face was no warmer when I informed him of this and he reminded me I had just lied to him and it was not acceptable.

He added that this would be dealt with later.

He gave a brief, forced, false smile and then he looked behind him and spoke to William. He informed him he would have to arrange for the mornings line up a little earlier than usual. I then saw a look on Master Adam's face that concerned me. I felt uneasy and looked at Edward who dropped his head down.

William nodded to agree with Master Adams who then told me to go with them to avoid Blackie. He added I was to stay in my room until I was called for and I did not need to come out for the blowing of the horn on this occasion.

They escorted me to my home and as I crossed the yard I saw the horrible hound pacing up and down with his head down and not making any sound.

When Blackie lifted his head to look at me I looked right into his eye and gave him my thoughts of anger towards him and he looked away from me.

I returned to my room and sat on my bed with consternation running through my head. I knew I was in trouble and the strange thing was it was for doing nothing. I had been taking the coins from the jar and hiding them and I also tore Master Adams shirt and then gave the blame to Blackie and these things were what I have done with deception. Yet staying with Edward was something innocent and it comforted me. The problem was I lied to Master Adams and I knew I was going to be taught that this was not to be tolerated.

I sat on my bed and I felt my stomach and it was moving and I knew my unborn child was talking to me. It was as though it was telling me everything would be fine. This was my only comfort now as I start to worry over my fate this morning.

I looked out of my window and I saw the clouds moving over the sky, they looked dark. I then saw a flash of bright light and soon after this their came a heavy rumble of thunder.

That was when the horn was blown and I heard Hannah leave to join the line. I stayed behind as ordered.

I waited and the worry started to make me feel sick and my mouth became dry. I thought back to how I had sat in a filthy squalor of the White building that kept me for many weeks yet this wait for Master Adams to beckon me was not ending and the longer it went on the more restless I became. I stood up and started to pace up and down my room.

My stomach and my back were hurting, I was starting to feel hot and I took the fan next to my bed and cooled myself down. I was never hot in the morning and so I knew I was elevating my concern the longer I waited for my fate.

Eventually I heard the outside door was opened and there were voices in the main sitting room.

I heard Master Adams voice and then the footsteps came towards my door.

A knock followed and I opened the door and I was told by William to walk with him.

I followed him along the hallway and I saw Master Adams was standing in the main room. He spoke to me as I approached.

He told me I was doing very well with my duties in his house and he also informed me that Mrs Adams liked me. He even told me that Miss Sylvester had spoken highly about me but what he did not like was the fact that I had stayed at Edwards home, and that when I was asked I did not speak the truth.

Master Adams walked up to me and he told me that for this I would have to be taught lies are not accepted. He then ordered William to bring me along and he turned and left my home.

As directed I followed him with William behind me.

Outside looked dark and as I stepped through the door the sky lit up with another flash of light and then I saw the rain was starting to fall. Moments later a loud rumble of thunder roared its deep noise and it was as though the sky was angry with me.

We walked towards the home of Martha and I saw the wooden

seat with the holes in it where Abel Bowleg was made to sit and I started to become nervous.

Blackie was walking at the side of me and he was looking at me and showed me his teeth. I don't know why but I looked down and I showed my teeth back at him and he yapped at me which prompted Master Adams to look back and shout at him.

I lifted my head and I felt the spray of the rain hit my face and I closed my eyes. I felt it was getting stronger and the wind then blew cold against my hands, chilling my fingers.

I looked ahead and I saw Edward was standing next to the wooden seat and I felt uncomfortable. It was at this point I hoped that my stomach and my unborn child could not be hurt.

Edward stood with his head down and as we approached and I saw he was shivering.

Master Adams told me to stand next to Edward and he then spoke to us about the rules of his plantation which was that it was not permitted for anyone to be away from their homes after the time of retreat.

He then spoke to William and asked him if he heard the way I lied to him and he replied to say he did.

Master Adams asked me about the tattle I spoke to Edward, about the pot of boiling water being ready.

I replied I needed the water to bathe Edwards wound to which Master Adams reminded me there was no water boiling when he arrived at Edward's home.

Then Master Adams asked me how Edward had caught his hand on a jagged barb of a cane when he had arrived from the field without any injury. He advised me he had just spoken to Augustus who was working alongside Edward and he informed him Edwards arm was without any wound when he left the field for the day.

Master Adams then thanked Edward for the gift of the drum he had given to him and he did not know how it worked but he was sleeping a lot better.

Then as the heavy cloud continued to shower us with its cold and wet drizzle, the door of Martha's home opened and out walked Augustus carrying a big pot which was steaming from under the lid. The pot was so hot that Augustus had cloths over the handles to stop the heat penetrating through the cloth through to his hands.

Augustus was struggling with it and he just managed to reach us before he placed it on the ground in front of both me and Edward.

Martha then stepped from the same doorway as Augustus and she was covering her head with a cloth. She walked over to stand near to William who nodded to acknowledge her.

Master Adams asked Martha to be vigilant and he then asked me to show him how I was going to treat Edwards wound.

I really did not know what I was supposed to do but of course he knew this. I never answered this question and I remained tight lipped.

I was asked again by Master Adams to tend to Edwards arm and he fortified this with asking me if I knew how to heal the wound and I shook my head to answer I did not.

He ordered Augustus to remove the lid from the pot and as he did I saw the steam flow out and reveal it was full of freshly boiled water.

The rain was pouring down and this was spitting onto the pot which made the steam flow more. Augustus was then ordered by Master Adams to leave us and he turned and ran back to the house from where he came.

Master Adams walked over to Edward and he told him he now had his boiling water he could use it to treat his wound. Edward looked at Master Adams nervously and he started to shake and this time it was not from the cold rain.

Master Adams raised his voice and he spoke to Edward with a sternness telling him to put his arm into the pot of water.

I could see Edward was holding back from Master Adams order as he had a look of terrific fright on his face. Master Adams then asked William to join Edward and help him put his injured arm into the pot of water for treatment the way I had wanted.

William walked over and he took a hold of Edwards arm and he pulled him towards the pot then he asked him to remove his rain sodden shirt.

Edward was slow to do this and when it was removed he stared at the steam rising from the water and then his eyes looked like he was in a state of shock.

Blackie barked as if he was joining in the giving of orders and Master Adams spoke again. He ordered Edward to put his arm in the water as the treatment I was going to give him.

The third request was received by a rejection from Edward and so Master Adams told William to help him.

William took Edwards arm and he pulled it towards the steam and as he got close I tried to look away, this prompted Master Adams to order me to look at my treatment to remedy Edward's injury.

He then spoke to Martha and he told her that I was the new root doctor for the plantation and this was my idea of healing Edward's injury. He added that with my own words the pot of boiling water was for "bathing Edwards wound."

This was not what I meant, my cipher to Edward had been taken at face value and now Edward was going to be scolded by the boiling water. I could not bear to watch.

William pulled Edwards arm closer to the water and he started to shake his knees. The rain was pouring quite heavily now and it was running off from Edwards face and dripping from his chin.

Master Adams looked at me and he shouted and asked me if this was the way to treat Edwards arm. He demanded an answer so I replied that it was not the way to cure the injury. As soon as I spoke this prompted Master Adams to cease with his treatment towards

Edward and he ordered William to stop. He let go of Edward's wrist.

Master Adams then spoke to Edward and he asked him what kind of friend I must be who was going to make him put his arm in a pot of boiling water and Edward did not answer.

He then told Edward that for this mistake I would have to be taught to pay for my lies and deception, and because I was going to make Edward suffer from wrong treatment for his injury. This was not true but what could I do? The problem was now if Edward did not put his arm into the water would it mean I will have to do it? Master Adams looked at William and he nodded his head. This prompted him to walk over to me. He then gave his order to take me to the nearby tree and tie me to it and Martha followed.

William walked up to me and then he went around behind me and he pulled the back of my dress, he started to undo the lace. I felt him tugging and this pulled my body backwards and I had to step back. Once he was done he pulled the top of my dress from my shoulders. As he did this the sky lit up from a bolt of lightning.

Master Adams took from his waist what looked like a coiled rope which was thick at one end and as he released it I saw it was the same type of lash the obroni used at the Nnonkonsuo River and I now knew my fate.

I was to be flogged by Master Adams but what about my baby, he could not touch me whilst I was with my child? At this moment I realised I was breathing heavy and shaking and I looked at Edward who watched me with the same eyes Fiifi did when I was chosen by Nana Apane.

William walked to stand in front of me and he pulled my top down and exposed my chest. I felt the ultimate humiliation. He then stepped aside to allow Master Adams to see me and my condition was clear at this moment. My breasts were swollen with the food for my baby and my belly was also on show to my audience.

My secret was out for all to see. I caught Edward looking in disbelief as his jaw dropped open as my exposure was the ridicule of my bare flesh.

Master Adams then asked William to wait and he spoke to me about my stomach and he gave out a great deep roar. He laughed at my round belly and spoke to William that he suspected I was carrying a child when he bought me at the market but he admitted he had forgotten all about it. He added he was so pleased I was going to have a child as he would have another field worker in a few years and he would not have to spend any money. I remember thinking at this time that my child would never go through this degrading shame and one day he will be free and will know about this wrong doing.

Master Adams face was suddenly beaming a huge smile and he could not take his eyes from me.

I was concerned about what was going to happen to me yet it appeared now that my unborn child was exposed it caused a change in Master Adams plans.

He stood in the rain looking at me and I felt his eyes observing every part of my body as the rain soaked my skin. He watched me for quite a while without a flicker of his eyelids. It was an intense look he gave me. I took my bitterly cold hands and I held them into a fist and I placed them whilst shivering in front of my body.

He could see I was becoming extremely cold with my shaking, but I was also extremely scared.

Master Adams was watching my body with more of an interest in just my belly and I felt embarrassed and uncomfortable so much that I actually wanted to cry but I knew this would not make any difference to my fate that morning.

Master Adams seemed not to care that we were all standing in the rain. He told William to take me to the hole in the ground which was next to the wooden seat that had accommodated Abel Bowleg when he had his punishment. William took my arm and I held it closed to my body. I tried to keep what little warmth I could and keep my chest from being exposed.

At this stage Martha spoke to Master Adams and shouted,

"Master Adams you are going too far, please don't do this!"

Master Adams stomped ahead and shouted back,

"Stay out of this Martha this is no business of yours!"

We walked towards the wooden seat and as we did this I walked past Edward who put his head down as if he was respecting my shameful exposure.

We past the seat and arrived at this muddy hole that was now filling with rain water. Blackie strolled over poking his snout in and he started sniffing the ground.

I looked down and William told me to lie over it with my stomach in the gap.

I thought what is this misery being given to me that it would make me to lay down on wet mud with my belly in a watery hole?

I crouched down and reached my hands out in front of me and then William ordered me to place them next to the wooded logs that were poking from the ground.

I did this and William tied my hands to the embedded stakes with a heavy rope.

I felt the cold of the water in the hole against my stomach and my body started to shiver. The cold rain was splattering against my back as it splashed the mud in front of my face.

Blackie started to sniff my head and then he licked my face and I got a scent from his mouth which smelled of rancid and mouldy bone. The beast then picked up his back leg and I felt the heat of his water spray over my face and some of the bitterness seeped into my mouth. Blackie trotted away as though he had given me his payback for the way I had showed my teeth at him. I showed them to him again and this time I growled at him as well. He looked at me and he snarled and then he walked away and hid under the seated bench that had kept Abel Bowleg shackled and tortured.

I heard footsteps and then Master Adams spoke and he advised me that my payment for telling him untruths was ten cuts from his whip.

The rain continued to hit the ground hard and it splattered against the muddy ground and this was flicking into my face. I closed my eyes and put my forehead on the ground as I waited for my beating. I looked up and I kept my back strong and I felt my belly hanging down into the hole below me. I heard William clear his throat and I knew he was standing at the side of me. I then heard Master Adams call to Edward to come and stand over me. Martha was also ordered to join the others and be at my side.

Martha spoke again,

"Master Adams I beg of you, I plead with you, please don't lay your hand on her!"

Master Adams shouted back,

"Don't speak to me now Martha. This is what needs to be done and so help me, it will!"

I knew the pain would come and so I braced myself and my teeth clasped together. I closed my eyes and I called for my silent drum to help me endure the pain. I heard it coming to the forefront of my head and it started to filter into my ears with its Bam Bam Bam.

The sharp bite from the leather tail of Master Adams whip had not stung my skin but I was ready for it to take its pain on me.

My silent drum was now beating and pounding to a thump in my head and I played it loudly.

Inside my thoughts there was nothing that could hurt me and there was a feeling of numbness like a shield over my bare back. I closed my eyes to better hear the Bam bam bam of my silent srum.

Then without any signal, "Crack!" came the first slash of the tail against my skin and it was like a hot knife had just scorched my flesh.

My drum fed me my beat as it pounded in my head.

"Bam Bam Bam Du Du Du Bam Bam Bam Du Du Du Bam Bam Bam Bam bam bam du du du bam bam bam du du du, bam ba",

Then again "Crack!"

"Bam bam bam du du du bam bam bam du du du bam bam bam du du du bam bam bam du du du"

Again, "Crack!"

"Bam bam bam du du du bam bam bam du du du bam bam bam bam bam"

"Crack!"

"Bam bam bam du arrgh bam bam du du bam argh argh," I was losing my control and this hurt.

"Crack!"

"Bam bam arrrghhh" this pain was ripping my shoulders away from my bone with each strike. I screamed and my eyes drew water immediately they were running from the pain as each lash ripped my flesh with its sting.

I felt one strike seemed to meld into another and my eyes saw a glazed flash of light as the lightning bolt lit up the flooded ground in front of me.

I did not know if or when it stopped as my body just hurt constantly with burning across my shoulders but I felt myself being pulled by my arms which made my bosom stretch in front of me and my stomach feel heavy as if it was pulling me down.

I could barely see but I heard a voice speak as Master Adams informed me that as I needed to rest at night in the same home as Edward then maybe I should have the silent drum Edward built in my own room for help with my sleeping. So this statement was to be the end of the coin collection and the game was over for Edwards dream.

My eyes struggled to open and a haze fell like a mist across them.

I felt myself being lifted from the ground and then I sensed my stinging aching body being placed on a soft flat cushion. I was laid on my side.

I could not lay on my front because of my unborn child and I could not lie on my back because of the lacerations that opened my skin.

Soon after I heard the voice of Martha and I knew I was going to be treated with her healing touch. I heard her speaking in a language which I did not recognise and saw her figure standing over me and it was as though she was raised from the ground with her arms stretched above her head. I could not see her face as it was blurry but she appeared to be wearing a mask and a strange robe.

Martha started saying something but I did not care to understand it as all I wanted was for the pain to end. She was speaking with a husky voice and she used words that sounded African.

I sensed something very powerful was happening and it was like Martha was chanting some kind of spiritual words at me. I managed to look out of the corner of my glazed eye and I saw her with a candle in her hand and then she blew some dark powder over me.

I was all confused and at one point I thought I saw some spirits wrapping themselves around my painful body.

I felt a cushion of numbness encase me and the pain eased at which point I wanted to tell Martha that whatever she was doing was working.

"Martha me daase" (Martha thank you), was all I could think of at this time and then I felt my eyes rolling and my vision vanished in front of me.

CHAPTER 22: Pockets

As I woke from my slumber I was more tired than from when a new day started. It was like I had taken some kind of herbal remedy that had forced me to sleep and as a consequence I had to fight to open my eyes.

I lay on my side and my body was hurting. The lashes felt like they had almost cut deep inside me through my back to my chest. My bosom were still exposed and my belly was swollen which was showing my naked skin from my waist up.

I heard something grinding and I opened my eyes and I looked up and I saw Martha standing over a table next to my bed. She was mixing something in a bowl and every now and then she sniffed and spoke to herself. I could not make out what she was saying but I don't think I was supposed to hear her anyway.

She sat beside me and placed something cold onto my back and I winced with the soreness around my shoulders. Martha told me she had smeared a cool soothing paste over my wounds. It would slowly heal the lacerations that marked me. She then added that she got the sap from a plant in the yard which she called maguey which she informed me had healing juice in its leaves.

I was also feeling a little dizzy and Martha assisted me to sit up and she gave me a tea to drink. As I took the cup from her my hands were shaking so Martha helped put the drinking vessel to my lips.

Martha spoke to me and her voice was not her usual one. Her words were mumbled but she was informing me she would heal me in no time at all. I just had to just absorb the pain and it would soon go away. Her sniffles told me she had been crying and I responded to her that my back was now stinging me and as I said this I felt my eyes release some tears. Martha then spoke something to herself as my eyes were closed and she said,

"Master Adams has been too cruel this time and he needs to be taught a lesson from our spirits." What did she mean by this I thought?

Martha responded by kissing my forehead and then another set of sniffles was greeted with her handkerchief taken from her apron which she place against her nose.

I managed to drink some more tea but I needed to rest my aching body and Martha help me to lie down again on my side.

I heard a voice outside my window and Martha asked who it was and the reply came from Augustus. Martha asked him what he wanted and he responded that he had brought something for my room. Martha took a bed sheet from a drawer and placed it over me before going to greet Augustus and as she left she kissed her teeth.

Moments later I heard some banging in the hall way outside and then my door opened and Martha held it as Augustus carried in the silent drum.

My heart raced quickly when I saw it and he placed it at the end of my bed on the floor. Augustus just spoke to say he had brought the drum on the orders of Master Adams and it was to be kept in my room to help me to rest. I knew what point Master Adams was making but he did not realise that to take the drum from his room had more of a meaning to me than not being able to sleep.

Augustus then added he would not mind borrowing the drum for himself if the power it contained was true and it would help him to rest at night.

He explained that after carrying it from Master Adams house it had made him tired. I did not feel the desire to reply until Augustus added he must have grown weaker as the drum was heavier than when he carried it to Master Adams home on his push trolley.

I had to speak and I reminded Augustus there was a slight uphill slope on the way from Master Adams home.

Augustus acknowledged my information and he left, however I knew the reason the silent drum was heavier was because it had coins inside. I also knew I was weak but my thoughts remained as sharp as a rodent's teeth and as clear as a blue sky.

Martha closed my door after Augustus left and she told me to rest, which I did. I closed my eyes and let myself relax.

I managed to sleep even though my body hurt. I woke when Martha opened the door. The room was dark. She walked into my room with a candle as the evening had arrived. She told me I had a visitor and I thought Master Adams was coming to pester me again and I closed my eyes ready for another battle of his mind.

I waited for his voice to invade my ears but I just felt Martha kiss my forehead again. Her presence alone made me feel better.

Another kiss and this time it was on my cheek and it scratched me and so I opened my eyes to see Edwards face flickering in the light of the candle flame.

I saw his eyes sparkle and for a moment the pain over my back was gone. Edwards smile then lifted my mouth to turn with his and he held my hand.

I had a warmness reach into my body which began with Edwards touch of my fingers and it flowed down my spine. It felt like it was healing me from inside and I knew with him being with me, and Martha treating me with the sap from the maguey leaf, I was going to recover.

Edward spent most of the evening with me as he did for the next five evenings from dusk until the time was up for him to retreat back to his home. Eventually I was told by Martha that I had to start my duties back at the house again and she had done her best to heal my wounds.

During the evenings Edward spent sitting with me as I healed he told me he was made to watch me receive my beating which almost broke him. His feelings for me were stretched to its upmost as he worried about my pain and the degrading way I was treated. My body being exposed in the way it was and with my belly carrying a child. He felt my humiliation and this made him angry to begin with which soon turned into words being spoken by him of a way to seek revenge.

Edward asked me how I was able to hide my belly from anyone knowing and I informed him I had taken some thread and a needle and readjusted my clothes to fit my ever growing waist. Edward asked me how I was at sewing material and I laughed and told him I was very good, which was so good that nobody even knew I had altered my dresses.

He spoke to me softly so nobody would hear us in my room that he was now even more determined to collect Master Adams money.

He informed me that one day Master Adams will have his day of humiliation and I would be there to see it. Edward said that we were going to continue to collect the coins. My first thought was that the silent drum was now in my room and it was not going to be used again. Edward told me he had another plan which would enable us to carry on with our secret task.

I was eager to hear what he had to tell me and I was also feeling the same as he was. My desire to take the coins, which I now saw as payment from Master Adams for the way he tortured me, had grown strong.

Edward explained to me that I would have to sew some pockets into each of my dresses and these were where I would place the coins on my visit to Master Adams room.

I would then bring them back to my room and as before I would place then into the clandestine slot in the silent drum.

When Edward told me this I felt a twitch of excitement in my belly until I realised my baby was moving which made me think maybe it was happy as well as it heard Edwards voice.

Edward said that I had to sow ten pockets into my work dresses. These pockets needed to have an over pocket so what went in stayed in. He then added these pockets needed to be spaced well apart to prevent them from chinking together whilst I was carrying them. He suggested I sow these folds into the lower part of my dresses so they would be easier to place them when hiding the coins.

So my dresses were going to carry these hidden purses and we were going to continue with our plan. We also had the silent drum in my room so it was not necessary to carry it to and from the house.

I told Edward I liked this secret contrivance and I would set about sewing my dresses straight away. Edward replied that I was a very brave woman and he found strength in himself which he drew from me.

I stood from my bed and I felt the wounds on my back had started to heal, yet they were still sore as the crusts of the healing scabs broke when my skin was stretched. I had to move gently but I found my first dress which was hanging from a peg on the wall and I showed it to Edward.

He pointed to the inside of the lower hem of the dress as an ideal place for a pocket and we then agreed on the same distance of each fold thereafter.

I had one more day to rest my wounds before Master Adams wanted me back in the house doing my duties and so I told Edward I would start making the dress purses the following morning.

Later that evening when Edward had left, I asked Martha if she had any sewing thread and she told me she did. She asked me what I wanted it for.

My answer was simple, I wanted to make some clothes for my baby and so Martha replied to tell me she would get the cloth and a needle and thread for me in the morning.

It was also my last day at the home of Martha and I had to go back to my own room at the same house as Hannah.

I rested and thought of the duties I had to start in the morning. My sleep was uninterrupted and actually quite heavy and I remember waking up after dreaming of my home in Africa.

I stretched my back and I felt some of the wounds pull in areas across my shoulders but apart from that I woke feeling a lot better. Martha looked at my wounds then applied some more cooling paste.

She also handed me a small light wooden pot with a lid and some thread she had taken from Violet Bowleg and some cloth she had sent for me. I removed the wooden lid of the pot to reveal some needles and a thimble. Now Violet knew I was carrying a baby she was keen to give me some material, however she only gave me a small piece because she insisted on making the clothes for my baby herself.

Martha left me and I began to sew the pockets on my dresses and I remembered how Kesiwaa had taught me when I was younger while sowing Nana Apane's robes and Kakraba's dresses.

I had to make some clothes as it was the reason for the cloth so I had to be quick. I had three dresses and there had to be ten pockets in each. I sowed all day until my fingers became sore from pushing the needle but I did not let this minor ache stall my production.

Finally I was done and it was time for me to have my final evening of rest and as I lay down Edward came to see me.

I told him the pockets were in place and he wanted to try one out so he went to the silent drum to take a coin. In no time he had one in his hand. I asked him how he took the coin from the silent drum so quickly and he just smiled and gave me a sweet eyed wink.

I showed him the dress and he looked for the pocket and he could not find it. He asked me if I was playing with him as he saw no folds on the inside of my dress, so I took it from him and lifted the bottom edge, I knew where to look. I asked Edward to give me the coin and manipulated it into the hidden purse that sat in a double fold in the dress lining.

I then showed Edward and he was scratching his head as he could not find the coin.

I took the dress and just as Edward did earlier in no time at all I had the coin in my hand. Edward looked at me with an enquiring face and I just smiled and returned the sweet eyed wink back to him.

Edward laughed and this made Martha shout at us to keep the noise down as she was resting.

We were ready to begin with the collection and I was prepared for my day ahead so Edward left me for the night. This was my last day to be treated by Martha and so I gathered my dresses.

Before I left I saw two golden shaddock fruit on the table and I thought how juicy they looked. I picked them up and as Martha was asleep and I carried them with me and I returned to my home. I knew that as I never asked Martha if I could take the shaddock then I should hide them so when I reached my room I placed them under my bed.

Soon afterwards Augustus brought the silent drum from Martha's home and he placed it in my room in Hannah's home. I went to sit with Hannah who was so pleased to see me and she wanted to throw her arms around me but I shook my head and she stopped. She knew I was fragile and this would only cause me to suffer even more pain.

I stood for a moment and thought to myself that I was at last becoming free from any pain. I was stripped of my decency, made to lie over a muddy sodden hole in a gale of weather, urinated on by a hound, and then my flesh was ripped open to the point of fainting.

I have been treated, cured, watched over and cared for to bring me straight back to be used again. I was then shown a greeting of friendship and love and I could not receive it.

I went to my room and took out the shaddock and I ripped open the skin to one of them but I felt so tired and needed to sleep so I put them back under my bed. I thought then I would eat it the next morning. I rested until the night's tiredness took me to sleep.

After a relaxing sleep I woke and I put on one of the dresses which contained the pockets and I looked for the shaddock but they were gone. I thought this to be very strange and I questioned where I placed them.

I was due to return to my duties at Master Adams home so I forgot about them and I made my way. I was greeted by Miss Sylvester who looked tired.

I was told to start my duties in the kitchen and so I went there to begin preparing some tea for Master Adams.

Miss Sylvester informed me that I was going to have a meeting with Master Adams during the morning. She added that I just needed to make him some sorrel tea and chop some fruits for his breakfast which he would take on the veranda at the back of the house.

I prepared this and I took it to Master Adams who was sitting down next to a table and he was writing notes in his book. I saw Blackie's tail wag and this made me nervous and my hand shook and rattled the cup slightly.

Master Adams did not look at me so I placed the tea and fruit on the table and returned to the Kitchen. I then told Miss Sylvester I would be going to the bedroom.

I started to make my way towards the stairs when Miss Sylvester shouted for me to stop and wait until Master Adams had spoken to me.

She ordered me to collect some eggs from the chicken pen and so I wandered into the hot sun outside. Blackie decided to follow me.

As I walked closer to the fowls coop Blackie took a bite at my dress and snagged his teeth into the bottom hem and I thought about the secret pockets being torn. "Does this nasty beast of a hound never give up on me?" My thoughts about the hound were never going to change.

I managed to pull my dress away and then I shouted at Blackie to get off me. I looked towards Master Adams for help and support but he was watching the show and laughing at me. My thoughts towards him were wearing me down as he seemed to constantly humiliate me and he appeared to enjoy it.

Blackie walked away and I entered the fowl pen and collected the eggs that I was asked to take back for Miss Sylvester.

I returned and Miss Sylvester informed me I needed to sweep the front of the house and then we were to meet Master Adams in his sitting room.

I did not know what I was called for and so I asked Miss Sylvester. She said she could not tell me as she had not been briefed either.

Whether she was telling me the truth or not I could not say but Miss Sylvester was not talking too much anyway. I felt that everybody had problems with me on this day.

I completed my chores and then I was summoned to the sitting room of Master Adams.

Miss Sylvester led me down the hallway and we both walked through the door. Master Adams was sitting upright in a long backed chair behind a large wooden desk.

I stood next to Miss Sylvester and Master Adams looked at us as we stood still.

I was slightly anxious at this meeting and I expected that Master Adams just wanted to ask me how I was feeling. I thought to myself about what I should say to him. Did I tell him I was well? I thought about this and came to the conclusion that he would maybe think his punishment was not enough. Should I tell him I am still in pain and therefore showing that I was weak? I just raised a tiny smile and held my chin down.

I pushed my thoughts to the side as Master Adams stood as he spoke, however he never spoke to me. He informed Miss Sylvester that I was with child and I was coming to the end of carrying 'The bastard' as he described it.

With this he informed Miss Sylvester that my duties would not include the climbing of the stairs and I would only be responsible for light work until further notice. As Master Adams announced this I heard a faint sigh in Miss Sylvester's throat which did not express any positive response at this announcement.

I was also not in favour of this as I would not be able to collect any coins and so the plan for the coins was again to be stalled without Master Adams realising what he was doing.

I left the room with Miss Sylvester. The rest of the day was quite unusual day as I was left to collect and chop vegetables and then fold some washed laundry.

I cut the ground provision ready for dinner, the potatoes and carrots were being prepared as we were making a meal called 'goat water' which Miss Sylvester said was based on an Irish stew.

Master Adams had gone to the plantation and I knew he would be away for most of the day. He also took that wretched hound Blackie with him so I knew I could have some peace.

Miss Sylvester was up and down the stairs all day and she looked weary. She was gasping for air on her last visit climbing to the level above.

I finished this day without doing much which was actually not so bad but I got nowhere near the jar of coins.

That evening I decided to visit Martha to thank her for what she had done for me and I knocked the door and she greeted me with a smile and invited me in. I started to speak of my thanks when I saw the two shaddock fruits on a plate on the table that I thought I had taken.

I finished what I was saying then I asked about the shaddock and Martha told me they had been on the table for a couple of days and if I wanted them I could have them.

I walked over and picked them up and one had some of the skin torn away. I looked at it and it was just the same as the one that I had started to peel the night before, exactly the same in fact and I held my fingers at where I had started remove the skin. I looked at Martha who smiled and I remembered the "Obeah" or as Master Adams called it "A form of magic," and also that Jack Spaniard spoke about her before. I knew Martha was good to me but this made a shiver run through my spine.

Later that evening I met with Edward who shared his disappointment with me at the decision made by Master Adams.

We sat together talking about it and we were both slightly

deflated. It was then I turned to speak to Edward and reminded him that it would only be until my baby was born and then I would probably regain my duties. As I looked at Edward I noticed behind him on the wall there was a spider. Now I was not afraid of spiders and neither was Edward, or so I thought, and I told him to take a look behind himself. As I did this I did not realise the reaction I was going to get as Edward stood up so fast he was like an unleashed hound racing for a bowl of food.

I laughed at Edward who was outside my door panting like Blackie when he had raced towards Master Adams to greet him. Edward was also shaking when he slowly edged his way back through the door.

I took the tiny light wooden pot which contained the needles and thread given to me and removed the lid. I tipped out the contents and covered the eight legged invader. I then took a piece of paper from my drawer and captured the scary little thing. Once I had done this I quickly replaced the paper with the wooden lid again.

I called Edward back into my room and his brow was beaded with sweat and his face was one full of worry.

I told him that he looked just as afraid of the spider as Miss Sylvester did when she saw one. I reminded him that she was so afraid she was gasping for air and breathing quite heavily with her fear from seeing this leggy beast.

I looked for a reaction from Edward and then slowly his mouth turned from a frightful frown to a beaming smile and I then felt his thoughts transfer to mine.

We both spoke the name of Miss Sylvester together, then Edward smiled at me and I returned one back at him as we knew what each other was thinking.

The way to get my duties back was to scare Miss Sylvester out of the room with the jar of coins. Edward and I were starting to think the same now and we shared the same joke.

That was until I turned the pot towards his direction and I

removed the lid to reveal the spider again and Edward yelled like a wild animal.

I laughed until my belly hurt me and I had to stop. I covered the pot with the lid again and I took the spider to release it outside but Edward came after me and told me to keep it for my trick with Miss Sylvester and so I went back with Edward shaking his head at me which made me smile.

Our plan was returning and all because of the worry from a tiny creature in a small wooden pot.

CHAPTER 23: Shock!

The next day I put on my pocket dress and my pinafore then I wrapped my head in a cloth. It was the first time I realised my hair had grown and it was difficult to tuck in to my head cloth so I asked Hannah to quickly plait it for me.

As she tidied my hair she advised me that William had passed by earlier with a message from Master Adams. I would not be needed at the house until later in the morning. I knew then I could take my time to prepare myself.

After my hair was done I went to find my spider and when I lifted the lid of the pot I saw my small leggy creature was still there but it was not stirring and its legs were tucked under its body.

I took the pot and I gave it a little shake and he did not move so I carefully took it out of the container and placed it on the table next to my bed. To make it look bigger again I gently unfolded its legs to spread it out a little bit more.

It was clearly not moving but this was not going to be a problem. I believed Miss Sylvester would not even notice this as it still looked menacing anyway.

As requested by Hannah I arrived at the house of Master and Mrs Adams later in the morning and the sun was quite high. I took my little creature with me in the pot with the lid over the top and I was careful not to jolt it around.

As I arrived I carefully walked past the fowl pen. The hens were quiet and it was then I realised that Blackie was not around. Whilst I was there I saw William's barn door was open and the wagon and horses were missing. I knew from seeing this that Master Adams and his wife were gone too.

As I approached the house I saw the upstairs window drapes to Master Adams bedroom were still closed so I had to be careful in case I was wrong.

I arrived at the rear door and then I walked over to some firewood that William had chopped the day before. It was stacked at the end of the veranda. I placed the spider pot on the ground next to it so it blended in. I could not let Miss Sylvester see I was carrying anything.

I returned to the rear door of the house and I entered. Miss Sylvester, who was on her hands and knees, was scrubbing the floor under where the food was prepared. She glanced up at me and she looked like she was tired and her face gave an indication she was crying for the help I could not give her.

I felt awful at that moment as I was going to play a cruel trick on her later. The guilty prank I was going to do will tease my good natured heart. I had to just keep saying to myself that Kesiwaa was goading me on to do it as I listened to her voice talking to me in my memory of her.

Miss Sylvester then stood up and she groaned and wiped her brow which made me ask if she needed some help.

Without any warning Miss Sylvester shouted at me. This was frightening as her voice was strong. She told me to stay away from the wet floor and if I were to tread on it she would,

"Cut my hip with a sweeping brush!" This was her way of telling me she would spank me. It was an aggressive tone of voice to warn me away but it was just Miss Sylvester's choice of words which I was starting to understand. Her bark was much worse than her bite.

Her shrill made me feel ill thoughts for a brief moment which were contrary to my thoughts of apathy moments before. I thought to myself about my guilt for what I was going to do but these thoughts were blown from my head by a strong blast of wind as Miss Sylvester screamed.

"Don't you just stand there girl, git to work?" She hollered.

I waited with my eyes lowered and out of her vision and I kept my mouth shut until I was instructed to collect some eggs from the hen's pen.

Miss Sylvester also told me to collect some for myself and Hannah as there were quite a lot laid and they were not going to be eaten. This was not to be missed. Anything given by Miss Sylvester was not to be turned away and Hannah would want me to bring home what I could.

I was also asked to bring some water to pour into the vase's that contained the flowers in the study. She added that I should collect a full pale of water.

I purposely asked Miss Sylvester if I should prepare some ground provisions after these duties. Miss Sylvester informed me that Mrs Adams had travelled to the next Island plantation very early in the morning and Master Adams had only just left recently to go to the field. I think this was also the reason Miss Sylvester told me to take the eggs as Mrs Adams was not around to say anything. Maybe this was because it made her look like she was being good to me.

I went to the store room to collect the wooden pale and I also took the wooden lid so I did not spill any water onto the newly cleaned floor I was warned about. I took the basket for the eggs and I knew what to do.

I casually strolled outside and I gathered the eggs and then I made my way over to the firewood and collected my spider pot. I then walked over to the water stored in the barrel at the side of the house which collected run off rain water from the roof.

I scooped some water into the wooden pale and then I floated the pot with the spider in the water. I placed the lid onto the pale and returned to the house.

Putting the eggs on the table I separated my eight and put them in a separate straw bowl in the kitchen. I then watered the flowers in the study and I returned and asked Miss Sylvester if the flowers in Master Adams room need to be watered as well.

Miss Sylvester told me to hand her the pale as she had been instructed to clean the bed of Master Adams. She had been so busy that morning she had not even managed to get up the stairs being so far behind with her duties.

I paused for a moment and I tried to think quickly until she walked over to me and grabbed the pale by its rope handle so sharply it snagged my hand.

Miss Sylvester then took a cloth and some powder from the storeroom and she climbed the stairs.

I did not know what to do at this point because my spider pot was inside the water pale and my plan was about to be discovered.

I had to follow Miss Sylvester so I walked delicately behind her and as she climbed the stairs with her big bottom wobbling in front of me, her heavy bulk making them creak with each step.

As we reached to near the top Miss Sylvester was breathing heavily and her knees were shaking which made her legs tremble as well.

She stopped at the top and grabbed the rail. I walked from behind her and I grabbed the pale and took her hand.

She looked at me with a squint in her big brown eyes and I spoke to her in a soft voice and said,

"Let me help you Miss Sylvester."

Her squint softened and she smiled and took her hand from the rail and she cupped my chin then she stroked my face as she took in a deep breath.

She informed me she needed to clean Master Adams bed as he had spilled his tea earlier that morning.

I reminded Miss Sylvester that I just needed to fill the vase with the flowers for her with some of the water and then I would carry on with the next duties she asked me to do. I added that I would carry the pale for her and she managed to nod as she could not speak for panting so hard. She just managed in between breaths to tell me to go on ahead.

I made my way to Master Adams bedroom and as I had been instructed I knocked the door first. I entered and I saw the curtains were closed as before but the room was lit by a flame inside a glass. The room had a strong smell which I had sensed once before which was fortified with a smell of body odour similar to Miss Sylvester's own.

I had to be quick as Miss Sylvester was soon to be coming so I removed the spider pot from the pale of water and took off the lid. I swiftly stepped over to Master Adams bed, pulled back the light bed sheet laid across it and I dropped the spider onto the bed in the middle. Just as I did this I saw there was a damp part to left side of the bed. I thought it was a strange place for Master Adams to spill his tea as I believed he slept on the right side because his clothes were always left there but I had no time to think so hard. I kept the spider pot in my hand.

I then turned and walked over to the vase of flowers and placed down the pale in front of them. I removed the lid quickly and as I did this Miss Sylvester opened the door. I was next to the curtain so I pulled it to the side and found the window was open, so I threw the spider pot outside into the yard. I proceeded to pour in some water to the vase and then arrange the flowers.

Miss Sylvester walked in and she went straight over to the bed and sat down. I told her she should be careful not to sit in the wet area of the tea spill and she replied by telling me she would be fine as the damp area was on the left side of the bed.

I was immediately confused on how she knew which side of the bed needed to be cleaned? She told me earlier she had not been able to climb the stairs this morning yet she knew where the tea was spilt.

I rearranged the flowers and I blew out the candle as the sun was now brightly shining through the window. I then approached Miss Sylvester with the water left in the pale and I placed it on the wooden floor at her feet. I smiled at her as I did this and she seemed to scowl at me in her response.

I then left the bedroom and I was pleased to be out of there as the musty smell was stale and sour. I thought about it and it was the same aroma which invaded my nostrils the time the bastard governor stole my innocence and it made me feel uncomfortable.

I made my way towards the stairs to return down them and then it came, just as I knew it would and what a shrill it was.

"Arrrrrgghhhhhhhhh spider!" Came the shout and then the bedroom door flew open and out came Miss Sylvester like a chicken that had just lost its head, full of disorientation.

I turned and walked back towards her. She could not speak and so I looked at her frozen and open mouthed stare and I tilted my head to the side in an enquiring manner until she finally spoke to order me to get the spider which was in the bed of Master Adams.

I returned to the room with a smile and laughter ready to burst from my belly and headed for the bed where I saw the poor leggy beast lying motionless and quite clearly dead.

I did my duty and scooped up this poor creature and dropped it out of the open window. I was about leave before I realised I was too quick and so I made a few feet thumping sounds on the wooden floor with my feet and shouted a couple of times at my imaginary prey before I sounded a triumphant call for Miss Sylvester to hear that all was clear and it was safe for her.

I returned to the landing to see Miss Sylvester wiping away a tear from her eyes, she had clearly been crying. She was really frightened beyond anything I ever saw before.

I wanted to scare her but to make her release tears was not my desire or indeed my intention. However I made her cry so I took her hand and I tried to comfort her and she was shaking. My guilt really did start to get to me and I felt terrible as I did not expect this to have such a frightening effect on her.

I escorted her down the stairs to the kitchen where I boiled some water and made us both some tea from the leaves of a lime tree. I offered Miss Sylvester a mango from the fruit bowl on the table but she refused. She then told me I should take them to my home as they were overripe and needed to be eaten. She also told me to take the cooked chicken carcass which still had its wings and legs as Master Adams had taken the bits he wanted already. She then added that Hannah could boil it up for a soup.

Miss Sylvester was being very giving yet she also appeared to be in a bad mood and worried about something and I had paid her with cruelty. I had to convince my head what I did was right anyway.

However, I felt there was something bothering Miss Sylvester as she started the day shouting at me then she was suddenly offering me foods to take home.

I pondered about this briefly then I brought my thoughts back to thinking my deed was done but I was unhappy with myself for the extent of Miss Sylvester's frightful condition and the result it brought to her.

The rest of the day we maintained the house by ensuring it was as Master Adams wanted it to be. I was then ordered to go to collect some fresh citrus fruits and ensure the chickens and goats were fed. This day went quite quickly really but this was because I started late but I was tired just the same.

My last duty was to boil pots of water and pour them in the large metal tub for Master Adams to bathe in. I filled this large vessel which sat in a room at the front of the house. The room had a heavy drape over the window. I was told to ensure this was drawn to close any light coming through and I was also to put a candle next to the tub.

The day ended for me when I saw Master Adams returning towards the house.

Miss Sylvester was looking anxious and she was hurrying me to finish with heating the hot water from the fire.

I poured the last pot into the tub when Master Adams walked through the door and yelled for something to eat. He saw the chicken carcass and he ripped off a leg and ate it as he walked around his house. He then enquired about his water and it was obvious from the tone in his voice that it was time for me to retire for the day.

Mr Adams called for Miss Sylvester and he made his way to the room with the water to bathe. Miss Sylvester ushered me to leave so I finished off what I was doing and put the pot away and Miss Sylvester looked at me and her face was frowning. She then told me I had to leave for the day and she was quite rude with her tone. She was almost pushing me out of the door. To me she seemed a bit irritated but I did as I was told and left the house and started to return to my home.

I walked past the fowl pen and continued past the tamarind tree. I reached the mangoes and looked up at the lovely sun setting with a bright orange sky as the sun started setting peacfully.

I reached my home and looked for a fruit on the table to nourish me before I served myself some broth Hannah had made.

There was nothing in the wooden bowl on the table. Then I remembered that Miss Sylvester had told me to take the mangoes from the fruit bowl in the kitchen at Master Adams house. I also forgot to take the eggs and the cooked and stripped chicken carcass.

I was feeling tired and my legs were aching but I needed to go and collect them so I returned to the house.

I walked through the door and announced my entrance but my greeting call did not meet with a response. I headed straight to the kitchen and I saw the fruits were still in the bowl and the eggs were in the basket where I had left them. The chicken carcass was sitting on the side table and only one leg remained. I picked the different foods up and placed them into a cloth and wrapped them.

I was about the leave and I heard a noise coming from the room with the tub of water and it was a sound I had not heard before. It was a groan and it caught my attention straight away so much so I wanted to know what it was.

I placed the food sack back onto the table and walked along the hall way towards the room where Master Adams was bathing. I managed to step stealthily to the door and as I approached I saw that a knot in the wood to the hinged side had fallen out so a tiny peep hole was telling my curiosity to look through.

I then heard a falling splash of water and then drips which slowly became less constant. I needed to know what was happening so I started my maco'ing which I knew I had been warned about and I knew the risk.

With my left eye closed I slightly bent my knees and lined my right eye with the tiny knot hole and I saw that Miss Sylvester had put a few candles inside so the room was lit quite well. I then saw the back of Master Adams standing naked in the bathing tub and the water was dripping from him.

I noticed his neck and arms were the shade of a Portugal fruit ready to be picked and his body was the colour of the goat's milk. I had a little smile to myself as I had never seen this before and at the time I thought how strange.

His back also had several round brown marks which looked like they were tiny lumps of soil stuck to him and his bottom had red blotches. The thing I found the most interesting was that he had the most hairy legs and they were bent outwards like they were buckling.

Miss Sylvester was not in view at this time then suddenly she appeared with a large cloth and she started to rub Master Adams back from the dripping water as she dried his skin. She then moved the cloth down to his bottom and she dried his lower body. Master Adams then turned to the side and Miss Sylvester took the cloth along his arms and down his waist to his legs where Master Adams then stepped out of the tub.

As Miss Sylvester dried his tummy Master Adams took the cloth from her and he threw it on the wooden floor and it was then he moved his hand and he grabbed Miss Sylvester's breast. I was so shocked by this oversensitive and revolting show that I wanted to push open the door and say something but this was not for my eyes to see and my voice to speak.

Master Adams then opened the blouse of Miss Sylvester who just stood and looked at him.

He continued to undress her from her waist up until she was fully exposed, then Master Adams took his head towards her and he started to kiss her lips whilst fondling her large breasts.

He stopped and he told her to follow him to his room to continue what they were doing and that is when I saw the manhood of Master Adams sticking proud from his midsection. I had to leave and quick as he took her hand and faced the door I was peeping through but Miss Sylvester held him back. She spoke to him softly, which I did not hear, then she removed her dress right in front of him. Miss Sylvester was completely naked and facing Master Adams. She told him to take his enjoyment on the long soft cushioned seat behind the tub under the draped window.

Master Adams did not refuse the offer and soon they were on the long cushioned seat with him rocking and weaving his mid-section against Miss Sylvester. She was looking over his shoulder at the ceiling and her face had no expression. I knew I should not have watched but I could not leave as I sensed I was seeing something that had an edge of secrecy to it. This did not take long before Master Adams built up his rhythm then he groaned loudly and stopped before slumping on top of Miss Sylvester.

I knew my time to leave was now due. They grabbed their clothes and headed towards the door but Miss Sylvester spoke to Master Adams and what I heard was very interesting. She spoke about her sleeping in his bedroom.

Master Adams laughed and told Miss Sylvester that they have all night just as they normally do when Mrs Adams is away.

Miss Sylvester then responded to inform Master Adams that earlier she was in such a state because she found a spider in his bed.

This made Master Adams laugh again and Miss Sylvester looked at him with a hard stare. Miss Sylvester then went on the say if it was not for me then she would not have been able to cope. I could not believe what I was hearing. She informed Master Adams I was her saviour and this amused him. He started to laugh quite loudly and she just carried on praising me.

Miss Sylvester then spoke above Master Adams laughter when she said to him it was the reason he had his enjoyment on the long cushioned seat just now. She added she was too scared to go to his room as they usually did.

Master Adams stopped his laughing as he realised Miss Sylvester was being very serious. I looked at her face and she was clearly frightened.

She told Master Adams that she wanted me to be given the duties back in his bedroom and when Mrs Adams was going to be away, she wanted me to spend a good time in their bedroom to check for these many legged frightening horrors before she slept in the bed.

This was said better than if I had tried to say it myself, but more interesting was Miss Sylvester and Master Adams were secretly sleeping together which I now knew. This was definitely the time for me to leave as I did not need to know any more or even want to anyway.

I turned away from the door and crept softly away and towards kitchen and picked up the food cloth, tucked it under my arm and went to the door leading to the back of the house and quietly stepped into the yard.

I managed to leave without making a noise and I walked away unnoticed and what a relief it was. I started to think to myself about what I just heard and saw and I was disgusted.

As I tried to understand what was going on with Miss Sylvester my concentration was interrupted, and who do you think came walking towards me? Yes, Blackie of course. His stare was evil as he looked at me and he showed me his teeth.

I was not in any mood to let him start on me so I reached into the food bag and I took out an overripe mango and held it just behind my shoulder ready to throw it. I looked Blackie in his eyes and as I stood still I remembered back to when I first met Fiifi and how he told me to throw a spear accurately.

I thought then it would be better to try and avoid any fight with this miserable hound so I turned to the side and moved away in a half circle from his snarling snout. I passed Blackie and then I started walking backwards to watch his every move. I carried on retreating. I passed the fowl pen and the tamarind tree. He followed me and he growled and that was it.

I stopped, stood still, and I put my feet apart and bent my legs slightly. I put my hand level with my shoulder and slightly behind me. I looked at his movements until he stopped for just a tiny bit too long. Then I just let my hand go. I flung the mango at Blackie just as though I wanted to point to his ugly face and it got him right on his miserable wet nose. "Plonk!"

"Now that shocked ya didn't it Blackie!" I said to him.

As the mango caught him he gave a whining cry before trotting away with his tail down. He went straight to his sleeping place which was the box next to the rear door of the house.

I held my laughter inside then I turned and walked on back to my home with excitement knowing I had my duties back and I just got one over Blackie.

These were the good parts of the day but after seeing what I did I felt bitter and quite disappointed with Miss Sylvester. What did not seem right was that Miss Sylvester was quite rude to me when I first arrived at the house which I now realised was after lying down with Master Adams during the night whilst Mrs Adams was away at the next island. Then she was kind to me by giving me the food but then she changed again and she was grumpy when Master Adams came back and I now know why.

I reached into my food cloth and took out a ripe mango and tore off some of the skin and bit into the sweetness of the flesh and just thought about my aim at Blackie's nose. I smiled and walked home. That evening I went to visit Edward in his home and I told him what happened with the spider and he was pleased but when he asked me if I thought I would get my duties back, I struggled to talk. I did not want to speak about what I saw with Miss Sylvester so I decided to keep this to myself and I just advised him that Miss Sylvester had spoken to Master Adams.

That evening Edward took me in his arms and he kissed me and he told me he will always be by my side. He felt my stomach and he looked at me and we knew my baby would be arriving soon. With these words I felt stronger for my child growing within me. This was my blood and I will show it the life of a mother I never had. I had lost mine and I never knew what it was like to have one.

Edward spoke to me about the African tradition of when a baby is born. The placenta is buried in the ground just as we had talked when we first met. I told him I remembered our conversation and he smiled at me.

I reminded Edward that a fruit tree is traditionally grown on top of this area as a sign that the child would never go hungry which of course he knew about as well. Edward told me there was a clear ground behind his home away from anyone passing by and he recommended it as a suitable place to bury my child's placenta in the earth and he would then plant a fruit tree. He added it was always in the sun and it was an area where he could see from his window. I agreed with this and he smiled and told me he would ensure my child was always looked after.

With Edwards support I would show my child the traditions of my forefathers and I would teach it the ways of my villagers. It would be proud of where I was from and it would know all I know and all I can teach. Edward never asked who the father of my baby was but one day I would tell him.

CHAPTER 24: Scion

The following day I arrived at the house and saw Blackie sitting in his box next to the door. I looked straight at him. I walked towards the door and my first thoughts were for Miss Sylvester so I knocked the door and went to the kitchen where she was washing some fruits.

She told me that Master Adams wanted to talk to me so she took a cloth and dried her hands and left through the door and asked me to join her. I followed along the hallway and then through to the study where she knocked on the door. A voice behind it invited us in and there he was sitting behind his desk.

Miss Sylvester entered first and I followed and stood next to her. Master Adams looked up at us and he then spoke to us to advise why the meeting was called.

He spoke to Miss Sylvester and he informed her that the reason was because he realised the duties he had given to her were too much and she was better suited in the lower part of the house and so my duties were restored. Once this was said he smiled and asked us to continue with our duties.

Miss Sylvester had been fooled by the spider I had placed in Master Adams bed and I wanted to burst out with laughter at this but I kept the thought to myself.

I was going to be back in Master Adams room and the collection of the coins would continue.

Later that morning Master Adams left the house and went to the sugar cane field to watch over the workers and I made my way to his bedroom. I immediately opened up the door to the wardrobe which contained the secret panel and I saw the jar which was full with the coins. I took it out and I opened the top. I counted out ten coins then I put the jar back and quickly replaced the panel again. This time I stopped to remember that Miss Sylvester would not be coming up the stairs and so I actually had more time for each collection.

I inserted the coins into the hidden pockets of my dress and then continued with my duties to clean the room.

Mrs Adams returned later in the afternoon from her trip to another plantation which I now knew as being on the island of Tobago which was formally known as Isla de la Asumpcion and also as La Concepcion.

I saw Miss Sylvester relight the smile back onto her face that was missing for the days that Mrs Adams was away. I recognised this when Mrs Adams was around as her husband did not pester Miss Sylvester and this was clear by the look on her face.

The day ended and I returned back to my home. I went to my room where I changed from my work dress. I then sat on the end of my bed next to the silent drum and I opened the secret compartment. I pushed the spear thrower to release the hidden slot then put in the ten coins I had collected.

I pressed this secret section back into its start position to seal it and my task was done. I needed to rest and so I lay on my bed. My baby was talking to me and I saw my stomach moving like the rolls of water over the sea. I was drifting to sleep when I was woken by the knock at the door and the voice of Edward who was asking to come in.

I opened the door and invited him into my room and I looked at him and he gave a replied raise of his eyebrows as he was asking me if I had managed to achieve my task so I smiled and nodded at him.

Edward threw his big arms around my shoulders and they weighed me down so much I had to push him away. All the work in the sugar cane field had built his arms to a strong and powerful size which I did not notice as much before.

I told Edward to be gentle with me and he told me he was sorry but he was excited. He then took me in his arms and softly caressed my cheek. He held my head in his hands and we kissed and with this a relief of tension drained away from me.

He had strong arms which any warrior would be proud of but with the delicate touch and tenderness of a gentleman. We spoke briefly and then Edward asked me to join him and the others outside to talk, which I had not done for a while so we went to sit with them.

We spoke with everyone and shared moments of our day and I spoke to everyone about Miss Sylvester being afraid of spiders. This was when Jack Spaniard spoke to his tormentors to advise them he was not the only one to be fearful of tiny creatures. The others agreed and they turned their mocking towards Miss Sylvester as they all joined in.

I realised then that none of the others liked her but they did not say why and I did not want to ask them. I could not tell them I had placed the spider in the bed as part of a plan as I was aware there could be a spy amongst them. Edward knew this as well so I just listened to them as they laughed and japed about spiders.

Edward asked the workers about an area of scrubland at the back of his home. He enquired about this unused earth and he informed them that he wanted to use it to bury the placenta of my baby after it is born which did not really get a response from anyone. Edward added to his plea by advising to the workers who were sitting around that he did not want anyone to disturb his plot as this would be a sign of disrespect to my child which would ensure that anyone who did would have him to answer to. One worker spoke in response to Edward with words of support and he made sure those workers who were not paying attention did listen. He did this by standing up and he raised his voice to them. He also knew of the tradition and he fortified Edward's words with his support for this to be respected.

The workers were too interested in mocking Miss Sylvester and the only comment I heard was that it would be great if Edward could find and capture a couple of creatures or spiders to be used for fun against Jack Spaniard who just kissed his teeth and told them all to be quiet. They did not realise that Edward was keeping his fear of spiders quiet and to himself but I knew.

This was when the spokesman shouted at everyone to stop mocking this tradition and suddenly they all became quiet. This man made the others listen and he continued to inform them about this and they should all be taking note. I felt that some of the workers knew this but they had, over the years, lost their interest in their family history and settled for the life which they knew and not what had been passed down to them.

This spokesman then shook his head and then he made his excuse to leave the group and he walked away.

I asked Edward about this man who stood up and spoke as I had seen him around but I had never spoken to him. He informed me his name was Tobias Jack and he was very knowledgeable about his African culture and heritage. He added that he arrived at the same time as his former love Catherine and he claimed to be the son of a great leader from my land. Edward told me he did have an African name when he arrived but he has never told anybody what is was in all the time he was on this sugar plantation.

I don't know why, but this man Tobias suddenly interested me and I sensed Edward saw this in my face when I made my enquiry. I did not ask any further questions but I knew from this time to watch the actions of Tobias Jack whenever I saw him.

The evening came to a close and I felt myself wanting to rest so I returned to my room and took away the day with my relaxation.

The days came and went and on every opportunity I had, I collected ten coins, never more than ten and never anytime fewer either. I started to recognise that some of these coins were slightly bigger than others. Some were smaller but slightly thicker. I did not ask why this was but when I went to market with Master Adams over the coming weeks he bought provisions and other things needed.

On these trips I noticed that when I was with him at a store or bartering with a vendor at the market he put the smaller coins from the provisions he bought into his little money purse and then into his large left side pocket. The larger coins he put into a small sack, these appeared to be quite heavy.

I started to observe which of the coins were of more value and it became remarkably elucidatory to my eyes which ones these were. I made a note in my head from the things he was buying and I was counting to myself these coins until I soon had a good understanding of what was used to buy the different items. I thought to myself that I was putting myself in danger for coins of little value just as much as I was for the higher value coins. Why should I take ten coins when I could only take one the same worth?

One evening I put this idea to Edward and he agreed that I should be selective and not take so many of the lesser value coins. So I became more precise with the ones I took from the jar. This went on for quite a while and the collection grew bigger. I could not be too eager though, and I made sure the coins I took were as much of a variety as possible.

I overheard on one occasion when Master Adams asked his wife to count the money jar. At this point I stopped collecting for a while.

The silent drum had filled up to a point that there was little room to get any more in it anyway and so I spoke to Edward about this.

Edward replied that as the silent drum could barely hold any more coins he needed to remove them from their safe holding and hide them. I sensed he had another plan to resolve this and he informed me to stop collecting them until he gives me the confirmation to start again.

Edward got to work the next evening after his duties in the field by clearing the area where he told me he was going to bury my baby's placenta behind his home.

He dug away a small clearing of scrub until the earth was free from any weeds and the soil was level. He toiled hard and he was tired. I gave him some pressed mango juice of which he poured the first drop into the soil for the dead.

I remembered back to what Kesiwaa did and I smiled to myself as Edward really knew his traditions carried down by his forefathers. Edward told me the plot was ready and he asked me to save the seed of the mangos that I had used to press the juice as he would bury them on the plot of soil he worked on.

As he said this Tobias Jack strolled along the side of Edwards home and greeted us both. He acknowledged Edward who introduced him to me and although I had seen Tobias on many occasions I felt a sudden rush of excitement as we met.

Tobias held out his hand and he had in front of him a tiny pot with soil in it and in the middle there was a green scion of a plant, a tiny little shoot that was ready to place in the ground to propagate. Tobias informed me it was grown from the seed of the shaddock which was a yellow bitter citrus fruit which grew quite large. He nurtured it for himself but he felt that he wanted to offer it for my baby.

I smiled immediately and thanked him then I looked at Edward who raised his mouth to smile but I knew it was a false grin. It was as though he was questioning the gift from Tobias which I found uncomfortable. I accepted the tiny shrub from Tobias who spoke to say that he wanted to make the offering as it was a part of his ancestor's tradition to do so. He said he believed strongly about what was passed down by our African forefathers. He added that he did not want these to be lost as this was our heritage and he would see a rage of fire with anyone who prevented these from being passed on to our children. Tobias then gave his parting words and left.

It was then that I saw a look from Edward which I had not seen before as his face sank and he told me he did not trust Tobias. Edward walked over to me and he took the pot from my hand and he threw it on the ground to the side of me. The soil spilled from the little pot and the small green shoot sat with it. This was interesting as I had never seen Edward like this and as he walked away I thanked him for his work but he never answered me. I scooped up the small green stem of the plant with its delicate roots and the soil and placed it back into the pot and then I returned to my room. I placed this small plant on the floor next to my bed then I lay down as I was tired. I held my stomach. I had no time for Edward's behaviour this evening and I soon found my sleep.

My pregnancy had almost come to its end and I was due to be relieved of my duties. This was a time I actually started to get scared as I was going to give birth and I did not know what to expect.

The next day Martha came to see me and she advised me William had been sent to deliver an instruction from Master Adams that my duties would stop until my baby was born. So I spent my time resting and sleeping.

That evening Edward came to visit me in my room and he brought me a beautiful red plant that he called a "Chaconia" which he told me he grew himself. He informed me that it was given its name in honour of a former governor of the island of “Le isle de Trinity.”

He added that the name of this governor was Don Jose Maria Chacon who was Spanish. I asked him about this title name of governor as this word I had heard before. It was this name ‘governor’ that made me uneasy as it was the title that the devil obroni at Elmina castle used.

Edward advised me that the previous governor of this land was a Scottish man called Sir Ralph Abercromby. He was killed recently in a battle in a place called Alexandria, and had nothing to do with Don Jose Maria Chacon.

He added that the British called our island “Trinidad” and he then advised me that this island was seized by the British recently but many people in different parts still spoke Spanish and French. I listened to him but my concentration was on this stunning crimson coloured leaf as its flower was pleasing to my eyes. I wondered whether this was to be a gift to show his choice was far superior to the one given to me by Tobias but I soon let this pass.

This plant was so beautiful and the bright red colour was such a pretty sight to see. It really made me feel happy and I placed it near to my window and then I kissed Edward and thanked him. He looked at me and smiled and he took me into his arms and I looked down behind Edward and near to the ground next to my bed I saw the tiny green shoot of the scion in the pot of earth that Tobias gave me.

I managed to move around and with my foot I reached out with my toe to nudge this pot under my bed without him noticing. I could not have any more drama over such small thing that really had no meaning. Edward informed me that the clearing he had worked on was all done and I thanked him then he left me and returned to his home.

I was tired and I soon found my pregnancy was draining me and I came to the point where I had just had enough of carrying my child and I remember going to sleep and dreaming this night that my child grew up to become a drummer. This made my head start to play my beat.

"Bam ba ba, bam ba ba bam ba ba bam, ba ba bam ba ba bam, ba ba bam ba ba bam bam ba ba, bam ba ba bam."

I was just enjoying this until this Bam bam bam became a little irritating until I heard loud banging and voices outside. I woke up and opened my eyes then I closed my eyes again and began again with my silent drum in my head.

"Bam ba ba, bam ba ba bam ba ba bam, ba ba bam ba ba bam, ba ba bam ba ba bam bam ba ba, bam ba ba bam."

This was soothing but there was a noise interfering with my concentration which was coming from outside. The brightness from the window told me it was the morning.

I raised myself from my bed and I ventured outside and heard the noise was coming from behind Edwards home. I walked closer to this banging noise and I saw several men around the clearing he had made. These men were joining wooden frames together with hammers and I immediately felt a rush of worry flow through my body. My akuma started racing. Some men had tools for digging so I walked up to these men who were looking at the soil.

They were men who usually worked in the field but none with whom I had spoken or knew their names. They had homes at the furthest part of the workers living area. These workers did not really sit with the workers I knew and they paid no notice to me.

I asked them what interest they had in this clearing and I was informed by one of them that Master Adams wanted them to construct another sugar cane holding barn on the site and he spotted this cleared area recently as he walked by.

I informed him the site was prepared by Edward for a garden for fruit trees which had already been chosen and was not to be touched.

My words were not heard as the men continued to prepare the

wood for their construction. I shouted for them to stop and my akuma built up speed as they all just ignored me as though I was not there.

I needed to speak to Edward to warn him and so I walked at speed towards the field for the sugar plantation which put pressure on my body. I was trying to run but I could not as my pregnancy weighted me down. I arrived at the field and my breathing was heavy, I was gasping just like Miss Sylvester did when she climbed the stairs. I shouted his name and the hot sun made me wilt until I felt my head spinning and my vision became blurred. Edward eventually came to me and I saw his face through a haze. I told him of the men behind his home then I passed out. I don't know what happened after that.

The next thing I felt was a sudden pain in my mid-section and I awoke in my bed and gave out an almighty scream.

"Arrrrrrggggghhhh!" I opened my eyes and I looked around and there was a face watching over me. My eyes then recognised it was Hannah, I lifted up my head and I saw Martha as she stood ahead of me and she was stooping between my spread legs that were bent at my knees.

I looked back at Hannah on my side and she was wiping my brow and holding my hand. I looked around and I was in Martha's home so I was being cared for but why?

I gave out another scream "Arrrrrrggggghhhh!" Then another, and then another.

My stomach froze with a hardness that was unbearable and the pain was strong. I felt that I was saturated between my legs which made me feel uncomfortable. I felt like my legs were being ripped apart like a cooked chicken being torn by a hungry pair of hands ready to feed its mouth. I looked at Hannah and told her that I was in great pain. Hannah advised me that I will be fine as they had an axe under the bed for me.

"An axe I thought an axe!"

The pain was unbearable and I reached for my silent drum and then forgot about it straight away as more pain came. Are they going to chop my legs off to kill the pain? I then remembered back to Bobo and I wondered what happened to my feet?

Hannah then told me that the head was showing. I thought what head is she talking about? This made no sense at all and my eyes closed to shut out this evil dream but then my senses came to me when I realised what was happening and I screamed the loudest of all. "Arrrrrrgggggghhhh!

I then snatched at some short breaths and felt the pain coming again.

The birth of my child was happening now and I was not only nervous but scared. I was going through an experience and I did not know how to deal with it. I was not aware until I was already pushing my child into this cruel world.

"My Onyankopon please watch me and guide me right now." I spoke softly to myself.

Martha gave her instruction and she was very clear as she told me to push through my lower section and after several strains and one more scream from my tired throat I felt the release of the pressure and my stomach dropped down.

All went silent then and Hannah squeezed my hand and wiped my brow as I snatched some quick breaths again.

My baby was born and Martha picked it up and as she did this she asked Hannah to bring her some paper quickly. I did not know what was happening but Martha took my baby and she picked up a small knife that was at the end of my bed and I saw her take it to my baby's face.

I shouted to Martha in terror of what she was doing but she told me to keep quiet. I could not move my legs from the pain and I was overcome with a panic which made my akuma race so fast my breathing became uncomfortable.

Hannah returned with a sheet of paper and Martha rubbed it over my baby's face and then she looked like she was unhooking a veil from around its ears.

Martha lifted my child over me and placed it on my chest and she then cut the cord.

Martha informed me that I had a son and my akuma flapped like the wings of the hummingbird.

I had a baby boy and as I held him I had a swelling of water in my eyes that started to drip tears of joy, and the dam burst from behind and I cried happiness uncontrollably.

I almost wanted to pass out again but I was also excited at my gift. This was the devil obroni's child but now I saw this child as mine. I had never thought of it like this until Hannah placed my baby in my arms. I saw the face not of the devil but of an angel. This was my son, my flesh and blood the baby carried by myself with nine hard months of difficult times. This was a life that I had just given birth too and I was very proud and happy.

I was given this gift by my mother and now I was the maker of life myself. My child was born but, just as the others on the plantation, my son was introduced into a world of captivity. With so many thoughts racing around my head at the same time I wanted to shout to everybody about what I had done but my arms, legs and stomach ached along with my back which was in such pain and I felt totally drained and weary.

I thought about my silent drum in my head but it was not needed this time as any pain needed to be absorbed by my emotion to cushion the soreness below me.

Martha was at my lower end and she had a knife between my legs.

I then looked at her and in her hands she raised a dark fleshy sac and the cord was dangling from it. I saw flashes of light from the window as a sliver of the sun sparkled into my eyes and I then received a cloth on my head from Hannah and my legs trembled without any feeling or control.

Martha spoke to me and she asked me to rest and this instruction was welcome but I wanted to look at my son. She handed me the paper and told me to keep it safe as my baby was born with a caul which she has placed on it. I had no idea what she meant but I agreed anyway with her and I nodded.

I gazed at my son and my eyes saw the sweetest face of the most treasured child ever.

My feelings at this moment were flying around again like a bird hovering in a clear sky. I just wanted to cry again and then a moment later joy filled my akuma and my eyes just focused on my delicate creation. I felt my channel of birth being dampened with warmth and then Hannah lifted my head for me to drink from a cup of bitter liquid.

My legs were then closed together and I was covered with the cloth which made me more comfortable. I looked at my new born miracle I caught a movement in the background and I saw Edward approaching.

My Edward was here and I looked at him for support and he came to me and kissed me which felt blissful.

Edward told me he was very proud of me which meant more to me than anything he had said before. It was then I remembered the clearing of the ground so I questioned him on it and he told me not to worry as it had been resolved and the ground was mine.

I felt supported by everybody around me and I was excited but I needed to rest and so I asked Edward to stay with me which he did and I felt his hand touch mine and I squeezed it with the little strength that I had.

I felt my excitement was too much and I asked Edward to take my son which he did and he told me to rest. After a short time Edward spoke about another reason for his visit as he informed me in a soft voice that he needed to collect the coins from my room. He asked me also if there was anything that he could collect for me from my room as he wanted to move the coins. He just needed a reason to go to my room so I thought what I could ask him to bring me. There was only one thing which came to the front of my thoughts. I told him to bring my "Chaconia" flower.

I saw Edwards face return a smile and he replied that he would come back shortly and with this request he handed back my baby son, wrapped in a soft cloth with just his face showing.

This was the first time I saw how light his skin was.

I looked at my son for as long as I can remember and all I saw was my tiny little descendant sleeping in my arms. His face was so soft and sweet and my gaze was mesmerised by him. My eyes looked at every tiny part of him and I traced my finger around his lips and chin then up to his tiny ears. I noticed then a mark on the back of his left lobe which was red and it looked a little sore.

Martha came to see me and asked if I needed anything and I replied to her that I would like a drink of water as my mouth was dry. I asked her about the red mark at the base of my babies' ears and she informed me it was the caul that had marked my son and there was nothing she could do.

She added that this would normally fade over time but in some cases it could leave a scar. I asked what this 'caul' was and Martha advised me that she saw it only once before. She told me that it is a sign that my son would be gifted. She added that it was like a veil over his face, like a membrane from the placenta. She added that she had heard many times that this was good omen and it was also a sign he would one day be destined for greatness. She added that some people sell their babies caul's to the men who sail on the sea as people born with these are said to never drown in water. People who therefore own a caul would never drown at sea. She added that people born with a caul are also believed to see people's auras and see things that no others can.

This was not really of an interest to me as I had heard a lot of these stories as a child. As she turned to get me the water I asked her what day it was and she told me the day was a Monday.

She looked confused at my question and she continued to go for my drink.

I looked at my son and my mouth said to his tiny ears.

"My son you are an African boy and your name is Kwadwo. The name means you are Monday born, but more importantly it also means that you will have good health, fortune and spirituality. Welcome to the world Kwadwo Kwaku son of Esi Takyiwaa Kwaku." I said.

I kissed my son and I placed him in the wooden cradle next to me. Martha returned with the water that was sweet.

Edward returned later in the evening and he sat down next to me and he looked at Kwadwo. He brought the chaconia flower which was just as bright a crimson as it was when I first saw it and he placed it on the table next to me and the petals gave brightness to the room.

Edward informed me with quiet words that the task was complete.

I asked him what deed he had done and he told me that firstly he asked Martha for my son's placenta to bury it which she gave him in a sack cloth.

He then went to my home and Hannah let him into my room and she was washing the cloths outside that were used in my childbirth.

He then informed me how he took the coins from the silent drum and put them into another sack cloth which he placed into the sack with the placenta.

I nodded at him and he looked excited as he was talking to me.

He then told me that as he had already dug a hole in the ground earlier in the day where he had cleared the scrub land near to his home. All he had to do was place the sacks into the hole and return the soil to cover the placenta and the coins. Edward then explained to me that the amount of coins was far more than he had anticipated and the sack was very heavy.

I questioned him further and he responded by telling me he separated the sacks before he added the soil. He told me the placenta was in the middle of the clearing and the coins were one stride to the left. I knew I would remember this from the mark from the veil left on Kwadwo's ear which was on the same side.

I smiled at Edward and he looked happy with himself. He told me that when I returned to my duties in Master Adams house I could start collecting the coins again as the silent drum was now empty.

I heard my son start to splutter and he was restless from his sleep so I picked him up and placed him on my breast to let him suckle. He was so eager to feed.

I spoke to Edward and I informed him my sons name was Kwadwo and that it meant Monday born and he smiled and replied that it sounded just perfect. I then added that it also meant he will have good health, fortune and spirituality. This made Edward smile broaden more than I ever saw before.

I told him he was my scion Prince who would one day be a profoundly sage man who was destined for greatness.

Edward told me that he found the little green shoot in the pot under my bed when he had to lay the silent drum on its side to remove the sack with the coins inside.

I looked at him and I told him it was a kind gift I kept for my son and it was not for me. Edward nodded and he said that he knew this and for this reason he did what he thought was right.

I asked him what he did with the little green scion and you know where he put it?

Yes it was planted into the ground on top on Kwadwo's buried placenta.

CHAPTER 25: Expulsion

Edward visited every moment he could and it was a true sign he was as excited as I was about Kwadwo. He wanted to hold my son and he told me he wanted to raise him as his own which was the ultimate compliment and commitment to me. These were the words which made the emotion flood from my eyes and I held on to Edward as he sat next to me and he placed his arms around my shoulders.

I sapped at him to be gentle with his heavy limbs as my body was sore with numbness and my stomach still felt lumpy which made me ache. At this time after the birth of Kwadwo I noticed that I was very emotional and I sometimes did not realise how sharp my tongue was towards Edward and although he noticed this he never complained.

On one occasion my baby showed signs of discomfort and he needed to be cleaned up from his messy rear. I prepared some water and collected a clean and folded cloth from Martha then started to disrobe the ones around him. When I removed the soiled napkin I washed away the mess from Kwadwo's bottom and to my horror I saw a blue bruise on the base of his back. I was so confused by this which made me wonder where it came from and I panicked. I shouted for Martha who came rushing in to see me.

I felt my eyes swell with worry as I thought that I must have held onto my son too tightly and this has bruised him. Martha looked at this mark and immediately she told me not to worry. She had seen this before on some of the new born babies on the plantation. It was usually mulatto babies, those of combination lineage who were marked. I did not understand this and I could not recall being told anything about this when I attended my puberty rites.

Martha informed me that as it was seen in my son's skin colour his father must have been a white man. She advised me that I must have conceived my son before I arrived in Trinidad. She told me that usually when this happens, they stop women carrying mulatto children across the sea. She added that they usually keep them in my homeland in a building not far from where we leave on the water.

She also advised me that she had never known this before and she was surprised I was allowed to travel. So I could have been held back if it was known I was carrying a baby but I was never informed about this either.

My conclusion to this information was it was not supposed to happen which is why I was not taught about it and why my queen Kesiwaa did not tell me.

After another emotional moment at the information Martha gave me I dried my watery eyes I thanked her for this and I picked up Kwadwo then made sure he was dressed again and snuggled him back to rest in his cradle.

I looked at Edward who held my hand and then he told me everything was now alright as he was going to look after me.

I asked him about his garden and how he managed to stop the workers building on his plot. He informed me that Master Adams had agreed to build next to the clearing prepared by him and not on it. What a relief this was as our plan had nearly been destroyed.

Edward informed me that he was asked by Master Adams as to why he wanted the soil that he had prepared, so he explained to him about the tradition of burying a baby's placenta. He added that although Master Adams agreed to this it was Mrs Adams who tried to stop it. Mrs Adams was complaining to him about African cultures and she wanted this sort of thing to be slowly removed from her plantation and her workers.

After a few days of rest I was visited by Master Adams who asked me the name of my child. I told him that he did not have one yet but I was looking for one from my home. I was so proud to speak this to Master Adams but his response almost made me choke.

Master Adams told me I had to choose an English name and he suggested I called my son Joseph. He ordered me to forget these African words and names which were a thing of the past. He added that my life was now in Trinidad and it was where I would stay and I should now accept my life the way it was.

He also told me it was Mrs Adams who did not like African words and names as she did not understand them. Master Adams then looked into the cradle of my son and he commented on his colour. He told me my son would grow up speaking English and so the words I knew would be lost anyway. He informed me that he would tell Mrs Adams I had named my son Joseph and she would be happy with it.

This made me think how my words and traditions were not good enough for them, but my hands that tidy their room and the feet keeping me standing over a washing table in the hot sun were worth dragging me from my homeland against my wishes.

I had to be careful though as I was not in my own country and I was not living by myself. I also had a responsibility now. I suffered the pain of eviction and all the horrors of my journey and I would be a fool to allow my son to suffer any humiliation and mistreatment as I did. I had to protect my son so he could grow up to the man he deserves to be. I could not make any mistakes and let my son be punished or robbed of his chance for a decent life. My son would always be my son so his name would be irrelevant anyway so I had to do as I was instructed.

Over the next few days I thought hard about what I was told and after an evening talking to Edward I decided I had to let go of my African roots and move on with my future. I would let go but never forget in my akuma of course.

I was living and working for Master Adams and I was eating well and I had to see my future on this soil. My son's safe keeping and wellbeing was paramount to me and as I belonged to Master Adams I had no choice and I had to take instruction from him.

So I decided to call my son Joseph as informed but I would keep the name Kwadwo in my thoughts at all times. I spoke to Edward about this and he told me he knew that it hurt me to have to change my sons name but he agreed it was a way of keeping Mrs Adams tongue from complaining.

After a few more days William arrived at my home and Hannah answered the door before she let him in. William came to inform me that my duties needed to restart but I was still feeling delicate and I was delicate from childbirth.

I asked William for a few more days to recover and I also reminded him that my son needed to be fed regularly. William left and he told me he would pass the message on to Master Adams.

William returned after a short while and told me that Master Adams needed me to go straight away to his home as he had duties for me to attend to. He added that not being in his home on time was similar to being in the morning line up after the conch shell was blown and I knew what that meant.

I asked William about the welfare of my son and he told me that Hannah would have to look after him. I explained again that my son still needed to be fed regularly, so I would have to take him with me and he agreed. I spoke to Hannah as she was preparing some tea and she told me to take my son with me as at least he would be inside Master Adams home. She told me that the other women had to work in the field and so it was extremely difficult because they had to tie their child to their back as they worked.

I went to my room and saw my baby asleep and I spoke to him to tell him he was coming with me and I called his name Kwadwo but then I slipped in the name Joseph.

"Kwadwo-Joseph come with Mummy." I spoke to myself and this made me smile. I wrapped him in some light cloth and then dressed myself in my work dress. My stomach was still swollen but it did not matter as my body still fitted into this garment. I took my son into my arms and walked out to join William and Hannah.

I felt so weak and needed to rest more but as my duty called me I had to go.

I followed William to the house and then he left me to return to his barn. Blackie was standing next to his bowl and he was lapping his water rapidly. He never bothered me as I entered the house where I saw Miss Sylvester in the kitchen and she gave me a smile then she came over to me. She wanted to see my baby and I felt a rush of excitement.

She looked at him with a really big smile and then she screwed up her nose in an expression of identifying the innocence that a baby carried with it. She commented on how sweet his face was and she spoke of how light skinned he was then she looked at me with an enquiring expression but I said nothing.

I looked at my son and his face slept warmly in my arms until a bark from Blackie at the rear door made his eyes open which made Miss Sylvester give a sweet sigh of her delight. Blackie started scratching at the door and his claws were scraping quickly and he continued to howl.

That was when Master Adams walked into the kitchen and gave Miss Sylvester a look from a grumpy face, and then he made his way to the rear door and went outside. Miss Sylvester continued to drool over my baby who encouraged me to place my finger into his tiny hand and this made him smile.

I was ready to lay my son down when suddenly the rear door burst open and Master Adams walked back in and he started to shout that Blackie had no water and he was panting for a drink.

Master Adams face had turned slightly red which I knew now was his anger showing and his voice was loud and frightening. He had in his hand Blackie's water bowl and he handed it to Miss Sylvester. He asked her to get some water for his thirsty hound and then she was to see him in his writing room. He walked away from us still shouting as he left.

I asked Miss Sylvester where I should lay my baby and she told me to put him on the cushioned chair in the room along the hallway which was the same one she had been in with Master Adams. I did not really want to put him there and I looked at her in a way which showed my disappointment at this room choice. Miss Sylvester spoke to me again and this time her voice was also slightly raised and harsh in tone.

I made no more remarks of refusal and took my baby as ordered and laid him down as he was sleeping.

Master Adams shouted for me to go and see him and so I

made my way to his room. Miss Sylvester met me at the door and I knocked and we both entered.

Master Adams beckoned us forward; we stood side by side just as we had done before.

He told me that my defiance to take his instruction from William to come when asked was completely unacceptable. I was about to open my mouth when he then told me that Blackie was crying for water and the sun was hot today which could have made him suffer.

I was again about to say something but he added that he found Miss Sylvester and I holding a little bastard that had no other use other than to prevent us from doing our duties.

I started to tremble and my legs felt weak by these evil words which made me want to be sick.

Master Adams then turned his anger on to Miss Sylvester as he told her to leave her brooding eyes from my baby as it was unhealthy for her. He concluded with his disappointment with us both and he ordered us to return to our duties immediately.

We both left and I went straight to Master Adams room to clean it and to tidy his bed.

This time I was weak and so I was slower and it was difficult for me to bend and collect things from the floor. My body ached and I pushed myself to complete my duties. I did not take any coins this time as I started to feel dizzy and my head was suffering like it was pounding.

Master Adams then shouted at me from downstairs as my baby was crying and I quickly made my way to the room where he was and I found him screaming.

He ordered me to go home for the day as I was annoying him with my inability to work efficiently. He told me to return the next day with a more positive attitude and to leave my son with Hannah.

I returned to my home with my baby and I told Hannah that I had to leave my baby with her after this day. She assured me she would take care of him then I went straight to my room and I lay down with Kwadwo.

The next day I did as I was instructed and I did my duties from the start of the day. I spent the whole day in a day dream thinking about Kwadwo and when I tried to stop I kept recalling him crying and this started to haunt me. I returned home in the evening and went straight to see him sleeping. Hannah told me that there was another woman on the plantation who had given birth only a month before me and she was the one who came and gave him his feeding.

This did not seem right as my son was being suckled by another woman, one that I did not even know.

I had no choice but to accept this, even though it ate away at my feelings and my bond for my son. Each day I left for Master Adams home I had to abandon Kwadwo and each evening I returned and I suckled him and then again during the night and first thing in the morning.

After a while he was sleeping through the night so this was becoming less and less of a natural mother's duty for me until my feeding became unnecessary. My breast lost the ability to provide for him.

I was not given the chance to choose my sons father, nor was I allowed to choose his name. Now I was deprived the privilege to feed him. I could cope with these first two denials but the third one made me very sad in my heart.

I continued to do my duties for Master Adams and I carried on collecting the coins until Edward had buried another full sack in the same spot as the first one and slightly to the left.

Edward grew very close to Kwadwo and he played with him and made little carvings for him to play with. One was a favourite which was a hollow wood with some grains of rice inside and sealed which made a noise and it rattled when it was shaken.

Kwadwo continued to grow and quickly he reached the point where he started to take his first steps and how funny he was. He was strong and he walked tall and when he did this he giggled and he started to touch everything, so he had to be watched.

One evening when Edward was with me and my son in my room Kwadwo stood up and he walked over to the silent drum. I watched Kwadwo and it made me smile. I thought that he must have a desire to accept his ancestry as he wanted to beat the skin to a new beat and I shared this humour with Edward.

I was looking at him as he stood balancing against it with his hands on the side and I had a thought in my head of him playing it.

Suddenly the secret compartment popped out and I was shocked. Kwadwo had opened the clandestine pocket of the silent drum and I wondered how much of a sign this really was. Edward looked at me and I raised my eyes in surprised and we both laughed.

Kwadwo reached his first birthday and Edward had buried many more sacks of coins and these each time were again to the left of the other sacks of coins.

Kwadwo was a very handsome little boy and he stole the hearts of the workers when he played in the yard. I wondered how my life was lived without him as he was my blood and my future and I loved him dearly. Edward also told me that he saw him as his own which made me happy but I saw it in his nature how he bonded with him.

I continued with my duties at Master Adams home. One day as I walked there Blackie was growling at me and I knew he was up to his tricks again to try and torment me.

As he came running up to me I made sure I stepped to his side and I avoided his aggressive leap. He soon left me alone and I continued to the house.

I entered the rear door and I delivered my greeting to Miss Sylvester and started with my duties in the master's bedroom. Mrs Adams had gone with William to the market that morning and they had left early. Master Adams was in the field with the workers but due to return soon.

I made my way to the wardrobe to collect some coins and my nose suddenly sensed a whiff of a smell which was quite nasty and sour. I looked around and on the floor I saw there was something that was not right. I saw a smudge of mess that was not there when I came in to the room. I took a closer look and it was the foul of Blackie. I then noticed that this deposit was under my slipper and I had walked into his nastiness after he leapt at me in the yard outside and I had trampled it in to Master Adams bedroom.

I panicked with what I done and so I removed my slippers and I made my way to fetch a bucket of water from the container in the yard.

As I returned I saw that I had trampled this mess with every step I had taken in the house. Miss Sylvester was outside washing some clothes so she did not see me.

I had to think about this as I knew Master Adams was soon to return and so I had to think what to do then I had the answer. I put down the pale of water in the kitchen and I returned to Master Adams bedroom and I found a pair of Mrs Adams shoes.

I then took my slippers and I scraped the hounds mess from my own onto those of Mrs Adams. This way I put the blame on Mrs Adams and I was clear of any trouble.

I wash Blackie's mess from my own slipper then continued with my duties and I started chopping some ground provisions in the kitchen. Shortly after this Miss Sylvester walked in and joined me. She had a chicken in her hands that was fresh and plucked ready for the pot.

She commented of a sour smell in the kitchen and I replied that I had also smelled it. Master Adams then entered the house and he walked towards his writing room then he stopped having noticed the mess on the floor.

He screamed at what he saw and his face turned red with his anger. He asked what it was that he noticed and I remained quiet. Miss Sylvester shrugged her shoulders which did not get a good response from Master Adams.

He raged at this as he informed us that it was the smudged muck of his beloved hound Blackie.

I offered to clean it straight away and I picked up the pale of water and started to clear the mess.

Master Adams then went to his writing room and I carried on with my duties.

That evening I left for my home and shortly after I arrived I was joined by Edward and I told him what had happened and he laughed at what I had done. I was quite satisfied with my little trick and I thought of how Kesiwaa would be pleased with me. I snuggled with Kwadwo and his playing with Edward's shaker made me smile. I sang a beat of a drum and we made a little moment of enjoyment between us.

That same evening William came to the door of my home and he did not have a look on his face which was cordial.

I was asked to go to the home of Master Adams. I returned at once and I stood in front of his desk. Mrs Adams was at her husband's side and they were looking at me. With Miss Sylvester by my side I waited to hear what warranted my recall.

Master Adams then delivered his speech to inform us that the mess from Blackie had been trampled all over the house and this had been done by one of us. He spoke to say that his beloved hound was stressed which is the reason that he scratched the rear door and he was crying until he was allowed into his home. Blackie then found the mess on the floor in the kitchen first then he followed the scent to every spot it had been trampled around his home.

He added that Blackie led him to Mrs Adams shoes that were found to contain this mess. He told us that he had first thought his wife was to blame but Blackie was growling which was not his usual behaviour and it was the same growl he gave me. He was going to just clean up the mess himself but it was Blackie's constant growling which made him realise his wife was not to blame. He then asked his wife about this and she told him she had not worn that pair of shoes that had Blackie's foul on them for over a week so one of us was guilty of transferring it to them.

I knew this was true as I had done this and I that my devious act had been discovered. Miss Sylvester immediately spoke up and she took the blame and I remembered back to Ifunanya when I had decided to take ownership of the situation. This prompted me to speak up to my actions and all went quite in the room. I admitted it was me that transferred Blackie's stool onto the shoes of Mrs Adams.

Master Adams then sent us both away and I returned to my home and that night I felt the comfort of Kwadwo sleeping with me. I saw Edward and told him about the situation and he advised me everything will be alright. I felt nervous and uncomfortable and although I tried to sleep I awoke many times during the night with worry.

I returned the next day to Master Adams writing room with Miss Sylvester standing next to me and Mrs Adams stood next to her seated husband. I was delivered a statement which made me swoon.

Master Adams made his speech which he told me was a decision made after he consulted his wife. He informed me that my behaviour was so conniving that it made him feel betrayed of his loyalty to me and my son. He then went quiet and I stood in silence with my sentence hanging in the air waiting to enter my ears with the punishment I was going to be given.

Then it came and I listened intensely but the only part I heard was when he then told me that he had decided to send me to another plantation on the island of Tobago. He told me that he would transfer me on the following morning. My heart sank deep into my chest and my thoughts went to Edward, then Hannah, then all the friends I had made.

I felt rejected and bitter at this discharge from the plantation that I had learned to live on and I felt like I was the victim of Blackie's revenge at being cast out as I had made this my home. I had adjusted well with my son and I was close to Edward.

I had no time to think about this and I just took a deep breath as I had to accept it.

Miss Sylvester touched my hand and squeezed it slightly as Master Adams started writing on a piece of paper on his desk and I waited for my instruction to leave. I thought about what my destiny was going to deliver me on the new plantation. At least I had my son and we would be fine to start a new life.

That was when Master Adams delivered his final word and he told me I would be going alone and my son would stay. He did not even look at me when he spoke to me which told me how cold his words were.

"What! My son will not go with me oh my Onyankopon." I said to myself.

I started to tremble and Miss Sylvester grabbed my hand again. I felt myself swaying and the ceiling started to rotate in a blur. I blinked my eyes and took another deep breath.

Master Adams raised his head and looked at me and smiled. It was almost as though he was laughing at me as if the pain he was giving me gave him satisfaction before he continued to write again.

Master Adams then told me to go and take my clothes from my home and then William would take me early in the morning. This really hit me at this point and I felt this dismissal was similar to being cast out of my home village. Can you imagine how I felt about this? My heart was crushed into a pulp of sadness.

It was then I decided to say something and so I spoke up to Master Adams.

I pleaded with him to let me stay but he was not interested and he just held his head down. I dropped to my knees and clasped my hands and begged with Master Adams to let me stay on the plantation and after a short time he raised his head and said that if I wanted to stay the decision was to be made by me.

Master Adams then said that if I wanted to remain then he will send my son away instead and I was to make the choice of which of us was to leave.

I had no answer to this question and my thoughts flipped around in my head. I recalled my own life and my security and then I gathered in my head the thoughts of my son Kwadwo.

What should I do? I was in a state of confusion because of a question that should never be asked.

I shook my head. I was in no better position as I was going to be separated from Kwadwo whatever I said so it was my son or me?

Master Adams prompted me to answer him and so I had to think quickly and I thought about the choice. Would it be better to stay and keep collecting the coins with Edward and let my son start a new life or did it make sense to leave Kwadwo with Hannah and I try the new life.

Master Adams then told me to hurry with my decision and when he spoke he gave me my answer.

"Well is it you or the Bastard mulatto child who is staying with me? Spoke Master Adams in a tempered voice.

There was no way I would let my son live with this man without me being around and so I made my decision for my son to start a new life away from this horrible and cruel man. Of course I did not know the place he was going to but I called on my Onyankopon for it to be a better place than this one.

I replied with my answer and Master Adams then tore up the papers he was writing and he took a new paper and began writing on a new one.

Whilst he did this I thought about my choice and I decided on myself staying and to let Kwadwo go was the better option. I believed that I needed to carry on with the collection as well. This would now also be personal and as a payment for my son.

Master Adams then told me I would need to go to my home and spend the last night with Joseph. I thought then that my son will never be called Joseph after this vile insult.

I thanked Master Adams through a forced voice of gratitude and returned to my home and I called Edward to join us.

I picked up my son and I spoke about my love for him and that he needed to be a strong boy.

"Yebehyia bio", I told him in his ear, which meant "We shall meet again."

I held him close for my hands to remember how his softness felt. I looked at him to savour the shape of his face around his eyes and his other features. I kissed him to taste his skin and then I asked him to speak to me so I could keep his voice inside my head to remember how he sounded. The most important thing was I smelled him.

I knew I would not have a visual memento, an audible one or one to taste or feel but I decided to keep some of his garments as they contained his smell which I decided to hold onto.

Edward and I played our games with the shaker that evening and it went by so quickly. Edward retired to his home and I cradled my son with watery eyes and the energy was drained from me with the drama which drew into a tiredness which I fought as I did not want to sleep. My eyes remained looking at Kwadwo with the help of a candle flame as he rested that night with me taking snatches of sleep.

The morning arrived and before I could wake properly Hannah shouted at me to advise me William was waiting at the door.

I had no time for fuss and I knew I had to do this and so I dressed Kwadwo and gave him a last squeeze against my bosom.

I then held back my emotion as I gave my son to the hands of William who gave me a weak smile which reflected a slight embarrassment at what he was forced to do.

I watched as William walked away carrying my child towards the master's house and then he disappeared out of sight and my son Kwadwo Kwaku was gone.

It then hit me hard. My son was gone and I felt profoundly empty and hurt. My heart was crushed to nothing more than an empty skin of a once full and ripe fruit. Do you know how it hurts to lose your child? A child alive but taken away from you, do you? I can tell you how it feels. It is more painful than losing someone you love to Onyankopon when they die and remove themselves from living as at least you know then they are at rest but when you know that your child is out there in the world and you have no control of their nurturing, the delight of seeing them grow and the joy of their learning then it rips at your chest, head and stomach like a savage beast mauling you. Do you think it hurts this badly? No, it is much worse than that.

CHAPTER 26: Malice

Hannah informed me that I had to go for my duties at the house and so I dressed and tidied my hair.

I arrived at the home of Master Adams and I saw Miss Sylvester who spoke to me but when I tried to reply my throat was too dry to respond.

Miss Sylvester asked what was wrong with me and I advised her that it was because my son was gone. She coldly ignored my reply to her and informed me of the day's instruction and then she left me by myself. I spent the whole day in a daze, thinking about where my son was taken to.

The hardest part was not being able to know the family who were going to raise him. If I could meet them then I may have been a lot more focused on my duties. I found myself paying very little attention on my day and when I washed some of Master Adams clothes I had worn the soap down to nothing without realising how long I was scrubbing the cloth.

I don't even know what happened to the next couple of weeks. I was numb with my loss.

I stopped collecting the coins from the jar and one evening Edward reminded me I needed to continue and I snapped back at him with my answer.

Edward knew how I felt and he apologised for pushing me with the collection and I forgave him and we soon got back to talking of our future.

This made me realise that the only comfort I had was with Edward who stuck by me at every occasion and each evening he gave me his full attention.

When I spoke to him about Kwadwo he listened even though I must have told him the same thing over and over again. I asked him how he would feel if his son was taken away from him and he always replied with the same answer, that his son was taken away also.

There were evenings when I just sat in his arms and smelled Kwadwo's garments with my eyes shut and there were evenings Edward and I spoke about Kwadwo's funny little mannerisms. What was interesting was Edward had noticed things about my son I had not seen. One was when he seemed to always know when it was about to rain. Edward and I laughed at this and it was then he told me my son would grow up to be a fine boy and he spoke to me very profoundly when he told me I would see my son again.

Edward knew how to lift my spirits when I was down and he knew how to make me laugh when I had been through a tiresome day at the house.

All this affection and attention made me soon realise I was in fact in love with him. With my son taken away I was replacing the love for my son with my love for Edward and one day my words fell away from my mouth when he held me and I told him I was in love with him and do you know what he said?

He told me that he knew and he was waiting for the pain I had suffered to ease before he told me he loved me also. He knew what I had gone through with carrying my child, loving my little boy the being torn from him.

One night he walked me to the spot where we stood underneath the stars and he told me had something to say to me that had been on his mind for quite a while. I had not any idea of what this was until he just came out and said it. He asked me to marry him.

Well you can imagine how I felt when these words filtered my ears I was absolutely lifted off my feet and I told him yes straight away.

I felt a great rush of emotion with the loss of my son and the way I had been treated during my recent life so this came as though it was a life line to embrace.

Edward told me he would speak to Master Adams and he would

tell him our intentions and I was so happy.

He called for William and he asked him to make him an appointment with Master Adams for an announcement.

I was so excited the next day that I skipped along the dusty ground towards Master Adams home and when I saw Blackie wagging his tail and standing in front of me I just laughed at him and he returned to his wooden box next to the door.

I walked through the rear door and I did not see Miss Sylvester but I heard voices and they were load. The heavy voice of Master Adams was competing in a battle of words with the shrill of Mrs Adams and I found myself walking towards the stairs and soon I was outside their bedroom door.

I stood and listened as Master Adams made his dissatisfaction of the visits his wife was making to the next plantation recently. He was complaining that she usually only travelled every month yet lately it was a lot more regular. She was visiting the other plantation now every week and he wanted to know why.

Mrs Adams retorted to say her husband was a miserable man and he had lost his control of the plantation as he let all the workers continue with their African traditions. She made it clear she did not like it and she felt concerned about the things she had heard.

She spoke about the witchcraft she called the curse of the slaves which she did not see on the other plantation where she felt a lot safer. She was also unhappy about the workers making African carvings and masks which she had previously warned him to put a stop to.

Master Adams then returned his shouting by saying that she did not show any attention to him anymore and he added he may as well be lying in his grave for the way she makes him feel. Mrs Adams advised him that he should not speak in a bad tone to her as these words could be his blight. She added that there must be someone on the plantation who she could arrange with to grant his wish of being in a grave.

I thought about Martha when Mrs Adams spoke this and it brought a sudden shiver to run through my body.

Mrs Adams clearly did not like African things being made which made me think of the silent drum and whether or not it would be taken away and destroyed. I knew when I returned to my home I had to inform Edward at what I heard.

The argument soon cooled down so I quietly made my way back down the stairs and I took a brush and I started to sweep the outside veranda.

Master Adams came outside into the yard just after me and called William to see him. I did not hear what they spoke about so I continued my day until it was time for me to retire to my home.

Later in the evening, whilst I was washing some clothes outside, I saw Master Adams approach the home of Edward and I noticed he was invited inside.

Only a short time passed when Master Adams left and Edward followed him outside. He came over to see me and he was looking stressed.

Edward spoke with tears in his eyes when he told me that Master Adams had rejected his request to marry me and he told him to find somebody else.

I could not believe this as I had just found the man I wanted to be with. I asked Edward what reason Master Adams gave to him and he replied that I was the house girl and I was not available.

What mean kind of rules are these I thought and my emotion turned from disappointment to the feeling of a fire in my chest.

I was enraged but there was nothing I could do. I thought back to what Kesiwaa would do and I tried to think how I could release my revenge on the bastard Master Adams who was stealing not just my body and my child but also my heart and future with Edward.

I held Edward as he sobbed into my bosom and I told him to stay quiet when he spoke to me of his happiness being stolen from him.

This was the second time this happened to him. I stopped Edward speaking when he rambled on about how he would not let Master Adams prevent us getting married.

"Only with his death I will be able to marry the woman I love." Edward spoke whilst sniffling and increasing his embrace on me.

That night I did not sleep very well and I thought about the herbs and medicines Martha had in her home and I knew then that I needed to see her to learn a little bit about them.

As I tried desperately to sleep I heard a little scratching at the side of my bed and I looked down and I saw a mouse scurry across the floor towards my door. I shrieked and this brought back the thought of the girl on the boat who became delirious and ate the rat that bit her finger. I needed to get this thing out of my home as I was not going to eat it.

The next morning I joined the line-up for the call from the conch's horn and Master Adams stood in front of the workers with a downturned mouth and he looked like he was in a temper again.

He spoke firstly about Mrs Adams desire to remove our African traditions, as they made her uneasy.

This prompted Tobias Jack to speak up and asked for him to think again about his decision.

Master Adams turned to William who was at his side and he informed him Tobias's tongue was too moist with words. He ordered William to make sure Tobias did not take any water whilst he worked in the field so his throat would dry up and prevent him from speaking when not required.

He then spoke to Abel Bowleg and he told him that if he saw Tobias take any water then he should report it or he would find himself back in the stocks.

Master Adams passed this instruction on to William and as his head was turned I glanced along the line and Abel's head had sunk to his chest. He was rocking slightly and was clearly distressed.

The line broke up after the spoken words of Master Adams and I went to visit Martha.

I was greeted by her with a smile and I informed her that I needed something to help me pass my food as I was not doing so for two days and my stomach felt a cramp. What I really wanted was to make Master Adams run to release his bowls just as Kesiwaa had done to Nana Apane.

I then added that during the night just gone I saw a mouse in my room and she gave me a look of concern.

Martha walked over to her shelf of jars and bottles and she removed two of them and placed them onto the table. One bottle was in a round shape with a cork stopper and there was a tag tied around the neck, the other was a slightly smaller one, it was darker and there was no tag.

She pointed at the larger one and told me to put a drop into some hot tea and it would help me to move my bowls. She then pointed at the second bottle and told me to put a drop onto some bread and place it in a corner of my room. The unwanted furry guest would feed on it and I would not see it again. It was a poison to kill the mouse.

Martha then took two cloths and she wrapped up the bottles, secured them with neat ties, and handed them to me.

I took both of the cloths and walked to Master Adams home. As I entered I held the cloths together so they looked like one. I saw Miss Sylvester scrubbing the floor.

She stood up to collect some more water and I asked if I should make Master Adams and his wife some tea. She told me the water had just boiled and it was ready and she would make it.

She told me to go and collect some eggs and then she saw the cloths and asked me what I had in my hand. I replied to advise her that Martha had given me some medicine to help me pass my stool and placed the bundle onto the table.

Miss Sylvester laughed at me and I left her smirking. I collected a basket, then went into the yard and gathered eggs from the fowl pen as she requested.

When I returned I saw that Miss Sylvester had the tea ready on a serving tray and she told me to take it to Master Adams.

She turned away to empty the bucket of dirty water that she used to scrub the floor and I quickly grabbed the bundles of cloths. Miss Sylvester turned back suddenly and I only managed to pick up one bundle. The other one remained on the table. I placed the bundle I had onto the tray then I left the kitchen.

I was unsure which bottle I had but I had to pursue my plan. My fear of Master Adams was eroding and it was being rapidly replaced with hate.

I walked toward Master Adams writing study and as I approached I stopped, placed the tray on a table, and I untied the cloth. I saw the bottle lying down on the tray and I prized out the cork.

I heard Master Adams cough from behind the door to the room of his study. I had to be quick.

I poured some of the liquid from the bottle into his tea, then pushed the cork back in the bottle and retied the cloth. I placed the cloth with the bottle inside on the table.

Picking up the tray I knocked the door to the study and I was invited in. I entered and placed the tray with the tea onto his desk and left. I picked up the cloth bundle from the table and then I went back to the kitchen to await my orders from Miss Sylvester.

I had a feeling of revenge tickle my stomach and it felt good. I felt justified for what I had done.

I picked up the other bundle from the table then I asked Miss Sylvester if I could be excused to return to my home to take my medicine. She gave her consent to me as she knew I had to take this medicine and with this she smiled at me.

I returned to my home and placed both bundles onto my bed. I unwrapped them both. Seeing the two together made me wonder which one was for me and which one was for the mouse. I picked up the smaller bottle and I noticed it was almost empty. I looked at the one with the tag and it was still full.

I had poured the liquid meant for the mouse into the tea of Master Adams but I was not really concerned with this as it was only to halt a mouse and so it could not be that poisonous. I took the bottle with the remaining drop of liquid and I poured some onto a couple of pieces of bread and placed them, as ordered by Martha, on the floor in the corner of my room.

I returned to the house and continued with my duties.

I never saw Master Adams again that day although Mrs Adams was complaining that he was being sick and he had to go to his bed to rest. She called for Martha to go to see if she could help him. Martha was with Master Adams for a long time before she left to let him sleep. I continued with helping Miss Sylvester around the house and then the evening arrived and it was time for me to go home.

I found my way to my room and I looked to see the pieces of bread were gone. I looked around and under my bed and there was the mouse still and quiet and lying on its side. I reached under my bed and pulled the tail and there was no movement so I pulled it again and dragged the tiny corpse out. I walked towards my window, opened the shutter and flung out the dead creature.

I felt a little bit uneasy with this and so I washed my hands then I went to see if Edward had returned from the field but he was not in his home. I asked the workers who were sitting nearby and they informed me he was comforting Tobias Jack who earlier in the day had fainted from dehydration in the field. I went in search of him and eventually I learned that he was in the home of Martha, and so I made my way there.

I knocked the door and Martha greeted me and I was invited in.

I saw Tobias Jack lying down and sitting beside him were Edward and Jack Spaniard.

Tobias was talking but he was clearly drained from his day of suffering. Edward saw me and he stood up and told me that Tobias was determined and stubborn enough to last the day without any water but it was too much and he collapsed. Edward then said how he had seen a strong side of Tobias which he admired and it was the reason he was there to give him some support.

He added that they were sure they could sneak a drink for Tobias at some stage during the day but Master Adams had sent William to the field to observe him. To make it worse he ordered everyone to give their water flasks to Abel Bowleg so he could be responsible for the orders given at the line-up.

As Abel was not allowed to supply any water to Tobias he watched as Toby slowly drained of his energy and Abel was at home feeling guilty that he had caused his slump into unconsciousness in the field.

He added that Abel was also in a bad way because he felt the other workers would blame him for this and so he had locked himself away. Edward then informed me that the workers tried to tell Abel he was not to blame as it was on Master Adams orders and this made him start mumbling about the punishment which he endured and his want for revenge on Master Adams.

I looked at Tobias and told him he would be well looked after by Martha and then sat down with the others and listened as Tobias spoke of his anger at Master Adams. I thought it was only me who had this resentment but I was wrong.

"My revenge will come." He spoke with a haunting tone in his voice. "I will make Master Adams pay for not allowing me to drink water during the day. His throat will be a dry as that of a dead man one day." Spoke Tobias with an angry tone with his words.

I could see that Edward wanted to speak about his fury with Master Adams but I pinched his hand to make him stop voicing his opinions for others to hear. Edward soon kept quiet and shortly after we left. I returned to my home and Edward went to his.

That evening the rain came down quite heavy so before I went to my bed Hannah and I gathered as many pots as we could and put them out side to catch the water.

As I did this I saw Tobias was leaving the home of Martha and I saw Edward closing the shutter to his window from outside. Edward did not notice me, but I saw him stand for a short while looking towards the big house of Master Adams. Before he returned to his home he shouted something which I did not understand but it sounded like a shout of anger directed at Master Adams.

I soon returned to my room and I snuggled myself together to try to sleep.

The rain spattered against the ground most of the night and I woke several times from the wind making the fences creak and rustling the trees.

The next morning I was so tired from a restless sleep that I just wanted to put the bed cloth over my head and let my comfort swallow me up but Hannah came to my door and she started banging it.

She was shouting and she would not stop and then she just opened it and entered my room.

I wondered what could be so important and then she told me something which hit me so hard I did not know what to think.

She spoke directly and sternly at me and said "Master Adams is dead!"

Well you can imagine how I felt at this announcement as my ears did not register the full consequences of what was informed to me. I had to ask again what Hannah told me. She repeated the information. I stood from my bed and I looked at Hannah who was now sobbing.

I knew it was my hand that had done this. I played with my thoughts and came to the conclusion, I had murdered Master Adams. I put the poison in his tea earlier that day. I turned my back to Hannah and pulled my bed cloth to tidy it and as I did this I spoke to myself "Oh my Onyankopon what have I done?"

I joined Hannah and we walked to the big house. She continued to release her tears and as we approached we saw William. He was comforting Martha. She looked like she was crying as well and then Miss Sylvester came out into the yard and her face was full of agony and streams of sad tears running down her cheeks.

The whole yard was full of dismay. Blackie howling like a frightened beast. This time he was just pacing towards and away from the house like he was a confused puppy and then he began whimpering sadly.

Some of the workers started drifting towards the house and William told them to stand where they were and remain still.

Among these were Jack Spaniard, Tobias Jack, Abel Bowleg and his wife Violet. Augustus and some of the others wandered up to join those already there.

They were all asking what had happened but I knew that I had murdered Master Adams. I had to remain calm. I was the one responsible and the more I thought about it the more my akuma raced.

We all stood talking about what we had heard and we hoped it was not true but the worry was about to be confirmed. We waited then all went quiet as through the rear door Mrs Adams appeared. She was joined by an obroni that I did not recognise.

Mrs Adams was standing in front of everyone and we formed a crescent line around her as she called for calm.

Her announcement was made with a trembling voice and a cloth wiping her face from the tears on her cheeks. She stopped and paused as she struggled to speak and the obroni placed his arm around her shoulders to comfort her.

Mrs Adams then announced that her husband was passed on from this world. She added all of the workers should go back to their homes and remain there and await instruction. She said that until further notice we will be taking our orders from the man who was standing next to her and she announced him as Master John White.

Nobody moved at this request until Master White raised his voice to fortify her command and with this the workers turned away slowly and they headed back to their homes.

As they did this there was talk amongst them. I saw Tobias walked alone and then Abel Bowleg held the hand of Violet.

Slowly, everyone dispersed and Hannah told me to go with her and Martha would remain with Mrs Adams as we were excused for now and we would be called on when needed. Edward looked at me and told me to join him as soon as I was ready. I noticed that he had a really worried and concerned look about his face.

Miss Sylvester came over to me and she took my hand. She asked me to go with her and she was acting like something concerned her.

I excused myself from Hannah and walked with Miss Sylvester. We made our way to her home which was at the side of the main house.

I saw a look on Miss Sylvester's face which I thought to be odd and I suspected she knew I had murdered Master Adams.

I entered Miss Sylvester's home which was a simple small wooden one roomed house and she asked me if I wanted to drink some tea and I obliged as I had to keep my actions as normal.

She placed a pot of water on a fire outside then she started to talk to me about the worries she had with the death of Master Adams and I could not believe what I heard.

Her face was full and swollen and I asked her what was wrong.

After taking a few moments to dry her tears Miss Sylvester spoke.

"Elizabeth, I cannot live with myself anymore and my secret needs to be told. You do realise that I have no children around me don't you?"

She whimpered and I acknowledged her information. She then told me she had in fact five children but they had all been taken to the other plantation on the island of Tobago as my son had been.

Miss Sylvester then spoke that she was once in love with Cleophus Hornigold and that Master Adams had stopped her relationship with him. She told me that she knew I had seen him hanging from the tree when I had gone to the market and it saddened her immensely.

Then she spoke to my ears something which added to the full drama of what was happening and she spoke with a voice which was soft but also one wanting to deliver information.

"Master Adams has taken me to his bedroom for many years and I have given birth to five children, and each time they were old enough he sent them to the plantation owned by Master John White."

I sensed something quite profound was going to be revealed. I sat and listened closely.

"My first born was a boy called Jacob and he had a sweet looking face but he was taken away from me. My second child was a girl who was sick. She was called Victoria and she was named after the then queen of England but she died just after she was born. My third was a boy and his name was Arthur and he lived but he was also sent to the plantation of Master White. My fourth child was another boy and he was called Thomas. He was a strong child who I struggled through child birth with. However, Thomas developed into a healthy child but there was a fire at Master White's plantation on the island of Tobago and he died. My fifth child was a boy again and he was called George. I have been informed he still lives, he is now three years old."

I nodded my head with acknowledgement that I was absorbing this information and I wanted to speak but she continued before I could say anything in reply.

"Master White was a friend of Master Adams but he can be just as nasty as him when he wants to be."

I listened with shocked ears as she told me that every time Mrs Adams went away from the plantation, either to the market for the day or to see friends, Master Adams called her to his bedroom which I knew for myself but I did not tell her anything.

After pausing to gain composure she spoke again.

"Eli when Master Adams asked you who to send away to the next plantation he knew you would choose your son. He bought you because he knew he would make a profit from your child just as he did with all of mine.

When I heard he took your child away I knew he was going to start taking you to his bedroom. Master Adams waited for your child to be born so as soon as he was gone I knew that your fate was in his bed. I could not let you suffer what I have been through and I could not let him touch you."

I could hardly believe what I was hearing and I felt a shock of sickness hit my head and it played heavily on my thoughts.

She spoke to me with nervousness in her voice which made me feel uneasy.

My eyes started to well with tears as Miss Sylvester came over to me and she took me in her arms as she continued her speech to me. She mumbled a few words then she held me tighter and I soon absorbed what she had confided in me.

Miss Sylvester continued with her story and she told me that she had done a terrible thing.

I asked "What did you do Miss Sylvester. What is it that you did?"

Miss Sylvester then told me something I will never forget.

"Elizabeth, I think I killed Master Adams. I poisoned his food with a clear liquid that I saw in a bottle marked with two lines which crossed like they were bones and a picture of a skull over the top. Of course I do not know what it was as I cannot read but I could not let him continue with you and take your life away. I did it to make him have a sickness so he would stay in his bed."

Miss Sylvester told me the liquid she used was the one that Master Adams placed on a dangling paper in his bedroom to kill the flies and insects. I remembered that it was the one Master Adams told me to not touch when he shouted at me so harshly.

As we stood facing each other she embraced me as a gesture that she had saved me from a real horror. She then stood back and continued talking and I absorbed her every word.

I was shocked and my eyes spilled over to let the tears flow. I cried heavily and embraced Miss Sylvester strongly as she also shed tears of sadness until her dress was soaked on her shoulder.

I asked Miss Sylvester if Mrs Adams knew anything about her husband taking his lust with her and she informed me she did not.

She spoke with nervousness in her voice and she sounded like she was scared for her life. I listened to every word intensely and I told Miss Sylvester that I would find my son one day and I would also find her living children. I also informed her that I would not say anything and her shared words were between just the two of us.

This confession shocked me and it made me think that maybe I was not the only one who sealed the fate of Master Adams. I still remembered the tea which I served him on the morning when he became sick. I may have delivered the fatal poison that was too much for him, but perhaps not.

I was so confused at this time and Miss Sylvester was showing me she was in a state of worry so I stayed with her for a while until it was about midday. I did not tell her what I had done and I was particularly appalled by what I had heard but it gave me the feeling that I was not alone to blame for the death of my owner.

I remembered hearing his wife, Mrs Adams also speaking ill wishes on him and how she could arrange for him to lie in his grave. Maybe she did go and see someone and there was witchcraft involved. Was that person Martha? This made me think what Martha had said the time she helped me recover from my lashes and humiliation of my pride over the watery hole in the ground.

"Master Adams has been too cruel this time and he needs to be taught a lesson from our spirits."

I thought about the workers too. There was Tobias Jack. Now he had a motive for seeing Master Adams suffer for preventing him from drinking water whilst working in the field. He spoke openly of revenge. Then, there was Abel Bowleg who was disturbed by his cruel treatment which he never seemed to overcome as he hid away and shook like a leaf in the wind when he saw Master Adams. Finally there was my very own Edward. He had his reason for seeing off Master Adams after his second love was denied him. He spoke about his love for Catherine and now it happened again and this time it had broken him.

Was it murder or retribution that was the end for Master Adams? I did not know but I wanted to find out.

CHAPTER 27: Guests

After I had spent my time comforting my now broken and weeping friend, Miss Sylvester asked me if I was coping with losing my son. I shook my head and she saw the pain in my frown.

I told her I would not have managed if it was not for Edward. She informed me that he was a good man who lost the girl he wanted to be with a few years ago. I told her I knew this. I then informed Miss Sylvester about Fiifi and I told her that he arrived on the same boat and he was sold in the same market as me.

She advised me that he was probably still on an island plantation somewhere or even on the next plantation owned by Master White.

I did not want to hear this as it made me feel confused about my feelings for Edward. I then remembered that he wanted to speak to me so I informed Miss Sylvester that I needed to visit him and she gave a nod of approval.

I informed her that Edward and I wanted to get married but Master Adams said no to our request. Miss Sylvester looked at me and she gave a tiny smile as she advised me that because he was not around to prevent it I should go and speak with Mrs Adams instead and make my plea with her.

I never thought about this before so I made my exit from Miss Sylvester and walked up to the home of Edward. As I made my way I thought about what Miss Sylvester had told me and if she was right then Edward and I could now be married. I felt at last something may give me some happiness and the love of Edward would comfort and support me.

I arrived at his home and he greeted me with a kiss and an embrace as I fell into his arms. I spoke to him about what Miss Sylvester had told me and he smiled, agreeing that we may now have a new chance. With Master Adams gone there was nobody to stop us. I did not tell Edward what Miss Sylvester had shared with me about the plans Master Adams had to take me to his room. It was neither appropriate or the right time to upset him. In fact it did not matter now Master Adams had gone from this world.

Edward asked me to sit outside with him. At this time work in the fields harvesting the sugar cane had temporarily ceased.

The field workers were gathered on their stools and there was only one conversation to be heard.

"Who is this Master White?" They asked between themselves.

During this day many of the workers just sat around talking about what they thought would happen.

Abel Bowleg was still keeping himself in his home but the others were speaking about an enquiry which would now be made about Master Adams death. I dared not share my knowledge of Miss Sylvester's confession or the fact I could also be to blame.

The day ended with a strange air around the plantation as some of the workers reminded us that although Master Adams was a rotten man it was better the man they knew than this man called Master White who they did not.

I thought about what my future would now bring and knew things could change either way and so I had to be vigilant.

The next day I was called by William to go to the house and I saw Miss Sylvester was already present. She was standing at a window at the rear of the house looking out. I saw her face was in a trance as her stare was unmoved. I asked her if she was alright and she told me to look at the breadfruit tree at the far side of the plantation. I asked her why and she just replied to me in a plain tone that every morning as the sun rises it creates twinkles of light through the leaves. She added that it was almost like the tree itself was greeting the heavens and welcoming the day ahead. I looked at the tree and I saw what she meant. It was indeed very beautiful. I saw the shafts of golden rays spiking the ground creating a wonderful and glorious pattern of morning light on the ground.

Mrs Adams came into the room and told us to prepare the

bedrooms for visitors. She told us there would be three people arriving shortly and they would be coming to stay for a night. Mrs Adams did not share the names of those people who would be visiting but I guessed they were coming because of Master Adam's death. After talking to Miss Sylvester it was confirmed that the people coming were a physician, a man from the governor's office and a holy man.

I was told to stay away from the room at the front of the house. Behind its closed door was where Master Adams body lay.

Mrs Adams told me to clean the writing study first as this was going to be used by the visitors so I went there straight away. I was going to knock the door but there was no need to as nobody was there so I just opened it and walked in.

I walked over to the drapes which hung over the window and pulled them open. Approaching the writing desk I picked up the tea that was left on the side and then I left and made my way back to the kitchen. As I placed the cup on the side I suddenly realised it was the tea I had served Master Adams the previous morning. The pot and cup were still full.

It was then I realised that he had never tasted the poisoned beverage I had given him therefore I concluded that I did not contribute to his death.

I felt a rush of relief from worry evaporate from my skin. I raised my head up wards and I thanked Onyankopon.

I began making sure the guest rooms were ready. I needed to place a water jug and a bowl of fruit in each room. I then had to go and cut some flowers from the yard. I knew where there were some pretty golden ones.

As I did this I saw Blackie lying down and he was looking like he was lost without his master and I felt pity for him until he growled at me. I then had a quick tiny thought to bring him the cup of tea Master Adams did not drink.

I found the flowers in the yard and cut them and then I placed them in each of the three rooms which were now ready for the visitors.

Now this was done I went looking for Miss Sylvester and she asked me to help her prepare some food for the guests.

As we peeled some ground provision Master White came in to make himself some tea and he saw the cup I had left on the side. He asked me why it had been left there and I replied it was a tea I had made for myself but it had gone cold and so I was going to throw it away. I was a little edgy at this moment until Master White told me to drink it or dispose of it.

He added that tea was very refreshing when it was cold with some lemon squeezed into it so I picked up the cup and carried it outside and poured it into the dusty ground. I felt uneasy with Master White as I did not know his character so I made sure I was extremely careful with everything I did.

I continued my duties and later in the afternoon the guests started to arrive.

The first guest to show was dressed in a black jacket and he was carrying a medium sized black leather bag. He stepped from his wagon which had a long wooden box on the back. I noticed he was quite tall and slim and he had bushy hair on the side of his face. Master White greeted him and he took him into the house and I served them a cup of tea in the sitting room. William then took the large wooden casket from the back of the wagon and carried it to the room where Master Adams was lying.

Miss Sylvester informed me this guest was a physician and I asked what this was and she just told me he was here to examine the body of Master Adams to try to understand how he had passed on. She added that she was concerned he would discover that she had poisoned him and I told her to remain calm and quiet about it.

Shortly after, the second guest arrived. He was another fine gentleman and I was ordered to make more tea, this time extra sugar.

I took the tea and saw this man who was quite short and stout and was bespectacled. His face was clean shaven and his hair was missing in the middle. As I served him his tea I could hear him breathing heavily. I placed his cup on the table and he touched my bottom. I pulled away sharply and when I did he smiled at me. Well I did not think it was at all amusing and this made me feel shaken.

I heard Master White talk to this guest and he asked him how the new governor was keeping. I thought about what I had heard. I had been told that the governor was a man called Sir Ralph Abercromby but he had recently died in battle. However the conversation between the men informed me that the new governor who was called Sir Thomas Picton.

Master White asked about his ruling at a garrison on the island and the guest spoke to advise that Picton considered this place to be inadequate. He also gave Master White his opinion about some form of corruption which was taking place as Picton had a mulatto mistress who was influencing his decisions.

I heard some interesting conversations between these men which I had to try to remember and it was clear the new obroni governor liked the dark skinned women but they did not like to show this in public view.

The third guest arrived and he was greeted by Master White who spoke to him with similar respect to the others. I could not see this man's stature as he wore a long gown and it was similar to the obroni from my home that brought us the word of the Lord.

I served the tea and then Mrs Adams joined the group. The second guest then commented on how charming he thought I was and that he had not seen me before.

Mrs Adams informed him I had been with her for quite a while now and I was brought from Africa as a slave girl.

The man informed Mrs Adams there were words spoken in the British Parliament about the trading of slaves was soon to be abolished. I was not sure what this word 'abolished' meant but I sensed something was going to change. I was curious to know if it was going to affect me. Mrs Adams responded in disgust and she asked what she would do without her workers and the guest then added that slavery would still be in place it was just the trade would be stopped so slaves could not be bought and sold.

This prompted the holy man to speak and he stated how he was in favour of the slave trade being abolished. He added that this sick and vile trade was a rape of a person's human rights. This drew a stunned look from the others.

"They are called slaves in the eyes of those who take their innocent victims yet they are captives in the vision of those whose lives were stolen wrongly from them." He spoke with strength in his tone.

"They are slaves now and they will always be slaves to me." Replied the governor's assistant and the holy man shook his head to disagree.

This stout framed guest then asked me what my name was and I paused at first but Mrs Adams spoke and she told me to answer the guest so I replied it was Elizabeth.

He then asked me what my African name was and I looked at Mrs Adams and her stare was frosty.

The man asked me again and I looked nervously at Mrs Adams and she ordered me to reply to this man.

I spoke that my name was Esi Takyiwaa Kwaku although saying the name made me a little bit awkward. It should have made me feel proud.

As I spoke my name the man from the church spluttered on his tea and then he told the others that the first African clergy of the Church of England was a man with the same surname as me. This man was called the Reverend Doctor Philip Quaque.

"Q.u.a.q.u.e." he spelled it out for them to hear but I knew the name was wrong but I dare not tell them that I could write it down for them and I could read.

This guest then added that Reverend Doctor Philip Quaque

was ordained as a priest in the Church of England in 1769. He also informed everyone that this man was very well respected and liked in the church.

Mrs Adams gave a look of horror at this and she spoke to tell everyone that blacks had no place as leaders in the church. I did not care for her words.

Well can you imagine how I felt hearing this? I felt a shiver run through me. The strange thing was this Philip Quaque was a man who was spoken of with an air of respect yet I was only a slave. I could not understand this and I wanted to know who made the rules for this man to be given the blessing of the obroni yet I was given the value of an animal.

Mrs Adams saw I was listening to this conversation and she immediately asked me to leave. I had heard things which gave me a hope of a better future.

I returned to the kitchen to continue with the dinner to be served and once it was ready Master White and everyone moved to the dining area.

Miss Sylvester and I served the food and the man from the church was still talking about Philip Quaque. I heard them say that he was from my country and I felt myself suddenly caught between a hope of freedom and a feeling of why I was in this position. I listened as I served Master White and the guests. When the diners saw I was listening too keenly they fell into silence.

Mis Sylvester and I were ordered out of the dining room and we followed the instruction without any question. However my curiosity demanded I listen to the conversation further so I held my ear to the door after I had left.

After some small talk about the plantations profits the real conversation came out as they spoke about the talk in the Parliament that the trade in African slaves taken from their home was going to stop. I wanted to know more about this.

As I stood next to the door Miss Sylvester joined me and I asked her to be quiet with a quick gesture by putting my straightened index finger to my lips.

Miss Sylvester pulled my arm and told me to go away from the door. I stood my ground and for the first time I defied my orders from Miss Sylvester. She turned her back to me and walked to the front of the house and towards the window which shone a beacon of light through the tree and she placed herself directly in the brightness of the sun and gazed towards the sky as if to absorb the direct sunlight.

"Never before in my lifetime has there been anyone here of such responsibility Elizabeth. We have three men who have arrived who all have their individual importance." Spoke Miss Sylvester. Her voice trembled as of a person who was in a state of panic.

"I now see my fate Elizabeth." She added.

I must admit those words scared me. I also started to feel the fear. I tried to laugh it off but Miss Sylvester did not join my jolliness.

I continued to be present for duty during the end of the afternoon until I was excused to leave and return to my home. I walked quickly as I was eager to speak to Edward about what I had heard.

I raced up to his door and I knocked loudly and he invited me in. I told him about the guests at the house and he looked at me with interest. I grabbed his hand and I spoke so fast he told me to slow down. After I explained everything to him he told me the time was coming when we would be free.

I looked into his eyes and I knew he was right and when I spoke to him about Reverend Doctor Philip Quaque he thought at first I was making up a story to amuse him.

I asked Edward if we should make a request from Mrs Adams to allow us to get married and he told me he would make an appointment to see her. He then told me he would not do this until the guests had left and Master Adams was laid to rest. I knew this was a good idea and so I agreed to it.

The next day I arrived early for my chores as there were the guests to attend to. I poured the water for the tea and I prepared some shaddock topped with some sweet sugar. Miss Sylvester was busy as usual in the kitchen and she had baked some bread and cooked some fresh eggs.

The physician man came to the table to eat first and then the others joined him. He had been examining the body of Master Adams that morning and he arrived from the room where he was lying.

The guest from the governor's office spoke first and he asked what conclusion had been made. The physician spoke directly to the others and informed them he suspected foul play. He suggested Master Adams was murdered.

Master White ordered me to leave the room immediately and I went to find Miss Sylvester. I told her what I had heard.

Miss Sylvester swooned and she looked clearly shaken by this so I took her hand and told her not to worry.

I took her outside into the yard at the rear of the house and I noticed some workers were digging at a clearing at the edge of the plantation on a raised piece of ground. Miss Sylvester advised me it was where Master Adams was going to be laid to rest.

Master White then called me to ask William to go and request that Martha and Hannah arrive at mid-day to show respects in the burial of Master Adams. He also asked for three of the workers to attend the burial to represent them.

He told me to collect more flowers for Mrs Adams to place at his burial site and he made a request for a wooden cross to mark the spot where he would lie which he wanted William to make. Mrs Adams called for Miss Sylvester to prepare food and drink for the wake and she asked her to bring some flagons of rum.

As the bright sun shone high in the sky above the workers arrived. They were Augustus, Edward and Jack Spaniard along with Martha and Hannah. Then out of the house I walked with Miss Sylvester then behind us followed Master White, Mrs Adams and the three guests. Master White called Augustus and Edward to the house. He also shouted at William who was carrying a wooden cross to join them.

They entered the house with Master White and moments later they returned carrying the wooden box which contained Master Adams body on their shoulders.

They walked slowly to the burial site as they waited for the words of the holy man. He started to pray as they approached which was accompanied by the howling of Blackie, who had decided he wanted to join the group.

The holy man took control of the service and he spoke of his respect and admiration for Master Adams with a tone in his voice which induced a sniffle from Mrs Adams.

Slowly the three men then slid the box with Master Adams into the ground. The holy man continued to speak his words of the Lord and Mrs Adams broke into a spluttering of tears which made her take a napkin to her face.

Master White took a shovel and he started to refill the earth over the wooden box and as he did this he spoke to say he would find the person who murdered his good friend Master Adams. He spoke to advise everyone that he vowed to catch this fiend and have them tried for murder. As he said this Miss Sylvester grabbed my hand and then I felt it pulling away. I watched helplessly as she slumped to the ground. I dropped to her side and her eyes were closed. Martha joined us and the others looked on.

Master White ordered Augustus to complete filling the soil to the ground and he asked Martha to take care of Miss Sylvester. He took his arm and placed it around Mrs Adams shoulder and escorted her back to the house. She was whining like a blustery wind. The three guests followed them and I knew I should also join them but I was concerned for Miss Sylvester.

Martha called for William to stay with her so Miss Sylvester could be taken to her home and William responded to say she was too heavy to carry. Martha asked him to collect some water then told me to go to the house of Mrs Adams which I did.

I arrived and was called to the sitting room by Master White and instructed to serve the rum to the guests.

I found the flagons sitting on the table in the kitchen and I took five cups and placed them on a tray. I took this to the sitting room. Master White told me that Mrs Adams was not there as she was too upset and so they only needed four cups. I guessed she was taking a moment to be alone.

Master White asked me to leave the tray with them and prepare some ground provision and fowl. I went to my duty and I could not help but hear the heavy cries of Mrs Adams and I wondered if the tears were real or was it false wailing for the guests to hear.

My thoughts kept going back to the holy man. I just wanted to listen to him. To hear what he spoke about the man he called Quaque. I knew that whilst he was around he might speak of something that would be useful.

I removed a fowl from the pen and chopped of its head and I plucked its feathers before I collected some ground provision and I placed them in a pot of water to boil. As this was cooking I walked to the door of the sitting room and I held my ear to the door for more maco'ing but I heard nothing except talk about Sir Thomas Picton and his lame rule. They spoke about the succession to this man and it looked likely to be made imminently. The man to take control was a man called William Fullerton.

I then heard something which was more interesting. They spoke about a French slave rebellion on an island which was being monitored. The conversation was about a revolution in a place called France. This was causing problems in Saint Domingue where thousands of French colonists were fleeing and they were bringing their slaves with them to this island. The governor's assistant told the others that this was being caused by newly purchased slaves and not the local creoles who were settled slaves, or born on their plantations and so Master White did not have too much to worry about.

I found this information interesting. If there was going to be a rebellion then it would be these men in this place called Saint Domingue who would be able to do it. I then heard the noise of footsteps coming to the door and so I quickly dashed back to the kitchen.

Master White found me and he told me to go to see Mrs Adams in her room and take her some sorrel tea.

I boiled some more water, made some sorrel tea, and took it to the room of Mrs Adams. After knocking the door I was called to enter and I carried the tea to where Mrs Adams was sitting. She was looking into the mirror brushing her hair. I saw that her napkin had fallen onto the floor and so I picked it up and I gave it to her.

She looked at me and gave me a weak smile. I wanted to express my sadness and I looked into her eyes and they were clear and dry. I passed her the napkin which I felt with my fingers was not moist and damp from drying tears. This was strange as I had watched as Mrs Adams sniffled and sputtered through the burial service and was whining for a while after wards. I placed her tea onto the table where she sat and left.

I continued to make the food and then later Mrs Adams returned to Master White and the guests. Mrs Adams asked me if the food was ready and I replied it was. She then ushered everyone to another room to sit at a dinner table and I took them the cooked fowl and ground provision. I placed it in the middle for everyone to help themselves. I later returned with some bread and fruits and I noticed that, when I placed the food in front of Master White, his words were slurring like those of Nana Apane when he drank palm wine. I saw the other guests were also full of sot and they were laughing like small children.

Mrs Adams poured a cup of the rum from the flagon that Master White had brought to the table and she smiled at the others. They filled their cups again and Master White held his cup in the air and he called the name of Master Adams. They all spoke his name together.

They continued with their food and they talked of the importance of plantations in Trinidad. They spoke of how they would be able to continue if the end of the slave trade was to be introduced.

I stood and listened and saw them drink from this flagon and slowly they started to speak about my people with no respect.

The stout bespectacled man from the governor's office asked Master White if I was available for sale before the slave trade was abolished and his reaction was to look at me and laugh.

He replied to the guest that he had no use for me and he should make an offer for me.

I looked at Master White and he saw me eyeballing him and I held my stare longer than I should have done.

Master White then spoke to me. He asked me why I looked so worried. I dared not answer until he asked me if I was spoken for and Mrs Adams advised him that I was not taken as nobody was interested in me.

Master White then asked the guest to make his offer and there was a paused silence which was broken by the holy man.

He told the others to remain quiet and he looked at me and he told the others to let me speak. This caused them to laugh and they shouted at him in disgust and he responded to them with a raised voice and arising swiftly from his seat he spoke sternly.

"In God's name let the girl speak!" As he did this he slammed his hand onto the table. All went quiet.

Master White spoke as the holy man sat down again and he asked me if I was betrothed and my heart started to race. I shuffled my feet as they all stared at me. I was ready to speak but my throat was so dry. I took a deep breath and I told them my pledge was with Edward.

The holy man then spoke his happiness with a small shout of support at my response and then he poked the stout guest with his finger. The room went quiet again until Master White asked why he did not know about my betrothal.

I told Master White that Edward had asked Master Adams to let us get married and he had turned down the request. Master White responded to me and he spoke to say that this must have been very sad news. He asked me how Edward felt about it. I did not know what to say until Master White asked me if we were in love. I replied that we were.

Master White informed me that if he was denied being with the woman he loved then he would be very hurt and disappointed and I nodded my head to agree. Master White spoke again to say that if he was denied being married to the woman he loved then he would be so angry that he could not imagine the pain it would bring. I nodded again and Master White then asked me how Edward really felt and he kept asking me and he goaded me to reply. I responded to say Edward was angry with Master Adams as he had once before given his heart to a girl and she was taken away from him.

Master White then stood up and spoke out loudly and he pointed his finger at me.

"Would Edward be so angry that he would murder Master Henry Adams then?"

The physician shouted for Master White to steady his accusations and the holy man agreed with him but the governors assistant spoke to agree with Master Whites claim. He spoke with a loud deep voice to say,

"Here here John I think what you say is a valid point."

Everyone in the room looked at each other and the holy man spoke to say that enough was said and I should be allowed to marry Edward as he was my betrothed. The governor's assistant interrupted to say that as slavery was still legal, that he had every right to make a bid to buy me. He would make an offer with Master White at a later time and when there were less people to interfere. This man was clearly making me nervous but I felt he would not be able to buy me as I was needed for my duties in the house.

Mrs Adams ordered me to clear the table and so I collected the dishes and left Master White and Mrs Adams to their guests.

I noticed the guests did not consume all of their food and there was some fowl and ground provision still not eaten.

I cleaned the kitchen and made sure in the morning there would not be too much for Miss Sylvester, so I decided to scrub the floor as well.

This took me to the late afternoon when I heard Master White call my name. He ordered me to ask William to load the baggage of the guests onto their wagons as they were leaving.

I went to find William and he did as he was asked. I stayed around to try to hear the holy man speak but I heard nothing again from him.

William secured each guests baggage onto their individual wagons and they each delivered their farewell. They all rode along the track leading away from the plantation.

Master White and Mrs Adams waved their hands to acknowledge the departure of each wagon and then they returned to the house and I saw out of the window that Master White was not walking in a straight line. I had to smile to myself as he looked like a fool, his face had turned red and his expression looked silly.

They entered the house and Master White spoke to Mrs Adams to say he needed to go and lie down to rest. Mrs Adams instructed me to leave and she helped him climb the stairs. I heard their steps as they walked along the landing near to the bedrooms.

I made my departure and I left from the rear door and I closed it behind me and I made my way to my house when I remembered I had forgotten the uneaten fowl and ground provision left by the guest from their dinner.

I returned to the house and let myself in through the rear door. The food was still on the kitchen table. I picked it up and wrapped it in a cloth and then I was just about to leave when I heard shouting from Master White from the floor above.

I also heard Mrs Adams; their voices were raised in argument. I thought it was best for me to leave as the quarrelling did not concern me but then I thought that maybe because I spoke to the guest I was going to be punished. I knew that Master White was not thinking straight with the rum that had soaked into his head and so I decided to listen. I could not hear clearly so I climbed the stairs and walked slowly along the landing and I heard the shouting coming from Master Adams bedroom and I was maco'ing again.

I crept to the door until I heard firstly the voice of Master White and he was being quite direct when he spoke and he said something which shocked me.

"Look Margaret we both agreed on this and in fact it was your idea."

Mrs Adams then replied, "I told you to take care of Henry away from the house and make it look like an accident but oh no you had to strangle him didn't you John?"

He then spoke again and it was difficult to make out his words. He paused as he had suddenly started to hiccup during speaking.

"Look when I strangled Henry he was already weak and he was in his bed and seemed to be suffering from a fever. He was at a vulnerable time and it was my best chance to make it look like the illness took his life." He paused again then said,

"I love you Margaret and now I have gotten rid of Henry we can be together."

Mrs Adams was calm as she said.

"I love you also John and yes we are together after our secret love of many years, I was just worried about you being found out as Henry's murderer."

Master White then replied with a softer voice,

"Well I gave our guests a taste of who could be a potential murderer today and it was that useless field worker Edward."

Well I could not believe what I was listening to as it was Master

White's confession of murder, yet he was making Edward sound like he was the guilty man.

Mrs Adams then asked what the physician and Master White had said about the marks around Master Adams neck.

Master White told Mrs Adams that he saw the bruises and this was why he spoke about murder. Master White added that he told the physician he did not want any fuss to be made so he paid him to ignore the marks on Master Adams neck.

My teeth were grinding together in anger at the conversation I had listened to. I had heard enough from this confession of murder from Master White and I did not want to get caught listening. I slowly crept back down to the kitchen and I left through the rear door. I did not want to be seen by Master White from the rear window so I walked to the edge of the yard where I knew from the bedroom window I could not be seen and I made sure I hurried.

I had learned through experience to listen to every word if I could, as this would help me judge any future occasions. I needed to have information about anything and any announcements being made.

I also remembered from my past there was a saying and I thought to myself,"Onyankopon aniwa hu asumasem biara", as you will know by now means "God's eye sees all secrets," which they certainly did this time.

As I returned to my home I thought about what I had heard and I was almost in shock. So the real killer of Master Adams was Master White and Mrs Adams was in on it with him. What concerned me now was that Edward was being blamed by them and this did not sound good.

CHAPTER 28: Wedding

I returned to my room and lay on my bed and tried to think what to do. I knew I had to speak to Edward and there were many things to tell him. I arose quickly and I walked over to Edwards home and he invited me in. When I walked into his room I was shocked to see William was there already but he was just leaving.

I did not ask why William had visited as I was too keen to speak about what I had to say. Edward looked anxious and I asked him if everything was alright and he took me into his arms and we kissed. This was just what I needed as I was feeling as though my thoughts were out of control like a leaf in a blustery wind.

He released his clasp on me and he held my arms and looked into my eyes. I knew he was interested in anything I could tell him from the house and he asked me what I had heard from the guests.

I informed Edward firstly about the man who spoke about the end of the slave trade and Edwards face brought a smile of excitement and he clenched his fists in front of him. I told him the Governor of Trinidad was now a man called Picton who was ruling in an inadequate way and he was being influenced by his mulatto mistress.

This seemed to be better news than before and Edward clapped his hands together. I was so shocked at this reaction but I carried on with my information as I told Edward that the physician had made a statement and in his conclusion he declared that Master Adams had been murdered.

Edwards face went into one of shock and he looked at me for more on this so I carried on and told him Miss Sylvester thought she had poisoned Master Adams. I knew the truth so I felt it was now alright to share what I knew with Edward.

I informed Edward I had overheard the conversation between Master White and Mrs Adams about them being lovers and that Master White strangled Master Adams. Edwards face was shocked and he questioned what I was telling him almost like he was unsure in believing me.

Edward scratched his chin as he showed he was deep in thought then he stared at me and he advised me to keep this to myself. He repeated this with quite a direct tone in his voice. He indicated to me that if I was to say anything then I would probably not be believed and punished for gossiping.

I repeated to him this was the truth and I also informed him Master White was now aware that we planned to be married.

I spoke about how one of Master White's guests had asked to buy me before the slave trade was abolished and this brought out the question about my betrothal to him among the guests. Again I informed Edward how I spoke to them of our wedding plans.

This made him smile so I continued with my information and told him that Master White suggested that he, Edward, would have been angry at Master Adams as he had already taken Catherine away many years before and was now being thwarted again in his search for happiness.

Edwards smile dropped at this and he put his head in his hands.

I took him in my arms and told him to be happy as I related the rest of the conversation and that we could now be married and he agreed. He was just concerned about Master White who he did not trust and I agreed that we both had to be vigilant. I felt Edward's tension from what I had said but he assured me he would be fine.

I wanted to stay with Edward that night but until we knew we could wed for certain we had to be careful so I wished Edward a goodnight and went home.

I found it difficult to sleep and during the night I heard a sound which I had not heard before. It was almost like a bird calling but I knew it could not be. Eventually the sound stopped and I slept.

The next morning the sun was bright and I made my way to the house. I started my duties in the kitchen and I fetched a brush to sweep the veranda. Mrs Adams came down the stairs. She was dressed and wore a hat and looked like she was going out. She then spoke to me and she told me she was going to the market. Master White would be in the field later if I should need him. She added that he was still delicate from his evening previous as the rum was still in his blood.

I asked Mrs Adams if she knew where Miss Sylvester was and she informed me she had not heard or seen her that morning. She told me to call William and to get the wagon ready. I felt it was my duty to look for Miss Sylvester as I thought that she may be feeling unwell.

I stepped outside and Blackie was lying in the sun wagging his tail. I saw William and he was bringing the wagon out of the stable. I asked him if he had seen Miss Sylvester, he shook his head.

This was not like Miss Sylvester as every day I arrived at the house she was normally scrubbing the floor or making preparations for food, I sensed something was wrong.

I returned to the house and I knew I had to get started on the bed sheets and to collect the laundry.

I collected some water in a bucket and started to wash the sheets and clothes for the widow Mrs Adams. As I did this I felt weary and I saw the ray of light, beam, through the window that Miss Sylvester had stood in before as she looked at the light glistening through the leaves of the breadfruit tree.

The room was too stuffy and I decided I should open the window to let some air in.

I walked towards the beam of light shining through the pane of glass and I pulled it open. I breathed in a gentle breeze which I felt cooling on my skin and looked high in to blue sky that had few clouds. I thought to myself what a beautiful day it was and I could hear a bird singing.

My eyes fell towards the tops of the trees and I saw a mot-mot bird fly away and I then lowered my eyes again until I saw the flora below. I was about to turn away but I saw a dark shape below the branches. It was indistinct against the dazzling sun. I shielded my eyes for a better view.

Then I knew exactly what my eyes had seen.

"Oh noooo!" I shouted and I raced along the hallway towards the rear door. Blackie started to bark but I did not care I had to be quick and I ran towards the shape in the breadfruit tree.

I arrived at the form of Miss Sylvester hanging from a rope supported from a strong branch. Underneath was the chair Miss Sylvester had sat on when she had spoken of her guilt at the murder of Master Adams. It lay on its side. I ran up to her and tried to push her body up into the air to take the strain from her neck but she was motionless and she was cold. I was screaming wildly in my frenzy and my eyes soon started to let the tears flow down my cheeks. I remember thinking this could not happen but there was nothing I could do and although I knew it was too late I still tried to help her.

I was struggling and I needed some strength as she was far too heavy for me. I looked back at the house and I saw the window Miss Sylvester had been looking from to see if anybody was there but my sight was blurred from my tears and I just screamed again for help.

"Miss Sylvester somebody help Miss Sylvester!" I cried at the highest my throat let me.

I found myself exhausted and gasping for breath. I was not getting Miss Sylvester to safety however my screams had alerted Master White and William who looked horrified as they ran towards me and my burden.

William took over and he jumped up with a cutlass and cut the rope suspending Miss Sylvester's body. She landed with a thump on the ground and her legs buckled under her large frame.

William laid her arms and legs away from her body and he looked into her eyes before feeling her wrist. Master White stood over them and I found myself sitting on the ground.

I knew I was flooding with tears but I did not know that my body was shaking with fear and I was breathless from the sudden rush of energy.

I looked at the breadfruit tree which took her life and it just stood there not knowing what it had done to my friend. This was the tree Miss Sylvester was observing on the day she stood in the window. She had chosen this spot to remove herself from her years of torment and abuse and the thought of being branded a murderer. I then remembered the bird calling during the night and what Master Adams had told me and I knew the Jumbie bird had collected her spirit.

William looked at me and his eyes were full of tears as he also had lost a friend. This strong man looked broken as he held Miss Sylvester's hand and sobbed like a child into his other. I had never seen William like this and he crumbled as his chest sank.

I looked at Miss Sylvester and spoke to myself she was now at asomdwoee which in my language was the word for peace.

My eyes had seen my mother and Kesiwaa taken away from me but I was surprised at Miss Sylvester as I thought she was a strong woman. I looked long and hard at her lying on the ground then I heard the voice of Mrs Adams asking what the fuss was all about.

I stood up and turned to see her rushing towards us. Master White explained to her what she had done and I dropped my head.

Then Mrs Adams spoke to everyone saying she knew this was going to happen. She spoke to Master White and informed him she had taken her life because she was in love with Master Adams and she could not bear to lose him.

I wanted to take my hands and squeeze them around Mrs Adams neck right there and then but I knew I could not. I thought to myself how wrong she was with what she had said. William looked at me and he knew what I was thinking then he shook his head at me to tell me to let it go.

I made my exit to leave and I took one last look at Miss

Sylvester's lifeless body before I closed my eyes, then I turned away and returned to the house.

I thought to myself profoundly as I walked back and asked myself if there was anything I could have done.

"Why did I not see the warning signs?" I asked myself.

I reached the steps to the house and as I walked through the door I was confused as to what I was to do. My thoughts were concentrated on the horrible image of my friend and protector Miss Sylvester.

I wandered in a daze back to the laundry and as I approached it Mrs Adams walked behind me and she spoke to me.

She ordered me to go home for the rest of the day and as I left the house I saw Master White and William laying Miss Sylvester onto the wagon.

I reached my home and went to my room and lay on my bed. My body was numb and my thoughts were all of Miss Sylvester and how she made me feel from when I first met her to the last time we spoke when she confided her secret with me. I thought about her children and how she had suffered from the lust of Master Adams only to have his wife blame her for his sins. She served them loyally to the end with her duties with commitment both in her head and with her body and she was finally driven by a dreaded fear she had become a murderer when in fact she was not guilty any more than I was.

Hannah came to see me and I explained to her what Miss Sylvester had done and she sat with me and lifted me to her embrace which brought back more tears.

A short while passed and then the door to my room was knocked and it was William who came to visit me and he expressed his sorrow with me. This day I saw a side of William I had not seen before and his usual obdurate character showed he had feelings as well. William told me they had taken Miss Sylvester to be laid to rest in an area for workers. There would be a few people invited to see her placed into the ground and I was one of them. I agreed to be present and I asked if the holy man would be returning and he shook his head to advise he would not be.

The next day I went to the house and started my duties. There was an air of emptiness which made the large white building lifeless and without character.

This time there was no physician, no governor's representative and no holy man.

There were no men digging a grave on the top of a small hill. Nobody of any importance would be present at Miss Sylvester's burial. Any form of dignity and recognition for the many years she had dedicated herself to the plantation to which she gave her life went unrecognised.

Later that day without a physician to examine her body I was taken by William to a clearing which I had not seen before. It was away from the house and was the burial site for the workers. Four men stood beside a hole in the ground with earth piled to the side.

I saw Martha standing over a roughly made wooden box which was quite large.

Martha took charge. She spoke words of love and she blessed Miss Sylvester's soul and wished that she rest in peace. This time my eyes poured woeful tears and William put his arm around me and walked me away as the four men struggled to lower her coffin into the ground.

The thoughts of Miss Sylvester stayed in my head and my love and respect for her found a place in my heart. I knew Miss Sylvester was a great woman and I wanted to keep her memory alive and so later that day I placed some flowers over her grave. I visited her on every occasion I could and I sat down sometimes and I spoke to her. I ensured her place of rest was always pretty and colourful. I planted some shrubs around her place of rest and I even put some food out as was tradition in my tribe. (agyina aduane-ghost food)

The weeks went by and Edward kept up his support for me that I needed and we spoke again of getting married. This time we both agreed on a date and we decided a Sunday was the best day.

Edward spoke to Mrs Adams and she agreed and gave her permission for us to go ahead and make our plans.

We decided to inform the workers and one evening when we sat outside Edward jumped up from his seat and he made the announcement and there was a great cheer from everyone and all wished us happiness.

Edward made a joke about the abolition of the slave trade and that he had to marry me quickly before Mrs Adams or even Master White sold either of us.

Abel Bowleg spoke up to say he thought we would make a great couple and he would get his wife Violet to make a pretty necklace from some beads for the day. Jack Spaniard joined in to give his blessing. He suggested somebody should play the drum which Edward had made but even before the idea settled into everybody's head Tobias Jack reminded us Mrs Adams would not allow it because of her dislike of African traditions. I looked at Edward who gave me a stare which we shared for the real reason playing the drum would not be a good idea. The sound would be muffled from what it was hiding inside.

Our announcement seemed to lift every ones spirit a little and the workers found smiles on their faces which had not been seen for a while.

So we had set the date and we had things to prepare. I spoke to Mrs Adams about our preparations and the day we had decided and she responded to advise me she would let some of the workers to be present as indeed she would be herself.

I spoke to Mrs Adams about me moving into Edward's home with him and she told me it was expected once we were married. I advised her that I needed to start taking some of my dresses and things to his home and she agreed this would be also alright to do.

Edward and I was a couple at last and it was recognised. I did think, however, Mrs Adams wanted me to be away from the eyes of

Master White as for her to be so pleasant was slightly unusual. I did not care, as I could finally find my happiness and be with Edward in the way I had wanted for so long.

Our day to be married approached and I took some of my dresses and the little possessions which I had and I carried them to Edwards home. He greeted me with a huge smile.

At last I could see my future looking like it would be a happy one and I spoke of my thoughts and feelings with Edward which he shared in his agreement.

The day before my marriage to Edward I was greeted by Hannah who made a big fuss over me as she had arranged some bunches of flowers for my room. She informed me that Violet had come to see me and when she walked into my room she brought a dress she had sewn for my wedding day.

She had put on some pretty bows and there was a frill around the collar and cuffs which looked very fancy.

I was as excited as Hannah told me to try it on. I could not wait and so I stepped into it and I let Hannah and Violet help me adjust it and I felt so beautiful.

Hannah held a tiny hand mirror for me and I was so surprised to see the reflection of a woman ready for her husband. I thanked Violet and Hannah and they told me they were so happy for me, and that Edward was a good man. I had to remember also that I had to be at the house to start my duties and so I took off the pretty dress and put on my working one ready to go to the house.

When I arrived I was asked to prepare to go to the market with Mrs Adams which is what I did. I found the hat which kept me cool under the heat, and on the wagon I ensured I carried a flagon of water as the sun was burning.

I followed Mrs Adams out of the front door. William had the horses ready and he was going to take us.

The journey was long and hot and when we arrived William

unbridled the horses and took them for some water next to the sea front. I noticed a ship had arrived and it was sitting on the water.

I followed Mrs Adams as she requested and she collected some things she needed for the house. I carried them and placed them onto the wagon. I was told to wait as Mrs Adams spoke to a lady and they were looking at materials.

As she did this I looked for William and I saw he was talking to a mulatto woman who I had not seen before. I saw him hand her a cloth bag and he was looking around as if he was checking to see if anyone was watching him. He looked very suspicious but it was of no concern of mine.

Mrs Adams retuned and she took me away again to walk around and help her carry things.

We walked for a long time until I struggled to carry anymore and then we finished loading the wagon and Mrs Adams called and signalled for William join us.

William came back and he bridled the horses and we returned home. I was puzzled thought at the time why William had unbridled and took the horses away but did not feel the need to ask.

The day was draining and when we got back to the house I just wanted to relax but Mrs Adams kept me late into the evening.

She said that as I was going to be away from the house with my wedding I had to do my preparations for her the evening before.

Once this was finished I made my way to my home for the last night before I was to join Edward. On my way William called me over. He was standing in his barn holding a shovel.

I was tired so I asked if I could speak to him in the morning and he insisted on talking right away. I asked him to let me go and rest as I had my big day the next day and I wanted to rise early. William looked at me with disappointment on his face but then Master White came out of the house and called him to assist with some wood for the fire.

I carried on to my home and rested. I found it difficult to sleep at first then the tiredness took me into my slumber.

The next morning I woke up feeling very weary and my body ached but the door knocked. It was Hannah. She told me the day was really special and as soon as the sleep left my thoughts I smiled at her as I was going to be married.

Hannah informed me that I would need to be ready and dressed for mid-morning and the person who would be performing my wedding to Edward was Martha. She told me to go and wash while she prepared my dress. She also had to plait my hair.

I went for my morning wash and took a bucket to the back of the house and into a fenced off area and I stepped into the cold water which made me wake up quickly.

I looked at where Kwadwo's scion was planted and I saw that a small bush had grown which I had not seen before. I looked again and I noticed the earth was dark like it had been disturbed recently but I did not worry about this. I thought it must be the way the plant shifted in the soil as it grew.

I was so excited and I thought about a drumbeat that I remembered from my village when a man and a woman were united and started to tap my feet which made the water splash. I started to sing to this beat and this caused Hannah to come out to me.

"Bam bam bam bam, bam bam bam bam, du du du du bambam bam bam bam, du du du."

I sang loudly and Hannah told me to calm down and to stop splashing the water.

I told her that I was too excited and she smiled at me and reminded me to save my energy for my husband. The word husband sounded so delightful and I was ready to start using this title for the man I loved.

I might be a slave but I would soon have a husband who would take care of me as he has done since I first met him.

I remembered then all of the kind words and things he had done for me and I also thought about how we worked together. I thought about the collection of the coins. I thought about our silent drum.

Edward was such a smart man and this was clear to me which fortified my desire to be his wife. He also made his priority my wellbeing after Master Adams stole my son away. I thought about us kissing and the brightest star in the sky which brought our love together. I then remembered Fiifi and I was sure in my akuma he would want me to be happy as did Edwards first love Catherine.

I heard a voice and it was Violet who came by to help me to prepare for my day. She came into the partitioned area and she brought me a soft cloth to dry my skin.

I returned to my room with Violet then placed a beaded necklace onto my bed and she told me it was her mothers and she wanted me to wear it as she knew my mother was not present.

Hannah then came in to see me and she gave me a chaconia flower which she said she would fix into my hair once she had plaited it.

I felt the rush of emotion take my breath away and I looked at both woman and I told them that I wanted to thank them for all they had done for me.

Then the door knocked and in walked Martha and in her hand she had a chaconia posy which she told me was for me to hold in my hand as my father was not there to take my hand and give it to Edward.

I felt so happy with all of this attention and I thanked everyone for their kind thoughts and gifts.

Hannah then told me sharply to hurry up and this was joined by Martha who wanted to get the wedding started soon.

I put on my pretty dress and the Hannah plaited my hair and I felt like queen Kesiwaa as I sat being pampered.

Violet took the necklace and fixed it so it sat just right over my shoulders. I picked up the chaconia posy as Hannah finished with my hair with the flower. I stood ready to go and Hannah smiled and said to me I looked very beautiful.

I walked to the door and stepped outside and there, everyone stood waiting for me.

There was Abel Bowleg and his wife Violet, Jack Spaniard, Tobias Jack, Leopold Gonzales, Augustus George and right to the side was Martha Callendar with a great big grin on her face.

I walked slowly towards her and she took my hand and asked me to stand and wait as Edward was not there yet. Hannah then joined the others and she wished me a happy day.

The sun was hot but I knew it was only a short time to wait. I spoke meaningless words to Martha and she knew I was nervous and excited about seeing Edward to look at how he was dressed.

The quiet air was then interrupted by a heavy noise which made the ground rumble and I looked to my guests who had also noticed it.

They started to gaze at each other and soon I noticed there was something coming up the hill towards my home. As it approached I saw it was obroni men on horses and they rode right up to where I was standing.

Martha asked what this was all about in a way only Martha could get away with and one of the horsemen asked for Edward Garcia.

Martha enquired what business the man had with Edward and the reply was that they were under orders from the governor to arrest Edward for the murder of Master Adams.

Well I was already hot under the sun with a heavy dress on and these words made me start to shake and I looked at Martha who told me to get inside my home quickly.

Somebody took my arm and I found myself sitting in my room and it was Hannah who spoke to me to say she did not know what was going on.

I was trembling and my throat had no air to make my voice release any words and my mouth went dry rapidly. I also felt like I wanted to vomit and I had a fit of coughing for no reason.

I suddenly had an urge to relieve myself and I asked Hannah to assist me. She told me to wait as the voices of the men on the horses were still outside.

I continued to shake and cough and I heard outside that the horses were spluttering and then the sound of the clip-clopping hooves told me they were leaving.

My coughing stopped shortly after as Hannah held my hand. So Edward was being hunted for the murder of Master Adams that Master White committed and I could not say anything to anyone.

I sat and started to weep. Hannah fetched me a cloth and then Martha came into the house. She saw I was distressed and she poured me some water and then she spoke of the men. She said they searched for Edward but he had fled the plantation. I tried to remember the last time I had seen him myself and it was true that I had not seen him for at least a day.

There was a knock of the door and Hannah went to greet the caller. It was William.

William spoke to Hannah as I saw through the gap in the slightly open door where she stood.

Hannah brought William to see me and he asked for us to be alone and both Martha and Hannah agreed to this and they left.

I looked at William and he paused before speaking to me. He asked me if I saw him talking to anyone the day we went recently to the market and I replied that I noticed he was talking to a mulatto woman.

William then told me the woman was the mistress of Governor Picton and she had warned him about his assistant who came to Master Adams funeral. He had heard I was getting married and he was determined to buy me and own me for himself.

He then used the words that Master White had spoken when he said that Edward had a perfect reason for wanting Master Adams to be murdered as he had refused his marriage to me.

I responded to William and I advised him that Edward did not murder Master Adams and William replied to me that he knew this.

I asked William what happened to Edward and he informed me that he had helped him escape the day before. He was safe with some rebellious French slaves who were in hiding on the island.

I asked if he was going to be alright and William told me that he was making plans to get aboard a ship to leave but he could not tell me anymore.

With this information William apologised and he told me the soldiers who came had orders to arrest Edward, and if necessary shoot him if he resisted. William did not know the extent of my hurt feelings and loss and I could not express it but he knew that my concern was for Edward, and also from him, so was his.

My wedding day was over and this was the final time I thought about trying to let my akuma be in the hands of any man.

My day was spent sitting in my room until Mrs Adams asked for me to go to the house to start with my duties again. My akuma was broken and it turned to the same heaviness of a stone that was dropped into water, and with it sank my hope for ever being happy and in love.

CHAPTER 29: Abolition

I cried for so long that my eyes became sore but I was comforted by Hannah. She brought me food and sweet tea. She talked to me about the loss of her husband which really never helped but I understood how she was trying to give me support in my pain.

I decided that I was not going to let my heart be ruptured with the hope of love anymore so I made a commitment to myself. A life without anyone would be better for me.

With Edward gone I spent more time limin' with the field workers as I often sat alone and this made me feel the pain of losing my love.

The talk among them was about the abolition of the slave trade. It was near approaching and after a while this was the only thing I had to think about as well. The only part I did not understand was what was I going to do without my home on the plantation if I was not going to be a slave? It was Augustus who first spoke about it when he asked what was going to happen to us when we would be free.

Tobias Jack spoilt everyone's hopes when he told them not to get too excited as the abolition of the slave trade was coming but not the end of slavery itself. Nobody really understood what the abolition of the slave trade was really all about. He spoke about his vision of the end of slavery completely but it would not be for quite a while, maybe not in our lifetime.

He also talked about people who came from a land close by where there were several uprisings among slaves who fought for their freedom and many of them paid with their lives.

He added that it was only going to be the end of buying and selling our brothers and sisters but we would still be owned by the plantation master. As this sank in to our heads our hopes fell. Like most of the other workers we would still be property of the plantation owner.

I kept my opinion about this conversation with the workers to myself and I continued to work my duties at the house. I knew the changes were happening and I heard Master White talking to Mrs Adams that a new governor was now a man called William Fullerton. He had taken over the rule of the Island and he had also removed Picton's assistant and sent him back to England.

I was relieved to hear this news but I was just as aware of the new governor as I was with the new master of the plantation. I did not know what to expect from him. What did ease my concern was the governors' assistant was not going to try to buy me.

The days drifted into weeks and then months and time slowly moved on and one day I was walking back to my home and I saw Kwadwo's placenta bush and it was thriving.

Tobias Jack was walking away and he was carrying a vessel in his hand. I called him and asked him if he had watered the tiny tree and he replied to tell me that he has done so since it was planted in the soil.

I just hoped at the time he did not know what was underneath. That there was more than fruit he was nourishing.

I asked Tobias more about the end of the slave trade and he advised me that one day he hoped to see the abolition of slavery all together. He then asked me if I would be able to support myself if the master of the plantation removed me from his land and I replied that I would have no other choice.

I told him about how Miss Sylvester had nurtured me to cook ground provision and if I had some chickens then I knew I would be fine.

Tobias reminded me it was a cruel world we lived in and it was more than likely going to become more dangerous before it got better. He added that we had the protection of the master at the moment but how would we be without this? I did not know whether Tobias was trying to scare me or warn me but he had never given me cause to mistrust him before so I took his words and saved them in my thoughts.

I thought to myself it could not have been any worse for me. I thought that if I survived my broken heart then my Onyankopon was watching over me.

The day of the abolition of the slave trade, when it came, was not so great. Nobody really sensed anything different so we carried on our duties as we always did.

Master White had gone to the plantation on the other island which concerned me slightly as I overheard him talking about some last selling of unwanted workers at the market to clear out those who he could not afford to keep.

He especially talked about those who were older and the very young ones who were just not productive. I thought about my son and whether or not he was still on the other island and for this I had to hold on to my emotions.

I was feeling really low at this point then one day there was a knock at my door and I had a visit from William.

I invited him into my home and he sat down. He was full of seriousness and he had things he needed to tell me.

Well I was shocked to hear when he informed me he had helped Edward escape. He heard he was alive and he managed to get to a different island. He and Edward had built a small boat many years ago and it was hidden next to the sea. Forethought saved Edwards life.

I was so pleased and I asked if Edward was a free man and William told me he was. He then added he had a message from Edward to tell me he really loved me and he was torn apart when we did not get married but to stay would have meant he would have been killed. This made me sigh heavily and William knew how I felt.

William told me he knew about the silent drum and the coins. At this moment I felt a little uneasy but he added the secret was safe with him. He then informed me the night before Edward left he dug up half of the coins and the other half was still under the shaddock bush.

I asked William if they were even worth anything to me as I was never going to have any use for them. I told him these pieces of metal were of no value if they were sitting in the ground.

He told me that as they remained under the earth they were not being spent and they were my investment for my future. He then told me something which shocked me.

Master Adams and Master White were smuggling gold which came from the ships at the docks. He added that he was responsible for transporting it to the plantation.

I did not see the point of him telling me this but then he added he also had his own part in this and he was taking some of the gold each time it arrived and he melted it down and mixed it in the metal shoes that he put on the horses hooves.

Each time he did this he took it on a journey to the market where he had buried his own investment in a hidden place. I remembered when I travelled to the market the shoes on the horse were firstly light yellow brown on the journey to the market and then grey on the return. Of course, this explained the reason for changing the horse's shoes twice in the day. This also explained why William unbridled the horses and took them away whilst Mrs Adams went to the market shops and stalls for supplies. William told me that he had also paid the mulatto girl at the dock for the information she had given to him about Edward which was the sack I saw him give to her secretly.

The gold was being infiltrated by him and because of this Master White thought it was Master Adams who was stealing the gold shared between them which accounted for the reason why he killed him. He then laughed when he told me that every time he took some of the gold he made sure he spilled his blood on it before he buried it. These beliefs meant that it would never be taken away. Master White and Master Adams did not know about this tradition and the gold did not stay with them.

I must say this was quite a shock to hear but it was great to know Edward was fine and William was not so loyal and more devious than I ever thought.

This conversation between William and I was never brought up again and after a while I settled back into living my life without any reason to question what my duties were. I did not desire freedom anymore and the coins in the ground, to me, were worthless as was William's hidden gold as it was never going to be used. I saw his dream as a mango tree which bears no fruit.

I knew not how long I lived other than by the season measures but I learned the abolition of the slave trade came in 1808. This was by the obroni dating method and many years passed until the end of slavery itself was coming upon us.

In the obroni year of 1838 there was emancipation and the dream I thought would never happen was here.

I was free from being a slave but there was a problem. In order to prove I was able to live as a free woman I had to serve a four year apprenticeship. This meant I was free but I was also not free. I could not leave the plantation until I could satisfy the master of the plantation I was capable of being self-sufficient. The only people who were allowed to leave were those aged six years and under.

Well how many of those at this age would leave by themselves? This new law of nonsense stared us in the face and laughed at us then showed us its tongue.

However the workers wanted to celebrate and so they organised a celebration and there was drinking and dancing. Whilst this was happening there was a lot of mocking the plantation owners who did not own us anymore.

Tobias spoke about a Saint Bacchus who was the God of wine and this brought us the term 'bacchanal' which was drinking, revelling and dancing. When we danced some of the men painted their bodies and some used the molasses as well to remind themselves of what they gave their hard earned labour for. We called our music kaiso which was a west African term meaning "bravo" or well done. We would say "Dat is kaiso" which was good calypso.

I served my four years of apprenticeship and eventually I was a free woman. I decided the only thing I needed to do was to search for my son Kwadwo and so I made the arrangements to travel to the island of Tobago.

I spoke to William who told me he would take me to the docks but first I need to collect the coins from ground.

I asked William for a spade and he told me he would dig for me.

In a strange way I was excited but also I had my fear of leaving the plantation as I did not know what the world was like after spending what I calculated to be thirty seven years in the same place. William told me he wanted to come with me as my chaperone and he also wanted to find a new life away from the plantation.

William took the spade and he dug down at the spot where the coins were. He dug to the right side and then he dug to the left but there was nothing. William looked at me and he scratched his head. He told me Edward said he had only taken half of the coins but it was now obvious he had taken them all.

Well I really had nothing left in my life now. I was free but I had no freedom, no money to travel with, nothing. William told me he would use his gold for us both and so we made our arrangements to leave the plantation.

I gave my tearful farewells to Hannah and Martha and the workers. Before I left I visited the resting place of Miss Sylvester and I laid a single chaconia on her grave.

William and I set of to the docks and we passed the place where Cleophus Hornigold once hung. I remembered this vividly and my body shook when I thought of the horror I saw on the journey past him.

We arrived at the docks at the capital city of Trinidad which was Port of Spain and we boarded a ship.

I felt slightly uneasy at getting on to this craft as it brought back to me the thought of my last journey by water from my home.

We arrived at the island of Tobago at a place which was simpler than Trinidad at its dockyard.

William told me he had travelled to this island before with Mrs Adams and so he knew where the master's plantation was and we made our way there.

I had a tense feeling inside me and I could not hide it from William who advised me everything would be fine.

We arrived at the plantation and the master's house was similar to the one in Trinidad but slightly smaller. William knew some of the workers and he discovered some of his friends had passed on which he was sad to hear.

I was introduced to one of the key workers who spoke his name as Nicademus D'Abreau. He looked at me and he knew my visit was personal. He asked if we wanted something to eat. We thanked him and walked to his home.

As we made our way I saw a group of men limin' on stools just as they did on our plantation.

We walked through the door to his home and Nicademus asked about our visit and William told him I was looking for my son who was brought to the plantation many years ago.

Nicademus handed me a drink of sorrel tea and he smiled.

"What is this boy's name?" He asked me in a soft but deep voice.

"I think they called him Joseph." I replied.

"Joseph ay, hmmm," came his reply. He then handed William his tea and the he told us to sit down at the table.

"Joseph the little boy came here many years ago is a mulatto boy? He asked."

"Yes" I said.

My stomach twisted and my hands trembled and I spilled my tea.

"Joseph, Joseph, well you just walked right passed him." He said

"He is sat outside with the others," added Nicademus.

I dropped my jaw and my cup slipped from my hand and dropped to the floor. My body shook and I felt a sudden rush of excitement run through my stomach like a load of butterflies had just been disturbed.

I stood up and I made my way to the door. William and Nicademus followed me.

I made my way outside and I walked up to the group of men and I saw one of them among the group who was mulatto.

"Kwadwo, is it you?" I spoke to him and he looked at me confused.

"Joseph I mean." I said and he responded to me as he knew he was called Joseph.

He then stood up and I could not believe how tall he was. I thought to myself if this was my son then there was something that would make me sure.

I placed my hand on his chin and I moved his head to the side and he had the slight mark just underneath his ears from when he was born which was caused by the caul. Then I knew he was my Kwadwo.

"My son!" I said.

I screamed and he then responded and we threw our arms around each other with a delightful passion. He knew who I was and he was so excited I had found him. I looked at William and I told him I was very thankful for him to bring me to the plantation and he smiled and told me I was welcome.

My son's face was the same as mine and he was very handsome and he was a fully grown man. My son was not only alive but he looked healthy and he had his own home where he took me. He introduced me to his wife Florence.

I spent the next couple of days talking to Kwadwo and his

family and I told him all about my homeland and he was so keen to listen.

He talked to me about a vision he had of me and a feeling he had from since he could remember and it was me always lying down near to the sun. This was a strange thing to tell me but I guessed I was one person who enjoyed the sun when it was high in the sky and I did not care much for the rain. He added he saw in his head thoughts of my dancing and then he started to sing the rhythm of a drum beating.

"Bam bam bam, Bam ma bam, bam bam bam, his foot started to tap on thc ground and I knew he had my style.

I told him what my name was and he replied to me by saying,

"So my real name is Kwadwo Kwaku?" I told him it was correct but I had to explain the way he would have to spell his last name should be "Quaque" as this was the way people spelt it in this country.

William and I sat and spoke and I asked Nicademus if there was a slave brought here by the name of Fiifi and he told me that someone of that name did come from the market but he did not settle and he kept running away saying he would never give up for his right to freedom.

After several times of doing this Master White lost his patience with him and he sold him at the market. However the man who bought him said he was taking him to another island where he disappeared and he was never seen again.

Nicademus added there was another man who came to the plantation and he asked about this Fiifi which was strange.

He said this enquiring man said his name was Edward. He came here unexpected and left pretty much the same.

Then Kwadwo spoke to say this man Edward met him and he told him about me and when anyone ever poured a drink of rum then it was the custom to pour some on the ground for the dead which was known as libation. He added that this drink was only a loan to the dead as it would be repaid in other ways. I responded to say I knew about this unwritten rule and he grinned at me.

Kwadwo said Edward informed him that when, if ever, he met me he had to tell me the following which was spoken like this,

"Because of this I lent rum." Kwadwo then pretended to pour a drink into the soil.

Kwadwo told me Edward informed him where his placenta was buried so he always knew where he was born. He added when he buried Kwadwo's placenta it still had some of my blood and this was spilled onto the sack buried with it.

I looked at William and this seemed to be a strange message to pass to me but I spoke to myself.

"Because of this I lent rum" again and again. I then realised what he was saying.

I spoke these words over and over again until I said,

"Because of The Silent Drum."

I spoke to William and Nicademus and asked why he spoke about Kwadwo's placenta plot?

I looked at William and I asked him if Edward used his barn before he helped him to escape and he nodded he did. Edward told him he needed to be left alone and he had to watch the barn in case anyone tried to visit and this was agreed by William who remained loyal and he kept his word.

Kwadwo spoke to say the sky looked like it was clouding over and it looked like it was about to rain which was strange as he felt there was a golden sun ahead. I remembered that he was born with a caul and as myth says the child will have a special gift.

I knew then what secret message Edward had passed to Kwadwo and the next day I left with my son and William and we went back to the plantation on Trinidad. I went straight to my room where I saw the silent drum in the corner and asked Kwadwo to move it out so I could look at it.

Kwadwo told me it was very heavy and he needed me to help him. We dragged it into the centre of my room and I looked all around it and I could not see anything to make any sense of what Edward was saying until there it was. It was right in front of my eyes.

Edward had carved a chacionia flower and I had never seen it before, right at the top next to the skin of the drum. I placed my finger onto it and nothing happened until I pressed harder and the drum skin rose slightly.

I looked at Kwadwo who was puzzled and I took my hand and with my fingertips I gently removed the drum skin and there it was.

It was a shiny circle that was the same size as the skin around the inside of the drum and it glowed like the sun in the sky and you know what colour it was? It was gold of course.

Kwadwo then reminded me that he had always had a vision that I was lying close to the sun and he was right but the sun was a circle of gold.

So the coins we collected from the glass jar in Master Adams room were really gold and were painted to disguise them. Edward had buried a large amount of coins directly with Kwadwo's placenta. With Tobias Jack constantly watering the shaddock tree it slowly washed away the layer of paint which sealed their true value. This was why my gold never left me because my blood had spilled onto the coins from Kwadwo's placenta.

I looked at my son and I smiled at him and he threw his arms around me and we both looked at our treasure which was hidden all this time inside the Silent Drum.

THE END